Winter's Child

a novel

RJ HERVEY

For my parents, and for Kesslan.

I don't know how to say thank you.
You told me to be who I wanted, to do what I loved.
You supported me in everything and always put me first.
You are forever the brightest stars in my night sky. You are my
guiaing lights.
I don't know how to say thank you, but maybe this is a start.

I hope I make you proud.
I love you all so much.

This is for you.

Contents

Winter's Child

I *am cold.*

So cold. The snow is still falling, slowly burying me where I lie beneath the white oak tree. I've wrapped myself in this black cloak, but it cannot stave off winter's grasp. There is blood as well, still pooling beneath me. Crimson is a strange color when set against the endless white landscape of Toscana – artistic, as if that mattered now.

Gazing through the trees, I can almost see the short towers of Firenze to the west. Through the snow, and through the morning fog, they must still be there. The city won't miss me though. No one will. Barely anyone is left who even knows my name.

Numb. My feet and hands have lost all feeling, but that feels right; it's been so long since I was in control. My fingers were once agents of music and art. My feet once danced through the golden pastures and sunlit fields of the Florentine countryside. That was so long ago – a lifetime, it seems.

My eyelids are heavy. When I close them next, I know they will not reopen.

I can no longer feel the cold. I can barely even feel the slowing of my heartbeat as darkness creeps ever closer. Behind the darkness – beyond the veil – fire is waiting for me. Dark fire. I know it with a certainty that sets fear upon my soul. Fire has borne me, so I suppose that to fire I must return.

My eyes finally close, shattering the frozen tears that I'd left there. In the mists of my memory, I see the ghosts of all those whom I've lost. I imagine their satisfaction at my fate. Death alone would be too kind a fate, after all, for a murderer.

Not just a murderer: a traitor.

A witch.

I turn away from them, and I flee to hide my shame. I flee to the open skies and wide hills of my childhood. Already I can hear my harp as it softly echoes against the stonework in the Piazza della Chiesa. In those days, I could hear the music in everything. In those days, my laughter was my song.

SPRING

I was born late in the year of 1429, or so I was told. It was winter when my parents left a newborn upon the stoop of a workshop in the small village of Montaione. I might have found my death there, beneath a different snow, had it not been for the kindness of fate. Many baby girls are so abandoned if their burden cannot be afforded, and most die unclaimed in a world they've barely come to know. We few that survive are called Trovatelli, for we were found.

The colors danced upon the canvas: hopping, sliding, gliding, and bending. My paintbrush conducted their intricate song, and I played the music to their ballet. Happy yellow flirts with radiant pink, spinning tenderly to the soft sounds of the psaltery. A tempo change, and purple bursts into action, twirling onto the stage in a sweet moonlit basse. Turn, turn, spin, explode. Slower now as a red and orange meet and move together, lost within the innocence of new romance. A motet – gold jumps forward joyously. A dirge – browns and blacks appear, shyly shadowing the other performers. The promenade skips forward again, then slows, then quickens. Movements become yet more intertwined as the dancers are pushed closer and closer together. Now they dance in unison. It is harmony; it is discord; it is serenity; it is beauty.

Exhausted, I lay down my brush.

"Well done." Matteo's voice appeared suddenly from behind me. "Molto bene."

"Maestro!" I nearly stumbled as I spun around, and I had to take a deep breath to calm my surprise. Seeing the grin on my teacher's face though, quickly made me giggle. "How did an old greybeard like you manage to climb up here without creaking and groaning with every step?"

"I had to chew on one of my socks to keep quiet," he replied. "It wouldn't do to interrupt you, after all."

Because of the chronic clutter in the workshop below, I often used the small balcony as a studio from which to paint or compose. The fresh air always served to free my mind, and the rolling hills of the Toscana countryside sang with a beauty to inspire even the most melancholy spirit. However, the steep cobble steps that led to my retreat had long since become difficult for my teacher to climb. Matteo di Francesco was no longer a young man. Though his eyes sparkled with a joy for life that survives in so few, his back was bent and his hair was grey.

"But what's a bit of sour tongue for the chance to see *this*," he muttered, absently waving me aside so that he could closer examine my painting. Seconds became minutes as his eyes explored every brushstroke. He was a master craftsman in nearly a dozen disciplines: music, architecture, literature, botany, zoology, medicine, natural philosophy, astronomy, and – foremost among them – art. His proficiency with a brush far surpassed all but the most renowned painters, and we were often engaged by patrons from as far as Firenze who sought an elegance of art that only Matteo could provide. I could not have hoped for a more masterful teacher.

"You have come so far, *farfallina mia*." Finally satisfied, he leaned back with a sigh. A cool spring breeze whispered through the balcony, brushing my short brown hair around my shoulders. Dusk had begun to fall. To the west, the hilltop town of Montaione was framed by purple-red rays of sunlight that swam languidly around the buildings and archways; its eleven towers reached into the painted sky like the prayerful hands of God. "Even with my many, *many* years—" he winked— "I am still surprised at the beauty of our world," Matteo remarked, his voice gentle in the stillness of the moment. He turned his gaze to me. "And at you, Amadora. This painting," he waved his hand over the canvas, "is the finest I have seen you complete."

"Grazie Maestro," I said. His words made me glow with pride. "Everything I know, I learned from you."

"Bah," he said, waving my comment aside. "You are too modest by half. One day you will realize what a gift you have; I only hope I'm still around to see it."

"I suspect you will be. You've never missed an opportunity to prove that you were right."

"I cannot help it. Stubbornness rides with age and wisdom." He reached out to lay a soft hand upon my head, and his face split into a wide grin. "I remember when you were no taller than my hip, and I was still new to fatherhood." He chuckled. "Such as the time you mixed together all my dyes. Mio dio, do you remember that? You told me that by doing so we would only need one paint."

I laughed with him. "A wiser man would have kept them on a higher shelf."

"Come no! Though I know you would have found your way to them regardless. You have always been a determined girl." His eyes sparkled.

Our laughter faded, and together we basked in the setting glow of the sun.

"Sing me a song, Amadora," Matteo said, voice both soft and tender. "Like you did when you were young. I miss the sound of your voice."

"Maestro, you hear me sing every day."

"But not to me." He sighed, his breath heavy.

Grasping his hand, I led him to a nearby bench. "What shall I sing?"

"Sing to my soul," he said. His voice sounded to me like the slow creak of an old tree, moved by a lofty breeze that only it could feel.

Turning to the sunset, I sung softly of hope and passion, letting my voice drift freely with the wind. My song took off like a bird to flight, and for a while I lost myself in it. The sun finally fell beneath the horizon. Upon that starlit balcony, Matteo's hand found my own.

"Promise me something, Amadora," he said, his tired voice barely more than a whisper.

"Qualsiasi cosa, Maestro."

"Never forget the woman you are in this moment."

Gently, I squeezed his wrinkled hand.

I continued to sing into the moonlight for some time, my voice warming the brisk air into the late hours of the night.

Light had not quite broken the horizon when I suddenly woke, yet the greyness that barely illuminated our small bedchamber foretold a sunrise not long off. I sat forward on my cot, somehow sure that I would not be able to return to sleep, but unable to remember what so abruptly pulled me from rest. Upon a bed parallel to mine, though several paces apart, lay Matteo. A dreadful, raspy snore accompanied each breath that filled his thin chest. I smiled, never knowing him to make any other sound when asleep. In its own strange way it comforted me.

My nightgown rustled softly against my legs as I folded my sheets and tucked them beneath the mattress. Quietly sorting through my chest that sat at the foot of my bed, I took my breeches and white tunic. Slipping away from my gown, I shivered as the crisp, predawn air bit at my naked skin, and I wasted no time before donning my work clothes.

Across the hall, at the rear of the workshop, was the combined kitchen and pantry. I claimed a piece of bread from the cupboard. As usual, there wasn't much from which to choose.

It hasn't even been a month, and we already need to visit the market again, I thought to myself. *Matteo won't be happy; he had wanted to buy new canvas.* I only took a few bites before returning my half-eaten breakfast to the shelf. *It's just been too long since we've had a big client. Soon we'll be choosing between paints and food.*

My stomach was still rumbling as I wandered back down the hallway, past the room from which I could still hear Matteo's raspy snore, and into the workshop's main chamber.

As was common, the workshop served not only as a place of business, it was our home as well. We composed ballads in the same room as we slept. We imagined architecture on the same table we sat to supper. We diluted our paints with the same water we drank. It was not an easy life, but though luxury was not a comfort we could afford, neither was it one we particularly desired. I know that, for both of us, our greatest joy was in our work. Being so surrounded with art and music and literature was comfort enough.

My worn leather boots slapped against the wooden floor. The sound might have echoed in the large, high-vaulted room if not for the accessories to our work that littered the vast space. Almost hidden behind duo of easels – each host to a partially finished portrait – was a remnant pile of unused canvas. The wooden dowels we used to build the canvas frames lay piled on a shelf near the wall. Nearby, a desk was littered with charcoal, brushes, and spare parchment, and on the other side of the desk sat a tall cabinet in which we kept our paints and dyes hidden from the light. Two long tables reached across the length of the floor, one of which was covered in architectural designs for renovations to San Regolo – the town church. At the head of the other table sat a large clay model that would one day be an awe-inspiring sculpture of Solomon.

In the back corner of the room sat a large tub of water from which we drew to dilute our colorings, rinse brushes, and other such work. Still groggy from my early awakening, I approached the basin and splashed some cool water across my face. There was but one mirror in the workshop, and Matteo had insisted it stand above the water tub. In it, I caught sight of my reflection.

I looked older than I felt, but younger than my age expected. My eyes – which seemed to oscillate daily between green and brown – were framed by chestnut hair that hung just past my shoulders. Reaching up, I tied it back with a bit of string, as I did every morning, so that the tail tickled the nape of my neck.

My slender frame was childlike in many ways – a thoroughly unpopular characteristic in my own mind. I barely crested the shoulders of most men, and though I was a woman by any other standard, my build seemed more suited to a girl of fifteen than a woman of nearly twenty.

Still, I was beautiful, I suppose, in my own way – or so I was often told by Matteo – though I never devoted much time to pursuits of fashion. In fact, I was often a topic of criticism amongst the townsfolk. Rather than the traditional shirt, dress, and stockings, I most always opted for comfort while I worked, donning breeches and a wool shirt with sleeves that bunched below the elbow. I must have been a strange sight to any visitors that walked through our door, for while I did not consider myself so unique as to think that

I was the only girl to be apprenticed in a workshop, my case was certainly among the oddest of rarities. I was an enigma to most in Montaione, and things of that nature spread quickly in a town where gossip is common and scandal is scarce.

I shook my head at the strange girl in the mirror. *The body is a prison-house of the soul,* I reminded myself, referring back to my early studies of Plato.

With a sigh, I turned back to the workshop. There were nearly a half-dozen daily chores I was tasked with, and to do them all would take several hours. Even starting as early as I was, it would be nearly midday before they were all completed.

First, I lit a fire in the hearth. We were rare in having two places at which to keep a fire: the hearth in the workroom and the stone crib in the kitchen. The hearth in the workroom had been an addition of Matteo's when he had purchased the workshop and was necessary to keep ourselves warm while working even in the depths of winter. Cold fingers made for sloppy brushstrokes.

We stored chopped tinder against the wall in the kitchen so as to keep it dry. I retrieved several pieces and lay them so that, if he wished, Matteo could continue the fire after he woke. Then, donning my thick woolen smock that I kept hung on a peg near the door, I removed the heavy terracotta jars that held our many colors of oil paint. One by one, I opened the jars and, with a wooden wand, stirred up the thick sentiment that had collected near the bottom. This was one of my most important tasks within the workshop; if the paint wasn't churned daily it would solidify and waste.

Over an hour passed before I was satisfied that each paint had been thoroughly mixed. In the meantime, the sun had broken free of the horizon, so I unlatched and opened the trio of windows that faced east, allowing the day's new light to cascade into the workshop. I also unbolted the double doors at the forefront of the shop and swung them outward.

We were situated on a grassy knoll just east of Montaione. On foot, it was only an hour to the Piazza della Chiesa, and on horse, even less. Standing in the entryway, I gazed out the town that I so loved and took a deep breath of bright air. I could already hear the distant sounds of the village as it began to wake. As I listened, the morning bells of San Regolo began to sing out their deep and vibrant song.

"Buongiorno, i miei amici;
il giorno ci convoca, le cantatrici."

I smiled. It was a good rhyme; I would have to write it down.

With the door left barely ajar, I retrieved the broom from where it lay against the wall and swept the workshop as thoroughly as possible. More than painting had been ruined by dirt and dust collecting on the surface as the paint dried. I took special care as I swept near the front of the workshop and the large painting that rested therein. The scene, almost five feet across, had been unfinished for nearly three years now. Matteo often called it the greatest of his creations – his masterpiece – and said that upon its completion he would never paint again. I did not doubt his sincerity, for the painting was beautiful beyond what words could describe.

The depiction was of Adam and Eve, the forbearers of mankind, as they toured the gardens of Paradise. Every line – every brushstroke – had been Matteo's and had been made with the utmost precision and care. I realized, with a touch of sadness, that the painting was nearly complete. In just a few short months it would be finished, and my master would lay down his brush forever.

Allowing myself a few moments of indulgence, I set aside my broom and lost myself within the scene. The landscape was framed by a beautiful mountain range crested with the most wonderful white snow. Beneath the endless sierra sat Eden with its vast flowering trees and vibrant florae. All manner of exotic fruit hung from tree to tree; I could almost smell the rich flavors soak the air. A whisper of wind softly scooped dandelion spores into the sky where they danced across the breeze like coryphées upon a stage. Songbirds perched upon the lower branches of countless trees. I could hear their morning refrain twirl along joyously. Underfoot was a soft bed of grass and moss that ran through park and meadow, tucking up against a river that rushed gracefully over smooth stones and white sands.

Hands intertwined, Adam and Eve walked the forefront of this scene, the quintessence of devotion and piety. I saw much of myself in Eve, as Matteo had used me to model the character. It was a choice that, at the time, had both confused and flattered me to no small extent, yet as I now gazed upon the painting I could not help but admit to his better judgement. He must have seen some hidden aspect of myself that I still could not perceive.

Eve stood before Adam, marvelously nude, gazing around herself with delight and open wonder. I could feel the grass tickle her feet. Upon her finger alit a butterfly with delicate wings of shimmering gold. Into her long chestnut tresses were woven a garden of flowers – white roses, orange lilies, yellow daffodils.

Behind Eve followed Adam – or what would eventually become Adam. Though not for lack of searching, Matteo had not yet found someone suitable to model the figure. In this, he was right to be meticulous and selective; were he to choose a model unfit for the scene, it would stain the otherwise flawless piece.

No matter how long I admired the painting, whether it be minutes or hours, I always felt as if there were more to see and experience. Inevitably though, I would find myself drawn back to the figure of Eve. I was attracted to her, though not, I think, for the skill of artistry she represented. It was not even the resemblance she held of myself. In her face I saw an emotion so perfectly drawn – so immaculately actualized – that it seemed to surpass the bounds of realism, yet however I tried, I could not describe the sentiment she portrayed. It was more than joy, or peace, or contentment.

Purity, perhaps? I thought to myself. It was as close as I could come.

Matteo once told me that he had been inspired by a fresco on a wall of the Brancacci Chapel in Firenze. The mural, he recalled, depicted mankind's banishment from paradise.

'Pain has been the subject of too many beautiful works,' he had said. 'That is not idealism. I will capture perfection, so that through it, we might know virtues lost.'

I closed my eyes for a moment, then, shaking myself, reclaimed my broom. I had indulged myself enough for one day.

Matteo woke just as I brushed the last bit of dust through the doorway.

"Buongiorno, Maestro," I said, my voice as bright as the sunrise that streamed through our eastern windows. "Hai dormito bene?"

He nodded absently and took a seat near the model of Solomon. A small breakfast of bread and wine was already in his hands. He said nothing about our dwindling food store.

"You woke early, Amadora," he remarked, eyeing my progress of the day's chores.

I shrugged. "The day seized my night before its time. Nothing more than a bad dream, I'm sure." My eyes turned to Matteo. "And you, Maestro?" I asked, noticing a slight ashen hue to his cheeks. "Are you feeling alright?"

"I'm plagued with old age," he replied, waving aside my concern. After a moment, he laughed. "I fear it may be the death of me." I tried to ignore the false nonchalance in his voice but resolved to keep an eye on him, lest he fall sick.

While Matteo ate, I excused myself outside. The morning air had lost most of its bite, though I still shivered as a breeze chilled my skin. Wrapping my small arms around myself as best I could, I made my way toward the well. Most townsfolk relied on the public well in the piazza, but we were somewhat unique in having our own source of water. Dropping the wooden pail into the well's dark mouth, I listened for the tell-tale splash it made as it reached the bottom. After a moment, I slowly began pulling it back to the surface using a system of pulleys that Matteo had designed. I despised this chore. Era noioso. One hand after the other after the other for what seemed like forever. I took the opportunity afforded by my boredom to drink in the beautiful Florentine countryside. Rolling hills and hues of vibrant green stretched into the horizon, glowing gold in the spring sun. Here and there, copses of Cyprus trees spotted the vista. To my left, Montaione sat majestically upon its knoll, like a king upon his throne, overlooking our little piece of Toscana. The breeze that so chilled me carried the undying scent of vineyards and flowering fields. Upon that wind rode the sound of morning birds. When I finally looked down, the water pail was already in my hands.

Smiling, I untied the container and carried it into the workshop. I suppressed a sigh of relief as the warm air of the studio washed over me. Matteo had finished his meal, and I was surprised to find him decorated in his Sunday robe and cape. "Are we going into town?" I asked. Careful not to spill, I tipped the bucket into the water tub, filling it nearly to the brim.

"A messenger arrived yesterday with a letter from Antonia. She asked to speak with me about a job, and I think perhaps we could use the coin."

Antonia Compagni was the matron of a prominent merchant family in Firenze, but she and her husband to spent most of the year living at their castello, here in Montaione. We owed much of our business to Antonia, and over the years our relationship had grown beyond that of patron and artist to become that of close friends.

"Should I come as well?" I asked, failing to entirely mask my excitement.

"Mi dispiace Amadora, but I think it best if you remain and watch the shop. Signora Tessa had thought to sit again for her portrait either today or tomorrow, and it would ill-befit us to be gone when she arrives."

My frown described my disappointment.

Matteo smiled, leathered wrinkles appearing at the corners of his eyes. He embraced me for a moment, then with a thin wave, departed. I sighed; the workshop seemed so much larger whenever I was alone.

Done, for the moment, with chores, I turned to my harp where it stood beneath the steps to the veranda. At the very least, I could make the most of my time alone. Removing the leather slip that covered my instrument, I went to work tuning its twenty-six strings. There were several pitch pipes lost around the workshop, but I had never needed them; I could simply hear when the strings were in tune. Matteo said I was blessed with the birthright of Apollo: un'orecchio perfetto.

While it was true that Matteo had apprenticed me in many fields of art and study, it was the realm of music with which I had most strongly resonated. I had taken to it like a fish takes to water, finding joy in its teachings and quickly rising to become proficient in its expression. It was at the crux of that course that Matteo bought for me my harp – a gift, he had said, to celebrate my accomplishments.

It was by far my most precious possession: simply made, carved from polished maple wood, and though it did not have the lavish inlay that many performers desired, its sound was clear and its tone was steady. The rest of the song, as Matteo often said, was in the hands of the musician.

As small as I was, the harp came up almost to my chest, and for several years I had been forced to rest it upon the floor as I played. Only recently had I begun bracing it between my calves, even though doing so pushed the shoulder of the instrument nearly above my head.

Finally satisfied with my tuning, I leapt into a quick carol to warm my fingers. I loved the feeling of the soundbox vibrating against my chest. It was erotic, in its own way. As I brushed my fingers across the coarse strings, loose fibers tickled the ridges of my skin and the notes reverberated into my diminutive frame. I closed my eyes, playing, as always, from memory. Song scores were rare, and much of my repertoire was self-written.

I moved into a slow, hymnal anthem. I tried to fill the workshop with the sound, then call it back to a whisper, then draw it out again. Next, a secular ballad, then a soft lullaby. I wove the songs together as best I could so that each flowed into the next without pause, just as Matteo taught me. I internalized the music, drawing it into myself. Soon, my heartbeat began to match the tempo of each song, and in some cases, dictate it. My cheeks flushed with passion. My breathing quickened. I began to sing – no words – just harmonious accompaniment. I laughed in the way you only can when alone.

Several hours passed. It wasn't until my weary fingers begged for rest that I allowed myself to stop playing.

I had found after years of writing music that I composed my most beautiful melodies immediately following a session such as the one I had just enjoyed – while I was still full up with passion – and so, carefully setting my harp aside, I reclaimed a half-composed sonata from where it lay within our desk of drawers. The echoing music in my mind ordered itself, and I transcribed it onto the page. By the time I had finished, the sun was well past its zenith.

Just as I was replacing the slip over my harp, I saw the shadow of someone enter the shop.

"Salve, Signora," I called out in greeting, assuming it to be the aging seamstress come to finish her portrait. I turned and was surprised to find instead the figure of a man. "Oh! Mi dispiace, signore. Come posso aiutarla?"

The stranger did not respond; he did not even pay me a glance, nor did my lack of permission seem to hinder him from touring the studio space and examining our work. My hackles rose, but I held my tongue. He was dressed well – very well. Even though I was not familiar with any trends of fashion, I could easily read the richness of his cloak – cut crimson velvet lined with the spotted fur of a lynx – and as he walked, I could see that beneath his cloak was a gown of equal exorbitance. The gown, his trousers, and his stockings were all woven from lavish serge fabrics, and from his cuffs and collar lay fine lace of a quality I'd never before seen in person. Upon his head rested a feathered cap sewn from smooth ormesino.

He was far older than I, and though not yet of an age as to be considered an elder, he carried himself with a sense of disinterested superiority. His narrow eyes, such I could see them as they gazed about the shop, demanded deference in a way that made me uneasy. In fact, everything from the fat of his paunch to the wastefulness of his wardrobe bothered me – grinded against my humanistic ideals – but as detestable as I might find him, his wealth was obvious and his patronage might feed us for years.

When he finally spoke, it was with a voice both deep and raspy. "You work alone here, girl?"

Girl. Something of the way he spoke made me feel as helpless as the word suggested. It took a moment to find my tongue. "Signor Matteo di Francesco is paying a visit to the Compagni family. I don't know when he will be back." I forced myself to add, "But I'm sure I can help you in his stead." The words sounded empty even to my ears.

If my insincerity bothered the man, he did not show it. His true thoughts – about which I was absolutely certain I did not want to know – were hidden behind a well-practiced smile that did not touch his narrow eyes. My body responded with palpable relief as his gaze returned to the workshop.

"When he returns you may let him know that I will have this painting," he said. Then, to my dismay, he gestured to Matteo's unfinished masterpiece.

"I'm sorry signore," I said, my voice uncomfortably shrill. "But as you can see, it is not yet complete, nor will it be for sale when it is."

He did not immediately reply, but almost as if without thought, his hand moved to perch upon the hilt of his sword. My breathing quickened.

"This figure has not yet been painted," he remarked as if I'd never spoken at all.

"Y—yes. It is to be a portrayal of Adam."

He nodded in the gross facsimile of understanding. "That is good, he will paint me in Adam's place."

I felt like a bird suddenly aware of the snake sliding into its nest, yet I could not quite get my wings to work. Still toting his empty smile, the man approached me. He stood too close. The sick smell of him filled my nostrils. Leaning down, he spoke to the top of my head. "I will return in two days."

I could neither speak nor move as, without another word, he turned on his heel and left the shop. The oppressive silence that followed seemed to quiver like the deep resonance of a bell.

A breath escaped my lips that I did not realize I had been holding. I muttered some unpleasantries beneath my breath, and I indulged myself with an obscene gesture that helped to turn my mood.

It did not take long before I again felt like myself. *How did he unsettle me so thoroughly?* I wondered, embarrassed at myself for my lack of composure. Yet, whenever I replayed the scene upon the stage of my mind, a sick feeling again appeared within my stomach.

I struggled to put myself back into my work, but when Matteo returned nearly four hours later, I was still troubled.

"Bentornato a casa, Maestro," I said as he ambled into the shop. "How is Signora Antonia?"

"Well as always, and sad to have missed you," he replied, grunting heavily as he sat down. "Santo Dio, I'm not yet old enough to be so weary!"

I forced a smile.

"What's bothering you, farfallina mia?" he asked, keenly measuring my unease. "Did something happen?"

I tried to speak, but my voice caught in my throat at the sight of his painting just over his shoulder. It was his masterpiece, his pride. I should have been more forceful in my defense of it. At that, I felt myself fill with shame. "No Maestro, I'm just tired is all." *I'll tell him tomorrow*, I told myself. I'll have to, *but not yet.*

Matteo coughed once into his hand, allowing me an opportunity to change the subject. "What did Antonia want?"

"It seems that her husband has brokered a rather impressive trade arrangement with a nobleman from Firenze," he replied. "The man arrives tomorrow to celebrate the new partnership, and she asked if I might play for the occasion." Matteo sounded tired.

I tried to be pleased for him, but could muster up only the likeness of joy. As he rested his feet, I excused myself to bed, hoping the solace of sleep would free me from the pervading sense of unease that I could not seem to shake.

As I drifted away, there began a dull aching in my chest that followed me into oblivion.

I will always remember that night at the Castello di Compagni. The laughter. The drinking. The secrets. I will always remember the face of Gilio Salviati and the way he made my skin feel cold.

I still feel cold.

There was a fire without flame. I could feel it slowly sear away my skin layer by layer until there was nothing left but bone, and even that turned to ash. Only then, when there was nothing else, my soul began to burn. I screamed – a soundless scream that would never end. My torment was infinite. In the throes of my agony, a figure approached through the darkness. He looked like a man, but was not a man. His skin was too taut; his eyes were too large; his fingers were too long. Abomination. Denizen of hell.

His voice, if you could call it such a thing, was soft– a serpent's hiss. "I see you, Amadora Trovatelli. I see the path upon which you walk, even if you cannot yourself see the ground beneath you. I see the end of that path, Amadora Trovatelli, and it is there that I shall wait." He arched his too wide mouth into the facsimile of a smile. "I am Moloch, the sceptered king, and I brand you as mine, Amadora Trovatelli." Reaching out with one finger, he touched me lightly upon the chest.

I woke with a sharp catch of breath.

My skin was coated in sweat. My sheepskin blanket had been kicked away in the night. More nightmares. I absently rubbed at my chest.

The sun was cresting the horizon, coaxed onward by the singing of the morning birds and the wheezing snores of my aged teacher. I lay upon the mattress for a moment, allowing the sounds of the moment to ease me from a restless sleep. Soon, the nightmare began to fade from memory, as such things are quick to do, but still there remained a tightness in my chest – a remnant of things forgotten.

As I rose from bed, so too did my spirits rise. Whether from the catharsis of sleep or the transience of anxiety, I no longer felt my unease from the night before, and by the time I had a fire roaring in the hearth of our workroom, I felt like myself again.

But I tried not to look at the painting.

As I stirred the paints, I thought about the celebration to be had at the Castello di Compagni that night. Excited now, rather than melancholy, I giggled. I wished so very much that I could go; it was certain to be an evening of romance. If the stories I so often enjoyed were any indication, there was sure to be all manner of dancing and bowing and handsome noblemen's sons and falling in love. In the privacy of my mind, I imagined myself wearing a wonderful linen gown – oh, I would be the envy of all the other women – and dancing with the finest of men. There would be one who understood me above all the rest. We would talk and dance and laugh into the deepest corner of the night. Then, when the celebration had become only ours, he would carry me away to his room and—

I blushed crimson. *Well, it would be nice to go.* I stood up and aggressively wiped my hands upon my apron.

As quickly as I was able, I finished my chores and retired to the veranda. There, I busied myself with sketch-work. In all my years at the workshop, I must have drawn and redrawn the surrounding countryside a hundred times over, but each time it felt as though I were finding something new. Of all my artistic exercises, it was by far my favorite.

While I worked, my mind wandered to the thing which I had known I could not avoid: Matteo must know about the man who had visited the workshop and his plans for the painting. *I should have handled myself better. He would be right to be angry.* My charcoal paused upon the parchment. *I am a fool,* I chided. *I know Matteo better than to think he would be upset. He will know what to do.*

That simply, the matter was settled in my mind, and as my anxiety at Matteo's response waned, relief grew to replace it.

With newfound vigor, I returned to my sketches. Several hours seemed to pass like minutes, and soon I was brushing charcoal dust off my fingers. A breeze swept the light powder into my nose, and I sneezed. The sound seemed loud in the silence of the workshop below. *Where is Matteo? He should be awake and preparing his instruments.* I suddenly realized that though the sun had risen well into the sky, my teacher still had not risen from bed.

"Maestro?" I called out. No response. Unease crept back into my chest. I descended the stairs into the workshop and made my way toward the room in which he still slept. Something was wrong; I knew it as soon as I entered. His raspy snore had fallen to a feeble wheeze. His chest fluttered a little too quickly, and his cheeks were grey. I ran to his bed.

"Maestro?"

He coughed, and then groaned. "Buongiorno farfallina mia," he muttered. Coughing again, he cynically added, "I may have fallen ill."

My heart dropped.

Matteo lay his hand upon my own. "Don't fret, I will be healthy as a young man again soon."

Sickness had struck our workshop before, but with each passing year Matteo grew weaker and illness more dangerous. "I'll go fetch the doctor," I said, turning for the door.

Matteo grasped my hand. "No need, Amadora. I will be fine."

"Don't be stubborn," I said. "He will be able to help."

"We have not the denari to pay him." The tone in Matteo's voice caused me pause.

"We can find it somehow—"

He interrupted me with a squeeze of my hand. "Perhaps tomorrow, farfallina mia, if it's worse." He coughed again. I could hear in his voice: this was an argument I could not win.

"Alright, Maestro." Grudgingly, I nodded. "Tomorrow." I knelt next to him. "Can I bring you anything? Bread? Water?"

"Some wine, I think," he said, "but that can wait. We must discuss tonight."

I frowned. "You cannot perform. I'll run the message to Antonia; I'm sure she will understand."

Matteo smiled and shook his head. "You will go in my stead, Amadora."

Words fell helpless upon my tongue.

"I had considered whether it was right to send you regardless, and it seems this malaise makes the decision for me." He coughed.

I was surprised, pleased, and nervous, yet as grateful as I might be, Matteo's confidence was not my own.

"You will perform beautifully," Matteo said as if I had spoken my worry aloud. "You always do. But we need to choose your selection for the night." Cough. "Fetch your harp. Time is short."

Several hours later I was clothed in my Sunday dress and departing for the gala. My russet hair was crafted into the semblance of braid which I had wrapped around my head in the popular fashion, and my harp was securely harnessed upon my back.

It wasn't until the doors of the workshop shut behind me that the gravity of my task made itself clear. Matteo was not with me. My music would be played not for the village square, but for royalty. I was on the cusp of a world made by princes and gold and such things as I had only before read about. Each step I took away from the workshop only seemed to jostle my emotions further; I was all at once anxious, worried, and proud. Too soon I stood before the Porta Grande, the great gate that faced east toward the workshop and, further afield, Firenze. Just within, I could see the unusual frenzy of Montaione's residents. Clearly I was not the only one with the festivities on my mind.

I took a deep breath. The next step felt like a plunge into icy water.

"Ciao, Amadora!" a friendly voice called out, breaking the spell as I strode through the cobblestone archway and into the town. "Have you come for the celebration?"

"Salve, Signora Tessa," I replied with a slight bow of my head, careful to keep an air of professionalism. I was there on behalf of the workshop, after all. "I have. I'll be performing."

The elderly seamstress stood before her small shop, before which was on display her finest dresses and her best cuts of silk and linen. She had decorated as well – ties of roses and poppies hung from above her door, and I could smell fruit shavings from where they were scattered upon her window sill. I couldn't remember the last time her shop had looked so nice.

"That's wonderful, child! My ears and heart would thank me for the chance to hear you play that harp of yours, but the palazzo is going to be closed to everyone except the council and the Podestà." Tessa made no attempt to mask what she thought of being disallowed invitation to what was sure to be the greatest festa in years. In fact, I very nearly expected the elderly woman to fold her arms and stomp her feet. "Can you believe that? Closed! Why if—"

"Mi dispiace." I cut in quickly with a curtsy before her lecture could gain too much inertia. Signora Tessa was known for her opinions almost as much as for her love of voicing them. "It wouldn't do for me to be late."

"Of course, you're absolutely right," she said. "You should know better than to waste time chatting when there's someplace to be."

I wanted to tell her that I had barely offered a word for every ten of hers, but I held my tongue. As I turned to leave, a thought struck me. "I'm sorry Signora, I almost forgot. Matteo has fallen ill, so we may need to wait for your last portrait sitting."

"Oh goodness, don't fret over that. The sitting can wait," she said. "Is it bad?"

I nodded. "He needs the doctor, but we do not have the denari." I sighed dramatically. "Perhaps after tonight we will be able to afford the cost, but..." Trailing off, I shrugged.

"It will be fine, I'm sure," she said not uncaringly. "Now you get along. It wouldn't do to be late to your big performance. Matteo is a stubborn old man. He'll be on the mend soon; you'll see."

I turned away to hide a small smirk. Signora Tessa was a shameless gossip, and I was sure the tale would get larger in the retelling. By tomorrow, the entire town would believe Matteo on the verge of death, and if I could convince even one of them to lend us a few denari, it might be enough to hire the doctor.

A few other friendly faces welcomed me as I continued my walk through town. Montaione was not so large that it would take more than a few minutes to walk from end to end, but I found myself savoring the trip. Tall stone buildings rose dozens of feet on either side of its three main streets, and smaller alleyways crossed here and there with little regard for symmetry or aesthetic. Everywhere I looked, second story shutters had been thrown open and doors swung wide. The cobblestone streets were clean, flowers had been laid out, and all of the people I saw were dressed in their nicest clothes.

I turned left into the Piazza della Chiesa, so named for the church of San Regolo that stood over the square. Across the piazza from the church was dug the town's one well – host to an assembly of women chatting as they waited their turn to draw water. The well itself, I remembered from my studies of the town's design, covered a cistern as big as the church – 20 paces on each side and half again as deep, with a central column to support its weight. I could hardly imagine so large a tank, yet it could hold almost thirty thousand barrels of water when full.

In the courtyard above it, children ran about playing games of chase, and behind them, I could see several young girls giggling as they conducted a mock wedding. Their ceremony was abruptly interrupted as a wayward game of devil's tail broke through their ranks. After a few moments of laughing and yelling, the game continued its chaotic tour of the courtyard. The girls, apparently having decided devil's tail to be more fun than an imaginary marriage, joined in the fray.

I smiled, remembering back to the days of my own youth spent playing with the other children in the piazza while Matteo was busy at the market. Several women waved as I strolled through the piazza; spirits were high.

The Palazzo di Compagni stood just within the town proper, on the furthest corner from the Porta Grande. Continuing through the Piazza della Chiesa, I passed a large building that served as the seat of our village's small government and traditional home of our elected Podestà, and soon found myself before the open gates of the Compagni manse.

Another deep breath. I walked inside.

If I had before thought Montaione was a bustle, it was only because I hadn't understood the full potential for chaos that I found showcased within the Palazzo di Compagni. Servants, paying me no notice, scurried about like mad as I walked the long, arched corridor that led to the palazzo courtyard. Many carried decorations, or supplies for the kitchen, but each moved with desperate purpose.

I entered the courtyard and very nearly gasped; the quad had been transformed into a lavish natural ballroom. The covered pathway that circled the open space had been scrubbed and polished until the marble floors gleamed like a mirror, and rich draperies hung from every column and archway. Finely carved furniture of walnut and ivory circled the grounds. Upon the tables were hung silken cloth, and they were decorated with intricate golden candelabra.

Potted roses – all somehow simultaneously abloom – had been placed in every available corner so that their fragrance infused the courtyard. In my many visits to the palazzo, never had I seen it so aglow with beauty.

"Amadora!" Antonia Compagni called out in welcome, appearing as if summoned from the palazzo interior. Her eyes sparkled in harmony with the cheerful lift of her cheeks.

"Antonia!" I replied warmly, all pretense of professionalism forgotten. We embraced.

Though she in no way pretended to be a figure of motherhood in my youth, Antonia Compagni had long been a warm womanly presence in my life. I was indebted to her for both her friendship and for her patronage, and as we embraced, I took courage from my need to repay her many kindnesses in my performance that night.

"Where is Matteo?" she asked, gently brushing dust from my cheeks. Her eyes caught mine, and I had to keep myself from looking away at the concern therein.

"He woke with a fever and sickly pallor." My voice wavered for a moment. "He sent me in his place with an apology and assurances that I will perform at the level he would have."

Antonia smiled comfortingly. "I have never doubted your talent, Amadora, and I see no reason to start now. I am truly glad to have you here." She brushed my arm. "Come, let's have you settled. I cannot fathom how you make such a walk with that instrument upon your back."

She led me to a corner of the courtyard where I gratefully set down my harp. As surreptitiously as possible, I stretched my aching shoulders.

"I shall have a stool fetched for you and food brought so that you may eat before everyone arrives," she said.

I thanked her for the gesture. I knew from Matteo that many patrons did not treat their entertainers with such kindnesses.

"Di niente." She waved my gratitude aside. "As for your recital, I fully trust your selection of music." Taking my hand, she continued, "But I would ask that you keep eye and ear on our guests. Should tensions boil, perhaps your songs may calm the foolish emotions of men."

It seemed an odd request. *Does she expect something to happen?* I wondered to myself as Antonia took her leave. In either case, I found myself in awe at the masterful way in which she ran her house. Though I would prompt no further attention by her guests than that of any other performer, Antonia had thought of a way to use my presence to guide the night to her satisfaction. Such acumen was the profession of patrician women.

I soon had my stool and a meal of roast pig with artichoke. As I ate, I could not help but continue to admire the courtyard, and I soon began to worry that my dress was not elegant enough for the occasion. In that course of reasoning, I also began to wonder whether I was elegant enough for the occasion – I was no noblewoman or gilded bard. I was just...me.

More for comfort than preparation, I retrieved my harp from its slip and began to check its tuning while my fingers warmed to the movements they would dance the rest of the evening. The feel of the soundbox as it rang against my body was enough to quell most thoughts of doubt.

Over the next several hours, respected residents of Montaione – no more than a dozen all together – began to trickle through the palazzo gate. From behind my harp, I espied Padre Curato from the church, our newest Podestà – a lesser-known banker from Firenze – as well as most of the town council all in their finest Sunday garb. Signor Roberto led the council in all but title, and usually it was within his inn that decisions were made and slights mended. Common gossip held that he was often too quick to scold, but I'd always had a soft spot for the old innkeeper. He and Matteo were long friends, and he would always bring a sugar coated nut for me to chew on whenever he visited the workshop. As he entered, he caught my eye and offered a small smile. *He must have heard about Matteo. That was quick, even for Signora Tessa.*

The rest of the council flocked around the man like bees to honey. Even for them, the occasion of a visiting Florentine noble was irregular, and they seemed no less awed by the state of the palazzo than myself.

For quite some time, the sound of my harp was the dominant noise within the courtyard. Few spoke, save in nervous murmurs. Antonia, for her part, drifted from guest to guest, greeting each in turn and making small talk as best she could. Under her care, the common tension began to ease, the townsfolk began to circulate the quad, and conversation began to find its stride. From what I could overhear, most spoke only of the visiting nobleman and his family – the Salviati, as I heard them called.

Many people vehemently articulated better days to come, citing the new trade partnership between the Compagni and Salviati families as a herald of wealth for all Montaione. A few stubborn pessimists voiced doubt about the nature of the trade agreement. The Compagni dealt mostly in blown glass, after all – a moderately successful export at best. What exactly did the Salviati gain? But those unpopular voices were quickly suppressed by the other guests.

I kept my head down over my harp, but I held onto every word. I'd once heard Matteo say that a bard's were invisible ears. I hadn't grasped the implication of his words until now. Within a half-hour, I was sure that I knew more of the common opinion than anyone else at the festa, even Antonia. Another of Matteo's adages echoed in my mind: *there is no wealth like knowledge.*

Just then, the sounds of an arrival at the palazzo gate drifted through the arched corridor that led to the courtyard. All conversation vanished. Antonia, full of grace and composure, placed herself by the entrance. Roberto, too, made his way forward, ready to welcome the Salviati to Montaione, and behind him followed the rest of the council.

So it was that when the patron of the Salviati family arrived, I could not see through the throng of people who surrounded him. Indeed, the man must have brought an entire entourage of servants, for the crowd seemed to double as he entered the courtyard.

Courtesies were exchanged, though I could hear frustratingly little of anything. And I could still not see the Salviati man, no matter how I craned or bent my neck.

"Signor Gilio Salviati!" All of a sudden, Jacopo Compagni, Antonia's husband and the patron of the Compagni family, burst from the palazzo full of cheerful welcome. I was often told that Jacopo had been a most beautiful boy in his youth, and while he could perhaps no longer be called the same, his age carried with it a handsome gravity that still ensnared the minds of most village women. He wore a smooth tunic of white serge, and upon his hip hung a ceremonial sword in a silver sheath. I had to pry my eyes away from the sword; I hadn't even known Jacopo owned such a tool.

As Jacopo called out his greeting, the throng that had surrounded the entrance parted, allowing my first look at Gilio Salviati.

My mouth went dry, and my fingers faltered for a moment upon my harp. There, leading the newcomers into the palazzo, was an uncomfortably familiar face. The man who had visited the workshop the day before. The man who had demanded the ruination of Matteo's painting.

Gilio Salviati: a name put to a snake.

His small eyes took in the courtyard with veiled scorn, but mercifully passed over me without notice.

"Jacopo," he finally replied, offering a slight bow of the head as his attention drifted back to the Compagni patron.

"Benvenuto, my friend! How did you fare upon the road from Firenze?"

"Well enough," Gilio replied. "Though I eagerly await my return to the city. I have not the stomach for the contado. It seems as though the tales of small towns and dusty roads all hold true."

Gilio's voice disturbed me, though it was not readily apparent why. As the two men spoke though, I began to realize the duality of the man: his voice and his visage. While he looked no different than the overheavy figure of conceit who had visited the workshop the day before, his voice almost seemed like it belonged to someone else. There was very little of the coldness and condescension that I remembered; it was veiled – adroitly – behind a guise of twisted geniality. The proficiency with which he wore that mask made my chest tighten and my stomach churn.

In my unsettled musings, I nearly did not notice as Gilio's train disappeared into the direction of the kitchens where I supposed the guards could be close and the servants would wait to be called. Only one retainer remained, a short man with thin lips whose head always seemed bowed toward the ground. I immediately mistrusted him. There was something about his smile; it never seemed to touch his eyes.

Introductions were made. Gilio didn't hesitate to hold out his hand for the council to kiss his ring at every opportunity, and it irked me that so many stooped to comply without hesitation. These were men of stature – of office, no matter how small.

Conversation followed introductions, and talk seemed genial enough on the surface. I busied myself with my music, careful to keep my head down, as the festa continued once again in full swing. My fingers continued to dance of their own accord as my mind wandered to the troubling places that this newest development led.

I had been so sure that Matteo could resolve the matter of the painting, yet Gilio Salviati was no common merchant. The painting was not for sale, nor was the figure of Adam a slave to auction, yet…the power Gilio wielded as the head of a noble Florentine family was not one to be easily refused. After all, law in the contado was that which noblemen made it.

Stop that. You're letting whimsy best reason. I closed my eyes for a moment to refocus myself, then I did my best to push the issue from my mind until there was something I could do about it. With passing interest though, I did wonder what Gilio had been doing in the workshop the day before when he claimed to have only arrived in Montaione that afternoon.

All around me, wine was light on the mind and laughter easy on the tongue. A duo of wine-heavy councilmen picked up a conversation near me.

"I should like to visit Firenze after this I think," one man exclaimed, his cup held high. "I've heard that the nobility often hosts events like this, sometimes twice in one week; can you imagine?"

"The city must be large indeed to hold such merriment!" the other replied, a bit of juice swelling over the side of his cup. "It must be ten times the size of Montaione. At least!"

I giggled under my breath. Matteo often spoke of Firenze in the same manner, but I doubted any city could be as big as either of them claimed. *Perhaps someday I'll see it for myself.* I'd never been further afield than Castelfiorentino, but I harbored dreams of seeing more of what I so often read about – of seeing the world.

"Come hear this pair of fools!" another councilman said, laughing loudly as he joined the conversation. "I traveled to Firenze in my youth, and I tell you now that the Castello di Medici is nearly half as large as Montaione by itself."

"You've seen the Castello di Medici?"

"Have you met Cosimo? Is he truly so great as men say?" There was wonder in the voices of both men.

"Sì, I met Cosimo," the man replied, clearly enjoying the attention. "And the tales are true. He must have been three—no—four hands taller than myself, and his eyes are as hard as diamonds. His voice was such that I believe he could tell mountains to move and they would do so—"

Jacopo laughed loudly, interrupting the tale the councilman wove. I hadn't heard him approach. "Cosimo is hardly all that! He is simply a man, i miei amici. A great man, surely, to shoulder the burdens of Firenze, but a man nonetheless." He laughed again. "Eyes like diamonds! Hah!"

"You have met Cosimo de' Medici, Jacopo?" one of the first two men asked, giving the third a sour look from the corner of his eye.

"Certo. Cosimo's son, Piero, and I have been confidants and close friends since our youth – following in the footsteps of our fathers. It is often at his castello that I stay on my visits to Firenze."

The three councilmen seemed awed by Jacopo's words, and I was not so sure that my face didn't share their surprise. Cosimo de' Medici was a luminary – the greatest name of our age. He had, in years past, singlehandedly kept Firenze from political ruin, and especially amongst artisans like myself, he was known for his generous patronage of art and philosophy. In fact, not too many years ago he had opened a library in San Marco that was welcome to the public – the first of its kind in the world. He was hardly 'just a man,' and it was his son, Piero de' Medici, who now led Firenze forward toward greatness. The legend of the Medici family was not one to easily wave aside.

As the conversation wandered out of earshot, my attention returned to my music. The festa, so far, had fallen short of my admittedly romantic expectations, and as my enthusiasm faltered, so did my vigor. I was beginning to sweat beneath the thick dress I was so unaccustomed to, and lingering worry for Matteo was beginning to find perch in the back corners of my mind.

I should be with him. The thought intruded upon the refrain of a particularly gentle ballad, and I struggled to quash the notion before it found my fingers and embittered the song. Matteo was not dying, no matter what tales I told Signora Tessa. This, like so many other illnesses, would pass in a week and leave my teacher again spry as a young man.

No...even as I considered it, I knew it was not true. Matteo was growing ever older, and his days of leaping around the workshop were long gone, no matter this malaise that held him. Eventually, whether tomorrow, next week, or next year, he would fall prey to a sickness he could not overcome. Someday, Matteo would die. Like a river to the ocean, the torrent of time flows ever on toward death.

> "Il sogno di vita is called to end,
> when il sole scaldare is called to ascend.
> Hades may, the king of death be,
> but 'tis Helios that bids the dreamers see."

The rhyme felt heavy upon my tongue. I belatedly realized that my ballad had taken on the face of a lament. Blushing, I quickly brought the song back to its intended pace. Nobody, it seemed, had noticed the misstep.

"Why don't you take a quick repose, Amadora?" Antonia had quietly approached while I was lost in thought. "Gilio has excused himself to see that his horses are well stabled, and I think it would be best if you were not fatigued. I'm not sure why, but my heart claims we will yet have trouble before the night is up." She frowned as if she had said too much, then smiled at me warmly. "The idle chatter of men could circulate for hours yet, in any case."

I accepted her offer with heartfelt thanks. Leaving my harp securely set beside the stool, I made my way toward the kitchens where I might find a spare slice of ham or bowl of minestra.

Even the palazzo interior, I noticed as I toured through room and hall, has been polished and prepared for the festa. Antonia had seemed completely comfortable, yet I wondered whether the Salviati partnership might be as dramatic a turn for their house as for the rest of Montaione. I had certainly never seen the palazzo so well cleaned or decorated, and if that was any measure of the matter, then maybe there was some merit to the scattered questions of why the Salviati were interested in the partnership after all.

The kitchens, being mostly noisy with the sound of sizzling meats and chopping knives, was neatly tucked into a corner at the far end of the castello. I noticed that Gilio's guards still lounged about the entrance. Apparently they had not felt the need to accompany him to the stables. As I ducked into the cucina, I was greeted with a crowd of idle servants – mostly Gilio's – and a chef whose moustache quivered in a way that made me wary of the large carving knife he wielded.

I found a place to stand against the wall for a time, grateful for the opportunity to stretch my legs, but it became quickly apparent that I would not be given the chance to whisk away so much as a piece of bread from under the wrathful eyes of the chef. He seemed especially hateful of the Salviati servants, and I did not begrudge the poisonous looks he threw their way. They made no move to help *(then why even bring them?)*, and in fact often impeded the chef's assistants with nary an apology. Several had even begun a game of dice upon a crate of salted pork. *As if this were a tavern!* If, as I'd heard said, the state of the retainers belayed the state of the lord, I could only imagine what such a scene suggested of Signor Gilio Salviati.

"—hard to believe the signore could find something worth his time in this dirt hill village." My ears perked up as a nearby conversation drifted my way.

"And they call them a lord and lady! Fortuna, I could leave for a village and be a lord m'self it this is what it comes to nowadays. Perdio!"

"Maybe if you could stomach life this far into the mud. I'd not stay one night longer in this cesspool than need be."

"Non lo so, I can think of a few reasons to lengthen my stay. Did you see the Signora? Per l'amore di Dio, I could spend a night up her dress and call it fair."

My face reddened, though more from anger than embarrassment. Before I could even think, I was in front of the man. My hand struck his cheek with enough force that he stumbled. The kitchen went abruptly silent. My palm stung.

"You little whore…" The man came up sputtering.

My reason returned with a frightening jolt of self-realization. Before anyone could say another word, I fled, my fists tightly clutching my dress.

Several rooms and hallways sped by before I allowed my feet to slow. Panting, I put my hand up against the stone wall to steady myself. A tall wooden cabinet stood alone in the passageway next to me. I no longer even knew where in the palazzo I was.

"Che stronzi!" I muttered between breaths. A deep fire burnt in the pit of my stomach; even through my embarrassment, fury still held me.

Struggling to control my anger, I nearly missed the rising hum of men's voices drifting down a nearby corridor. Alarm upset rage, and in its absence I suddenly felt very small. I took stock of myself. Dress disheveled, hair askew, angry tears upon blotchy cheeks; I was hardly in a state to be seen. I thought about retreating back toward the kitchens, but the prospect of facing those men again was too daunting to overcome. As the voices grew louder, I went to work straightening my hair. *Hopefully they will pay me no mind.*

My hands froze. One of the voices had convalesced into that of Gilio Salviati. Rising, inexplicable panic threatened. The man inspired a sick sort of fear in me, and I knew that I could not bear to let him near me – not as I was now. My eyes grasped around myself for some escape. There was no time to run.

The cabinet. The thought came to me like a quiet gesture of salvation. I swung the doors open. It was empty, save for a moth-eaten dress and some dusty portraits. The voices were closer now. They would show their owners at any moment. I leapt into the armadietto, pulling the doors softly shut behind myself.

For a few moments, I worked to still the wild drumming of my heart. Dust swirled around my nose and mouth, and I desperately suppressed a cough. As the tension stretched on, I began to feel childish. *I'm far too old for acting like this,* I chided myself. The words were empty though, for fear still gripped me, and I knew that to step out of the cabinet now would be even more absurd than entering in the first place. *Sono puerile.*

Despite my self-admonishment, my breath still caught as the men turned the corner and their voices rose to sudden clarity.

"—don't understand why you must align yourself with so meager a man." The voice was foreign to my ears, yet I was sure it must belong to the small-eyed retainer that had accompanied Gilio within the courtyard. "Pass the reigns, and I promise I can find you much more profitable associates within the city. No need to dirty your boots this far into the contado. If you would only allow—"

"Be silent!" Gilio's voice cut through the other's tirade. "Jacopo holds no interest for me. He is a pawn on a chessboard, and a fool besides."

I began to sweat. The two men had stopped walking and stood just paces from where I hid. I was barely able to breathe, yet I felt a sudden, strange satisfaction; these were the words – the voice – of the snake I'd met within the workshop, not the approximation of a man that claimed geniality at the festa before.

"So you say," replied the retainer, "but I see no profit here. What use is a country lord, and at so high a cost? The crates—"

I heard the crunch of fist on flesh only moments before the body of Gilio's retainer smashed into the cabinet. I bit my tongue to stifle a scream. My heart was now beating so loudly that I began to fear that the sound of its drumming might give me away.

"Tacere! Never speak to me as if you were my equal!" Gilio's voice quivered with rage. Another crash was followed by a low, pained moan from the retainer, then another. "Remember your place, cretino," Gilio continued somewhat more quietly.

"Mi dispiace, signore," the man returned, his voice strained.

Prolonged silence followed. I struggled to keep my arms from shaking. Finally, Gilio sighed. "You wander like a blind man into a den of lions. Were you any more a fool…" He paused.

"La mia vita è al servizio di tu," the retainer muttered as best he could. It was sickening to hear his complete verbal prostration.

"Of *that*, I have little doubt," Gilio responded, ice upon his tongue. Lowering his voice, he continued. "I am not in the habit of explaining my motives to mice, but perhaps knowledge of the precipice upon which you walk will tame your tongue."

I held my breath; my attention suddenly focused.

"My reasons do not concern you. All you will know is this: it serves me well to discredit and dispose of Jacopo and his house."

A chill ran across my skin. *What have I stumbled into?* Abruptly, a sharp pain stabbed at my chest, its intensity blurring my vision.

"For reasons that do not concern me," the retainer echoed carefully. "Does it, perhaps, concern me how you intend to fashion his disrepute?" He spoke slowly, testing every word before giving it voice.

Gilio snarled. "This partnership is no more than a veneer – a means to my invitation here. Mentre sono qui, I will plant a series of letters within his affairs. That, coupled with the chests of weapons that have already found their way into his storeroom, will be enough to convict him of treason."

"You will see him exiled," the retainer said.

"Executed, if I still hold any influence in Firenze. Either suits my cause."

There was a long moment of silence broken only by muffled breathing that sounded too loud for my ears. *Executed?* My mind was frozen in shock. Even my arms forgot to tremble.

"I suspect this information is not free." Perhaps the man was made of stronger mettle than I'd thought, for his voice did not waver.

Gilio laughed cruelly. "You have joined your small worth to the success of my design. Now, perhaps, you will step more softly." His unpleasant chuckling faded down the hallway as he continued in the direction of the courtyard, echoed by unremitting vows of faithfulness by his retainer.

The spell broken, my body began to shake uncontrollably, and my mind raced through a fog of panic. I began to gasp for breath. *I can't breathe!* Frantically, I burst from the wardrobe and collapsed onto the floor, wheezing through a flurry of dust.

My thoughts reeled as I lay upon the stonework – searching for answers to questions I didn't fully understand. After a few moments, I pushed myself to my feet, still dazed. Brushing dirt from my dress seemed so mundane, so ordinary, that I found myself fighting back what might have been a mad sort of laughter – the kind found not in joy, but hysteria.

Breathing in through my nose, I filled my diaphragm, held the breath for a few seconds, then slowly released the air through my mouth. It was a technique Matteo had taught me to improve my singing. In, hold, out. In, hold, out. I don't know how long I stood alone in the corridor, just breathing, but by the time the fog of my mind began to disperse, it felt like hours had passed.

Vaguely I remembered the gala still being held elsewhere in the palazzo, and I began to amble, thoughtlessly, in that direction. Meanwhile, my mind raced, struggling to make sense of the mire I found myself in.

Gilio Salviati, head of one of the most powerful noble families in all Firenze, was plotting to tear down the Compagni – Jacopo and Antonia – my friends and patrons. For some unknown reason, he wanted them dead or gone. From what I knew of Firenze's courts, an anonymous accusation of treason would be enough to warrant a search of the palazzo. Then, if they were to find the letters or weapons Gilio had left for them...

A quickly suppressed image of Antonia swinging from a gibbet made my stomach churn.

Run and hide. My instincts, like those of some hunted animal, fought to be heard. I was under no obligation to act; surely no one could know that I'd overheard their conversation. *Yet to do nothing is an act all its own.* I squared my shoulders. There was no way I would let harm come to Jacopo or Antonia. I wished my arms would stop shaking.

My resolve hardened as I walked into the courtyard and to whatever fate might bring.

The quad had not changed much in my half-hour absence, though I felt as though it should have. Flowers still bloomed out from ornate pottery. Men still laughed over the rims of their goblets. I saw it all with an eye that suggested nothing was real, but the ache in my chest and the chill in my legs were not the ailments of a dreamer.

Against the wall, in full view, stood Gilio, already returned to the festivities. His retainer was nowhere to be seen. My heart missed a beat, but I carefully kept my composure. For a moment, I thought his eyes veered my direction, but they flicked back so quickly that I soon doubted whether they had moved at all.

Jacopo. Where is Jacopo? There he was, right beside Gilio. Odd that I hadn't noticed him, but there was no course for me to approach him with Gilio so close. *Antonia, then.* I quickly decided. She would be easy enough to pull aside.

The Compagni matron was circulating amongst the guests – still playing her role as hostess. It seemed strange to me that so little could change in her world while mine had been cracked to its core. Step by step, I made my way to where she stood with Signor Roberto.

"—is a Roman distillation, from a vineyard just north of Tivoli," Antonia was explaining to Roberto.

"Che lascia senza parole," he replied. "You must give me the name of the man who trades in this delicacy!" The innkeeper noticed me in the corner of his eye. "Ah, Amadora! I have thoroughly enjoyed your performance so far. Molto meraviglioso! I daresay Old Matteo would be proud." Lowering his voice, he added, "I heard he has taken ill. Do not worry, little one, he will soon recover; he always does."

I offered a tense smile I hoped he took for worry about Matteo. "Grazie, Signore. I pray you are right." I turned to Antonia. A deep breath. "Mi dispiace, Signora. May I speak with you privatamente?"

She nodded graciously. I could feel sweat beginning to form on my brow. "A presto, Signor Roberto."

The innkeeper took his leave. Antonia turned to me with concern written plain in her eyes. "Stai bene, Amadora?" She placed her hand upon my cheek. "You're pale as a corpse! Come, we will find you a bed. You may have taken Matteo's illness as well."

I shook my head, frustrated by my body's betrayal. "I am healthy, Signora, only nervous." I took another deep breath. I had to force the next words to come; it was as though my tongue suddenly belonged to another. "There is something…" My voice trailed off.

With extraordinary gentleness, Antonia took my hand. "Amadora," she said softly. "What is wrong?"

Matteo has not raised me to be a coward. My hesitation was suddenly my shame. I clenched my fist.

"I overheard…" I almost didn't recognize the voice for my own; the words had come without thought. "I overheard Signor Gilio speaking with his manservant." The more I spoke, the easier it was to continue. "He means to betray you and Jacopo." The words were falling out now. "He said there were letters, and crates of weapons. That when they're found you'll be exiled or killed…I didn't mean to listen, but he scares me so much and I wanted to hide." I expected to feel relief, but I only felt more apprehension. "I didn't know what else to do." The last was a whisper.

Antonia's grip tightened uncomfortably on my own. She gave me a long, searching look. "I believe you," she finally said. Indignation flashed through the muted maelstrom of emotions within me. She relaxed her hold on my hand. "Do not give me that look, Amadora; what you have just said takes much to accept, but of course I trust your word." She looked across the courtyard at her husband. "Jacopo and I were suspicious of Gilio's offer, and it seems as though our fears are realized."

The next breath I took was one of belated release. My chest felt as if a large weight had been lifted from it.

Antonia passed me a warm smile, though the corners of her eyes were tight. "Rest now, la mia amica, your part in this ugly thing is over." Her brow furrowed in thought. "I must not let tell that yours was the ear to hear of this conspiracy. I think I must tell my husband of this plot as if

I were in your stead – that should satisfy him and protect you. Did you hear anything more?"

I shook my head.

"No matter. If it comes to our word against his, I believe the advantage will be ours." As Antonia spoke – mostly to herself, it seemed – I was awed by her composure. The conspiracy that had nearly driven me to hysterics seemed to wash from her like oil over glass. She hardly seemed nervous, only thoughtful, and perhaps a touch weary. Her strength fortified my own. "Go Amadora, return to your music and know that your courage may have given us our lives."

My adrenaline finally began to ebb as I returned to my stool, surprised to find a small plate of pork rind and a bowl of minestrone set upon the flagstones beside my harp. *The cook—?* The turmoil of my mind barely gave me the opportunity to question its appearance, and my stomach was no longer in any state for a meal. As Antonia had said, my part in the matter was finished, and though I still struggled against anxiety, more comforting, I found, was the presence of my instrument. The feeling of tightly wound strings, the chill of the maple soundbox against my arms, even the familiar way in which I crossed my legs beneath the large frame reassured and calmed me.

Almost out of absent habit, my fingers returned to their dance. They were tense and rough upon the strings at first, but I forced them to relax – forced myself to relax – and slid into a smooth ballad.

With newfound focus and veiled curiosity, I cast my cautious gaze around the courtyard. Antonia was no longer where I left her, but had already drifted to Jacopo where he was in conversation with Gilio. I kept my head down, but I couldn't look away as Antonia pulled Jacopo aside.

She whispered in his ear, calm as a spring pond. So too was Jacopo, at the start, but as her story – my story – developed, his composure was replaced with angry apprehension. Even from across the courtyard, I could see the fury in his eyes. Knowing what I knew, it was easy to imagine the reply he issued in a barely contained undertone. 'Are you sure?' he appeared to ask. She gave an almost imperceptible nod.

I held my breath, and my song slowed to almost nothing as I waited for whatever would happen next.

"GILIO!" Jacopo's thunderous voice rang out across the quad. The fire in his words made me shiver.

Several councilmen flinched in surprise, and at once everyone fell deathly silent. Only years of practice kept my fingers plucking their song. Soon, nothing could be heard except a concert of nervous breathing and the quiet melody of my harp.

"What say you to this?" Jacopo raged, spinning on the man. "Betrayal?"

Gilio was quick to don a mask of confusion, but hesitated just a moment too long in his response.

With a lion's roar, Jacopo slid his sword from its sheath, and within a moment had it against the Salviati's throat. "Traditore maledetto!" I was vaguely aware that my song had turned sour and tense.

Antonia gripped the front of her dress so firmly that her knuckles turned white but otherwise looked on with cool impassivity. Faces in the courtyard offered a range of emotions – frightened, confused, angry – but only Padre Curato seemed posed enough to step forward.

"What has happened, Jacopo?" the priest asked in soothing tones, unease not quite hidden just beneath his words.

Jacopo seemed not to hear the man, intent as he was upon Gilio. His arm quivered, as if he were fighting for control. Gilio's eyes bulged.

"Jacopo! To take a life is no small thing!" Padre Curato shouted, desperate to be heard.

The tension in the room was palpable. Every visible muscle was drawn tight in apprehension, every person's breath shallow and hushed. Suddenly conscious of Antonia's earlier instruction, I altered my song to fit the mood. The melody slowed almost to a standstill, waiting for the right moment.

"This man has conspired against me and my house!" Jacopo finally declared. At his words, my song burst forth in a steady battle march. Full chords resonated thoroughly amongst the columns and archways, and baser tones thrummed along with pulsating consistency.

"It is not true!" Gilio managed to cry out through the sword at his throat. The key shifted. Sporadic minor chords snuck here and there to an inconsistent tempo, surging forward and pulling back deceivingly.

"You lie!" Jacopo spat. The battle march returned full of righteous fury, slicing through Gilio's theme. "My wife has your designs from your own filthy mouth! You would see us executed for treason!" *Crescendo the bass.* Thrum. Thrum. Thrum. Indignant arpeggios took off like swallows disturbed from rest.

"Signora?" Padre Curato quietly entreated.

All attention flew to Antonia. The song fell to a sweet whisper – that of infallible femininity. The melody hopped forward timidly. I allowed the notes to echo into silence for one long, apprehensive moment. "It is true," she said. "From his mouth, he has come only to plant upon us false evidence of sedition."

All at once, the song returned full of righteous fury. Overlapping musical phrases housed barely contained chaos that slowly resolved into the original battle march. I saw the features of nearly every guest darken, and several began to call out in anger.

My heart raced. My chest ached.

"Bah!" Jacopo said, thrusting Gilio away onto the hard floor. "You live only because I do not want your vile blood staining the stonework. Take your men and go, bastardo. Scurry back to your nest in the city and know that this will not go unremarked within Firenze."

Humiliation battled wrath for dominance upon Gilio's face, his mask of false geniality long forgotten. Climbing to his feet, Gilio screeched for his manservant, who scampered forward from his hiding place within the shadow of a palazzo door. His face was bloody and bruised.

Even from where I sat, I could see Gilio's body shake with indignation as he sent the man to fetch his entourage. Spittle flew from his lips. "I will kill you for this, Jacopo! You are nothing to me! This means nothing to me!" he shrieked. Councilmen, incensed beyond reason, hurled curses at him. One threw a goblet of wine that sliced open his lip and streaked across his rich clothes. "Stronzi!" he practically screamed as he fled the palazzo. "I *will* see you dead!"

He turned and, for the first time that evening, looked directly at me. In that moment – that moment which seemed to stretch on without end – I knew with unfailing surety that Gilio knew of my role in what had happened. Somehow, he knew.

And with that he was gone.

This mortal affliction only reifies the death I suffered so many months ago. That part of myself – so full of emotion, so saturated with life – has long abandoned me, and the vacuum of its departure has since been a fate worse than even this.

I welcome the overdue embrace of death, but I equally dread what must follow. Fire. Anguish. Guilt. Those faces that shadow my nightmares await in the darkness of perdition. They are the faces of those whom I have loved and betrayed. Many will be there. Many will watch with satisfaction as I am cast into the void, but one will stand before the rest.

Matteo's death haunts me even now.

The festa came to a sudden and disturbing end, and I had been the secret conductor of that dénouement. No matter how Antonia assured me, no matter the thanks she gave, the harrowing prophecy of Jacopo's farewell words were what followed me on the long walk back to the workshop.

"This was not the last we shall see of that man."

Gilio Salviati. He made my stomach roil. Even as I stood upon the threshold of the workshop and the last vestiges of auburn sunlight faded into the western horizon, the hatred in his final gaze occupied my mind's eye. *This was not the last,* I silently echoed.

"Amadora?" my mentor's voice called from the bedchamber as the door to the workshop swung closed behind me. My thoughts immediately and with some measure of shame turned to Matteo; in the excitement of the night I had somehow forgotten his illness. I raced to his bedside.

"Benvenuto," he said as I entered. His voice was tired and weak, but still, palpable relief swept over me upon seeing his smiling face. "I did not expect you to return for another few hours. How was the celebration?"

"How are you feeling?" I asked, ignoring his question.

"Better, I think," he replied with a comforting grin. I tried to ignore the sickly color in his skin or the slight quiver in his voice or the thin sweat upon his brow. His smile faded as his eyes searched my own. "What happened, farfallina mia? You have the look of one hunted. See here, your hands are trembling!"

Exhaustion, which I had been suppressing all night, suddenly and with full force stole the last of my strength. My legs gave way, and I collapsed onto my cot.

I did not immediately begin to talk, and Matteo did not press me for an explanation. For some time I just lay there in the security and stillness of my home. When I did finally speak, I was not interrupted, a mercy for which I was grateful. I first told Matteo of Gilio's visit to our workshop the day before – of his demands and his disposition. Then I recounted the events of the night at the palazzo. I told him of my performance, of my hiding place within the empty wardrobe, and of the exhibition that followed.

"I don't know how to feel. I'm tired, I think more than anything else." I closed my eyes. "And I'm scared. I'm scared of Gilio and what he might do."

Matteo studied me under drawn brows. "Farfallina mia," he finally said in a deep and somber voice. "I have never been so proud of you as I am right now."

I shied away from his gaze. I knew that I should be content with his words – I had, after all, likely saved the lives of both Antonia and Jacopo – but at the moment I felt something less than pride. The Greek philosopher Heraclitus had written about the world in terms of balanced exchanges. If he was right, then what reply would my actions this night elicit?

"Remember Amadora, courage is not found in the absence of fear, but in the conquest of it," Matteo continued as if he could read my thoughts. I wondered why I did not see in myself the strength he seemed so certain of. "But even then, I expect Gilio will now return to Firenze. His plot foiled, there is little to keep him here."

His words did not comfort me. Gilio had already proven he was no slave to logic. Perhaps he had nothing left to salvage of his plans for Montaione, but I doubted that would stop him if he ever discovered my role in what had happened. It was to the lulling cacophony of this internal debate that I eventually drifted to sleep. Matteo left me alone with my thoughts, and I think that he too was soon slumbering, though his rumbling snore was again absent from the night.

Sleep may have been slow to come, but so too did it seem reluctant to go, for I did not wake until long after daybreak. The sun, having hidden itself behind clouds, allowed me my rest, and even the morning birds seemed to have muted themselves on my behalf. Yet what I woke to, when my eyes did flutter open, was unsettling quiet and gloomy grey light.

My muscles ached, so I lay upon my cot for some time before finally rising. I had slept in my dress, much to my chagrin. The wrinkles would take hours to flatten out, and I would need to be presentable when I returned to the palazzo to fetch my harp. Last night it had seemed too much to carry home on top of my mental burdens.

I wiped blurriness from my eyes, and for a moment, my gaze brushed upon the still form of Matteo. My stomach flipped; immediately I could see that something was amiss. His breathing had regressed into no more than a weak gasp, and his ashen face had been drained of whatever little color it had left to it the night before. Rushing to his side, I tentatively reached out and lay my wrist across his face. It felt as if he were on fire.

I gritted my teeth, but dare not try to wake him. From my studies, I knew that his body needed rest, and the reassurance I would gain from hearing his voice might be at the cost of what little strength he had left. I rose to my feet and began combing through my mental tomes of medicine. *Reduce his fever*, I told myself firmly, shaking away the anxiety that threatened to rise within me.

Movement helped – it gave me something to focus on. I quickly collected a cold pail of water from the well and a few strips of woolen cloth. With cautious haste, I wet the wool and lay it across his wrists, forehead, and neck. He didn't budge as the chilled rags touched his skin – he didn't even twitch.

Now I could only wait. I wracked my brain for any other medicine – anything else that might help Matteo to heal – but nothing came to mind. We had so few options, and I didn't dare leave him to fetch the doctor.

Minutes seemed like hours, and in the suspended silence my mind went to work fanatically manufacturing the many possible outcomes that might lie ahead. Would the night's moon see me twice-orphaned? I shook my head. *I can't think like that.* Yet another voice followed shortly behind, *But if the worst happens, what then?* I didn't have the answer, and my unease deepened.

I never knew my parents. As Aristotle would say, they were not present to etch themselves onto the blank slate of my infantile mind. In their place, I only had Matteo. I suppose my psyche had supplanted him into that role by necessity, but I was happy for the need. He was a man of wisdom, talent, and integrity. I valued him as a warden and loved him like a father. To lose him…to lose him would orphan me in a far more real way than I already laid claim to.

Eventually, I gathered a stool from the workroom to sit upon. Looking around, I realized how much I owed to Matteo. To be sure, he had stayed a child's death by taking me in, but he had given far more than the small life he had saved. My craft, my education, even my name were all gifts from the great man that lay beside me. Amadora: the gift of love. He long said I was a gift to a man with no children of his own, but I truly believed that the blessing had been mine. I would be a master artisan someday, and that end I owed all to Matteo.

Settling into my place at his side, I watched diligently for any sign of change. Every so often I would reach out and feel his cheek. His temperature was falling, though not as quickly as I would have liked. I wrung out the rags, dipped them again in cool water, and reapplied them. It was all I could do as hours passed and inactivity drew me closer and closer to the temptation of sleep. As my eyelids drooped, I began to search about for anything to take my attention. Somewhere lay a transcription of Apuleius' novel, *Metamorphoses* – a comedy that I often enjoyed to lose myself in – but the drama at hand seemed inappropriate for a story redubbed *The Golden Ass* by Saint Augustine.

In the corner of my eye, I noticed several letters perched upon Matteo's nightstand. My name upon one of the pages caught my gaze. They were freshly inked. Brimming with curiosity, I hazarded a glance.

Antonia, I fear this illness brings into sharp relief the vulnerability of my age. Should the superficial systems of this body fail and my time upon the Lord's fair earth be expended, I ask that you act upon an issue I've long been postponing.

The letter was in my hands now.

I bequeath my workshop, and all the items therein, excluding only that which Amadora lays claim to, unto you. They are to be sold and the returns used as dowry. Please see that she is married well. Signed, Matteo di Francesco.

My mind went blank. My eyes glazed over with a film of angry tears. "Married well?" The words fell softly from my mouth, though I hardly recognized them as mine. I felt confused, betrayed, and undeniably angry. "Married *well*?" My voice carried a sharper edge this time.

"I did not mean for you to read that, Amadora," Matteo's weak voice drifted up from his bed.

I looked at him, furiously searching for the man who had raised me in the workshop – in the ways of art and music and philosophy – but I could find no trace of him in the pale form that lay below me. My relief that he had awakened was buried beneath new mountains of pain and doubt. What had my life been for? Was I worth so little to him? Did my hopes mean so little to him?

"Did you think I didn't have a right to know what you were planning?" I crushed the letter in my hand. I felt my voice rising. "Or do I no longer have any place here? How could you do this?!"

"Amadora—" he began. I could not stand to hear his voice.

"This workshop is my home! I've never asked for anything other than to be by your side. I've supported you, learned from you my entire *life*…and for this? For you to marry me off like some bastard daughter?" I was on my feet now, blood practically boiling. "Did you ever think to ask me? Would you have even told me at all, or would I have been interrupted in my grieving by an unwanted marriage?" I hurled the crumpled letter at Matteo. He tried to speak. His mouth worked, but I didn't want to hear what he had to say. "Tell me, do the years we've spent together mean anything to you? Did you ever imagine me as someone who could follow in your footsteps, or were my lessons just a way for you to pass the time?" My voice fell quiet. Tears now fell unchecked from my eyes. "I had hoped that I might be like a daughter to you, but it seems the only legacy you mean to leave for me is a lifetime of regret and wasted talent.

"You should have left me upon the stoop." The words were out of my mouth, and I could not call them back. I was too angry. I was too hurt. The pressure in my chest was too great. With a gasping sob, I turned on my heel and fled the room, leaving Matteo to grasp weakly at the air as if to pull me back to him.

It was with a sore mindlessness that I ran into the workroom, so it was no surprise when I stumbled and crashed to the hard wooden floor. Angry splinters pushed into my cheek, but I found that I did not want to move. I just lay there – lay there and struggled to breathe.

How could I say that?

"Pathetic."

I screamed as a claw tangled into the back of my hair and painfully lifted me off the floor. I blindly scrabbled at an arm. But as the scene before me swam into view, a terrified chill froze me in place.

My face dangled mere inches from that of Gilio Salviati.

"We meet again, mocciosa," he growled. I could feel his warm breath.

I couldn't breathe. I could barely move. A suffocated shriek tried to escape my chest, but panic had closed my throat.

A weak voice struggled out of the bedroom. I could pay it no mind.

"Please…" I whimpered. With a hateful laugh, Gilio released me. I collapsed onto the floor.

I closed my eyes as I struggled to reclaim my breath. "What…what do you want?" I asked pathetically.

Gilio crouched down and leaned toward me. His eyes absently wandered downward, and I became abruptly aware that I wore only my nightgown. I uselessly tried to cover myself with my arms. Naked and helpless.

"Do you not remember?" he said. "I said I would return." His voice was calm, but I quailed at the intensity in his eyes.

"The painting?" I asked. His parting words of condemnation from the night before echoed through my mind.

"Ah yes, the painting," he said, turning away to examine the partially finished work. I took the opportunity to push myself to my feet and back several steps away. I would not give him the satisfaction of standing over me.

"Yes, I will have this painting."

I cringed. I wanted to give it to him – to see him gone from the workshop. *It is just a drawing*, I told myself. *I will give it to him, and he will leave. I will. I must.*

"It is not for sale." *Why did I say that?* It seemed that I could not abandon Matteo, even now.

"Then I will not be paying for it!" He donned a cruel smile. "Nevertheless, it is mine. Consider it remuneration for your...*performance* last night."

My heart skipped a beat, and the last hopeful vestiges of doubt left me. *He knows.*

"I don't understand—"

In an instant, he had crossed the workroom floor and struck me across the face with the back of his hand. My vision blurred as I cracked into a nearby cabinet. "Liar!" He screamed. His sword escaped its lavish sheath with an ear wrenching squeal.

The last of my barely maintained composure fled, and I fell backward onto the floor. Mind reeling, I clambered to get away from Gilio and the sword he held at my throat. As if from a distance, I heard myself pleading, supplicating for my life. *I'm going to die. I'm going to die.* I began to hyperventilate, desperately sucking in every breath as my mind fell further and further into a fear-induced haze. Through it, I watched Gilio stalk me in my pathetic scrambling across the floor. His eyes were wild. His mouth was curled into a smile.

"Stop this!" another voice rang out. Time froze for just a moment, all of us puppets upon suspended strings. "The painting is yours." Gilio slowly turned – having forgotten me for the moment, it seemed – toward where Matteo was standing near the hallway that led to the bedchamber. His face was white, and he struggled for every breath as he sagged against the wall, but his stare was vivid and harsh.

I scurried as far away as I was able, my heart still a bursting mass of terror. Slowly, my faculties began to return. My legs did not want to support my weight, but after a moment of struggling, I forced them beneath me.

"The painting is yours," Matteo repeated. He did not move, but his voice was strong.

"Truly, wisdom is a birthright of the elderly, vecchio," Gilio said scornfully. "You give to me that which I have already taken."

"Nevertheless, take it," Matteo replied. "Take it and be gone."

"No!" I yelled, unable to contain myself.

"Be quiet, Amadora!" Matteo fixed a commanding glare upon me.

"*Amadora.*" Gilio tasted my name – wrapping his tongue around it like a viper. "You would do well, bitch, to heed your master," he said. "He understands the way of the world. Everything has its price, does it not, vecchio?"

Matteo remained silent.

I could only watch as Gilio turned and again approached the painting. The scene called to me. White snow. Flowering trees. Rich flavors. Soft grass and rushing river.

The world seemed to slow until the air around me swirled and oozed like mud.

No!

I screamed as Gilio's sword tore through the painting. He laughed as he hacked at my teacher's beloved creation again and again and again, until the canvas was shredded beyond any lingering hope of repair. One of the clay pots of paint behind me cracked, and crimson dye seeped through the gash.

Shrieking wordlessly, I lunged at Gilio. My world was a blur of single-minded hate.

I threw myself against him, striking him with my fists and feet. It was with an almost absent distain that he threw me aside. My body slammed into the table, but I kept my feet beneath me.

"Whore," he growled. His sword was suddenly at my neck. I could see flecks of paint upon the blade's edge. I spat at Gilio, my fear momentarily displaced by loathing.

"You think this is righteous fury?" He mocked me. "It was your useless meddling that brought me here." His dark, sordid eyes held firm my own, and in them I felt as if I were caught in a whirling cesspool. There was something else there as well – deep within his gaze. Something sick and full of lust.

"Her actions have been accounted for, by my reckoning." Matteo's tired voice broke the spell that seemed to have been laid upon me. My short-lived courage was already melting away. Gilio's sword drew blood where it rested against my throat.

"Perhaps." Gilio licked his lips vulgarly, his gaze wandered down my body. "It would seem such a waste..."

His sword moved away from my throat, but my stomach curdled as Gilio used it to brush aside my sleeve, uncovering my pale shoulder.

"Stop!" Matteo yelled, struggling to move across the room. "Do not touch her!"

I shivered, but distaste kept blushing humiliation at bay.

"I always get," Gilio muttered, as though to himself, "what I desire." His sword brushed softly across my chest, sweeping aside my other sleeve. Nearly the full breadth of my bosom was uncovered, but the fear that again held me would not let me cover myself. Gilio's thin eyes devoured my exposed skin and slight breasts. Tears raced down my cheeks as shame overcame me, but still, I could not move. My heart quivered and tremors wracked my body.

Suddenly, Matteo stood before me. He swatted aside Gilio's sword, ignoring the deep gash it earned upon his palm. Blood dripped from his hand freely.

"Have you no modesty?" Matteo roared, anger free upon his tongue. "Vattene! You have done enough!"

Gilio snarled deep in his throat like an animal put off from the hunt. "Move aside, vecchio," he said quietly. The silence that followed was deadly. He was a snake, coiled to strike.

"I will not." Matteo's voice was labored, but not with frailty of resolve. "You are a small man, Gilio. A small man to tower so injudiciously. Your decadence betrays your insignificance." His words burnt against Gilio like fire. "Leave us! Your depravity will find no place here!"

The viper struck with nary a sound.

I screamed as the hilt of Gilio's sword smashed into the side of Matteo's head. Blood flecked my cheeks as his body was full hurled through the air. It collapsed into the tattered remnant of his painting, pulling the easel to the ground atop it and laying, as though lifeless, beneath the shredded canvas.

The wordless shriek that erupted from within my chest filled the workshop and fled into the countryside. As though from a distance, I watched myself take hold of a clay pot. Goat hair brushes clattered from its mouth as I raised it into the air. Gilio's back was turned.

I smashed the urn against the side of Gilio's head – just before his left ear. It shattered on impact, scoring a large gash across his brow. He roared in pain. More blood splayed out across the floorboards as he spun. Searing rage. Excruciating fury. Fire in his eyes.

My head cracked against the ground as he threw me to the floor. Dazed, concussed, teetering on the edge of consciousness: clarity came in flashes.

Cold wood against my stomach. My nightgown was torn away. Splinters slashed at my breasts.

Large, sweaty hands wrapped around my throat. I screamed, or tried to. My head whipped against the floorboards. I sputtered in a warm pool of blood that poured from my nose.

The blood ran into my mouth as I was lifted into the air. My nails dug into the hands at my neck. I writhed, desperate for air.

The table slammed into my stomach. I gasped and coughed up blood as my throat was freed. Something clenched my hair – another hand. My face smashed into the table. One of my teeth came loose.

A warm body pushed against my lower back. I struggled, and something heavy struck my leg. I heard the bone snap. Screaming, I went limp upon the table.

New pain surged within my abdomen – worse pain. The table heaved again against my exposed stomach. Again. Again. Warmth ran down my leg.

Helplessness. I was a doll. A puppet. No more screaming. Barely conscious. Barely alive.

Pressure gone, I collapsed backward off the table. Through a fog, I saw the oil lamp in his hand – saw it shatter against the floor. Fire. White tongues licked the walls and tables. Blank canvas burst aflame. I heard the paints gurgle and sputter.

Behind me, Matteo's tattered painting began to smolder. The wood frame cracked and buckled. At the corners of the canvas, bright paints bubbled and burst into sickly streaks of brown and yellow. The world within the painting collapsed as the rot shrunk inward. Blue skies turned to dark storm clouds of sulfur and brimstone. Untouched snow melted away as fire burst from the mountaintops. Trees cracked and fell, their fruit no more than withered husks.

The wonder of Eve's aspect: now horror. The butterfly upon her finger was gone. Cut away, or seared away. The canvas warped, and her face stretched into the façade of agony. Her mouth demonically distended.

Screaming. There was screaming as the last of the painting burnt away and the flames rose high above its corpse. She was screaming. A gnarled leg stuck out from beneath the pyre. Screaming.

Across the inferno, the mirror crashed to the ground. In its fissured face I caught side of a broken image. A naked body upon the floor. Nearly dead. Staring back with empty eyes.

I shut my gaze to her. The back of my eyelids glimmered with flickering light, but the darkness was comforting. I could feel the flames prowl closer and surround me. I prayed for a quick end.

There was an enveloping white light and a glaring pain in my chest. Then, darkness.

SUMMER

Notes on a Tuscan Workshop

The artisan atelier – the workshop – can trace the lineage of its tradition to long before even the Romans and their grand empire. It was the Greeks, in fact, sometime around the 8th century before the birth of Christ, who pioneered the concept of a workshop in their pursuit of artistic pottery – those Greeks who also brought mathematics, philosophy, and politics to humanity. In many ways, their work signified the birth of modern art and the since constant attempts to understand and reveal the beauty and mysticism apparent in the world around us. It is often said amongst painters that realism in art is not a reflection of nature, but an exploration of it.

The workshop of today's Toscana is not much different than that of Classical Greece. A master owns and manages the shop, directing those beneath him – both apprentices and paid artisans – in their duties so that the shop runs smoothly. Instruction, typically, is a matter of passive absorption; the longer a student is with the shop, the more he is entrusted with, the more practice he gets, and the more he learns. Eventually, a student – many of whom are apprenticed as young as ten years old – may attempt a work

Il maestro al lavoro

of such talent that the guild under which all painters submit may consider it a masterpiece. This marks the graduation of an apprentice to becoming a master himself, one who may now legally own his own workshop and take on his own apprentices.

To be sure, this system is not unique to Firenze, nor even to Italia, and while many argue that Firenze perfected the method, one must wonder whether the system itself may be flawed in some way. There is no common knowledge amongst artists. One master teaches one student, and so the knowledge of any artisan is only a pale reflection of the teacher under whom he studied. In the long journey of time, knowledge has, and will continue to be, drained away through the gaps and fissures between each generation. What is not taught, is forgotten, and should a master die, his techniques are lost along with him.

Have you ever been woken from a dream? The haunting imperfection of reality is never more apparent than at the cusp of consciousness, where the lingering comfort of sleep – so often unappreciated – is upset by the harsh colors and sharp lines of the wakened world.

It is in the wakened world that I now dwell.

Long I swam in darkness. Around me were half seen visions – haunting phantoms that spoke with a terrible voice. "You are mine, Amadora Trovatelli." They were so familiar.

Fire. Fire all around me.

Screaming.

I woke, gasping. Light burnt against my eyes. Screaming. I was screaming. Something upon me – a hand; I writhed to get away. *Don't touch me!* I choked and my lungs plead for air. Screaming turned to desperate sobbing. I was trapped. Something lay upon me, holding me down.

"Amadora!"

A voice. I sobbed. The light hurt my eyes.

"Amadora!"

Antonia? I searched through the fog around me. She was there, laying across my arms, clinging to the bed. I stopped thrashing, but shivers still wracked my body. "Antonia?" I repeated, my voice a dry whisper. My tongue was swollen, and my throat ached.

My panic began to subside, but desperate confusion was quick to replace it. My thoughts felt slow and sluggish. *Where am I?* A room. Not my room. The bed was too soft, and the blankets that lay upon me felt too heavy.

A weight lifted from me. Antonia had moved. She sat next to me, her expression that of deep concern. Sadness lay thick upon her eyes.

"Where am I?" My voice again. It sounded so wrong.

Tentatively, she reached for my hand. I trembled and almost jerked it away, but she grasped it and held me firmly.

"Amadora," she said softly. "Little one, how do you feel?"

I was so confused. Silently, I struggled to make sense of everything. *How do I feel?* I was sweating, and my body ached. I shifted, and my leg cried out in agony. It was bound, I realized, tightly bound so that I could not move it. There was another pain too, a deep burning pain between my legs. I could not remember why.

"Where am I?" I repeated. "Where is Matteo?"

Matteo. Where was he? I needed to know. I needed so badly to know.

"You are in the palazzo," Antonia said softly.

The palazzo? "Where is Matteo?"

"Amadora…"

"Where is he? Where is Matteo?" I was almost yelling, though my voice cracked and broke around my swelled throat. Was I crying?

My sodden eyes caught a candle as it burnt upon the nightstand. Fire. It consumed my vision. Fire everywhere.

I began to weep as tardy memory swept through and drowned me. The shredded painting. Matteo's body as it lay beneath the broken easel. At the memory of Gilio, I curled into a ball and began to moan. My fingers raked against my abdomen. I could still feel him inside of me. Invading. Tearing.

For what felt like an eternity, I did not move. I wept for a time, then my tears dried up and I lay as if dead. Vaguely, I knew Antonia still sat beside me. I could hear her cry, feel the tears upon my arm as she still grasped my hand.

I felt empty.

Hours, surely, passed. Antonia never left my side, but I felt no comfort in her presence. In fact, I felt nothing at all.

"How?" The sound of my voice – so even, so empty – surprised even myself.

"What?" Antonia replied, confused. She sounded sad.

"How did I get here?" My skin was unbroken, yet I could clearly feel the memory of flames upon my body. I knew I should be dead, burnt away to cinder. Something in Antonia's face agreed. There was a secret there – a whisper of something amiss.

"We…found you," she said.

I nearly pressed for whatever she was hiding from me, but I found that I could not bring myself to care. *What does it matter?*

"Amadora," Antonia prompted, her hand gently caressing my own. The gesture seemed surreal, even nonsensical, in this new world I had woken into. "Amadora, the fire…what happened?"

I looked at her, yet didn't really see her. My mind wandered through a field of mist. I could not speak, could not move.

"I'm sorry little one. I should not have asked so soon." She sounded tired. "You do not need to say anything until you are ready. I've sent for the doctor. Until then, you should rest."

She brushed my cheek in a way that would once have comforted me.

I said nothing as she left, yet in the stillness of her absence, I could not find sleep. My mind wandered aimlessly. I fixated on the mundane as if the placement of my clothes as they had laid within my chest of drawers was a lifeline to my uncertain sanity.

Mentally, I walked every foot of the workshop I remembered. Every brush, I stooped to touch. Every floorboard creaked familiarly beneath my feet. Yet it was empty. Try as I might, I could not conjure even a ghost of Matteo to haunt the halls of my memory.

I killed him.

The realization did not erupt within me like a sudden inspiration. I *had* killed him, of that there was no doubt. My little game of virtue at the festa had writ the decree of his death, and my craven indignity in the workshop had delivered the note. I was a murderer. Patricide of the ugliest sort.

Still though, I felt nothing. Perhaps I was numb, but it seemed to me more likely that I had simply fallen to a hell beyond pain and guilt.

The doctor came and went, or so I was told. Twice, in fact, though I remembered nothing of each visit. Full consciousness frightened me and unconsciousness eluded me, so I spent my days and nights as if in a dream, wandering the workshop of my mind – searching for something, though I knew not what. Perhaps it was Matteo I searched for, perhaps not.

Only when Antonia attended me could I rouse myself from my apathy. She sat by my side for long hours with few words, for which I was grateful. At times I let her hold my hand as well. It seemed to comfort her.

As the weeks passed, a new horror occurred to me, yet one that I could not face, so I shut my eyes to the signs and dove again into the slim comfort of my memories. However, I found that I was no longer able to wholly avoid the waking hours of consciousness from which I had thus far hidden myself.

It was almost a month before Jacopo paid me a visit. Antonia was at my side when he came, hesitantly, into the room they had given me.

"Amadora," he said in solemn greeting. His eyes darkened as they took me in. My condition had worsened in many ways since waking, I knew. I hadn't eaten, had barely thirsted. I supposed that I looked like a husk of myself.

I said nothing, but something in my gaze must have unsettled him for he shied away almost as soon as our eyes met. Nevertheless, he settled himself behind Antonia, who more firmly grasped my hand beneath the blankets piled atop me.

"Amadora," he repeated, "how are you feeling?"

I did not respond. By his face, I didn't have to.

Jacopo sighed sadly. "Little one, I cannot make you tell us what happened the night of the fire." He paused, as if to offer me a chance to speak. When I did not, he continued. "But while your tongue lays silent, others gossip and speculate. Many were there when we found you—"

"Jacopo!" Antonia interrupted, as if to forestall his words.

He took a deep breath. His eyes again met mine, and again shied away. "Very well, I will not pry, but should you find your voice again, please come to us." Reaching forward, he lay a comforting hand upon my arm.

My world exploded. Skin aflame, my heart seized with terror. I flailed, desperately throwing my body away from his touch. I was screaming, I realized, and shaking. I cracked my elbow as I fell from the bed, yet still I struggled to get away. In a mindless haze, I found the corner of the room. Curling into a ball, I fought the tremors that wracked my weak body. No more screams, but I was crying now.

"Amadora!" Antonia cried out, rushing to my side. Quick behind her was Jacopo, but at his approach, I again found myself screaming. I was trapped – an animal in a cage. I lashed out with my broken leg, and my shrieks climbed even higher as it struck the floor.

Antonia threw herself atop me. "Jacopo! Leave! Now!"

He hesitated for only a moment before retreating from the room. As he disappeared, I collapsed into a pile on the floor. Hugging my knees to my chest, I cried. I cried, and I shook while Antonia took my head in her lap and cried with me.

I did not see any more of Jacopo; Antonia was careful to keep him from my room after that. Even the doctor was disallowed after his touch too – a touch I was now aware of in full consciousness – ignited another episode of terror.

I have been broken, I realized. *Not just my body, but my mind. I am a cracked vase and of no use to anybody.*

Days that I had before spent intentionally half-aware were now suffered slowly in wakefulness. I still could not sleep, but now too the haven of my memories eluded me. I was left alone, for hours, with naught but the discomfort of my psyche – a poor bedmate indeed. And with every passing day, that which I most feared crept ever closer, ever more certain. Before long I found myself eager to escape my narrow bedchamber and the nightmares that haunted me within.

Still, two more weeks passed before I could put weight upon my leg enough to brave a visit into the familiar alleys and piazzas of Montaione. I left without a word to Antonia. Limping – clinging to the walls of the palazzo for support – I made my way out from my prison room. At the door to the palazzo I found a walking stick, a staff likely forgotten by some long-gone traveler. I took it, and clutching to it, I walked out into the town I once loved.

I do not know what I expected from the people of Montaione. Pity, compassion maybe, or even anger if they lay cause for the fire with me, but I could not have imagined the looks that awaited me at every corner and in every gaze.

What evil thing have I done to earn this?

Fear. Fear painted the face of every man and woman to watch as I shambled and limped down Via Cresci. Mothers – women who had offered me sweets as a child – hurried their children into shops and homes. Girls with whom I had traded secrets around the well in the piazza shied away as I passed. Every face was that of a brother or sister, father or mother, but now it was as if they were strangers to me.

I turned into the Piazza della Chiesa, mindless in my desire to escape the palazzo, yet as I shuffled through the square, my leg began to call for rest just as my heart begged shelter from the fearful glances that felt to me like the piercing of knives. *Why?!* Closing my eyes, I pleaded for an escape, yet the darkness only replaced sight with sound.

"There she is."

"I know what she is. I've always known."

"Stay away from her.

"*Strega.*"

The world spun. Desperately, I fled for the church – San Regolo whose large doors shadowed the piazza. I collapsed against them, tears falling to the cobblestone beside my walking stick as I grasped the wrought iron handle.

The door suddenly opened into me with such force that I was thrown backward. I cried out in pain as I fell and my leg struck the ground.

"Strega! Witch!" Padre Curato stood in the threshold of the church. His pious expression, that safe, calm, holy look that I had seen so many hundreds of times, now looked down at me with revulsion. "I will not allow your filth within this house of God!"

I fought against the pain in my leg as I struggled to push myself to my feet.

"Wh—." I sucked in breath. My heart was racing. "Why?" I finally asked, my voice strangled. "What have I done?" *I just want to understand.*

"Leave her be, you fools!" a new voice rose above the rest – a familiar voice. *Signor Roberto?* I wondered as the innkeeper managed to separate himself from the crowd.

"You cast your lot in with the devil, Roberto?" Padre Curato asked, feigning sadness, it seemed to me.

"Is sympathy the lot of the devil? Are not we taught to love? Amadora is one of us – she is as much a part of this village as any of you – yet you all condemn her without trial. You have no proof, I say! None!"

A short silence followed Signor Roberto's speech. A few faces had the grace to show shame, but Padre Curato only seemed to grow angrier.

"Evil is without law, and so deserves no trial." Curato announced. "We must be vigilant and purge such putrescence from our midst." His small eyes turned to

Roberto. "And we must not suffer those who would defend evil in the name of justice. Lucifer has a serpent's tongue!"

"Foul witch!" a voice yelled out. "Strega!"

"Signora Tessa?" I asked in quiet disbelief as the aging seamstress cursed me with bared teeth. She spit in my direction.

"Leave this place, witch!" Padre Curato called out. "You are not welcome here!" With his arms outstretched, as if to ward away a demon, he approached me. I saw his hands, his gnarled fingers, his untidy nails, and knew what would come next; I saw it as though we were actors upon a stage, yet I could do nothing to stop myself as I tripped backward and fell to the ground, scrambling away from his touch, whimpering as panic gripped me.

"There! You see?" the priest called out as I struggled to compose myself. "Do any of you still doubt? See how she flees from the hands of God! She is a witch! A strega!"

A chorus of curses rose around me. Even Signor Roberto looked now at me with uncertain eyes.

"Flee, strega! Slither back to your hole!"

Sobbing, terrified, and nearly paralyzed by pain, I slowly crawled back into the Palazzo di Compagni. My knees and elbows were raw from pulling myself across the flagstones, harried by curses. Some had even thrown rocks. The gate closed behind me, and I lay within the entryway, chest heaving, as someone ran to fetch Antonia.

The world is rotted – a corpse that parades about in the guise of life. Of all else, I have learned this lesson with the most certainty: evil is not a plague, something to be either succumbed to or sloughed off. Depravity is a defining quality of humanity.

If we are truly the Lord's children, it follows that he must be a whoreson.

I thought I had run dry of tears.

"We found you." I remembered Antonia's words, spoken as I first woke in the palazzo. There was a secret there, a reason to explain this new condition. I hadn't cared before, but now...now I needed to know.

So when Antonia arrived with a pair of her servants (women both, for which I was thankful), gasping, to find me skinned and bruised upon the stone floor of her entryway, my questions were poised.

"Why?" I asked, voice cracking with something between anger and sorrow.

"Mio Dio!" she cried out, dropping to the ground beside me. "What happened? Oh Amadora, what did they do to you?"

She expected this. "Why?" I repeated harshly.

"Come now, let's get you to your bed and clean these scrapes," she said, ignoring my question. She motioned for the women with her to help me off the ground. I gripped her arm so tightly that she cried out.

"Why?"

Her eyes held mine for a moment, then fell. I wondered at what was now so plain in my gaze that people could not bear to see it. Her shoulders slumped, and she leaned back against the cold wall of the corridor. "You can go," she said, waving away the pair of servants with a flick of her wrist. They left quickly, and I didn't miss the look of relief they shared with each other at doing so.

"Tell me," I demanded. "How did you find me?"

Antonia closed her eyes. Her brow wrinkled, and a concerned look painted her face. "The fire," she finally said, "was worse than I've ever seen. The flames rose like pillars into the sky, and it burned so brightly that it lit the streets of Montaione all through the night." She opened her eyes, and forced herself to meet my gaze. "And it did burn all through the night. From dusk 'til dawn, your workshop cackled and spat and seared the clouds. We tried to put it out – every man in the village came with water and bucket – but we couldn't even get close.

"We were certain you and Matteo hadn't escaped. No one had seen you, and we'd searched the fields around the workshop. We gave you up for dead."

"Where did you find me?"

I waited while she composed her next words.

"After. In the charred ashes and glowing rubble." For the first time, I saw fear in her eyes.

Even you, Antonia? I think it was then that I truly despaired. My last refuge had burned away.

"You were naked, pale as a ghost with blood upon your face and thighs. Your leg was broken, but there was not a burn or blister upon your entire body. Not one." Antonia looked away. "No one could have survived that—that inferno, yet…" She struggled with herself for a moment. "It was as if the workshop had folded down around you."

The hallway, Antonia, my bruised body, all of it faded away for just a moment into nothingness. I could almost remember. It was so close. The fire. The white flash. Something had grabbed me.

And just like that, the memory was gone. *I was saved,* I marveled to myself. *By…something.* I desperately tried to bring back the vision. I clawed at my mind, but all I could recall was the feeling of hands around my chest. Hands and…*wings?* I shook my head. *What was it?*

Antonia laid a hand upon my arm, gently bringing me back from my wonderings. "What happened, Amadora?" she asked, quietly yet with soft apprehension. "We do not believe you are a witch, as Padre Curato claims. There must be some explanation."

I couldn't answer. I tried, but I couldn't. *I don't know,* I silently shouted. *I don't know.*

That night, I slept for the first time since the fire. I dreamt of hands lifting me away from my bed and into a great white light. There was a voice, but I could not hear its words. If I could only hear its words, I might remember…something.

When I woke, it was to the silence of an empty room. I hated silence – I always had. I much preferred the soft sounds of a flute or harp to its lack. For a moment, I allowed myself to mourn my harp and its fate of cinders. In my mind, I looked to where my harp had sat in the workshop, hoping for one last look even if just in my memories, yet when I cast my mind's eye to the spot, it stood empty.

My harp wasn't in the fire, I realized with a jolt of something that could almost be mistaken for happiness. *I left it with Antonia after the festa.* I'd almost forgotten. My harp was still here, in the palazzo somewhere.

I rose from bed upon uneasy legs, but I was strengthened with new determination. *I haven't lost everything. Not yet.*

It was just a harp, a tool, an instrument of no real value and easily replaced. It could not belittle, in even the smallest part, what I'd suffered or hide the looming symptoms of a nightmare I still refused to acknowledge, and yet…it was something. I was like a woman dying of thirst; to me, even one drop of rain was a miracle.

For the second time in two days, I set out from my room. Like before, I clung to the walls to steady myself. The scabs on my knees and elbows cracked and threatened to bleed, but I could not find it in me to care. Room after room, I searched, starting with the courtyard. From there, I made my way to the studiolo, then to the storerooms. As I wandered through chamber and hall, I found myself needing to rest often. *You were not this weak before.* I ignored the voice in my head, and what it was trying to tell me. There were a few servants about, mostly cleaning. I could have asked for help, but I didn't. I needed to do this on my own.

Finally, as I limped down yet another corridor, I spied my harp through a wide doorway, sitting proudly within the great room at the heart of the palazzo. Beside it was a sculpted hearth of marble – cold and dusted free of ashes – and elsewhere in the room were stationed luxurious pillowed benches. I remembered the place well, for Matteo and I had worked for weeks upon the frescoes lining the walls that I could not quite yet see from the hallway.

I hesitated when I heard voices drifting through the doorway – the voices of Antonia and Jacopo as they sat, still out of sight, within the room.

"…says he has written the College of Bishops in Rome. Who knows what they'll do."

"The question is, what do *we* do? If they call a court…we don't want the inquisition here."

"We can't do anything until we know what happened."

"Jacopo, please, she needs time. She's been through so much."

Silence.

"I'll talk to her." There was a moment of silence, then a rustling of footsteps that soon faded away.

I knew the conversation had been about me, but I paid it no mind. My only thought was of my harp. I continued through the doorway, and it was into an empty room that I hobbled. Antonia and Jacopo must have left by another exit.

My limp was almost forgotten as I walked across the tiled floor. It was so close. It seemed like a monument of hope, singing to me of what once had been.

I was unnaturally conscious of my hands as I picked the harp from the floor and carried it to the nearest bench. Sitting, I braced the instrument between my calves. It felt harder than I remembered – its corners sharper. For some time, I simply sat there, waiting for the reassurance, the comfort, the passion that had always come with holding my harp.

It never came.

Desperate, I attempted to strum the strings. My fingers were irregular, clumsy, too brash and at the same time too timid. The coarse fibers caught in my nails and scratched my skin. And the sound...*oddio, the sound*. It was horrible – grating and cacophonous and excruciating in the highest degree.

My arms went cold. A cry of despair tore my throat. In one lurching motion I cast the instrument away. It seemed to hang in the air, flying, for too long a moment; all the while, I watched with the suffocated apprehension of a man upon the footsteps of the gallows. After what seemed like an eternity, it crashed to the floor, bounced once, and then clattered to an end almost within the empty marble hearth.

Gasping, I pulled my knees to my chest. Finally I understood: there was nothing left. Nothing of myself – of the life I'd lived or the women I'd been – had survived that fire. Even my music had been burned away; I knew it deep in my heart with a certainty beyond faith.

Then, for the last time, I cried. I cried like a child – eyes clenched shut, fists beating at my thighs, sobs wracking my breast until I could barely breathe.

Minutes, hours – I lost track of time. Even when the tears had gone and the shivers calmed, my head continued to ache. After a while, I opened my eyes. My harp still lay prone within the inglenook, feigning death.

I stared at it – lost myself in it. What a joke. It was not a monument to hope, it was the tombstone of my former life. A cruel souvenir from a sadistic god.

God did not do this to you, a small voice whispered from the back of my head. *That's right, God may have let the fire burn, but he did not light the tinder.*

"Gilio." My whisper was a dark prayer.

For the first time I realized, as I gazed upon the harp, there were two of me – the Amadora that had danced through Tuscan hills and painted with innocent passion, and this new, harsher Amadora whom I barely knew. I could feel myself tearing apart as they fought for dominance within me. They could not both exist, and I suddenly understood – with stark clarity of hindsight – that the conflict between them had been shackling me since I'd first awakened after the fire. It was so obvious. So obvious, and so inescapable.

And so, in that room, before an empty hearth and a harp that belonged to another girl, I let the dead die. The woman I'd once been fell away without the whisper of a struggle, and I accepted the reality of what I'd become.

It felt as though I had woken from a dream. Off from my shoulders I sloughed the larger part of guilt, regret, and despair. I was lighter now, disburdened of a weight I hadn't known I carried. Away from me I cast the feeble coat of hope and piety, and beneath I found myself to be hard – like iron tempered by the flame.

I had been scared, so scared, every moment of every day since I'd woken – scared of what I'd done, scared of what was yet growing inside me, and above all, scared to admit the emotion that always threatened to overwhelm me. *I'm not scared anymore,* I told myself. *It's his turn to be scared.* The floodgates opened, and out poured my repressed anger and tardy hate. White hot rage burned within my chest – embers of the fire that had killed me – and through the fog of my fury I saw his face, the face of the man who had done this to me. I held it close to my heart with a mindless fervor. I would not let it go. His face was the only one that mattered to me anymore. His face was the only one I allowed myself to see.

That was how Antonia found me, alone, curled up upon a bench in the great room, my teeth bared and my resolve focused to a deadly point.

"Amadora! Little one, you had me nearly in a panic! I've been searching everywhere for you." She saw the room in a glance – my harp upon the floor – and rushed to my side, eyes full of concern.

I looked at her, yet still his face was the only one I saw. Slowly, I tested his name upon my tongue.

"Gilio Salviati."

It tasted like a sweet wine. I relished it, working it around my mouth to savor its feel.

"What did you just say?" Jacopo had followed Antonia into the room, and it was the forceful snap of his voice that broke the stillness. Antonia, I realized without truly caring, had frozen, her hand just above my arm.

"Gilio Salviati," I repeated, letting his name fan the anger that now filled me. "He came to the workshop."

Neither Jacopo nor Antonia so much as breathed into the deathly silence that filled the spaces between my words.

"He knew I was the one who foiled him at the festa."

Jacopo's eyes flickered to Antonia, but he said nothing.

"He destroyed the painting. He murdered Matteo. He set the workshop afire."

The next words formed in my mouth without even a thought. What did I care? These were the tortures of a girl I'd left for dead.

"He raped me."

At that, Antonia began to cry, and I found that I hated her for it. When she reached toward me, I struck her hand away. Abruptly, as they had so many times over the last weeks, sharp pangs of womanhood wracked my venter. I nearly gasped from the sting, and my breasts ached as if bruised. I could hide from the truth no longer.

"I am pregnant."

Notes on an Unmarried Mother

It is a failing of modern culture that women are the sole proprietors of virginity and so pay in its entirety the price for misplaced lust. It was not always so. In many of the earliest recorded love songs of Egypt, sexual romance – especially that which precluded marriage – was lauded as a thing of beauty. Virginity was of social inconsequence, and in fact, the Egyptian language has not even a word to explain the concept. To be a bastard – born of unmarried parents – was there irrelevant, and thus the role of an unmarried mother differed little from that of her marital counterpart. This, when taken alongside the merciless social abuses modernly toted as proper behavior, begs the question: what changed?

To be sure, it is a question worth considering, for the plight of the unchaste woman is dire and without prospect. They are devalued, and so demand a higher cost of dowry – one that, if not met, disqualifies them from marriage entirely. As marriage is a cornerstone of Italian life, to be barred from its institution is crippling in the highest degree. The unmarriageable in most cases are left with two divergent paths. One is that of the reformed, to take the holiest of

*Le lacrime annaffiano la muratura
vicino L'Ospedale degli Innocenti*

oaths and cloister themselves within the house of God. The other is the path of the outcast, to take on the face of a whore and throw off the habit of honor.

These roads are unsatisfactory enough that to be forced upon them should be considered cruel, and yet for the unwed mother – that poor wench who upon the act of sexual misconduct is cursed with the progeny that sometimes arises from such – there is no option at all. The convent will not have her. No dowry will sell her. So it is to the brothel with her and her issue, to be reminded of the manner by which she fell from social grace until the end of her corporal usefulness.

Firenze, the perceived Italian capital of abstract sexuality, is a city of self-deceit, for while prostitutes are called upon with a frequency that borders upon addiction, they are simultaneously abused by social opinion and legislative directive. A whore is not allowed to enter many districts of the city, nor is she allowed to wear jewelry or don a gentlewoman's veil. She cannot ride in a coach or frequent a wine shop, and the penalties for unlicensed solicitation are extreme indeed.

The city is a cesspool of willful ignorance and hypocrisy. 'Permit not the unchaste,' they write with their right hand while caressing the breast of an unmarried mother with their left.

I have not found love to be a natural disposition. The few times I've experienced it have been the product of lengthy social construction, and if you can measure the primacy of something by its persistence, then the fragility of affection seems to disprove its inherency.

In the absence of love is only hate, just as dusk waits in the shadow of light. All candles burn away to darkness eventually.

I never loved you, Adamo. You were a pestilence from the first moment I knew you. Perhaps one day you will forgive me for that.

"He is gone, Amadora – for good – and you shouldn't dwell on him." Antonia's words sounded much the same as they had so many times over the past month. I ignored her, choosing instead to continue reading the text I had laid out in front of me.

"Per altra via, per altri porti verrai a piaggia, no qui, per passare," I read aloud, hoping that Antonia would take the hint and leave. She sighed heavily.

"You are as stubborn now as you ever were." Her words were stern, yet softened with a small smile. I was surprised she still cared to offer me such kindnesses; after so many weeks, it should have been clear that I no longer cared for them.

"You cannot dissuade me from this, Antonia. Nothing can. He deserves to suffer."

Her look turned sour at my words. "You talk of murder so casually. It isn't right," she mumbled, yet thankfully she said no more. Eventually, she stood. "Suor Maria says the child you bear is healthy. She warns you to avoid any distress, though you clearly mean to ignore her. You should think more of the child and less of yourself."

It was unlike Antonia to snap at me, but I supposed it was long overdue. As she left, I wondered if now she would stop visiting as often. *I can only hope.*

For the moment, it seemed, I was alone. Closing my book, I took a deep breath, enjoying the silence.

As soon as Antonia had learned of the pregnancy, she'd sent for a midwife from the nearest convent. Jacopo had, at the same time, written of my plight to Firenze, and while no response from his letters had yet arrived, the convent Santa Lucia had almost immediately obliged Antonia's request with Suor Maria – a woman of impossible gaiety and infuriating optimism. For the last month, she had lived within the palazzo, and so far her every word had been repulsively happy.

"The Lord has given you such a blessing in this hard time," she would offer whenever she talked of the growing child within my womb. "You will make such a fine mother." I could almost laugh were the joke not so cruel.

I am no mother, I told myself. *I never wanted that domestic life, and I'll be damned if I change my mind for this.* No, I would never mother this foul thing within me. As soon as it tore itself free, I would be rid of it. Antonia could give it to the church if she wanted, or she could leave it for the wolves. I did not care. As soon as the child was gone, I planned to leave for Firenze. For Gilio.

Nine months was too long a wait, and I often thought of leaving sooner – of taking the Porta Grande and traveling east. I knew, though, that I wouldn't get far before Antonia's people would catch me up and take me back to the palazzo. "For my own safety," she had said. Until the birthing, I was practically a prisoner.

Returning to my book, I waited for the next unwelcome interruption.

It was not long in coming. Only a few hours later, Suor Maria arrived to check on my health, as she did every day around the same time. I noted that Antonia was absent for a change; maybe she would finally give me some peace after all.

"Buon pomeriggio!" the stout nun exclaimed upon entering. "Have you seen out your window? It looks as though summer might come early. What a gift!"

The woman bewildered me. She was hardly much older than myself, yet she took to her habit and wimple with a happy fervor I rarely saw even in the older nuns. With a muted sigh, I resigned myself to another checkup.

"I've been resting," I told her before she had a chance to ask. "And I've not had any fruits."

"Bene!" she said. "But your humours are still unbalanced; this is why you are so melancholy." At that, I bit back a hateful laugh. "Have you eaten any venison?"

"No. We've had guinea fowl for nearly a week now."

"That's good. Deer is known to unsettle the stomach. You ought to eat warm, moist foods." If possible, she smiled even more brightly. "I'll talk to the kitchen about bringing you some boiled greens. That should settle you right up."

I didn't bother arguing. Best to let her do what she would do; I never managed to dissuade her anyway. *God, I hate this woman,* I thought to myself.

"I'm glad I can be of help," she continued, voice bubbly. "I'll never mother children of my own, after all, but I'm blessed that at least I might help bear so many other children like yours. In that way, I suppose, I'm a mother to many!" She chittered away. "Goodness, what would my sisters think to hear me talk like that? Sometimes I think I may not be as humble as I should be." She winked as she stood to leave.

"When did you take your vows?" The question slipped out before I could stop it.

"Oh, how sweet you are to ask." She returned to her seat, brushing the folds of her habit away so she could sit down. "I was a little girl – couldn't have been much older than four or five. It was so wonderful, I remember. I have never known a happier home than that of the Lord." Her eyes lit up. "Are you considering a life in the convent? Oh, you should! I would be so happy to have you as a sister!"

I ignored her. "Where did you live before that?"

She shook her head and shrugged as if my question were silly. "My parents were farmers near Gambassi, though I hardly remember them. My family is the church now."

"Allora non sì sa." I was speaking to myself, but of course Suor Maria thought my words were directed at her.

"I don't know what, amica mia?"

I took her eyes with mine and held them, searching. They were bright, but empty. I realized that, to me, Suor Maria wasn't even a real person. The girl knew no more of life than what she could find in her convent. She was a doll, I thought – pretty, but useless.

"Anything," I said, mostly to myself. "You don't know anything." *Neither did I, before the fire. The world is far fouler and more hateful than you'd know, Suor Maria.*

Her smile was sad, as if I were the one who knew nothing. Part of me wanted to reach over and strike the condescending smirk from her lips. "The Lord has shown me all that I need to know through the gift of scripture. Within it I've found love, forgiveness, and compassion – the fullest fruits of knowledge."

"You cannot possibly understand those things from a book," I replied, struggling to keep my frustration in check. "You have no idea of forgiveness, thinking it's available to anyone. It isn't. There are some things that even God can't forgive – some things that aren't his *to* forgive."

"Amadora, you are so wrong," she said, still smiling her sad, stupid smile. "You need only ask, and you shall be forgiven. 'If we confess our sins, he is faithful and just to forgive us our sins, and to cleanse us from all unrighteousness'," she quoted.

"You would not say that if you knew what it was like to have a family." I didn't know why I was so desperate to make her understand. "You don't even remember your father. You couldn't know what it's like to lose him and to know that your last moment with him was one of anger." I couldn't stop myself. "There is no forgiveness for that. The only person who could forgive me is murdered, and I'm to blame."

Leaning forward, she gently lay a hand upon mine. "Let's sing our scriptures, sister. I think there is much that the Lord would say to you."

Almost instinctively, I shook her away. "I think not, Suor Maria. I see no love or compassion, and I call fool the god who claims to give it to me."

For the first time, the nun's smile disappeared. "I—I'm sorry to hear that, Amadora. I will pray for you."

Not long after she left, a bowl of boiled spinach was delivered to my room. I poured it onto the street outside my window where someone might mistake it for the contents of my chamber pot.

Visitors came to Montaione that week, but I was so sequestered in the castello that I didn't hear about them for nearly half a day. It wasn't until Antonia appeared, anxiously rushing me into a dress far nicer than I'd worn the night of the festa, that I first thought something might be wrong.

"They're here to see you," she said when I asked, not really answering my question.

"Who?"

She didn't reply. Pulling me along, she led us silently and quickly through the palazzo.

We paused just before the great room. "Please, little one," she said, straightening my hair, "for your own sake, put on a good face." Gently, she cupped my cheeks and kissed my forehead. "Everything will be fine."

I almost said something scathing in response, but I got the feeling that Antonia had been talking more to herself than to me.

As she ushered me inside though, any thought of an eventual reply vanished. Padre Curato was waiting within, standing behind an empty chair. I could see the muscles in his neck tighten as I entered, but I caught his eyes and held them, watching with a sort of satisfaction as his body became more and more rigid. Finally, he looked away.

It was only then that I noticed the man in the great room beside him – a Spaniard by his dark eyes and hair – and wearing a black cloak that identified him as a Dominican Friar. "Tomás," he introduced himself to Antonia with a polite smile and nod of his head. His accent was heavy.

Antonia acknowledged him with a low curtsy that surpassed polite respect. "Benevenuto, Fra Tomás. I'm glad to welcome you to Montaione." Her voice was supplicant, almost beggarly, and the uncharacteristic show of timidity was a little bit unnerving.

The man seemed blind to her posturing. "Would I be right in assuming this is Amadora?" he asked with a smile, now looking to me.

I said nothing, though I was clearly expected to. Antonia was quick to fill my silence. "Oh, yes! Of course, Fra Tomás. This is Amadora. Though clearly you knew that. She is still suffering from the accident, forgive her rudeness. She really is a sweet girl."

Antonia was stumbling over her words like some sort of drunkard. I wondered at what sort of man could unnerve a woman who entertained nobility for a living. So far Tomás seemed courteous, if not entirely sociable. Certainly he didn't seem threatening.

"Please, make yourselves comfortable," Antonia said as a servant entered with a tray of cakes and wine.

Fra Tomás accepted with a gracious nod and settled himself onto the couch. Padre Curato, however, remained standing, his eyes again turned upon me. The servant offered him a glass of wine.

"Enough of this!" he growled, striking the cup away. The young woman who had offered it squeaked in surprise, and the remainder of her tray tumbled out of her hands, splashing pastries and crimson wine across the floor. "There's no need for false courtesy. We're here for the girl!" His long gnarled finger pointed toward me as if he were passing judgement. "The strega!"

Tomás stood, and calmly reaching out, he seized Curato's arm with a grip fierce enough to make the older man wince. "You are embarrassing yourself, Padre. Worse, you are embarrassing the church. Sit down." He spoke quietly, but with an edge that made me shiver.

Humiliated, Curato's cheeks blushed cerise. In his haste to sit, he nearly fell into the couch, and I had to choke back a snicker. He glared at me savagely, and through my amusement, I knew that his embarrassment had only further fueled his hatred for me.

Without hesitation, Tomás knelt to the ground beside the terrified serving girl and began cleaning the mess of food and drink upon the floor.

"Addio! No, Fra Tomás, there is no need for you to do that!" Antonia seemed horrified, and quickly tried to call in more servants to clean the mess and pull the first girl away from the room.

"Do not interrupt me, woman," he said with a heavy voice that brooked no argument. Instead, we were left to sit in silence as he cleaned the floors and wall. Antonia's eyes seemed to bulge larger and larger with every passing minute, and when Tomás began mopping up the spilt wine with the front of his cloak, I almost expected her to faint. Curato, meanwhile, watched the scene with angry impatience.

Finally finished, he returned to his seat as if nothing had happened. "The Apostle Matthew instructs us that 'he that is greatest amongst you shall be your servant'," he said by way of explanation.

I watched Antonia out of the corner of my eye. *Why does this man frighten you?* I wondered. *He's just another fool of the church.* Yet even as I thought the words, something within me told me that I was wrong. There was more to this Tomás than I had thus far seen.

"Despite his rudeness, Padre Curato is right, we can dispense with the pretenses. You know what I am here to do."

Antonia froze in the act of calling for more wine. I could see the sweat begin to form on her brow. "Sì, lo so," she replied hesitantly.

Tomás reached into his habit and retrieved a folded piece of parchment. "The formal charges are as follows," he began, opening it. His stony voice did not betray the gravity of his words – a discrepancy most unnerving. "The girl, Amadora Trovatelli, is accused by the Holy Catholic Church of maleficium, also known as witchcraft, patricide by those means, and of fornication with demons – which is an abomination before the Lord."

Silence followed. Padre Curato, I absently noted, carried a look of triumphant satisfaction. I wanted to say something – anything – but found that I couldn't. My mouth worked, but no sound came out. Antonia's hand found my own, and for once, I held it.

This will come to pass. I found myself chanting the passage over and over in my mind. It steadied me.

The Spaniard continued as if he was commenting on the weather, and for the first time, I felt fear creep into my stomach.

"We, of the Holy Apostolic See, hereby appoint Fra Tomás de Torquemada as Father Inquisitor and grant him the authority of the Church until this heresy has been resolved," he finished reading.

The inquisition. The thought hovered foggily in my mind. Antonia clenched my hand even harder. Standing up, Tomás bowed respectfully and offered a practiced smile so empty that my stomach turned over. Padre Curato wore a far more malicious grin.

"My investigation into the validity of these accusations will take some weeks," Tomás said. "You will be summoned to trial when I feel I have adequate testimony to confer judgement."

"I assure you, Fra Tomás, that Amadora is innocent of these allegations. Surely as a member of the nobility, my testimony will absolve her." Antonia's voice almost didn't quaver.

"We will see," Tomás replied. "I have often found that women, least and last of our Lord's creations, are quickest to sin and easiest swayed in temptation." Turning to leave, he added, "You were not glad to see me, Signora, as you claimed when we met. For one who lies so easily, I should wonder at whether your testimony will mean anything to the court at all."

I didn't sleep that night. Antonia didn't either, so far as I could tell by her disheveled hair and the dark spots under her eyes. It was unheard of to see her in such a state of visible distress, and I think the unbalance her anxiety brought to the palazzo only further fueled my own unease.

The inquisition, I repeated again to myself, as I had done a hundred times since meeting Fra Tomás. Just the thought cowed me. The inquisition was the hammer of the church – a weapon against heresy and apostasy with no room for the grace or compassion of the Catholic doctrine. Inquisitorial courts were known for being swift, cruel, and unbothered with the actuality of guilt. False confessions under torture, executions arranged before trial: common occurrences if the stories were to be believed, and after meeting Tomás, I could believe them all.

Fear.

I was a fool. I'd thought that my emotions had been purged – scoured away by the fire – but it wasn't until I'd met Fra Tomás that I realized what true apathy was. It was as if he had never known compassion, or dread, or anger. That sort of freedom…it made him a wolf in a world of sheep.

I was still afraid, but the more I feared Tomás, the more I lusted to be like him – to have that detachment, that power. My own emotions were a crutch; I was sure of that now. *He could do anything, and I can do nothing.* I began to claw at my arms until blood appeared. Fueled by pain, I dove inward, mentally attacking my fear, and my worry, and my sorrow. They didn't disappear, but I wasn't going to give up. I would rid myself of them eventually.

All but my rage. That, I would keep.

What is it that makes us human? What God-given gift is there to separate us from oxen and sheep and baser animals? I have seen into the bodies of men, and truly our corpses differ little from that of pigs. Heart. Lungs. Intestines. Brain. Where is that holier piece – that ultimate contrivance which sets us apart? I have not found it, and even have begun to wonder whether it is there to be found. Could it not be that our humanity is something ethereal? It is true that we perceive life with our minds rather than our bodies. How we act, what we say and do, the things we feel: could not these be just as integral to our claim of a higher purpose?

What is it that makes us human? I have often wondered.

The sun was hot; I could feel it burning my skin as I walked across the Piazza della Chiesa with an accompaniment of Compagni guards. It was the first time I'd been outside since my ill-fated excursion into the piazza, and I certainly wasn't comforted by the armored men on either side of me. Antonia had told them to keep a short distance, but still, I was nervous.

Of course, it wasn't the guards that made me nervous. Not really. After weeks of waiting – painful days spent with no word of what Inquisitor Tomás was doing in the village

– I had finally been called upon. Not to trial quite yet, but to give my testimony of the night of the fire.

Fear threatened to rise up in my throat, but I crushed it as I had done so many times over the past few weeks. It obeyed with nary a struggle.

The door to the church opened easily, and I stepped through. The guards waited outside, leaving me alone to face whatever lay within. Antonia had tried to prepare me – had spoken with me of what I should say and what questions I might be asked – but I only needed to conjure a thought of the Spanish inquisitor to know that no matter what I did, I would not be ready to face him. His was the spider's web, and knowing the trap could not prevent its close.

The church was dim. Even in the noonday sun, little light seemed to pervade the two westerly windows above the door. Before me stretched the building's main chamber.

For some reason, my attention was immediately drawn to the design of the room – elements of architecture I had studied with Matteo in my youth. The symmetry of the chamber was both immediately apparent and oddly satisfying. Closed windows lined the north wall, and even though the south wall adjoined the belfry, false windows had been cut and placed there as well. The black and white marbled tile on the floor was patterned in a checkered design, and the darker tiles created long, stretching lines that, coupled with the symmetrical trim along the walls and the imagined line of points created by archways along the ceiling, seemed to draw the eye to a vanishing point on the other side of the room.

And there, right at that point, sat Fra Tomás. Beside him sat Padre Curato, as well as a young man who seemed to be Tomás' scribe. No one else was in attendance. I was thankful, at least, for that.

"Come, Amadora," Tomás said, gesturing. His voice was no less casual than if he were inviting me to dinner. It was unsettling, but I was in control of my fear…for now, at least.

This will come to pass, I chanted. *This will come to pass.*

Squaring my shoulders, I approached. Cold needle pricks crawled along my legs as I crossed the room; the dissociation felt odd, as clearly my legs were feeling a panic to which I had already numbed myself. My stomach flipped. Maybe I was not so in control as I wanted to believe.

There was no chair, so I had no choice but to stand.

"Amadora Trovatelli," Tomás began. "On this, the second Sunday of June, we call you to testify the truth, in his house and before the Lord, on that matter of witchcraft which you have already been charged with. Do you swear to give true your testimony in fear of the Lord?"

I do not fear the Lord, I thought to myself. "Yes," I said aloud. "I swear."

"Then touch these four gospels," he said, holding up several books I had seen often during Sunday mass. "And give us the truth of your name and birth, so to show you are bound by the scripture."

Feeling a little silly, I reached forward and lay my hand upon the worn volumes. "My name is Amadora Trovatelli. I do not know the day nor place of my birth."

"Who are your parents?"

"I do not know."

"Are they alive or dead?"

"I do not know."

"Did they die of natural causes, or were they burned as witches?"

"I do not know," I said, frustrated.

"Then you could have been committed to the devil at birth?"

"Of course not!"

"Really? Then who are your parents?"

"I don't know!"

"Then you have no defense." Tomás motioned to his scribe, who leaned down to write something in his journal. "Where were you brought up?"

My fists clenched, but I held my anger back as best I could. "In the workshop on the hill just east of here. I was raised by Matteo di Francesco; he was a master craftsman and painter – a good man and well respected by everyone."

"I did not ask by whom you were raised. Only answer what I ask of you." His eyes were pitiless.

"We attended mass every Sunday," I continued, becoming more and more frustrated. "Ask Curato! Ask anyone!"

"Be SILENT!" Tomás yelled. His voice echoed through the chamber. Beside him, Padre Curato smiled a sick smile. The scribe wrote urgently upon his paper.

I vibrated with anger but forced myself to stop talking.

"Good. Do not interrupt these proceedings again, or I will be forced to continue without your testimony." It wasn't a threat. He spoke what was, to him, a simple truth. Somehow, that made it worse. After a moment, he continued, "Why do the people of Montaione fear you?"

"I survived the fire," I answered, careful to control my anger.

"How did you survive?"

I hesitated. "I do not know." I could hear the scribe's quill scratching from where I stood.

"Many people have testified to the severity of the fire, so I'll ask one more time: how did you survive?"

"I really don't know." I repeated, beginning to feel the first pangs of desperation. "I was unconscious, I don't remember anything.

"This is the fire that claimed the life of the man who raised you – Matteo di Francesco – yes?"

I was slow to reply, "Yes."

"How is it that you survived when he did not?"

"There was another man there, Gilio Salviati. He attacked Matteo. He was the one who started the fire."

"Do you have any proof of this?" Tomás asked. His voice made it clear that he did not believe me in the slightest.

"He forced himself on me. I'm pregnant with his disgusting child; isn't that proof enough?"

"Ah yes, the pregnancy," Tomás said, rifling through several documents on the table in front of him. "So you admit the child was conceived on the night of the fire?"

"What?" The turn of topic made me hesitate. "Yes, it was."

"And that the conception was undertaken in a manner evil and contrary to what is natural?"

"Yes!"

"You are also charged with intercourse with the devil. Do you admit to this as well?"

I froze. "No, of course not."

"Strange that you confess to all but the object of your sinful lust. No matter."

It was becoming harder and harder to breathe. My chest stretched tight as if I were slowly drowning.

"Let us return to the matter of Matteo di Francesco," Tomás continued, unaffected. "For what reason did you murder him?"

A jolt ran through me. "I didn't murder him."

Tomás' eyes narrowed.

"I didn't kill Matteo!" I repeated, both enraged and desperate. Harder to breathe. Pain in my chest.

Slowly, Tomás collected a sheet of paper from the desk in front of him and began to read, "Under oath, it is so testified that Amadora Trovatelli, by words spoken from her own mouth, has admitted to the circumstances of Matteo di Francesco's death. She confessed in confidence to the witness that Matteo di Francesco died as an object of her anger, as well as that she was guilty to his death."

Silence. Even the scribe's quill stood unmoving – a black sentinel watching all.

My mind raced, but no answers came. *What?* I wanted to ask, but my tongue felt numb. "Wh—who…?" I finally muttered.

Tomás sat back in his chair as if my question alone had decided the outcome of my case. "Suor Maria, of the convent at Santa Lucia. She is your nursemaid, is she not?"

Pieces fell into place, and suddenly I was aware at just how impossible my situation was. I must have been the last to realize: there was never any hope that I would walk free.

It was obvious though, wasn't it? I chided myself. *You aren't innocent, after all.* In my mind, I replayed the conversation I had with Suor Maria. I had told her that Matteo died while I was angry with him. I had told her I felt guilt at his death. I had never expected those words would be the ones that undid me.

A sudden rage flared up within me, though I was careful not to let it show on my face. The nun had betrayed me.

"Do you have any more questions for me?" I finally asked. My anger boiled, but I was not about to let it flow over. Not here.

"No, you are free to leave."

"What?" Curato exclaimed, speaking for the first time since I arrived. "She all but confessed! Surely she should be held in custody until her trial."

The priest fell silent at a single look from Tomás. Even so, the inquisitor seemed to consider what he had said. "It is true: there is enough evidence already to warrant imprisonment." He looked at me, and a chill ran down my back. "However, I hardly think it necessary. I have already been in contact with Signora Antonia, who has vouched for the girl. If she flees, Antonia will be tried in her stead. And do not forget," Tomás continued, "Our own soldiers watch the palazzo. She will be apprehended if she tries to escape."

That did not seem to placate Curato at all. If anything, the thought of Antonia on trial seemed to make him visibly ill. The Compagni were still extremely respected by the village – respected *and* relied upon. If Antonia were to be convicted by the inquisition…an inquisition that Curato had invited, no less… Well, I could see how he might be nervous. I sneered at him maliciously, and the blood completely drained from his cheeks.

The guards were waiting for me in the piazza as I reemerged from the church. If they were surprised at how quickly the hearing had been, they did not show it. Within minutes, I was safely back within the Palazzo di Compagni, Antonia holding me in a way that was meant to be comforting as she asked about what happened.

She sat quietly as I finished, but the panic in her eyes was thinly veiled. "I—I need time to think," she said after a while. "This is not good."

That's an underestimate of the situation, I thought to myself, but I left her to her thoughts. Tired from the excursion, I slowly made my way toward my room. Meanwhile, my mind ran rampant, desperately searching for any way for me to escape the fate that now loomed seemingly inevitable. *I'm going to be convicted; there's no way to avoid it,* I realized with chagrin, but the rest of my thoughts were cut short as I opened the door to my room. Inside, waiting for me, was the last person I could have expected.

"Amadora!" Suor Maria called out warmly. "How are you feeling today? You're starting to widen around the waist! That's good!"

For a few moments, I was too stunned to speak. Then, all at once, I was bursting with a white hot anger. "YOU!" I screamed, taking a threating step toward her. Maria's smile disappeared instantly. "How dare you come back here?! How dare you?!"

Maria nervously backed away. "Wha—whatever do you mean?"

I could barely speak. "Il tuo deposizione." I bit every word off.

Clearly, by her look, she hadn't expected me to find out. She tried on another friendly smile. "Oh Amadora, don't you see? They want to help you. Fra Tomás is a good man; he'll bring you back to the Lord so you can truly be forgiven! This is—"

I didn't wait for her to finish. Rage that I had been barely suppressing for weeks – rage that I had stoked into a frenzy and kept bottled up inside of myself – finally, and violently, boiled over. A visceral scream escaped me as I leapt forward and struck Maria across her face. Again, and again. She tried to protect herself – tried to push me away – but I could not be stopped, I was so enraged. She was on the floor now. I tore at her with my fingers, my nails tearing great red gashes across her skin. Several of her teeth were missing. Blood poured out of her nose and mouth.

Suddenly, there were arms around me, pulling me away. I thrashed against them, but they did not move.

"Amadora!" a voice was yelling. "Stop! Get ahold of yourself!" Some part of me recognized Jacopo's voice, but I was too frenzied to care. I writhed, struggling to get to Maria. My vision was red; everything else but her was a blur. Other people were there, I think. Antonia's voice echoed as if from a distance, and then Suor Maria was being carried away. I fought even harder to get to her as they lifted her out of my room. I spat on her as they passed, and tried uselessly to kick her even though I knew I was too far away. Suddenly, Antonia was upon me.

"AMADORA!" she yelled, slapping me hard across the cheek. Stunned, and with Maria now gone, I stopped thrashing. Jacopo let go of me with a tired groan and sunk into a nearby chair.

The fog in my mind was beginning to clear, though the echoes of my anger still vibrated through me. I looked at the blood pooled on the floor and almost gasped. *I did that?*

"You fool," Antonia whispered, looking at the mess around us.

I was still quivering with the last vestiges of my anger. "She deserved worse," I said, voice strong with emotion.

Antonia nearly collapsed onto my bed. "You fool," she repeated. "Do you realize what you've done?"

I did not.

"You've given him exactly the proof he needed to convict you."

"Tomás?" I scoffed. "His decision was already made."

"He didn't have any real evidence!" she nearly yelled. "All he had was gossip and the remains of a fire that no one could

123

prove you started! We might have still proved you innocent, but now…" she didn't seem able to say more, so Jacopo continued for her.

"They will say you are possessed," he explained. "You must be, to attack a holy woman like Suor Maria." His sharp gaze pierced me in place. "Amadora, I don't see any way for you to be acquitted now."

As I pondered his words, I absently realized that Jacopo's attempts to hold me back had been the first time since the fire a man had been able to touch me without sending me into a fit of panic.

"What are we going to do, Jacopo?" Antonia asked, but her husband gave no response. Desperation tinging her voice, she continued suppliantly. "Maybe if she offered an apology? Surely they can understand the strain she is under."

"I will *not* apologize," I said heatedly, glaring at Antonia.

"You will do whatever we tell you to!" she screamed, my refusal having apparently pushed her over the edge of self-control. "Non ti vedi? Do you think all this ends after the trial? That you'll get a slap on the wrist and go on chasing your revenge as if nothing changed?" Her composure was completely lost now, and I was so taken aback that I couldn't respond. "They're going to hurt you, Amadora. They don't even need a confession; they'll cut you and break you and make you bleed for no other reason than because they think that somehow the pain will clean the devil from your soul! *Then*, after you've screamed just enough to satisfy their morbid tastes, they'll drag your body through the town and hang you from a rope to set an example!"

I knew that she was watching the scene play out in her mind. Tears ran unchecked down her cheeks, and her hands shook violently where she clutched them in her lap. Hesitantly, I reached out and patted her arm. "I know, Antonia." And I really did know. There just wasn't any easy way to tell her that I didn't care anymore.

Jacopo stood up and moved toward his wife. Panic gripped me at his approach, and I hastily moved away. Apparently I was no longer exempt to my new phobia. Antonia, meanwhile, was so distraught that Jacopo had to nearly carry her out of the room.

"Get some rest, Amadora," he said as they left. "I'll send a servant by to clean up all…this." He gestured distastefully to the blood that was slowly seeping into the floorboards. "We'll talk more tomorrow."

Then, rather abruptly, I was alone.

The next morning arrived like any other, with cooing birds and warm morning light. I didn't leave my room. For some reason it felt as if I should enjoy the comforts of privacy and autonomy while I still could.

In my mind, I imagined what now awaited me – the impending trial and its almost certain outcome, the days of torture that would soon follow, and my death. None of it frightened me; no matter how violently I forced myself to envision the worst that was to come, I felt nothing except a deep, bitter resentment that I would not be able to hunt down and kill Gilio Salviati.

"Gilio." Even now, after weeks of obsession, the name tasted sweet upon my tongue. I closed my eyes and relished the vision of plunging a knife into his heart. *He killed Matteo.* As if summoned, my teacher's hazy visage interrupted my morbid daydream. It was painful to see him, but with little doubt could I interpret the look upon his face: disappointment.

This will come to pass.

Hurriedly, I brushed aside both Matteo and the shame that threatened to rise up within me. I wasn't the girl he had loved and raised; I had no right to her indignity.

It wasn't long before Antonia came to see me. She carried with her a tray of fine salted pork, a glass of wine, and even a bit of melon tart. It was a small feast, and as I hadn't eaten since before being summoned by the inquisition the day before, I was grateful for the deliberate show of kindness.

She said little as I ate, and I could tell that there was something heavy on her mind. The solemnity was tangible and somehow made me feel as if I were enjoying my last meal.

"Jacopo and I talked long into the night," she finally said when there was nothing but crumbs left upon the tray. I tried to relish the lingering satisfaction of a delicious meal, knowing full well that whatever news was coming would not be good. She paused, either collecting her thoughts or waiting for me to respond, I didn't know which. After a moment, she continued, "Amadora, you can't stay here."

I looked at her — really looked at her — and I saw the strain those words put her under. She seemed to want to say more but was having trouble finding the words. "You're telling me to leave the palazzo," I offered on her behalf with a shrug. "I understand. There's no hope for me, and you need to distance yourselves."

"No!" she exclaimed, horrified. "Of course we wouldn't do that! You are my friend, Amadora, and I would stand by you to the end if I thought it would help. Can you not understand that by now?"

She seemed upset, so I said nothing.

Antonia took a deep breath. "You must flee, Amadora. That is what I mean. If you stay here, you will die." Another breath. "I have a sister in Pisa who has agreed to take you on as a ward. I meant to send you to her after your pregnancy, but with what has happened…" Urgently, she grasped my hand. "You must understand, Amadora. I did not mean to keep it a secret, but I knew that with everything that had happened – the fire and how everyone has treated you – you would not want to stay in Montaione. If I thought it was best for you, I would gladly have you remain with us." Tears were forming in her eyes.

"I don't want to stay in Montaione," I agreed. It was true enough, but I certainly wasn't leaving for Pisa. My prey was east, in Firenze.

"The circumstances are less ideal than I had hoped, but it is the only way," she said, struggling to manage her emotions. "Jacopo does not want me to do this, so we must keep it from him. He worries at what will happen to me if you escape."

"Tomás said you were to be tried in my place."

She waved my words aside. "Don't worry, little one. That was only said to scare you. He would not dare go that far."

I thoroughly disagreed, but I kept my thoughts to myself. I had told her of the risk; it was not my fault if she chose to ignore it. Besides, this might be the only way for me to follow Gilio, and compared to that, nothing else – and no one else – mattered.

"When?" I asked.

"As soon as possible," she answered. "In the evening, either tomorrow or the day after, I think would be best. We won't have long before your trial is called – a week or two at most – and I'll need at least a few days to find a group of men I trust to get you away from here safely *and* keep it a secret. Gallo maybe. And Marcello. I'll want to send you with a handmaiden or two as well, though that might be trickier." She was talking mostly to herself now, but I didn't interrupt. I was already wondering how I was going to get to Firenze if the soldiers Antonia sent with me were on orders to take me to Pisa.

"Remember," Antonia told me, drawing me out of my deliberation. "Not a word of this to Jacopo, understand?"

"I understand."

Smiling, she cupped my cheek. "Don't worry, little one," she said softly. "Everything is going to be fine."

I looked back only once. Only once, and yet that last view of Montaione is with me still – as vibrant and alive as if I had painted it upon the canvas of my mind.

I knew I was asleep. I was dreaming of the fire again, as I had almost every night over the past two months. The flames crept closer, surrounding me. Even in the dream, I could feel the heat. The smoke caught in my throat, choking me. Starving for air, I waited.

In a flash, the heat disappeared. The whole workshop disappeared. White light enveloped me. I felt the arms around my chest, holding me, protecting me. No, not arms – hands. I was being held in the palm of a giant hand. I beat my wings. Large, wonderful, colored wings that fluttered like the finest silk.

"Not yet," a voice said. It was so familiar. "I will keep you from harm, Amadora Trovatelli." I strained to look at whatever held me, but I could not quite see it.

"AMADORA!"

I jolted awake, my heart pounding. Antonia was standing over me. Her eyes were wide in panic.

"Amadora, wake up!" she cried under her breath. She looked over her shoulder furtively, as if expecting someone to come barging in.

"What's happening?" I asked, adrenaline quickly washing away the last vestiges of sleep.

"They've come for you!" she muttered frantically. "Fra Tomás is here, with soldiers. They're looking for you!"

"What? Why?" I leapt out of bed. I refused to let myself feel the fear that tried to creep under my skin.

"He set the trial! For tomorrow!" She grabbed my shoulders. "His soldiers are already here. Amadora, if they take you now, you won't have a chance. You must go!"

"How?"

"Put these on. Quickly!" she said, thrusting a pile of clothes at me. I made out a pair of tan pants and a worn, tawny brown tunic. I threw myself into them as fast as I could. As I finished, Antonia pulled a short black cowl over my head. "I only hope you'll be mistaken for a serving boy if no one looks too closely," she muttered, glancing over me with a doubtful eye. "Come, we must go!"

Nearly running, she led me through corridor after corridor. After a moment, I realized she was leading me *away* from the palazzo gate.

"You can't leave by the front," she said quietly. "There are too many soldiers, but there is another way." She didn't say any more, as muffled voices suddenly came drifting through from a nearby room.

"This way!" Antonia whispered frantically, pulling me the other direction. More voices soon followed, and we had to change our course again. I caught sight of soldiers down a passing corridor. They started shouting, but we were gone before they could follow.

Antonia turned and backtracked, trying to find a path forward that was not blocked. Finally, after minutes that seemed like hours, we stopped.

The great room? I wondered skeptically. My harp sat silently – watching me, laughing at me – from its corner next to the marble hearth. We were in the middle of the palazzo. From the sound, it seemed as though we were unwittingly surrounded. It was only a matter of time before they found us.

"Now what?" I asked. Anger, constantly flowing and ebbing, replaced caution. "We're trapped!" My words, too loud, must have carried, for they were soon replied to by the shouts and clambering of inquisition soldiers nearby.

"Shh! Here!" Antonia whispered, urgently moving past the harp and groping at one of the engraved wooden panels that circled the room. Her fingers scratched clumsily at the wall as the beginnings of panic began to set in. The voices without the room were becoming louder; I could almost hear the strings of the harp hum in resonance.

With a click, the panel fell away from the wall. Astonished, I looked within to find a narrow tunnel leading downward between the walls of the palazzo.

"Get in!" Antonia cried out, eyes wide.

I didn't hesitate. Rushing forward I thrust myself into the passageway. It was even smaller than it looked, forcing me down to enter on my arms and knees. I could see nothing in the darkness further in, though the overwhelming smell of damp and stale air suggested that the tunnel receded deep into the earth.

It was only then that I realized the harp was in my hands. *When did that happen?* I marveled with an eerie shudder, unable to remember taking it from its resting place by the inglenook.

"Follow the passage down as far as it goes," Antonia whispered, dragging me from my reverie as she fumbled trying to replace the panel. To my surprise, a small collection of needle-sized holes in the wood allowed me to see the room beyond even after the false panel clicked back into place. Crouching down, Antonia spoke through them to me, "The tunnel will take you into the hills east of town. From there, you can make your way to my sister in Pisa."

Then, as if finally exhausted, Antonia fell to her knees and rested her head against the hidden doorway. She was mere inches from me, so I could not ignore as tears began to fall from her eyes. "I am so sorry, little one," she wept, voice barely a whisper. "Questo è sbagliato. This isn't how any of this should be. I cannot imagine the weight you bear, and I weep for what I know waits for you still. You are a beautiful girl and a gift, Amadora, and though you may not remember it now, you will find happiness again someday; I am sure of it." Reaching up with a hand, Antonia put her palm to the door. "Go now, little one. Go and do not think any more of this wretched place. You will be a mother soon." Tears were falling freely now from her cheeks, but a look of contentment suddenly swept across her face. "I wish I could have met your child," she whispered with a teary smile. "I wish I could have been—"

She was interrupted as the door to the great room burst open to the sound of splintered wood.

"Go! Go now!" she muttered frantically under her breath as a half dozen soldiers filled the room, closely followed by a figure that sent tendrils of ice crawling across my skin. I froze, hidden in the wall, unable to move, unable to suppress the fear.

This will come to pass. I gripped the harp tight to my chest as a drowning man grasps the wreckage of his ship. *This will come to pass. This will come to pass.*

"Where is she!?" Tomás yelled as a soldier with his sword in hand roughly pulled Antonia to her feet. The monk's eyes darted around the room as if to find me stuffed in some corner. "Where have you hidden her?"

Behind him stood Padre Curato, the priest seeming for all the world like one caught in a nightmare. His legs shook when he saw Antonia, and from then on he avoided looking in her direction, as if that could hide him from his fate.

"She has been gone since last night," Antonia spat, trying and failing to wrench her arm from the grip of the man that held it. "She is halfway to Firenze by now and far from your evil hands!" She lied convincingly, still thinking that I meant to travel the opposite direction to Pisa.

Tomás' eyes were wild, dark, and horrible. I tried not to look as he slowly made his way toward Antonia. He seemed to grow in the mind with each step. "You have set a strega loose upon Italia," he whispered dangerously. Antonia struggled against the man that held her, desperate to pull away from the inquisitor. "I name you, woman," he declared, "a heretic in collusion with the devil."

The silence that followed was interrupted by an uproar from the doorway as Jacopo was escorted into the room. "Antonia!" he yelled, trying to claw his way past a duo of soldiers that were struggling to hold him back. "Antonia!"

"SILENCE!" Tomás screamed. He flicked his wrist, and a guard struck Jacopo hard across his jaw. His legs buckled. "You are both arraigned on charges of abetting the escape of a known witch!" Tomás yelled. "Resist and I will pass your sentence here, now, and without trial!"

My hand was pushing against the hidden panel as if trying to get to Antonia. I had to force myself away from the door. *What do I care?* I growled to myself over the thunderous nausea in my stomach. *She knew,* I told myself over and over again. *She knew. She knew.*

Things happened so suddenly that I could not help but cry out in horror.

Jacopo, fueled by mad desperation, leapt to his feet and pulled a sword from the belt of the nearest guard.

In moments, the blade was red with blood. Three were dead upon the flagstones: two soldiers, and one pitiless priest.

Antonia shrieked. Jacopo seemed only to grow more frenzied. He fought to get to her. His sword was a blur. His eyes were wild.

There were too many. I knew it. I knew it. I shut my eyes. Antonia's screams reached a fever pitch.

She was still screaming as they dragged her away. I could hear her as she was pulled from the room. The echoes found me from the hallway and the courtyard and out the palazzo. They echoed all throughout Montaione that night.

As I laid in the tunnel, eyes closed, I stamped out my fear.

I laid in the tunnel and broke myself of sorrow for the last time.

The sun had risen and nearly set again before I finally emerged from an abandoned well in the hills east of Montaione. It was strange; I realized with almost passive disinterest that I was near to where the workshop had once stood.

I do not know what agency possessed me to find that burnt abode, but it most surely was not reminiscence. Curiosity, perhaps, drove me forward, step after step, my worn boots dwarfed beneath trousers that had never been made for a girlish figure. I was in no great rush, so my steps were slow – deliberate. My harp weighed me down, but for some reason I refused to set it aside.

The smell made itself available to me long before the charred corpse of my former life came into view. The pillars that had once supported the workshop appeared first over the horizon, now like broken black bones rising into the sky. My balcony, from which I'd charted and composed and drawn the Toscana countryside, had collapsed and scattered into dust. The roof was completely seared away. Only two walls remained, and even those looked as though they too wished to fall and be done with.

I walked into it all with the sense that someone waited for me within, yet I found the foundation empty save for ash and the memories that had been made there. I put a hand to my stomach, reaching for my womb within. The evil of that night was being made flesh within me. My fingernails dug into my skin, revolted at the new life I harbored.

Looking down, I realized that this must have been where I was found. Yes, there, in the center of the wreckage, was a circle of space in which no ash or debris lay. Fascinated, I moved closer. It was like a window to what had been; the wood floor was unburnt and undisturbed, pieces of shattered pottery lay here and there, and I could even make out the stains of blood – my blood – where it had seeped into the grain of the wood.

This... I realized for the first time. *This is not natural.* I moved even closer. Even after so many weeks the edge of the space was clean and sudden, untouched by rain or wind, and the circle was perfectly round, as if drawn by a giant hand.

In a flash, I remembered my dreams from the night before – dreams that had been plaguing me since first waking in the Palazzo di Compagni. There had been giant hands, I remembered; giant hands had held me. Except, it hadn't been me, at least not like I was now. I'd worn wonderful wings of colored silk.

I shook my head, and looked down again at the circle in the ash. Would I ever know what had truly happened? Did I want to?

My eyes slid to a small pile of debris nearby. I instantly knew what it was. My gaze lingered. Of course they had not thought to search the wreckage for Matteo's body. There was no one else to bury him anyway, and likely nothing of him underneath left to bury.

I turned away – away from the cinders and away from the questions. I turned south, to the one thing in my life that I any longer cared for. I would take the south road to Gambassi, then turn north to Castelfiorentino. From there I could make it to Montespertoli, then to San Casciano, and then…

"Firenze," I whispered. A grim smile stretched across my lips. "Gilio."

I looked back only once. The eleven towers of Montaione, which had once seemed like the fingers of God, now raked the sunset sky blood red as if they were the claws of a demon.

"Seldom, this will come to pass that one of us
Ventures the road upon which I fall.
Into that which is the final region and the darkest,
And farthest from heaven, which encircles all."

AUTUMN

Notes on a Florentine Execution

The death of a criminal is no private matter. Truly, it is understood by many in power as a means by which to showcase the cost of crime – an exhibitionary deterrent – and as such, it is dramatized with all the pomp and ostentation to rival that of the most sensationalist theatre.

First, the condemned is brought from the prison, Il Carcere delle Stinche, to be paraded before God and man around the city of Firenze. Trivial as this path along the Via dei Malcontenti may seem, it is, to many who walk it, the most painful of their last day's events, for the derision and scorn they solicit upon the journey is that of their friends, their neighbors, and their enemies. To be ridiculed by those who would rejoice in your death is worse still than to be lamented by those who relied upon you in life.

The tour, perhaps too long for its cruelty, continues from the jailhouse to the Palazzo del Podestà, where the person to die is read her condemnation in full view of the assembly. This too seems a simple enough matter, and would be if not for the reality of the situation – these events are not intended to cow the condemned; they are meant to deter the masses.

Il rogo aspetta, ammassato in
alto con legno e paglia

A quiet acceptance of charges is tiresome and less memorable than a scene of outraged denial, thus often are added to the conviction additional crimes uncommitted by the accused. It is here that the refusal of charges becomes an arranged drama, performed unknowingly by someone who does not grasp the irrelevance of her frustration.

From the Palazzo del Podestà, the journey is nearly complete. East along the Via Ghibellina, south for a stretch, then east again along the Via dei Malcontenti – no more than twenty minutes to walk, yet the path seems to stretch longer with each step taken along it. Finally, the condemned arrives at the place in which they are to die, the Piazza della Forche. This forum, nestled beneath the Torre della Zecca and beyond the Porta della Guistizia, falls just outside the city's great walls. To be taken beyond those walls feels much like being taken from the arms of a mother. In the end, the city turns her back upon them all.

Unhappy soul, it is here the performance reaches its climax. A thief or murderer might be led to a heavy rope swaying beneath the long, unbending neck of a gibbet. This is a common death, and the hanged man's dance is one observed with judicious appreciation. For the traitor – a man whose crime was of politics – a nobler death awaits upon the headsman's block. It is swift, and dignified, and wholly unpopular in all respects.

Years may pass with none but these deaths played out within the Piazza della Forche, yet upon rarer occasions, more horrifying and more exciting dramas may be performed. For the citizen turned bandit, the man who by his actions threatens trade and livelihood of a city so desperate for it, no prop upon the stage awaits – only the executioner and his blade, and the long, gruesome, harrowing death of quartering. That bloody show is well-liked and long-lived, for it can take almost an hour to cut and prune a body into four parts. This is true, and yet it somehow falls short of the excitement reserved for the favorite of all displays, that which is most treasured by the sickened masses that make such a city their home. It is an end fit only for the worst of criminals, those who have shown treason against God himself.

For them, a pyre awaits, piled high with the driest of wood and straw. Within the center is planted a stake to which the condemned is tied. This is the slowest of deaths, for the executioners often work to hinder the flames once they have begun to touch the woman's feet. This beacon—this bonfire is enjoyed by all in attendance for the spectacle it offers. Bright flame. The sour smell of burnt hair and acrid flesh. Screams that only seem to further goad the energies of the crowd. These are the true festivals of Firenze, wherein are punished your heretics, your blasphemers, and your witches.

Firenze. What is there to say about that fervid city that has not already been said a thousand ways by a thousand tongues each more quick to eloquence than mine? I did not love her, yet I find myself in awe of her nudity. Art and decadence. Music and lust. Piety and Pride. She is a palette of opposites in union, and without shame in all aspects. To no one does she hide any part of herself – neither amity nor vice – and I yearn for her like one so yearns for the embrace of a favored whore. Had I made my memories of that place by a different light, I might have found a home within her walls. Now I find only my death upon her doorstep.

It never stopped raining. Not once, on the long trip from Montaione to Firenze, did the torrent hesitate or lessen. It continued day and night right up to the moment I first saw the wide walls and cut towers of Firenze crest above the wooden hills north of San Casciano. Then, like an omen, it withdrew.

That first look at the city was more wonderful and more expansive than I could ever have imagined. Indeed, while the endless expanse of Firenze did bring upon me a sort of marvelous stupefaction, my awe did not lessen as my journey continued. It held to my experiences, resurging and retaking me with every corner I turned.

The walls: nearly six miglia long in their patrol of the city. They reached further and further into the air the closer to them I came, and as I finally stood beneath the southernmost gate – the Porta San Pier Gattolino – I had to look upward nearly three stories to the top of the wall as it towered above me. The effort. The *architecture*. Even as I walked through the tall iron doors of the gatehouse, I marveled.

Next came the Arno: the river that rushes ever west through the very center of the city. The four bridges that span the wide torrent of Firenze's lifeblood stretched tenuously out before me. I could hear the rush and swell of the river. I could *feel* its force upon the stones beneath my feet as I traveled across the Ponte Nuovo.

I continued on that road for a while.

Santa Maria Novella: like a great ivory monument of God, it shone brightly across the piazza. I cannot even remember my approach, but I remember with intense clarity the vision of its tall façade. I had never before seen a structure look so like a painting. Pure, aesthetic beauty.

I turned right. Into the heart, I hoped, of Firenze.

The Baptistery of San Giovanni: towering golden doors, laden with masterful panels depicting scenes of old scripture. The artistry was beyond splendor – beyond perfection. I lost myself there for a long while.

But the towering shadows of the Cathedral of Santa Maria del Fiore could not be ignored. The Duomo di Firenze: the cathedral – a wonder of the modern world by any standard. It had taken one hundred and forty years to build, being finished only a dozen years before under the watchful eye of Cosimo de Medici. Even now, the exterior decorations – towering marble facades and sculptures – were still incomplete. I could not imagine the scope of such a task, and as I gazed upward at the impossible dome that had earned the cathedral its name, I again marveled at the wonder so common of Firenze. There were people around me that did not even look up. How many years must it have taken for something so grand become commonplace?

From there, I followed the road south. I thought I could see the kiosks of a marketplace to my right, but the crowds dissuaded me from exploring further.

The Piazza della Signoria: the true heart of Firenze, I'd found it at last. Grand. Expansive. And above it all towered the Palazzo della Signoria, home to the city's rulers. I watched as hundreds came and went, flowing like blood through the veins and arteries of the city streets. There were so many people.

Firenze was far more massive than I'd dared to believe in my wildest fantasies. The entire of Montaione would have fit within just one district of the city a dozen times over, and there were over a dozen districts within the city's walls. I still struggled to comprehend the sheer size of it. There were so many people. So many possibilities.

Yet in it all, I sought only one man.

Hefting the heavy rucksack I'd stolen from a clothesline in Gambassi to hold my harp, I started off down the nearest road.

I had expected Gilio would be easy to find. In my dreams he always waited for me, but the reality was much different. There were no signs leading to the Palazzo Salviati – no maps or guides to take me where I needed to go – and even asking directions from the women I passed was more fruitless than not. Not many, it seemed, knew much of the nobility. It was strange, after the simplicity of Montaione, but I supposed that with so many magnates within the city, it was too much for any one layman to know them all.

Still, I was getting closer. I knew I was. Several women, now, had at least recognized the name of the Salviati, and one had even suggested a street – Via Ghibellina.

My feet fell hard upon the cobbled roads, reminding me of the long days spent upon them. On horseback, the road to Firenze was only a few days, but I was on foot, I was pregnant, and my fear of being seen had often kept me off from the easy roads. For me, the journey had been over a week – a week of no food, little water, and even less sleep. I was nearing my limit, but so too was I nearing my goal. I could push myself a little further. I was almost there. He was so close.

A faded plaque caught my eye. *There! Via Ghibellina!* My heart drummed loudly as I turned down the narrow street. Elegant palazzos passed me on both sides, but there was no discerning which might be the one for which I searched. "Scusa," I muttered nervously to a woman who'd just emerged from the nearest building. "Where is the Palazzo Salviati?" She gave my filthy garments a look of disgust before hurrying away.

"The Palazzo Salviati?"

It was a man's voice. I spun around and had to contain a small shriek of alarm. A monk, dressed in the same grey habit as Fra Tomás; I hadn't even heard him approach. My pulse quickened.

"Sorry!" he exclaimed. "I didn't mean to frighten you, I only overheard you asking for the Palazzo Salviati."

I took a hesitant step back, ready to drop my harp, about to flee, but something stopped me. *Stay calm. Look at him! He can't be from the inquisition.* Forcing my heart to slow, beat by beat, I took another look at the man. He was young, I realized – probably even a bit younger than myself – and though he wore the habit comfortably as one who had taken his vows as a child, he held himself as if he were unsure about his own body, which was, admittedly, rather tall and lanky.

He apologized again, clearly upset, "Mi dispiace! Fra Giovanni always says I lack *gravitas.*" He scrunched up his face as if trying to understand exactly what that meant. "If you *are* looking for the Salviati though, you're wanting that one there." He pointed past my shoulder to what must have been the most ostentatious building I'd ever seen.

I turned toward the palazzo. Tall marble columns decorated the building's façade, each adorned with intricate golden embellishments that had been polished until they gleamed. Between each column were marble plinths upon which sat masterful sculptures of men who I could only assume were the patriarchs of the family. High windows above the street boasted fine stained glass in the design of the Salviati crest, and to either side of that sat an additional two sculptures – a cherubim on the left, and a gargoyle on the right. Additional gold furnished every piece of trim and ornamentation possible, creating the sensation that one was walking up to the gates of the most wealthy home in Firenze.

The gates themselves – heavy iron this time, rather than gold – were closed, locked, and flanked on both sides by a pair of guardsmen. It felt strange that such ostentation would be guarded by two of the most unpleasant looking men I'd ever seen in my life.

He's in there, I told myself. I almost couldn't believe that I had finally arrived. Suddenly, nothing else existed but that one, driving need to find Gilio – to kill him. I dropped my harp and approached the gate. "I need to see Gilio Salviati."

The guards looked at me with a mixture of distaste and disbelief, as if a rat had stood on two legs and suddenly begun to speak. "Levati dalle palle," one of them finally said in a deep voice.

"I need to see Gilio Salviati," I repeated.

"I said get lost!" the one replied. "Isn't any way Signor Gilio has time for the likes of you."

"I…I have a message for him."

They both laughed. "Yeah?" the other asked snidely. "A street urchin like you?"

"I need to see him!" Desperately and without caution, I tried to run through to the gate.

Their laughter disappeared instantly. "Rogna sporca!" One of them leveled the butt of his spear into my chest, and I hit the ground hard. I gasped for the air that had been knocked from my diaphragm. My chest aching, I stood back up and turned again for the gate, but both guardsmen had positioned themselves between it and myself. The panic of my new phobia was beginning to rise. I began to shake. My heart raced, and I yearned to flee. Something, though, held me in place. I was too close now.

"GILIO!" I screamed in desperation, blood pumping. "GILIO SALVIATI!"

There was a tense moment of surprise before the guards could respond. "Shut the hell up!" one bellowed, eyeing the palazzo behind himself as if worried someone might hear. The other one growled menacingly. He raised his spear, there was a flash of movement, and the world exploded in pain and bright white light. For a while, I couldn't move; I couldn't think. I tasted mud.

"Mio dio! Are you alright?" a trembling voice asked from somewhere above me. "Mio dio," the voice said again. Slowly, the face of the boy-monk swam into view, crouched over me anxiously. Panic surged through my still foggy mind, and in a terror I leapt away from him. I yelped in pain as the sudden movement jarred my already throbbing head. Stumbling, I hit the flagstones.

The boy-monk, surprised by my reaction, had fallen as well. "Oh no," he muttered, rising and futilely trying to wipe the mud from the back of his robes. "Fra Giovanni is going to kill me." Cautiously, he gestured toward me. "Are you okay?"

My head hurt too much to nod. Slowly, I pushed myself to my feet and turned again to the gate of the Palazzo Salviati.

"What are you doing?" the boy asked apprehensively. The two guards were eyeing me warily from the gate.

Ignoring him, I took a step forward.

"Stop!" he yelled, grabbing for my arm. I cried out as his fingers brushed my skin, and he jolted back as if burnt. Nervously he continued, "They look like they're going to really hurt you if you go up there again. Please, don't."

I looked at him for a moment, then back at the palazzo. My chest and head throbbed from where I'd been struck. *He's right.* The focus – the adrenaline – that had been sustaining me disappeared in a moment, and I reeled as fatigue, hunger, and thirst all suddenly crashed upon me.

"Per favore," the boy-monk said, eyeing me as if he worried I would collapse at any moment – which, I supposed, wasn't entirely implausible. "If you want, you can come with me. The monastery has food. And beds!" He seemed to get more eager the longer he held my attention. "It's just down the road there." He pointed somewhere behind himself. "I'm sure we can help!" Drawing himself up, he added in a rehearsed voice, "Care of the sick must rank above and before all else, so that they may truly be served as Christ."

I looked one last time to the Palazzo Salviati, with its glittering façade apparently impenetrable. *I will be back,* I vowed. *I am not giving up.* Then, turning back to the boy, I nodded.

A broad smile lit his face from end to end. "Bene!" he said, clearly relieved. Then, as if remembering just how filthy and malnourished I was, he regained some of his prior solemnity. "My name is Timo, by the way." He gave a small start. "Uh, I mean my name is Fra Timo. Fra Timo da Arezzo."

"A—Amadora," I replied. My voice scratched my throat.

He stood there for a moment, watching me, then jumped when he realized what he was doing. "Sorry." He blushed. "Follow me?"

With another furtive glance, he started off down the road. I collected my harp and followed at a distance, studying him. The boy, Timo, seemed as nervous of me as I was of him. Somehow, the reflection of my own anxieties was comforting.

The road came to an end, but rather than turn down a side street, we continued across to a simply styled building with one large door. On a plaque beside it read,

"Each one who bears the insignia
Of the great baron whose name and whose renown
The feast day of Saint Tommaso keeps alive
Has, from him, a knighthood and its privilege."

I recognized the words – from Dante Alighieri's *Paradiso* – but they did not soothe me. If anything, I only felt more apprehensive as Timo led me beneath the classically styled arch pediment, through the large wooden doors, and into the abbey.

"There's the atrium," Timo said, breaking the silence as he eagerly gestured to a wide courtyard to our right, flanked by colonnades on two sides. "The Pandolfini Chapel is just around the corner. And here," he said, waving through a door on our left, "is the church. I can show you that later; it has the choir and the San Mauro Chapel and the chapter house."

I caught a glimpse of the church through the open door. It was enormous, and light flooded through the high windows cut above the chamber. A number of robed monks occupied the room, though none saw me. Just for a moment, I thought I saw grand frescos decorating the far wall, but Timo urged me forward and I lost sight of them.

"We need to see the abbot first. He's in charge of the abbey," Timo explained. "He should be in the Cloister of Oranges this time of day."

The what? I wondered, amazed by the sheer size of the monastery. It was so large. Far larger than it had seemed from the street. Looking up, I spied a belfry towering a hundred feet above us. San Regolo back in Montaione couldn't begin to compare to a place like this.

Continuing on, Timo led me left around a corner and for a moment I thought I was back in the Tuscan countryside. An aroma of bright citrus washed over me – ensnaring me. It was another courtyard, but rather than flagstones, this one was paved with moss and the greenest grass I'd ever seen. A collection of small orange trees dotted the space, and even as I watched, monks were moving to and fro, caring for the plants in the wake of the last week's rains.

As we continued into the cloister, I spied a large stone well rising out of the grass. Several monks were talking around it, including one who wore a silver pectoral cross around his neck. It was to him that Timo hesitantly approached.

"Salve, Father Abbot," Timo said, bowing his head.

The other men excused themselves, and I shuffled frantically aside to avoid them as they walked past. One or two glanced at me curiously, but seemed wholly unconcerned by my presence. Still, I stayed back, nervously hugging the shadows of the courtyard.

"Fra Timo, I see you have returned from the market. And so quickly, too. Were you able to find the vegetables that Fra Mariotto asked for?" The abbot surveyed Timo with a stern eye, but his voice, while deep as a rumbling drum, was not unkind.

Timo's mouth worked silently for a moment. "The vegetables? Oh, those! Well…no. I forgot." Something of the way he said it made me wonder whether forgetfulness was not a common occurrence with the boy-monk. Certainly, while the abbot's countenance grew very stern, he did not appear surprised – only exasperated.

"You are no longer a child, Fra Timo. You are a full brother of our order, and it is a cornerstone of our way of life that we serve one another in humility. Many of us struggle with humility, but somehow you continually manage to stumble over the concept of *service*." He affixed Timo with an unyielding gaze. "Why is it that you cannot remember a simple errand?"

Timo opened his mouth to explain, but the abbot continued without giving him a moment to speak.

"It is because you lack focus. You allow your mind to wander and dwell on earthly things. 'Set your minds on things that are above, not things that are on earth,'" he quoted with an air that he had given this same lecture many times before. "We are taught to seek patience and abhor violence, but I believe that if the apostle Paul was here today, he too would feel tempted to thump your head until this simple lesson was learned." The abbot sighed heavily. "You have the makings of a wonderful servant, Fra Timo, but you lack discipline."

The younger monk had turned a bright shade of pink. "Please, Father Abbot—"

The abbot stopped him with a raised brow. Timo made a small sound of frustration. "I apologize for my shortcomings, Father Abbot. Please have patience. I will work to do better." This too sounded rehearsed. After a moment, the abbot nodded to indicate he accepted the boy's apology.

"Very good. You must also apologize to Fra Mariotto. I'm afraid he will be missing a few ingredients for tonight's soup."

Timo was practically vibrating with impatience. "Please, Father Abbot," he said quickly as soon as the abbot had finished speaking. "This is Amadora." He gestured to where I was still waiting, almost out of sight. Indeed, it seemed as though the abbot had not noticed me before then. "I found her just down the road."

"I'm not a stray dog," I said, taking a few steps forward. Timo looked horrified that he had insulted me, but the abbot let out a deep, booming laugh that made us both jump.

"Well said, young one!" He bowed his head toward me, still chuckling. "I am Abbot Simone Pellegrino. It's my pleasure to welcome you to our abbey." He made no move to kiss my mud-caked cheeks in greeting, which I was thankful for.

I didn't know how to respond, so I awkwardly shrugged my rucksack higher onto my shoulder. Timo, though, was quick to fill the silence. "There were guards, and…" he trailed off. "Well, I offered her food and a place to rest." The abbot turned his considering gaze to Timo, who puffed up defensively. "Care of the sick must rank above and before all else, so that they may truly be served as Christ," he said firmly, repeating what he had said before the Palazzo Salviati. "And all guests are to be welcomed as Christ," he added, tentatively repeating another lesson. He seemed much less certain of himself the longer Abbot Simone studied him.

As if finally finding what he was looking for in the face of the younger monk, the abbot gently smiled. A strange feeling filled me; something about his smile was so familiar. *Matteo smiled like that whenever I would sing for him*, I realized. *Like that last night on the balcony.* I pushed the thought away. I didn't want to remember any more.

"You are absolutely right. It is kindnesses like those that embody the love of Christ we all must strive to imitate."

Abbot Simone reached out a lay a rather large hand upon Timo's shoulder. "I am sorry for my earlier criticisms; I should have allowed you an opportunity to explain yourself." Timo's mouth hung slightly open. He looked as if he had never heard the abbot apologize before in his life. "Go on and tell Fra Mariotto that I will need him to prepare a room for our guest before dinner. Go on!"

With a last hesitant look my way, Timo departed.

"Now then," Abbot Simone exclaimed, turning to me with a stern expression. "Fra Timo mentioned some trouble with guards—"

I opened my mouth to explain myself, but the abbot waved me off.

"—but that does not matter here," he continued. "We welcome any and all in need. You are free to stay with us for as long as you like. You will find we have few rules save those commanded of us by the Lord, and we ask only of you that you respect this place of contemplation and worship while you are with us."

I nodded. My throat was too dry to speak, and after so many hours on my feet, especially carrying a harp which seemed as if it were becoming ever heavier, I was becoming worried that I might collapse. Abbot Simone, sensing my fatigue, continued quickly, "But enough of this talk. There will be plenty of time for such things later, and you look as if you could use a hearty meal and a bit of rest."

The next hour passed quickly. Conscious that I seemed hesitant to meet anyone new, the abbot himself led me to a room above the cloister that had been prepared. Though not as lavish as my chamber at the Palazzo di Compagni, it seemed a heaven compared to a week of traveling through mud and dirt. There was a soft bed made with newly washed blankets, a small writing desk, a pair of sturdy wooden chairs, and a chest backed into the corner. Upon the desk already waited a clay pitcher of water and a meal of bread with cream, grilled cod, and a peeled orange. I barely waited for the abbot to excuse himself before I set upon the food with an animalistic fervor, and before I knew it, the meal – as well as the entire pitcher of water – had disappeared.

Then I slept – a deep and dreamless sleep – until I was woken by the sound of soft knocking upon the door a few hours later. I struggled to wipe the sleep from my eyes as Timo's voice hesitantly called from the hallway, "Um…Amadora? Are—are you awake? Can I come in?"

I yawned so widely that my cheeks hurt. "Sì, vieni avanti," I said, voice cracking – I was still thirsty and, I realized as my stomach chose that moment to grumble loudly, still very hungry.

As if in answer, Timo entered with a tray of food and another pitcher of water. The smell of it immediately filled the room, and I had close my mouth or begin to drool. I watched warily as he set all he'd brought on the desk and began to collect my previous meal's dishes.

"How are you feeling?" Timo suddenly burst out all in a rush. I jumped, not realizing until then that we had been standing in an ever-lengthening silence.

"Better," I replied honestly. I did feel a bit sick to the stomach, but that had been happening more and more in recent weeks. I was pregnant, after all – a fact I didn't quite feel like sharing.

"Good!" Another long silence followed, during which I hungrily stared at the tray of food he had brought. "The Father Abbot says I'm to help you with anything you need while you're here." He sounded quite pleased. "So if you need anything, just come find me, okay?"

"Okay," I said.

"And I'm supposed to read you the Divine Law of our abbey," he continued without taking a breath. "But it's a bit boring."

It seemed like he wanted me to say something. I shrugged. "Okay."

"Yeah," he laughed nervously. "So can I just summarize it for you? Only, you can't tell the Father Abbot!"

"Ma certo."

"Great!" he seemed more confident. "Basically, the Lord commands us all to repent, and we should love our neighbor or suffer the…" he scrunched up his face, "pain of eternal damnation. Um," he paused to think. "No trial is more than we can bear, and all sufferings are the work of God in order to prepare us for the kingdom of heaven."

I listened absently while eyeing the food, but some of what he said caught my ear. I looked up coldly. "You believe the Lord causes all suffering?"

The boy seemed terrified. "Y—yes. That's…that's what it says."

"And that he assigns souls to eternal pain and damnation?"

He nodded, unable to speak.

I didn't look away. "Then I wonder why we all so fear the devil."

Timo opened his mouth a few times, then closed it, apparently at a loss of how to respond. Finally, I turned away. He had done nothing but be kind to me.

"Thank you for the food," I offered. The smell of it was beginning to overwhelm my restraint. Timo relaxed a bit, though his brow was still drawn in thought.

"Sì figuri. Fra Mariotto – he's the cellarer – wanted me to tell you there will be more food in the kitchen if you're still hungry after that."

"The kitchen?"

"Oh, right. It's just downstairs – the big door on the west side of the cloister."

"Sure." I nodded.

The silence stretched on. Timo watched me awkwardly, clearly wanting to say something. Meanwhile, my patience was running low. I was so hungry. I opened my mouth to tell him to leave, but he excused himself before I got the chance.

"Well…enjoy your food," he said, fidgeting with the front of his habit. "A presto." He hurried out of my room so quickly that he forgot to close the door. With a sigh, I stepped forward and latched it shut.

The food was the best I'd ever smelled, I decided as I sat down to sup. There was another orange, some boiled cabbage, and a large bowl of steaming soup. Looking at the soup, I felt the sudden and almost immutable urge to laugh. It didn't have any vegetables.

I have seen things that cannot be explained – things that struggle against the humanistic ideals instilled in me by Matteo. I have begun to doubt even my most basic understanding of the natural world. Who we are, why we are here: do these questions even hold any meaning?

We are, as it turns out, only the playthings of greater spirits.

B reakfast was, if possible, even more delicious than supper had been. There was bread and honey, a bowl of thin milk soup, and another pitcher of water. No orange accompanied my meal, though the monks had thought to send a small carving knife to spread the honey. In no time at all, I had cleaned my plate of even the crumbs.

I looked around my room, amazed that they had been able to quietly deliver not only a tray of food without waking me, but also a large washbasin. Peeking inside, I saw it was half-filled with warm water, which by the smell of it, the monks had mixed with milk and herbs. I shivered with delight as the fragrant steam warmed my face.

It was with something dangerously approaching joy that I stripped naked and lowered myself into the tub. After a week of hard traveling – of sweat and dust and sleeping in the mud – I desperately needed a wash, yet for a moment it was nice to simply sit and soak.

Closing my eyes, I almost fell back asleep, but before long the water began to cool. With a sigh, I reached for the washrag. Dipping it in the now tepid bath water, I began to scrub the thick layer of grime off of my feet and legs. The water had soon lost its milky-white pellucidity in favor of something approaching the semblance of brown tea dregs. When I was finally satisfied that my legs were clean, I attacked my arms, scouring the skin until it smarted.

I winced, unthinking, I tried to wash my chest with the same fervor. My breasts had become even more tender, and, I noticed with a hateful eye, rather larger than I was used to. Biting my lip, I ignored the pain and continued to scrub, yet I couldn't ignore the sudden, concurrent realization that my stomach had begun to swell as well.

The subsequent jolt of shock stopped me dead. "It's in there," I whispered to myself, laying a trembling hand over my venter. Ice chilled my heart. Of course I'd known I was carrying a child, but this…this was the first time that it had truly felt real. There was a *thing* inside of me. Growing. Gestating. I struggled to suppress wave after wave of fresh, sick horror, but finally succumbed. Reaching over the side of the washbasin, I vomited my breakfast onto the floorboards.

My chest heaved as I gasped for air. Slowly – painfully – I forced myself to relax. Shutting my eyes as tightly as I could, I sat back into the tub and waited for my breathing to calm. After what seemed like an eternity, I dared to peek out again from beneath my lids. I took a deep breath, clenched my fists so hard that my nails dug into my palms, and forced myself to look again at my stomach. It seemed somewhat less threatening now, though my heart still raced wildly in my chest. *Accept it!* I silently screamed. *This is going to happen!* My hands shook, but with a few deep breaths, I no longer felt as though I was going to again retch onto the floor.

I knew that my midriff needed a thorough cleaning, but I couldn't bring myself to touch it, so I instead bent to begin working on my hair. The tangled mess was by far the dirtiest part of me, having started to knot together in dark clumps after a week sleeping in the mud. I soaked and scrubbed and brushed and soaked and scrubbed, but it barely made a difference; having been without clippers for more than three months, it had grown well past my shoulders, and the extra length only made it more unmanageable.

Frustrated, I tossed aside the washcloth and instead took up the carving knife I had been sent with breakfast. A few deft strokes, and the surface of the dirtied bathwater was covered in matted hair. Shaking my head side to side, I decided that I liked this new length, which was far shorter than I usually kept it. *I must look like a boy*, I thought wryly.

Careful to keep the floating hair from clinging to my skin, I slowly climbed from the tub. Tentatively stepping around the pool of vomit, I dried myself off on one of the towels the monks had sent with the washbasin.

I eyed the pile of men's clothes I had worn since Montaione with newfound disgust. Now that I was clean, they seemed even grimier than before. For a moment, I considered washing them in the tub, but one look at the now murky, hair-glazed bathwater told me that would not help them at all. I had no choice but to give up for now. Once dressed, I did, however, use the towel to scrub up the spot where I had been sick and rinse it off in the tub water; I didn't want the monks asking questions I was not ready to answer.

As I finished, my stomach grumbled loudly. Having lost my breakfast all across the floorboards, I was newly hungry, and I had no idea when my next meal might arrive. Remembering Timo's offer from the night before, I hesitantly stole my way out from my room with the kitchen in mind.

The sun was well into the sky already, but the monastery was silent. I moved across the hallway to the railing that overlooked the Cloister of Oranges below me. There wasn't a single brother of the abbey to be found. Curious, and grateful for the chance to look around in peace, I followed the railing around the perimeter of the cloister. The fragrance of oranges was no less pleasant than it had been the day before, though it now also incited within me fresh hunger. Soon, I found myself heading for the stairs that would bring me back to the courtyard's ground level, but was temporarily held up by the magnificent mural that circled the second story walkway. With a full night of sleep behind me, I found that my attention much more easily flitted from thing to thing, and so I spent nearly an hour moving slowly from one scene to the next, engrossed in the exquisite style and proficiency at work behind the artist's brush. It became quickly apparent that the work depicted the life and trials of Saint Benedetto: receiving the monk's habit, breaking a glass of poisoned wine by making the sign of the cross, resurrecting a monk who had been trapped beneath a collapsed wall. As the author of the Benedictine monastic code, I supposed an account of his life must have been both inspiring and enlightening to monks who made this abbey their home. Pulling myself away, I descended into the main courtyard – still empty – and continued through it to the westernmost door.

"Salve?" I called out, hesitantly pulling open the heavy door to find a kitchen that seemed no less empty than the rest of the abbey. Wide worktables spanned the length of the room. Along the walls were hung a carefully organized assortment of iron cookware, and from the ceiling was suspended a string to which was tied a collection of dried herbs. Barrels of wine peeked out from beneath a cabinet to my left, and shelves of pots lined the right wall. On the far side of the room, I spied a large oven beside another door. I made toward the door, wondering where everyone had disappeared to.

"Ciao ragazza!" a bright voice called out, suddenly accompanied by a portly-looking man who leaned out from where he had been working – unseen – behind a large pile of carrots on the other side of the room. His eyes were large and soft, and he smiled kindly. Bowing his head, he introduced himself as Fra Mariotto, the cellarer of the monastery. "I tend to the kitchen and cellar and such," he explained, in case I had not already gathered as much. "And you must be Amadora, am I right? Still a bit hungry?" He chuckled kindly. "You look like you haven't seen a decent meal in weeks. Don't you worry girl, I'm not one to let a little thing like you go around on an empty stomach."

I nodded, unnerved by his bubbly personality and nervous that he might set off another bout of panic. Beyond him being an agent of my newest phobia, I'd never before met a monk who showed such enthusiasm – most carried themselves with rather more reservation as, I had thought, they were directed by the monastic code.

"Let's see," Mariotto mumbled, opening and closing cabinets as he searched for a suitable meal. "I'm afraid I already gave the leftovers from breakfast to the porter for alms, but I'm sure we can find something else for you, eh?" He winked at me, then ducked back into a cabinet. "Hmm…I thought there was…Oh yes! I think we've found it!" Beaming, he reemerged with a large tart in his hands. "Never known a girl your age to say no to a bit of herb tart, and this one's fresh." My gut let out an enormously loud grumble as if in response. Mariotto laughed. "Sounds as though you agree! No need to hesitate. Go ahead, dig in!"

My hand began to shake as I approached, but my stomach had charge of my stronger drive. I was happy for it in the end, because I had never before tasted a pastry quite so fine. Buttered dough, egg, cheese, raisins, mint, ginger, a sprinkling of sugar and pine nuts – I could pick out the flavors of every ingredient, and they came together to create something far more delicious than the sum of their parts. "Thank you," I muttered after licking my fingers clean.

"Di niente," he replied, waving away my comment like the buzzing of a fly. "I hear quite enough of that, thank you very much." He chuckled. "There's too much formality around here as is. Please. Thank you. *Bah.* Most of my brothers are a bit boring, I'll be the first to admit." He put on a rather dramatic impersonation of the somber lay-brother, then laughed at himself for it. "I cannot stand that nonsense. The way I see it, the Lord has given us plenty to be cheerful for; seems a shame to deny him a laugh every so often."

"Doesn't that upset the other brothers?" I asked.

"Hah! A bit of discomfort is good for all of them – they take themselves too seriously. And as it so happens, the abbot is a bit sympathetic to my particular brand of piety," at that, he gestured to the herb tart and smacked the bulge of his stomach jovially. "It's in the best interests of their bellies, see? Once was a time that they tried to change me – were pretty firm about it too – but the Father Abbot said it didn't accomplish much except to ruin the pies." He laughed at that. "Now as long as everyone has a good meal, they leave me be."

I finished off the tart, thinking about what he had said. *He sees so little of the world from within these walls. His joy is just a different sort of ignorance,* I decided, yet I couldn't help but accept the offer of a sweet-smelling apple tourte to take with me as I left.

"Amadora!" Timo called out excitedly as I emerged from the kitchen and back into the cloister. "Amadora!" He ran up from the direction of the chapel, followed slowly by several other monks who continued on past us to their destinations offering neither word nor glance.

"Buongiorno," I offered as he skidded to a stop beside me. "Have you been busy?" I motioned to the other monks.

"Not really. It's just the morning liturgy. We do them every day." He studied me for a moment, then said, "You look totally different all clean. But—but it's nice! You look nice, I mean." His gaze brushed my boyishly short hair. "It's different, but I think it makes you more...you."

I didn't know how to respond, so I said nothing. Timo shifted awkwardly in the ensuing silence. Finally, if just to stop his fidgeting, I conjured up a thought. "Can you show me the rest of the monastery?"

The smile that broke out upon his face dwarfed any that I'd so far seen. Brimming with excitement, he motioned me to follow him back the way he had come. "You only saw bits of everything when you arrived yesterday," he exclaimed happily. "There's really so much to see. Come on!"

First he led me back to the atrium, all the while talking about the abbey. From him, I learned that it had been built at the end of the 10th century by a widowed Florentine woman from the Pandolfini family. Her generosity was remembered in the naming of the Pandolfini chapel, which as Timo showed me, was a large, domed oratory off the east side of the atrium.

The Badia Fiorentina – as the abbey was called – used to be a center of the city's politics before the construction of the Palazzo Vecchio. Timo explained that while the governance of the city now rested in much larger buildings, the monastery had not suffered. Rather, they had turned their attention to almsgiving and philanthropy, trying to lead the people of Firenze back to the Lord through the example of charitable good work.

"Sometimes we even work with the Confraternity of Blacks," he continued, leading me now into the main church. He was cut short, though, at the gasp of wonder I could not help but let escape as I first saw the chamber. The painstaking attention to detail in both design and architecture was almost beyond belief. A small, half-enclosed chapel to the right sported stunning moldings across its ceiling, all embellished with gold lacquer. Even the candlesticks were ornate and carved in wonderful design.

At the far end of the church room was the chancel – within which sat the altar, covered in shimmering golden frescoes – and behind that was the alcove intended for the choir. It was into the choir that I wandered, curiously studying the ceiling. The main chamber was in the gothic style with an open-timber roof, yet the ceiling above the choir was an enclosed, plastered dome. It was blank, unpainted, and yet I still had the distinct and vibrant memory of spying large frescoes within that same space as I had walked by the day before.

I turned around to ask Timo, but he had not followed me further into the church room. I could not even see him from where I stood. Something flashed in the top corner of my eye, and I spun, my gaze locked intently on the ceiling. It was still white, and yet…it also wasn't.

I was beginning to feel dizzy. Were my eyes playing tricks on me, or were there actually colors adorning the blank plaster? I squinted, struggling to focus. There were shapes – figures: several of them along the bottom of the painting. They were praying, prostrating themselves to another figure that sat above in the sky. I could hear their voices calling out, pleading for mercy and giving exultations of thanksgiving.

A breath of fresh air tickled the nape of my newly-trimmed hair. The fragrance of oranges from the cloister had somehow made its way into the church. The fresco had grown much larger– the characters along the bottom disappearing from sight as the sky above them overcame my vision. The figure there had grown larger too – and much more lifelike.

The wind picked up for a moment, and dandelion spores burst up into the air.

All of a sudden, reality crashed back in upon me. I gasped, disoriented as if being suddenly pulled from a dream. *Where am I?* My mind was reeling, desperately looking around at the rolling hills and vibrant colors of the Italian countryside that had somehow supplanted the church choir I'd been standing in only moments before. *How did I get here?* An orange tree was rooted beside me atop the hill upon which I found myself upon, giving off the familiar citrus-scent of the abbey's cloister.

My gaze shot around, and ice ran through my veins as I became suddenly aware of someone standing beside me. It was the figure from the half-imagined fresco – the one seated high in the clouds. Rich, blue silks were wrapped around his naked body, and he held himself with unquestionable dignity and noble poise.

Another gust of wind blew over the hill, brushing against the thick, white feathers that adorned the two enormous wings upon the creature's back. Too frightened to scream, I fell backwards onto the soft grass and scrambled away until my back was to the orange tree.

He looked down at me with a mixture of fondness and disappointment. It was as if his features had been chiseled by a master sculptor, for no façade of man, I was sure, had ever been so perfect. His hair sat upon his head in waves of glistening golden locks. I could hardly breathe.

"Amadora."

His voice was deep, yet with a tenor that could never have before been pronounced by either man or woman. I trembled as the thick vibrations of sound washed through me.

"Amadora, where is it you go?" he said it with the reproach of a worried father, and for a moment I heard the echo of Matteo's raspy voice in his words.

"I—" my voice failed me. Wordless, I stared up into the face of this creature and found the truth of his question as apparent as if I could read it from a book. He held my gaze with intense power. I could not look away.

After a moment, he spoke again. "Speak freely, Amadora. Do not be afraid. Where is it you go?"

It felt as though a giant hand was squeezing my chest. "I'm looking for…Gilio. G—Gilio Salviati," I finally managed to say. Each word was easier than the one before.

"Amadora, do you know who I am?"

"You—are you…" my voice trailed away.

"I am Oriel. I am an angel of the Lord."

My heart, if possible, drummed even more frantically.

"Why is it that you lie, my child? You do not seek Gilio Salviati. You seek vengeance – that which is the sole privilege of God."

A light spark of anger flickered in my chest. "Yet…" I hesitated for only a moment. "Yet he does nothing. Gilio is alive."

"He has plans beyond your understanding – plans that do not ordain the killing of evil men. Their reparation is not to you, but to the Lord, and he will have it in full when your kind stands before him on judgement day."

I responded heatedly, without thought. "If he does not interfere on behalf of those who suffer, then he has no right to judge us at all."

Oriel drew himself up to the full extent of his grandeur. Throwing his wings wide to either side, it seemed as though all else but him in the world became shadowed and dark. He spoke with anger, and it was like molten fire swept across me. "Know this, you who would oppose the will of the Creator: if you continue down this hateful path, you will meet sorrow and ruin."

"What more sorrow could I meet when there is nothing left of me to ruin?" I asked, anger growing more within me with every passing moment.

"The influence of demons is already upon you," the angel replied. "Should you kill Gilio Salviati, your unborn son will never live."

His words echoed forebodingly across the hilltop. One small orange fell from the tree into my lap. Then he beat his wings once with a rush of wind like that of a hurricane, against which I was forced to cover my eyes.

When finally the storm had passed, I opened my gaze to find myself once more within the church of the Badia Fiorentina, staring up at the white-plastered ceiling of the choir.

For many moments, I sat upon the tiled floor of the cathedral, breathlessly pondering what had just happened. *Have I gone mad?* It was a fair theory and not wholly unfounded, but as I looked about myself at the church, my vision seemed no more senseless than it ever had.

I pushed myself up from the floor. *Surely that must have been some sort of dream*, I thought, yet as my legs straightened, one small orange fell from my lap.

"Amadora?" Timo's voice called out from the entrance of the church.

"I'm—I'm here," I managed to respond, though my voice betrayed my uncertainty.

I could hear the sounds of him hurrying over. He emerged from behind the altar looking somewhat worried, but spying the orange on the ground, he laughed. "Oh, is that where you've been?" Stooping over, he picked up the fruit and deposited it in my hands. "You should have told me! I've been looking everywhere for you."

"You've been looking for me?" I repeated, confused.

"Well sure. I lost sight of you while you were exploring the church, and when I came to find you, you were gone!" He chuckled as if it made for a fun story. "We must have just passed each other around the altar. I've been searching for almost half an hour!" He scrunched up his face. "I must not have seen you when I searched the cloister."

I muttered something incoherent in reply, but my gaze was locked on the orange in my hands – an orange that had not been grown in the abbey.

It was real.

That night, as I lay upon my bed, I slept not a single moment. My mind raced – exploring, delving, speculating. Much that I had before thought true was now in question, but that did not frighten me as once it might have. I was beginning to uncover the secret of the fire – of my unearthly escape from the flames – yet above that, I knew with quiet certainty that my course would not be deflected: I would kill Gilio Salviati. I cared nothing for the angel's words nor the thing in my womb. Its death would be a blessing.

Music was once the lifeblood of my soul – an expression of myself in both pride and pleasure. Now I find myself utterly unaffected by its incessant ramblings. Yet sometimes, when I am least myself and most disarmed, I can almost pretend at the unbridled passions I used to enjoy.

What is this sound, so wonderful? It whispers to me as if from a long quiet dream. Have I heard it before? I think I have, and yet I cannot place it. I wish to know it. I wish to sing with it, and dance upon feet that are no longer my own.

But I know that these are the hauntings of the unquiet dead, and I will have no part of them.

"What does the church tell us about the angels?"

It wasn't until the abbot had invited me to sup at his table for the third time in the week since my vision that I finally dared ask for the answers I so desperately needed. I was reluctant, mostly because I still struggled myself to believe that what I had seen could be real, yet my hesitations brought me no closer to my goal. After all, I was forced to admit that, absurd or not, I could not ignore the angel himself, even if I could not accept his warning.

"The angels?" Abbot Simone replied after finishing his bite of smoked pork. He set down his tableware to ponder my question. "That's a more difficult question than most people realize, for while the church does indeed offer truths about the seraphim and cherubim, these have come to be corrupted by fantasy and popular superstition." He waved my words aside before I could ask him to continue. "But of course, I will tell you what I can."

In the background of our conversation was the constant thrum of one of the monks reading from the scriptures, as was the rule during every meal. None of the other brothers spoke at all. Across the small dining hall, I knew Timo was casting furtive glances my way when he thought I could not see – as he had done every time I sat to eat with the Father Abbot.

"Well, first I suppose is this," Simone said, "the word, *angel*. It is not meant to describe their being, but to describe their office. They are sprits of a divine nature, but not each is an angel." He furrowed his brow. "Many fell, at the beginning of the world. They are called demons, but in truth, they and the angels are the same."

"But…well," I hesitated. "Are they *real*?"

At that, Abbot Simone laughed. "Now there is a question that should be asked more!" He shook his head, still chuckling to himself. "The church tells us they are, so I should tell you the same, but truthfully, my answer is that I do not know. I like to think they are watching over us – protecting us, should it be the Lord's will – but I have certainly never seen one."

I have. "They guard us? Against what?"

"Against ourselves, I should think, but that is not their only role. They are messengers by almost every account. Messengers of the Lord to men."

"And…" I was getting close to the heart of my questions. "Are they all the same? The angels, I mean."

Abbot Simone raised an eyebrow quizzically. "So many questions! But, in answer: no, they are unique, or at least have some manner of individuality. Otherwise, how could some have fallen and some remained with God? Different choices are made by different people, and I think the same should hold for them as well. In any case, we are taught that each angel has a distinct aspect to his work."

That caught my ear. "What do you mean?"

"Well, some angels are concerned with nature, with crops and weather, while others still are warriors. Most, it seems, tend to the many spiritual needs of men."

"What about Oriel?" I asked, perhaps too quickly, though it didn't seem as though the Father Abbot noticed my eagerness.

"Oriel. Hm." Abbot Simone paused to consider before continuing. "He is called the Light of the Lord, if I remember correctly, as well as the Angel of Destiny." Another bite of pork. "And I believe many expectant mothers call upon him with childbed amulets, considering him a protector of unborn children."

I did not reply. *Protector of unborn children.* My hand, unthinking, drifted to my womb – to the thing within. Abbot Simone watched as I urgently returned my hand to my lap. Whether he guessed at what the gesture meant though, he made no sign.

After a moment, the abbot returned to his meal, and I returned to my thoughts. *So that is it then.* Surely, the mystery was solved. It must have been this Oriel who saved me from the fire, but for what purpose, I could not guess. *Could the seed planted within me have already taken root, even then? Was he protecting the child I would one day carry?*

Anger filled me, and revulsion. This *thing* I carried was higher in the minds of angels than I had been, or Matteo, or Jacopo. *Bastardi*, I thought. Not for the last time, I cursed at heaven – at the twisted inaction that allowed so much despair and evil, and yet only intervened for the sake of evil's progeny.

In the end though, I decided that truly, the vision changed nothing. There was no message that would deter me from my path, and this Oriel was a fool if he thought the death of this thing I carried held any distress for me at all. I felt nothing for it. Nothing.

With renewed focus and clarity of mind, that night I took again to the task of planning how I might gain access to the Palazzo Salviati. I had already delayed too long – thought too long on the angel and his words. I needed Gilio's death more surely than I needed food or air. I needed to find him, and to do that, I needed to first find a way inside his palazzo. After my last encounter with the guardsmen though, I had to admit that entrance by the front, especially while I looked so ragged, was unlikely. And I immediately discarded the thought of lying in wait for him somewhere in the city; I doubted he was ever outside the company of his soldiers in public.

My largest roadblock, I finally decided, was in the state of my wardrobe. There was no chance I could gain an audience with Gilio while wearing pauper's clothes. I needed to look the part of a damsel, or a courier, if I sought even a chance of admittance. *Clothes cost money. Money I do not have.* Frustrated, I stood from my bed and begun to pace the small room. *I could steal what I need*, I thought, yet already I knew that would be useless. A beggar like myself in a fine shop? – I would be watched like a hawk. It would be impossible to make away with a pair of stockings, much less a full outfit of my size.

So distracted was I by my meandering thoughts, that I unwittingly tripped over my harp, bruising my shin and stumbling into my cot. "Merda!" I cursed, wincing at the pain in my leg. Angrily, I aimed a kick at my harp, wondering for the hundredth time why I had brought it with me at all. "I should sell *you!*" I yelled.

I froze. "I *should* sell you." The thought seated itself firmly in my mind as if it had always been there. What other use for the harp did I have? I couldn't play it anymore – not really – but it was a fine instrument. I could easily find a buyer for it, and the money from the sale would be more than enough for the clothes I needed.

Finally, a plan – an actual, realistic path forward. I smiled, alone in the dimly lit room. For once, it seemed like fate was in my favor.

The next morning, I hitched my harp upon my back and stole away from the abbey while the monks were still reciting their morning lauds. Retreating into my mind, I let my instincts take over as I wandered in search of the marketplace I thought I had spied on my way into the city over a week ago. However, as I continued to turn down street after street with no luck, I finally had to admit that my memory had been clouded by exhaustion that first day in Firenze.

I don't even know where I am any more, I realized, suddenly aware that few people accompanied me upon the street, and those that did looked increasingly less friendly. Many were dirty, or ragged, and almost all carried a haunted expression. I kept my head down, but was sharply aware of the furtive glances occasionally stolen at the bag which carried my harp. Once or twice, someone actually stopped to watch me pass, caution clearly battling greed in their eyes. It seemed that I had unwittingly wandered into the slums, though what turns I had taken to do so, I could not remember.

Stepping quickly, I tried to retrace my path, but it seemed that every corner only led me deeper into this dark district of the city. I saw swords at people's hips, and a few times I thought I even saw hands drift to them as I walked past.

My heart was beating fast. I ducked down a nearby alley.

What now? I berated myself. Closing my eyes, I tried to re-walk my path from the monastery in my mind. After a few minutes, I finally decided that I must be east of where

I'd meant to go, but just as I was about to step back onto the street and hazard my new directions, the curious echoes of a woman's voice from around the corner made me hesitate.

"Ciao bello!" I heard her call out with no reply, her voice ringing loudly along roads and vias that were otherwise silent. A few moments later, she called out again, "What do you have time for, signore?" Curiosity caught me, and I peeked out from the alley, unsure of what to expect.

The woman was standing in front of some sort of shop not far down the road from where I hid. She like a noblewoman, her fanciful gown of so rich a cut, yet something of the way she held herself bid me hesitate. As I watched, she called out to a passerby, "Come now, amore. Don't you like girls?" When the man didn't reply, she laughed. "Am I not pretty enough? Come on then, I'll have no need of these any longer." Then, with a cheery twitter, she swept up her blouse to expose the full measure of her pale white breasts. "Do you want them, amore? It seems I am not using them correctly, after all."

I was so stunned that I forgot to look away. Crimson rushed to my cheeks. By the time I had again regained control of myself, the man had been spirited inside the shop – *the brothel,* I suddenly realized – and the woman was alone on the street once more, giggling as if the whole show had been intensely amusing.

So—so she's a—a whore? I was singularly fascinated, so much so that I did not even have the grace to be ashamed of it. The courtesan was barely older than myself, and while I could not call her an exceptional beauty, she held herself with such attractive self-assurance that I doubted many men could resist.

Suddenly, a pair of soft green eyes met my own; she watched me, a playful grin on her full lips. My chest tightened so hard that I squeaked, and I ducked back around the corner. Breathing hard, and feeling more than a little childish, I leaned against the cobbled wall and focused on salvaging my composure; by this point the blush in my cheeks felt as though it might become a permanent feature.

"Did you see something that you liked?"

I jumped nearly out of my skin and let out a sort of strangled scream that was only hampered by my heart leaping into my throat. The courtesan popped her head out from around the corner, laughter in her eyes.

"I—no! I mean—I didn't—sorry." I had to force my mouth closed before my words became completely incoherent.

She giggled. "Where are you trying to go, dolcezza? You look lost."

"I—" but I was interrupted before I could say anything.

"Oh! Is that yours?" The cover of my harp had slipped a few inches, exposing the instrument within, and it was at the instrument that the woman was now pointed excitedly, all pretense at composure gone.

I nodded.

"Really? Are you any good?" She bent over and gingerly touched a corner of my harp. "I've always wanted to learn."

Not knowing how to respond, I brusquely blurted out, "The market! I'm looking for the market."

She laughed. "The market? Dolcezza, you're going the wrong way." Eying my harp longingly for another moment, she straightened, but as she did so, her already low-cut bodice slipped even further from her bosom. A soft spot of pink emerged upon the bud of her left breast. My eyes darted away, and blood again flushed my cheeks. But while neither my blush nor the snap of my gaze were lost upon the courtesan, she did nothing to correct her blouse, only watching me with amused interest.

"You want the Mercato Vecchio. That way," she pointed down the street behind me. "It's not far."

I kept my eyes firmly locked upon the air above her head, futilely trying to return my face to its previous hue. She sighed as I resituated the cover upon the harp and swung it over my back. Then, offering a small nod of embarrassed gratitude, I took my leave toward the marketplace, absently considering that I should have asked the courtesan if she was interested in buying the harp, but unwilling to turn back.

Before long, the darker roads and dangerous people faded away behind me, the ominous silence being replaced with raucous merriment and the hawking of goods. I turned a corner, the noise reached an explosive crescendo, and I found myself facing the Mercato Vecchio, the old market of Firenze.

The sheer energy – the endless activity – was overwhelming. There were more people in the piazza than I had seen before in my life, each moving and talking and buying or selling, flitting to and fro, happy or angry or hopeful or sad. It was as if all the roads of the world led here. There was so much to see that for a few minutes I could only stand and stare.

Eventually, I continued into the marketplace. Letting my attention hang on only a few things at once, I was able to navigate the maelstrom without being overcome. Stalls surrounded me with their owners behind, or in front, shouting out their wares only when they weren't busy with a sale.

"Meat! Salted pork and veal!"

"Stay warm this winter! Thick pelts and furs!"

"Fresh milk and eggs!"

"Candles! Household oddities!"

I wandered for nearly an hour, exploring the different stalls and shops, continually frustrated that I could not get to the heart of the piazza, for the thick throng of people – of men – was too dense for my phobia. Yet I listened intently as I circled the outermost stands, and became fairly confident that none of the shops in the interior dealt in artisanal tools or musical instruments. In fact, very few stalls sold anything besides food, clothes, and other common necessities.

It was to one of the latter shops that I finally approached. Cookware, washing tubs, charcoal sticks, thick hay brooms, and a random assortment of other goods littered the expansive booth. The man behind the booth did not yell to advertise his merchandise like the other shops, but still it seemed that he sold two things for every one of the stalls around him. It was a long time before the crowds waned enough for me to hesitantly approach.

"Um…salve signore," I said, careful to keep my distance.

"Ciao ragazza! Anything to buy? As you can see, I've got whatever you might be looking for." He was loud, but though his words were kind enough, his eyes seemed permanently thin and his lips thick and pouty.

"No, sorry. I'm looking to sell," I replied. At my words, his smile disappeared.

"Oh alright then," he said resignedly, all trace of invitation and cheer gone. "Something good though, I hope."

I shrugged, not knowing what he might consider "good," and set my bag upon the ground in front of him. Taking a comforting step back, I gestured for him to look.

He raised a humored eyebrow at me, but did not say anything as he bent down to extract my harp.

"Ah, I see," he said, turning the instrument over to inspect it. "I'm sure it is well made, but unfortunately, I do not want it."

"What? Why not?"

Setting it back down and rewrapping the slip around it, he gave me an apologetic shrug, but one that left no doubt at the finality of his denial. "It will not sell. None looking to buy a harp would think to find one here."

"There's no way you would take it?"

He sighed. "I might for," he paused to think, "four soldi, but I think I will be losing money."

I sputtered. *It's easily worth ten times that!* I was desperate to sell, but the miserly offer would not even begin to cover the clothes I needed.

Scowling, I left without another word. The sun, having risen well into the sky, beat down on me in earnest as I wandered the market one last time, desperate to find a stall – any stall that might be interested in the harp, but I had no luck. Finally, I was forced to seek shade beneath a marble column, upon which was placed a wonderfully carved statue of gray sandstone, depicting a woman that must have been chiseled to represent abundance. Fitting, I thought, for the Mercato Vecchio, though it seemed that none of her bounty would benefit me that day.

Hiding in the shadow of the pillar, I watched the throngs of people surrounding me with disgust. Of course I could not find a buyer, it seemed so obvious now; none of these people were the type to find any use in music or art. They were farmers and beggars and peasants with no higher calling. If I was to sell my harp, I would need to find someone with the right appreciation of it.

A bright thought alit in my mind. I knew exactly the sort of person that might purchase a fine instrument. So, after a few questions and a short walk, I found myself in front of a familiar scene.

The workshop was different than Matteo's in every fashion, yet in every corner – upon every easel and stool – I found painfully comfortable familiarity. There sat a young boy busily churning paints. Beside him lay evidence of a morning spent translating manuscripts, and notebooks of charcoal sketch work and half-finished wood carvings were scattered around him.

The rest of the shop suggested to me that the master specialized in goldsmithing, a practice I knew to be reserved for the most prodigious artisans. Matteo had taught me the fundamentals of the craft in the course of my training, but we had never the materials to apply those teachings any further. He had said, however, that to be a goldsmith, one must be the master of many talents – art, woodcarving, sculpture, metallurgy. I just prayed that music ranked among this master's faculties.

"Niccolo Torrini," the man introduced himself, appearing from a back room with his hands full of parchment. His eyes did not leave the drawings upon them as he spoke, "Though of course you knew that, or you would not have come to me – I, who with only these hands create the most beautiful works in all Firenze. As even the great Cosimo de' Medici agrees, none other can compare." He gave every word the weight of a grand presentation.

"Salve signore," I offered. At my voice, his gaze finally left his work. Clearly I was not his vision of expectation, and he looked me up and down curiously, his gaze lingering for a moment, it seemed, upon my hands.

He was in all things dissimilar to Matteo. Much younger, he still boasted a full head of hair and his beard was well manicured, even if singed and gilded in places where it had absently fallen into gold lacquer. Yet even for all that and his brusque, proud mannerisms, there was something undefined of him that reminded me of my late mentor.

"What do you want, girl? I'm very busy." His grandstanding was seemingly for the benefit of others, for it had quickly disappeared. The boy, stirring paints, glanced curiously up from his chore, but visitors must have been common, and it wasn't long before his attention wandered back to his task. Meanwhile, Niccolo Torrini returned to his papers, seeming for all the world as if he had already forgotten I was there.

"I—um…" I hesitated, unsure if he was listening.

A moment passed. "Go on, girl. Out with it already."

"I need to sell this," I said, bringing the harp out from its leather slip. "It's a harp."

"Yes, in fact I know a harp when I see one, you little dullard. Do you know the craftsman?"

"I…no. I don't know." Silence followed, and desperately I added, "But I know it's well made! I—I bought it from a merchant. In Montaione."

"Montaione?" he asked. Niccolo's eyes appeared for a moment over the top of his work then disappeared again. "Play it for me," he said.

"I—what?" I asked, confused. "No, I need to sell it."

He rolled his eyes and sighed dramatically. "And I need to hear its tone before I know what the instrument is worth, yet I'm rather busy, as I'm sure even a simple urchin like you can see." He huffed. "So play it for me, if you can, and perhaps I will buy it if the tone is fair. Otherwise, go return it to whomever you stole it from and leave me to my work."

His condescension irritated me, but I didn't want to waste more time finding another shop. So, giving him a sharp glare, I picked up the harp. It seemed heavier on its own than it had inside the slip – silly, I knew. *Might as well get on with it,* I thought to myself, looking around for someplace to sit, yet the only stool I could see was appropriated by Niccolo almost as soon as I saw it. He still had not looked up from his papers. I glared at him as hatefully as I could, but he did not move. Frustrated, I kicked over the nearest, empty crate and took as seat there.

The harp was in my hands, but as suddenly as the harsh corners of the soundbox touched my chest I knew that I would not be able to play it. I had not been able to play it when first I discovered it in the Palazzo di Compagni, and I would not be able to play it now. I could still feel the coarse strings upon my stiff fingers, could still hear the rank maelstrom of noise. I could not play it – not anymore.

I began to form the words of my resignation, yet I stopped when saw the goldsmith, still hidden behind handfuls of parchment, with his haughty eyes and patronizing carriage. *Arrogant bastard.*

Grinding my teeth, I forced my fingers to the strings. They rested there uncomfortably. For quite a few moments, I sat like that, struggling between my dislike of Niccolo and my desire to leave. Finally, I plucked a string.

My nails – long and jagged and dirty – caught on the gut cord and snapped it so that it twanged piercingly. I flinched and cursed under my breath. I glanced upward, but Niccolo had still not looked away from his work. Angrily, I refocused on the harp and tried again. The string vibrated heavily under my clumsy touch, but the sound was clear.

Hesitantly, I moved to the next string, then the next. Slowly, but with no more embarrassing missteps, I tuned the instrument for the first time in over three months, trusting my ears to know when the sound of each string was good.

By the time I was done, I was practically shivering from the effort of trying to soften and control my clumsy fingers. I looked up again, half expecting Niccolo Torrini to send me on my way, but he only waved me on with absent thought. "A song now, I said."

Not bothering to hide my distain, I settled my hands into the traditional position. Fingers poised uneasily upon the strings, I decided on the simplest melody I could remember – really no more than a child's study piece – and tried to play it in my mind before attempting it on the harp, yet even then, the imagined tones were harsh and unnatural. I ground my teeth, and with great effort, forced myself to begin.

My fingers were ungainly as ever, clumsily falling off some strings and violently yanking others. They crashed against each other, stifling chords and muting strings without purpose or design. I refused to give up. Growling deep in my throat, I trudged forward, struggling with every note and butchering every arpeggio. I closed my eyes so as to better concentrate; I could feel my face scrunched in an angry scowl. The song finally ended in a cacophonous slur, the last notes mercifully dying away into the floorboards. I glared at my knees, my face flushed with embarrassment, refusing to look up and see the disdain that I was sure waited for me.

"Again," Niccolo said with an uninterested drawl. "I had wax in my ears and could not hear. Play it again."

Fury chilled the back of my neck. *He's mocking me*, I thought, and yet he still had not looked up from his paperwork. "Fine," I growled back, my breath heavy.

My patience had run out, and so I barely bothered with my fingers as I began the song anew. Ignoring years of patiently learned technique, I rushed through the first few lines with abandon. My breath caught, and I had to focus to keep my fingers moving as I realized, very suddenly, that the sounds from my harp were not the clumsy filth of before; they were nearly pleasant – almost melodious even. For some reason, my music had returned, yet no sooner did I have the thought than my fingers tripped over themselves and the song regressed back to its newly familiar cacophony. My hands fell away from the instrument, but there, just for a moment, I had been playing again – really playing.

Without looking up, I took to the song again. Ugly cacophony. I tried again. Discord. Again. I needed to find it. I needed to understand. Again

"You force yourself upon it. Let the music be its own." I had neither seen nor heard Niccolo approach, but he now stood beside me, curiosity in his eyes.

I said nothing, but as I started the song anew, I tried distancing myself from it – pulling myself away from the music in a way I'd never done before. I struggled to lose my focus; to do so was to fight against twenty years of hard-won habit, but slowly – ever so slowly – the song began to emerge from the dissonance around it, like a vine pushing through a crack in stone. I fought harder. I imagined my arms going numb; they were not mine and could play however they wished. The music was forming, flowering. My vision blurred as I lost focus. I gave up myself. And finally, as I let go of my fingers, the song burst into elegance.

So long had I been suppressing my emotions, that even then I felt only a muted parody of joy, but pride was enough to put a smile on my face. Excitedly, I moved to another song, and another, allowing them to weave together as I'd once done on the balcony of my small workshop in Montaione, but now I was not the conductor; I wasn't even the musician. I felt more like the instrument, letting myself be shaped and directed by the music. Yet even then, I think, I knew something was missing. It was not truly the passionate harmonies of my youth come again – only an approximation of them. The melody, it seemed, moved around me, but not through me as it once had. I felt no more of the music than I did anything else. No passion. No thrill. No surge of sensation. Pride, perhaps. Satisfaction, definitely; and in the end, that was enough for me – more than enough.

I set down my harp and winced as my sore, blistered fingers once again became my own. The workshop swam back into focus, and for the first time since I'd begun to play I remembered where I was. *I got carried away,* I realized, slightly embarrassed. The boy was staring, wide eyed, his mouth hanging slightly open and his paints forgotten. Before me stood Niccolo, a strange, softer expression drawn across his face. I looked down, and for a few moments the workshop was silent, save for the muted sounds of people from the street without.

"Andrea, vieni." Niccolo's voice finally broke our frozen scene. The boy jumped at the sound of his name, and Niccolo bent to scratch something upon a piece of parchment. I watched with apprehension.

"So…will you buy it? The harp, I mean," I asked, but Niccolo did not look up from his quill. Frustrated, I continued, "You said you would buy it if the tone was good. You said—"

"I said only that I *might* purchase it," he interrupted, setting down his quill and folding the letter. "And as it happens, I have decided against."

"Why?" I asked angrily, indignation flushing my cheeks.

He did not answer right away. Taking a nearby candle, he poured a dollop of wax upon the fold of the letter and imprinted it with his ring. He handed the letter to his apprentice, then turned to me. "I have no use for a harp like yours, but I believe I know someone who does."

"You led me on!" I accused. "There's nothing wrong with my harp, and you know it! Why bother with wasting my time?"

He calmly spoke to his apprentice as if he could not hear my yelling. "Take her to Piero and give him this letter. Don't leave until she is seen, understand?" The boy nodded dutifully. To me, Niccolo said, "Follow Andrea here. He'll see you to where you need to go." He waved us off with an absent flick of his wrist, his attention already back on his drawings. "Go on then. Off with you."

I was too frustrated for words. I wanted to scream, or hit the man, yet in the end all I could do was pack my harp, all the while stringing together angry curses under my breath, and then sullenly follow the boy, Andrea, out of the workshop.

He was waiting for me in the street, bouncing excitedly on the balls of his feet. "That was amazing, signora! I didn't know girls could play music! Where did you learn?"

"Just show me where we're going, alright?"

He seemed somewhat put off by my attitude, but as he led me down street and alley, his enthusiasm soon returned.

"I haven't learned much of the harp yet; I was only apprenticed to Signor Niccolo last year and he won't let me do much besides chores and sketches. I think I could do it good though! I sometimes play on his harp when he's gone—" His eyes flew wide. "But you won't tell him, will you? He'd be so mad if he knew, and I don't want him to stop teaching me! My mother can't really afford much, after all. I don't know what I'd do." He puffed out his chest. "But I'm going to be a goldsmith and make lots of soldi so she doesn't have to worry about any of that! I'm really good, I think. I especially like painting – I'm better than any of the other apprentices. Signor Niccolo told them all so. I'm going to learn more and be the best so that no one could ever paint better than me. I don't even think I'd want to paint anymore if I couldn't be the best. Can you paint too? Are you an apprentice like me? I never knew a girl musician or a girl painter!"

I let the boy prattle on without responding. I very much doubted whether he was allowed to talk much under the tutelage of a man like Niccolo Torrini, and it seemed that he had saved up his extra words to use at the earliest opportunity. He seemed so intent on his constant torrent of questions and explanations in fact, that he did not even seem to notice as I nervously sidled away from other men on the street, trying my best to avoid the ever-present threat of panic within me.

We walked for some time, all through parts of the city yet unknown to me. I thought we must be somewhere north of the Mercato Vecchio, but I couldn't be sure. In any case, there was very little by which to guess at where I was being led. The tenements and stores that flanked us seemed neither extravagant nor destitute. The people that passed us on each new street were convivial, lacking in the fearsome nature that characterized the slums I'd toured that morning.

"We do lots of work for the Medici. Well, Signor Niccolo does at least. He didn't even let me meet them until recently, but they're always really nice. I told all my friends that I had been to see them, and of course they were all jealous. I expect that I will do a lot of work for them when I'm all grown and a master goldsmith or painter. And I'll only take on the very best of apprentices like me so that they can help with all the work I'll be doing."

It seemed that his monologue had no end, yet only a few minutes later he came to an abrupt stop and fell silent. He looked at me expectantly.

"Cosa?" I asked, not having listened to the last few dozen sentences of his soliloquy and realizing, somewhat belatedly, that I must have missed something.

"I said we're here," he explained, excitedly waving me forward. Looking up, I saw that we were standing in the shadow of a massive palazzo, though one lacking the more ostentatious stylization of the Palazzo Salviati. In fact, had Andrea not pointed it out, I'm not sure I would have seen it in passing at all, but now, upon inspection, I was nearly taken breathless just to see its sheer size. It stretched all the way from one cross-street to the next, and it seemed nearly as high as the steeple of San Regolo in Montaione.

Andrea led me through the wide gate of the palazzo, outside of which were stationed two guardsmen – though guardsmen that could not have been in starker contrast with those of the Salviati family I had run afoul of the week prior. They were obviously well mannered, well outfitted, and even offered a respectful nod as I nervously passed between them. Through the gate, we came to an courtyard somewhat similar to that of the Palazzo di Compagni, but so grander in elegance that the comparison was laughable. It was ringed by a wide arcade, sporting columns which I knew from my studies to be decorated in the newly popular composite order of architecture – having both the broad volute spirals of the Ionic order as well as the classical chiseled acanthus leaves of the classical Corinthian order. Within the arcade were impressed niches that housed intricate sandstone sculptures; I supposed they must represent important individuals to the family that lived here, though I recognized none of the depictions. Meanwhile, in the center of the courtyard stood a large marble statue of David – naked, as was the popular style – and smoothly polished. Whoever lived here had a great appreciation for the arts, of that there was little doubt; I spied a fortune's worth of work in just the mouldings of the immediately visible courtyard, and I very much expected the decorations extended through the rest of the palazzo. Vaguely, I wondered at who in a place such as this would want to buy my simple harp, but I couldn't hold onto the thought for longer than it took me to become enamored by the next construct of elegance.

I was deaf to the rest of the world as I lost myself in the art and architecture that surrounded me, so it wasn't until Andrea tugged at my shirt that I saw a servant had come to lead us further into the palazzo. I followed silently, realizing rather late that the lad's touch had induced no bout of terror. He was only a boy, I supposed, and not quite yet a man. Strange that to my subconscious such a distinction should matter.

My expectations were met, and exceeded. The palazzo became no less majestic as we passed further and further into its interior. Grand paintings along grand hallways. Magnificent tapestries and gold sculptures. Marble engravings to decorate intricate archways. Extravagant, yet tasteful; the manse was like a living exhibit of every principle of architecture and art I had ever been taught. All too soon, my tour was done; the servant was knocking on a stout wooden door, and at the reply — "Vieni avanti, per favore!" – we were led in.

"Andrea del Verrochio!" the man within exclaimed in greeting, emerging from behind a desk piled high with journals and ledgers to tousle the lad's hair as the servant excused himself. The room itself was clearly a study, though larger than most and well decorated. Within waited the man who had first greeted us, as well as a young woman – not too many years older than myself and well dressed in clothes fashioned modestly after the style often taken, I knew, by Florentine nobility. She smiled kindly, and I saw a twinkle of indisputable intelligence in her eyes. More and more, I began to think that Niccolo was having some sort of game of me.

"Salve, Signor Piero!" Andrea replied happily. To the woman he made his best impression of a bow and spoke with attempted severity. "Buongiorno, Signora Lucrezia."

She coughed loudly to hide a chuckle. "Salve, Signor Andrea," she replied, imitating his solemnity.

"So, young Andrea," the man named Piero asked after their greetings were exchanged. "Where is grumpy old Niccolo? Don't tell me he's asking for more time on the tile engravings. He's already three months behind schedule."

"Oh, no it's nothing like that," Andrea replied. Reaching into his tunic, he pulled out the letter Niccolo had given him, which was noticeably more crumpled than it had been, and handed it to Piero. The nobleman took it with an air of curiosity, broke the seal, and silently read its contents. After a moment, he handed it to the woman, Lucrezia, and turned his studious gaze to me. To his side, I could see Andrea furtively trying to peek a glance at the letter.

"So," the woman said, carefully setting down the letter and joining her piercing gaze to Piero's. She said nothing else though, and as the silence stretched out, I wondered whether they expected me to speak.

"Um…Niccolo…he said you would buy my harp," I hazarded, feeling more than ever like the dirty urchin I appeared to be.

"Buy your harp?" the man repeated, raising his eyebrow as if the question was absurd. "I certainly will not." The woman nodded beside him in agreement. Something within me snapped.

"Then why am I here?" I exclaimed, all pretense of patience lost. I was angry, and frustrated. "I only need to sell my harp so I can buy clothes! If the goldsmith won't buy it, and you – *whoever* you are – won't buy it, then *what the hell* am I doing here?!"

Silence followed my tirade. Andrea watched me, eyes round as wagon wheels, looking as if I had lost my mind. After a moment though, the man let out a bright laugh, and the tension in Andrea's shoulders evaporated.

"You don't know who I am?" he asked, laughing uproariously as if that were the funniest thing in the world.

"I may just kill Niccolo for this," the woman beside him said, fighting to be heard through his fits of laughter. "No explanation? Was that really necessary?"

Tears leaked from the man's eyes as he fought to speak through his laughter. "I'm sorry," he said, "For laughing, that is. It's not at your expense, I swear it." My scowl must have shown my disbelief, because he quickly continued, "It's only, my name is Piero…Piero di Cosimo de' Medici."

My breath froze in my chest. *Piero…de' Medici? The son of Cosimo de' Medici?* I was reeling. *That means…this is the Palazzo Medici? Truly, the Medici?* Even through my shock, I knew that what I'd seen, the wealth and ornamentation, certainly suggested it was true. The Medici, though, were the rulers of Firenze in all but name. It was as if I had suddenly found myself standing before a king. *Yelling at a king.* I shivered.

"I—I didn't know," I finally stammered, attempting an awkward curtsy in my filthy tunic and trousers.

"And trust me, I intend to have a talk with Niccolo about that," the woman said, offering me a comforting smile. "And I am Lucrezia Tornabuoni, if you hadn't gathered as much already. Piacere di conosceria; it's a pleasure to meet you."

Of course, I had immediately known who she must be. Lucrezia Tornabuoni – wife to Piero de' Cosimo, and the most powerful woman in all of Firenze, if not all of Italia. Without thinking, I attempted another curtsy.

"That's *quite* enough of that," Piero said. "I am not my father, after all." *Cosimo di Medici.* I fought down the sudden urge to curtsy again.

They're only people, I told myself, and in fact now that the shock was waning, I was surprised to see how ordinary they both appeared. Lucrezia was firm, not beautiful to look upon, with a slightly sunken nose, a high-pitched voice, and a deep chin. Piero, on the other hand, looked nothing if not sickly. Dark bags shaded his bright eyes, his cheeks were fat and stretched in contrast with his thin, almost delicate, frame, and there was a subtle redness and swelling to his hands that suggested the rumors of his being plagued with gout were steeped in fact. Yet even so, the more I looked, the more I realized that there was something undoubtedly and undefinably regal about the pair before me – a certain strength of will that shone from them. These were not noblemen like the Compagni or the Salviati. I became, if possible, more nervous.

"No, we will not buy your harp," Piero repeated. "I am of a mind with Niccolo on that, if what he says of you is true; it would be a crime to part a master musician with her instrument."

"A master musician?" I echoed.

"That is what he says," Piero explained, gesturing to the letter that now lay open upon his desk. "And for all his faults, I trust him in such matters. I do wonder, however, what tale of desperation might lead a master of the harp – a woman, no less – to sell her instrument." Above his shoulder, I could see his curiosity mimicked in the eyes of Lucrezia. Andrea, too, watched for my response with interest.

Almost as an afterthought, Lucrezia added, "He says you hail from Montaione, have you visited there recently?"

Montaione. If I had not already been so taken by the enormity of the situation I was in, the word would never have caught me off guard, yet the mention of it was so abrupt that, for a moment, I was forced to fight down the memories that threatened to surface. Lucrezia's sharp eyes were piercing, but I was careful to keep my expression composed. "No. I haven't been to Montaione in years," I lied, proud that I kept my voice even.

After a moment of studying me, Lucrezia turned to Andrea. "I think you ought to get back to old Niccolo, don't you think?"

"A good idea, I expect he should not like the idea of you wasting time here with us. Be sure to give him our thanks," Piero added.

Andrea looked as if leaving was the last thing he wanted to do, but the dismissal in Piero's voice was clear as glass. "Sì, signore," he said reluctantly. "I suppose I should." He hesitated for just another moment, then with a last look my way, grudgingly took his leave.

Meanwhile, my mind was racing. Something – some latent instinct – tried to speak to me in the silence that followed Andrea's departure, but I could not decipher why I should worry. All they knew was that I hailed from Montaione, and I very much doubted that either of these two were an agent of the inquisition. I hurriedly compiled a biography that they might believe.

"I'm afraid I never learned your name, ragazza," Piero said.

"Amadora," I answered, glad for the safe question. "Amadora Trovatelli." I wanted to leave – to follow Andrea and find someone else to buy my harp – but I knew that there was something to gain from Piero and Lucrezia. Niccolo *had* said they could help me, after all.

But Lucrezia's eyes had missed nothing.

"You lied." It was not a question. "You were in Montaione recently."

Piero looked mildly surprised, but said nothing right away, instead choosing to study me with renewed interest. I couldn't quite swallow my alarm. "I—I didn't..." I stammered.

"You did," she insisted. "And I would know why."

My mouth worked, but no sound came out. For a moment, it was as if I were frozen, then all at once I panicked and leapt toward the door, harp forgotten in its slip upon the floor, my every instinct screaming at me to flee. Part of me was surprised to see neither of them raise a hand to stop me.

"Is Jacopo Compagni alive?" Lucrezia's question cut through me like a knife, halting my flight mid-step. "Tell us." Again, she did not voice it as a question. My eyes flickered toward the door. My feet twitched.

"Let's not bludgeon the poor girl," Piero said, calmingly trying to soothe his wife.

"No Piero. We will hear what she has to say."

I took another hesitant step away from them. *Run!* I yelled to myself. *Escape!* Instead, I asked, "How do you know Jacopo?"

"We've been friends since we were just boys," Piero answered. Through his level voice, I could tell he was on the edge of his seat. He looked at me as though I were a butterfly he feared would fly away before he could catch it. "Both he and Antonia we count as friends."

The memory of Antonia screaming and being dragged away by inquisition soldiers flashed through my mind.

"We haven't had word from either of them in over a month, and there have been rumors that a nobleman from that part of the contado has been killed." Lucrezia held my gaze with a force like iron. "Now you come to us, a harbinger of our worst fears. *So you will tell us* what has become of Jacopo and Antonia Compagni."

My mind wandered back to the night wherein my nightmare first begun – the festa at the Palazzo di Compagni. It was true: I had overheard Jacopo say he was a friend to the Medici. I still wanted to run – in fact, my legs begged for it. The door was just behind me. I had seen no guards on our way into the palazzo. There was nothing to stop me.

"Jacopo is dead." Was I speaking? I should be running. "Antonia too, I think by now."

The news visibly deflated Piero. He sunk back and closed his eyes. Lucrezia could well have been made of stone, yet her fingers clutched the back of Piero's chair so tightly that the knuckles turned white.

"How?" Her voice was stretched thin.

It was because of me. My hand was to the door in a moment. I threw it open and was sprinting down the hallway before her question had died in the air. Voices called out behind me, but I could not stop. Turn. Stairs. I burst out blindly into the courtyard.

I crashed against something soft, and suddenly I was rolling across hard, cold stone. Andrea groaned from the ground beside me. My head throbbed, and my vision was blurred. Gasping for breath, it was a few moments before I even noticed the blood that was dripping freely from my nose and running across my cheek.

By the time I managed to push myself to my feet, we were surrounded by half a dozen servants, and one of the guardsmen from the gate had appeared. I backed myself as far from everyone as I could, one hand desperately trying to stem the flow of blood from my nose, but there was no longer anywhere to run. Within just moments, Lucrezia, then Piero, appeared, both hurrying from the same direction I had come.

"You alright, lad?" Piero asked of Andrea, who, already on his feet, was being fussed over by a trio of stout housemaids. The boy nodded vigorously, clearly pleased with the women's motherly affections.

Lucrezia ignored them both. Quicker than I could believe, she had cornered me, wrapped my arm in a vice grip, and was leading me through the western archway into a wide garden. I did not struggle. All around were sculptures that made me think of men trapped in cages of stone. At the end of the garden was a fountain, and it was at its brim that Lucrezia pushed me to a seat. With one hand I was struggling to contain the blood still dripping from my nose, but I met her iron gaze nonetheless. My heart was still pounding from my flight.

Lucrezia did not speak, and I had the unsettling feeling that her eyes could see right through me. After a moment though, she sighed. Smoothing her skirts, she took a seat next to me on the fountain's rim. "Come, little one. Let's get you cleaned up." Pulling a square of white cloth from within her blouse, she wet it in the fountain and tenderly began to clean the blood from my face. There, for just a few moments and regardless of their many differences, she reminded me of Antonia.

"I'm sorry." The words were mine, but I did not know from where they had come. Lucrezia did not reply. After a while, I began to wonder if I had spoken aloud at all, or if the words had been just in my mind.

The bleeding had stopped by the time she was done washing my face. My already filthy clothes were now stained crimson down the front. We sat in silence for a few minutes. Finally, we were joined by Piero, though he merely watched and did not speak.

"You need clothes, you said, and money I should think." Lucrezia's hard voice broke the quiet. Piero nodded.

I stayed silent. A soft breeze wafted through the grass that carpeted the garden and tickled me through the holes in my boots. My face throbbed where I had struck the ground.

After a moment, Lucrezia continued, "And we need to know what happened to Jacopo and Antonia." She let the offer hang half-spoken in the air between us, but I knew I was trapped. My harp still stood in the study from which I had fled. Without it, I had nothing. No path forward.

You can't tell them. A voice whispered, but I ignored it. I was tired, and I was out of options.

The words came slowly at first. I started with Gilio, with the night of the festa. By their faces, I could tell they had already heard of the foiled Salviati plot, but neither of them interrupted me as I explained my role in it.

Then, the fire. The rape. The inquisition. My words were short and blunt. There were many things that I did not say, but thankfully, they did not ask for more.

Silence followed the final words of my story. Piero looked at me with such a look of sympathy that my stomach churned. Lucrezia, meanwhile, seemed lost in her own thoughts.

"I remember hearing tales of a secret tunnel leading out of the palazzo," Piero remarked absently. "An old lover's tunnel, they called it. Jacopo and I tried to find it as children." He sighed, then continued, "Thank you. For telling us what happened. We already had word of the Salviati plot from Jacopo by letter, but we could not have imagined that it would end as it did."

"You should know, it is almost certain that Gilio targeted Jacopo only as a means to attack us – to attack the Medici," Lucrezia said. Her voice was level, but the wrath in her eyes was alive and thunderous.

"She doesn't need to know—" Piero hesitantly began, voice full of sadness.

"I *do* need to know," I said firmly, interrupting him. To Lucrezia, I asked, "Why?"

"The Salviati consider themselves our greatest rivals in the city," she continued. Piero did not interrupt, though he looked as though he wanted to. "Our advantage over them is our reputation, which it would seem they meant to sour by criminalizing a family to which we have so many close ties. If Jacopo had been branded a traitor it would have been the perfect opportunity to accuse us of being sympathetic to his cause. That we might even be traitors ourselves. With a new seat opening in the Signoria, casting doubt our direction might have gained him much." She met my gaze. "That is why Gilio was there, and it is the cause of everything that followed. You deserve to know, and to blame us if you wish."

It was all for that? For…politics? My anger hardened, but not at the two before me. "I don't blame you," I said. I wanted to, but in my heart I could only lay those crimes at two pairs of feet. Gilio's, and mine.

"I'm glad," Piero said. "I swear, we will bring Gilio his due. You have my word he will see justice."

I did not say anything at first. I looked first to Piero, then to Lucrezia. "He deserves death. If that is justice, then I want to help." Approval flashed across Lucrezia's face and was quickly veiled.

Piero moved to set a comforting hand upon me, but when I flinched away, he stopped. "I understand your anger, Amadora, but you have been hurt enough by our problems. You should begin a new life here in the city. I will find you a husband – it would be only right – and you may even find there are opportunities for a master harpist in Firenze. Give up this fight, it is not yours."

"It *is* mine," I insisted loudly, anger lending power to my voice. "It *is* my fight, and after losing everything else, it is the only thing I have left."

Piero looked at me with pity, and my anger rose. "You can have more than that, Amadora. You can have a new life here – you and the baby; I will see to it."

I spat. "I *had* a life. I want no charity replacement. Accept my help or not, but I will keep hunting him until he's paid for what he did to me." I turned to Lucrezia. She had to understand. She had to. "Please," I said. "I have nothing else."

She said nothing, and her face did not betray her thoughts. Piero, meanwhile, looked on with sad eyes. "I believe we owe you for your story," he finally said.

The dismissal could not have been more plain. Anger flared up into my chest, but I managed to keep it at bay, if only just. It was with barely a thought that I took the bag of coins Piero conjured out of a coat pocket. A servant was sent to fetch my harp. Then, without a word, I was gone, the palazzo looming behind me.

I have nothing else. My words echoed through the deep spaces of my mind the entire walk back to the monastery. *I will kill Gilio Salviati.* I clutched the purse tightly within the folds of my tunic, and I shrugged my harp further up onto my shoulder. *With this. Somehow. I will kill you.*

I never harbored any expectations of a return to happiness after Gilio's death, but neither did I expect the agony that was to come. I should have expected. I should have known. The path I traveled was spoilt with signs. Not the first, nor last, of these came to me in sleep. Every night. A dream. The same dream. He waited for me even then.

My chest hurt. That was the first thought to which I awoke: of a sharp pain in the center of my chest. '*I brand you as mine, Amadora Trovatelli.*' Dreams again. I rubbed my eyes. I'd had the dream before. There was a fire without flame and a monster, twisted into the approximation of a man as if molded in mud by the hands of a child. *Moloch.* His name came to me suddenly and with an intensity that did not fade even though the details of the dream were already melting into mist. *Moloch. The sceptered king.* An immense yawn took me, and with it escaped the last dregs of the dream and my lingering interest in it.

The monks no longer spirited breakfast into my room each morning (in an attempt, I think, to draw me out), so after donning my all too familiar servant's garb – filthy, bloodstained, and threadbare as it was – I made my way to the kitchens. Fra Mariotto was always glad to see me, and I had come to suspect that the stout cellarer was the one sneaking in the treats that often awaited me when I returned to my room each night.

I couldn't stand the dining hall; it was too crowded and there was always a monk asking to sit and pray beside me, so I'd taken to having my meals in the kitchen with Fra Mariotto. "Here for breakfast?" Without waiting, he pointed me at a plate already piled high with food. "You are too small for a girl your age," he said, watching me eat as he absently prepared another, smaller dish. "You must eat more! More!" He laughed before excusing himself to deliver more meals to the adjoining dining hall.

While he was gone, my hand impulsively drifted beneath my tattered tunic to brush at the large purse that rested beneath my swollen breasts. I hadn't counted it. I hadn't even opened the drawstring pouch to peer inside, but even then, I knew it was a lot – more than I needed for a dress, and certainly more than I was willing to leave sitting around.

Fra Mariotto reappeared, his arms full with empty dishware, and my hand snapped back to my side. "It seems that today you will not be the abbey's only guest. There's a woman come to see the abbot." he said, depositing the plates onto a counter where I knew another lay brother would come to wash them after breakfast. He winked and nodded his head toward the door. "She's sitting with him now, if you cared to introduce yourself."

I didn't. Taking my time, I cleaned the crumbs from my dish only to have Fra Mariotto ladle another serving in its place. He seemed determined for me to eat it, so it was a long while before I finally emerged back into the cloister, stomach full to bursting.

I had become used to the smell of orange trees that followed me everywhere in the Badia Fiorentina – after only a week, it was becoming familiar, even comfortable – but so too followed Fra Timo. After my disappearance the day before, he was even more relentlessly worried than usual.

"Where did you go, though?" he asked, not for the first time. "At least say you stayed in the city!"

I sighed, the sun warm upon my cheeks. I was sitting on the moss that paved the cloister of oranges, but in the time it had taken for my tail to numb, Timo had given me no more than a few minutes to ponder the best use for the money I'd acquired. I'd finally had enough.

"I visited a whorehouse." While he fished for a response, I tried to envision different scenarios that might gain me access to the Palazzo Salviati. Absently, I added, "It was extremely eye-opening." *I could play the part of a courier. That might work.* Though, I had to admit I'd never seen a woman delivering messages before. The oddity of it might ruin everything before I even got inside. A small squeak wrested me from my thoughts, and I looked up to find that Timo had turned a very unnatural shade of pink.

"A—a brothel—you—why—?" He seemed to be having trouble with the words. "You—you shouldn't have!" There was unexpected heat in his voice. "You don't have to go there! I—I don't—I can help! I've been working with the Confraternity of Blacks! They—they sometimes pay dowries for…for…" he trailed off.

For women like me, I silently finished for him. I was surprised with the sudden force in his stuttering words.

"Anyway, I know they can help! You know…if I ask. So you don't have to go do – go do that…thing." His eyes shone, and he looked like he wanted to grab my hand, though thankfully he did not try.

I almost laughed. I had only mentioned the brothel to make him stop pestering me, and I told him so.

"Oh!" His blush darkened from a pink to an embarrassed vermillion. "Erm…sono contenta."

"That's the second time you've mentioned the Confraternity of Blacks," I said, offering him a chance to change the subject. "I've never heard of them before."

He jumped on the opportunity. "Are you sure? They're really well known around here. We give alms to the poor and such, but mostly we're known for spending time with criminals before they're executed." He failed to suppress a shiver. "I haven't had to do that yet. Father Abbot says it is the Lord's work, but it just sounds so…horrible. Some people call us comforters, but I can't imagine anything comforting about it. I hope I never have to comfort someone about to die. I really hope I don't."

I didn't say anything, but I wondered whether his fears might not be the very reason Abbot Simone had arranged for him to join the Confraternity of Blacks in the first place.

"Where else did you go yesterday?"

Grunting incoherently, I rose to my feet, searching for a quieter place to sit and think, but Timo refused to leave my side. Finally, I retreated to my room, his incessant questions harassing me the entire length of the arcade.

"You aren't leaving again, are you? It's just, Firenze can be dangerous if you don't know where you're going. I could come with you, next time you go...I mean, *if* you go anywhere again. You shouldn't, you know, if you can help it. I mean, I know it's your business, but I'm supposed to be your guide and you didn't take me with you, so I'm curious where you went. Were you safe? I hope no one bothered you; like I said, there are some places that are more dangerous than others. If you can't tell me where you went, can you tell me what you did? Was it—"

"Goodbye, Timo," I finally interrupted him when we had reached my room. I sidled inside the door, careful not to give him a chance to enter as well.

"Oh, can I come in? I still wanted—"

I near slammed the door between us, and did not hear whatever he had been about to say.

Flickering light danced upon the closed door. The candle upon the desk was lit. I spun around and found that I was not alone.

Lucrezia Tornabuoni waited for me, sitting gracefully upon one of the two chairs that furnished the room. She was not wearing noblewomen's regalia as she had the day before, but was instead adorned in a common riding dress and cloak that would not have looked out of place anywhere in the city. She made no move to stand, watching me with her bright and intelligent eyes. After a moment, she nodded in the direction of Fra Timo.

"A friend?"

"A child."

"That's a pity. Sit." She gestured to the other chair, which was placed just too close to her for comfort, but not so close that I could move it without betraying my unease. I sat.

"How did you find me?"

She swept my question aside with a light twiddle of her fingers. "I had you followed."

"Why?"

"Because I'm not done with you yet." She glanced around the room. "This seems a good place for you to stay, for now. The abbot is a good man; as good as they get, anyway. You will not be noticed here."

"Noticed?"

"The inquisition is still looking for you. Or had you forgotten?"

Never. "What do you want?"

At that, she paused. Crossing her fingers before her lips, she quietly studied me. "I am not Piero."

"Are you not? That explains the dress."

Her lips twitched. "I am not Piero," she repeated. "And I would not shackle you as he would."

"I didn't expect chains," I said, voice heavily laden with sarcasm.

Her eyes flashed angrily. "I understand you better than you know, Amadora. I am no porcelain woman. I know strength when I see it, and I know when it is better to sate a need than pay an orphan a few soldi for her *story*."

Silence.

"This fight *is* yours," she continued, somewhat more composed. "But you are not as alone in it as you think, whatever Piero would have you believe. I, for one, will not turn you away. I do not like to waste tools so freely given." She held my gaze in a steel trap. "So tell me, were your words yesterday only air, or would you truly help us bring Gilio to justice?"

"I want him dead." I replied. "Those were not empty words."

"Good." She smiled thinly. "But that isn't enough. Gilio must be brought to justice within the law, or his family will only grow more dangerous. I can see that his justice is death – I do have that power – but it is on the executioner's block that he must die, not before. Can you accept that?

"I—"

"Do not answer unless you can swear to it. What you seek will not happen right away. It will take time – years maybe – before we are ready to make our move. Can you trust me enough to wait? Because if you cannot…" She trailed off. "If you give in – if you betray my trust – I will leave you for the inquisition without a second thought."

"I can. I swear." It was as if my path was being wrought by the hands of an unseen architect. This was it: my way to Gilio; I knew it with clear certainty, yet the vow I'd just sworn was not flush with purpose. Lucrezia asked for more than she realized. Vengeance is no bed-friend to patience, and my strength was in my anger. I would follow her for now, but I wondered, when the time came, if I could wait for her justice.

"Good," she said, and for the first time, she smiled. "Come to the Palazzo Medici tomorrow. There are a few pieces to set in place first, but I believe I may have the perfect use for you."

With that, she was gone, and I was alone.

Several hours later I emerged from my room, having meditated overlong on Lucrezia's intent, and searched out Fra Timo. It seemed that my dismissal of him that morning had somewhat subdued his curiosity, and in fact he seemed rather sorry about the whole thing. Even so, when I asked him to accompany me into the city, he agreed with enthusiastic fervor.

There was one place I needed to go. Timo showed me the way, and the next morning when I set off alone for the Palazzo Medici, it was not in the tattered rags of a servant, but in the style of garb I grew up wearing: a tunic and vest, breeches, and a pair of sturdy leather boots.

The warmth of the day sent shivers across my arms. I stretched, reveling in the familiar feel of the clothes I wore. For the first time since fleeing Montaione, I once again felt like myself – or this new version of myself I'd become – and I was proud to know that, today, I would not be coming to the Medici in the rags of an urchin, but with some measure of dignity.

Lucrezia waited for me in the garden, surrounded by men of stone and their well-tended verdure.

"Piero believes I have befriended you in the hopes of your reformation," she explained after a quick greeting. "As long as he finds no reason to doubt it, you will be able to come and go freely."

"Io capisco."

She smiled gently, and lay a calming hand upon my arm. "I've thought long about the tale you told us, of Gilio and the inquisition." Her fingers were soft where they traced soothing lines across my skin. "I know you do not want sympathy, but still…I am so very sorry for the pain my family has caused you. I swear, I will help you make it right."

I did not know what to say, so I simply nodded. After a moment, she continued.

"Did you ever learn why the inquisition sought you out?" she asked.

"Never." The lie came easily. There were some things she could not know.

"They were likely sent by the Salviati," she suggested. "In which case, I doubt you will see them again, now that Antonia and Jacopo are—are dead." She hesitated just a heartbeat's length, and while I could see how deeply upset she still was by their deaths, I was impressed to see none of that sorrow upon her face.

"In any case," she continued, "the Salviati must be stopped, or yours will not be the last tragedy left in their wake. I said before that Piero and I mean to bring Gilio to justice before the law, but it is not as easy as it sounds. We have no proof of his wrongdoing, no link between him and any of the hateful things he has done, including what happened in Montaione. He is too careful to leave loose ends where we can find them."

Where, in all this, can I help? I wondered silently. Lucrezia smiled as if she could hear my thoughts.

"It was your tale of Antonia's festa that first gave me an idea of your usefulness," she explained. "*A bard's are invisible ears*, you said. And despite what followed, your ears that night heard quite a bit – enough to cripple Gilio's plans with Antonia and Jacopo, am I right?" her fingers tightened excitedly around my forearm. "Invisible ears…with those, we might just find what we need to put an end to the Salviati."

"You want me to do what exactly, listen?"

"I want you to do what you were trained to do. You still have your harp, do you not? I want you to play it – play it at every gathering, every festa I can get you to – and listen. Noblemen are notorious for gossip, their women are even worse, and in both cases they rarely pay a thought to anyone below their station. You will hear more in a night than my best agents could learn over the course of a year."

"I…" Words failed me. I hadn't known what to expect when I begged Lucrezia's patronage, but certainly I had never thought she would use me so familiarly. *Play and listen.* I could not help but admit, it was an adroit use of my skills. "I can do that."

"Good," she said. "With this, we may eventually be able to bring Gilio to court, before the Podestà, and see him to the block."

My pleasure was so intense that I laughed aloud.

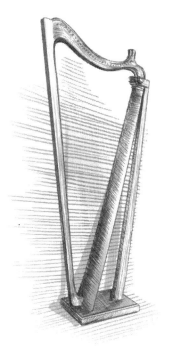

Le orecchie della musicista sono invisibili

Notes on a Florentine Gala

You have not lived, not truly, until you have attended twice the galas for which Firenze is so well known. I say twice, for the vibrancy of each festa invariably leaves first patrons with a deep inebriation, to such an extent that remembrance of the night hardly surpasses that of a wine-drunk child. No, it is the second night that one truly experiences the flavor of unchecked nobility – the music, impassioned; the food, ambrosial; the dancing, erotic.

Men, as always, tend toward exhibitionary displays of physicality, but even those pageants have been polished into entertainment by years of transcendent Florentine culture. Jousts showcase the virility of noble youth and lend a sense of danger to the processions. Injuries are common, yet even those are for the better; blood upon the flagstones pumps more heatedly through the breasts of those who see it. Life validates death, and how better to celebrate it than by the thrum and shiver of couplings made upon the dancefloor.

Art, of course, is the sweet wine of the evening's palate. Women yearn for the words of a poet no less than the gentle touch of a man, and men cherish the tenor of fervent language for what loves it offers that they otherwise lack. In all, these passions sweep through the patronage like waves across a stony shore, orchestrated in their movements by silent fingers upon soft strings.

Yet never has it been for the patronage that such festivities are held. Whoever hosts the gala is the true payee – paid in praise, notoriety, and status. Take note, the ostentatiousness of my palazzo, he says without words. See the golden florins that decorate my courtyard, my rooms, and my corridors. See the ease with which I hire the banquet, and pay special note: my marriageable daughter; no doubt she will want for a husband as wealthy as I.

Those silent conversations are had by yet few. For the rest – happy fools – the only words that matter are those furtive whispers uttered upon the ballroom floor, where they wrongly believe not even God can hear them, for none see a bard's invisible ears.

Secrets are everywhere – hidden in whispers and little gestures, dances and songs. In the end, they are rarely secret. Mine never were.

Smooth ormesino lay across my arms in waves of glaring crimson. It was far lovelier a dress than I had ever owned, yet already I yearned for the breeches and tunic that were so familiar to me. Lucrezia had insisted I wear the gown whenever I was performing, and quickly I understood why. The gala had been far beyond my expectations – more extravagant, more formulaic, and far larger than my singular experience in Montaione had led me to believe possible.

Even now after three concerts, I still left the ballroom feeling somewhat lightheaded, as if I had been pulled up into a whirlwind and was only now drifting back down to earth. My breathing was heavy, and though my night had been spent upon a stool, I yearned for my bed at the Badia Fiorentina.

But still, I could not go back to the monastery, not yet. Lucrezia had been firm on this point: I was to report to her immediately after each event, no matter the hour, and share anything I may have heard while it was still newly purchased upon my memory. Yet so far I had heard nothing of any real value – nothing to lead us to Gilio, in any case. I had, however, learned of torrid affairs, furtive business exchanges, and about a dozen conspiracies, each with a different plan to overthrow Medici rule. In the case of the first few, I had thought these learnings urgently serious, yet Lucrezia only laughed at what I found so dire. "It is a favorite pastime of the nobility to collude against us," she explained. "Tell me if one of these houses ceases to scheme, and then I shall worry."

She's been right about so much, I thought as I approached the palazzo, careful to keep my hood up. I had to be wary – if I were recognized it could unravel weeks of work.

I was not associated with the Medici, not on paper, anyway. Lucrezia had been immovable in her belief that a Medici-employed servant, even a musician, would be kept under scrutiny. Instead, she had set me up as a court bard to another, less prominent Florentine family that were not known Medici supporters. They, at her direction, lent me out for events across the city.

"How was the night?" Lucrezia wasted no time in asking as I slipped inside her private bedchamber. It was common, I knew, for wealthy couples to have separate rooms to sleep, but after spending most of my life with my cot beside Matteo's, I thought it sounded rather lonely.

"Well enough," I answered. "Adrea de' Pazzi boasts, as ever, of your friendship, yet I know for a fact that he and Riario are still trying to buy informants from inside your house."

Lucrezia's eyes twinkled. *She enjoys this — the thrill of the game.*

"Perhaps I should give him one," she answered with a sly grin. "I know a few serving girls who would be up to the challenge. I'll put a mouth to his ear, and he won't know the voice is mine." She laughed aloud. "That's a fine gift you've given me, Amadora. Anything else?"

"Much and little." It was true enough. I heard so many things, but few were worth my breath. "The Capponi boy has broken his leg in some scuffle. His father is furious that it should happen a week before that joust he plans to host." She waved me on. "Most else was hearsay. Signora Alba has been courting a new husband since her last died, it seems. She's been seen sneaking, by night, into the home of somebody called Mario il Topo. I've never heard of him."

"Il Topo?" Lucrezia's voice took on a strange tenor. "You're sure that's what you heard?"

I nodded.

"Mario il Topo…" her voice trailed off, and I could see her mind working. "I thought he was dead. I was sure he would be." She fell silent for a while.

"Who is he?" I hazarded to ask. Lucrezia's eyes flicked to me, and it felt as though I were being studied.

"You've met him before," she finally said. "Mario il Topo – Mario *the Rat*, we called him. He was in Montaione, with Gilio. You described him to us when you first came here: 'a short man with thin lips and small eyes, always hunched over his own feet.' That's no surprise, I suppose. He always had his eyes on Gilio's boots."

"That was…he was there?" *Is this it?* I wondered, feeling a bubble in my chest.

"He was," Lucrezia answered absently. "But no one has seen him since Gilio returned from the contado. After hearing your tale, I was certain he was dead and his wife widowed. Gilio doesn't leave loose ends, I've told you that before, but if Mario is still alive somehow…"

My heart was pounding. "Would he help us?"

Lucrezia grinned again, but with darker joy. "I will *convince* him, have no doubt on that. If he were to tell the Podestà about what happened in Montaione…well, it would be more than enough proof to bring Gilio to trial." She turned to me. "I'll work on this. If he's in the city, my people will find him."

"What about me?"

"Do not do anything," she answered, her tone brooking no argument. Seeing the look upon my face, she sighed. "You are doing well, Amadora. I've heard from several people now about a wonderful new harpist gracing ballrooms all over the district. You're good at this, there's no doubt, and already you've given us a lead. Eventually, you will be asked to play at more events —larger events – maybe even by families aligned with the Salviati." She gripped my chin firmly in her long fingers. "You are invaluable where you are, and I will not risk that to have you gallivant around the city looking for a man who may or may not already be dead. I have other people who can do that. Just wait, be patient, and I will send for you if I find anything, understood?"

I nodded, but inside I wanted to scream.

Lucrezia insisted on an escort back to the monastery – unmarked guardsmen all – so it was nearly sunrise by the time I crawled into my bed and gratefully fell asleep, visions of vengeance dancing through my mind to a melody only I could hear.

"You are mine, Amadora Trovatelli."

The dream was every night now, though I paid it no more mind than any of my other recurring nightmares. It was a symptom of the fire, I knew. Just a mental construct to torture me with visions of flame and guilt. I ignored it, yet another voice was quick to take its place.

"If you continue down this hateful path, you will meet sorrow and ruin." The words called unbidden, as if whispered in my ear. I shivered, still unused to the strange visitation of Oriel's message in my ear most mornings. I still could not decide whether the words were real, uttered by an unseen angel on my shoulder, or if it was instead my latent subconscious speaking unchecked through the cureless clefts of my mind.

Indistinct angels and illusory demons. I laughed at their uselessness.

It was well past noon by the time I snuck out to the cloister to steal an orange from a low-hanging branch. The sweet juices dribbled down my chin.

"Buongiorno, Amadora!" Timo smiled, clearly glad to find me out of my room. Truthfully, I had been avoiding him the last few weeks. "How was the festa?"

I conjured my best impression of a return smile. "Good enough, though Signora Pazzi kept me on the floor until the eighth hour of the night." I yawned for good measure, fully aware that he would not take the hint.

"If you think that's bad, try waking up at the tenth hour every night to recite the morning vigils!" He smiled broadly, but then his eyes snapped to something over my shoulder. In an instant, the smile was gone, replaced by the panic-stricken look of a child caught stealing sweets.

"How predictable."

Timo's wide eyes followed the monk as he approached. I recognized him as the prior of the abbey, Fra Giovanni – second only to Father Abbot Simone in terms of authority, but first by far in his application of it.

"Our youngest brother: yet again an embarrassment to his habit. You now add slandering the holy offices to your résumé." His scowl enveloped the boy in its grasp. "For anything, I cannot see why the Father Abbot thinks so highly of you. You are loud, uncouth, childish, and if I were abbot, you would soon find such behavior met with a rod. I suppose you are lucky, then, that the Father Abbot thinks himself above corporal punishment, because I, frankly, do not."

Timo was practically quivering beneath the older man's unyielding glare. "I—I was just making a joke. I'm sorry."

"You apologize like a fool. Worse than, because even a fool can learn to dance. You, it seems, cannot even learn the barest of courtesies. This is a place of godliness, not imprudent laughter. Your jests insult the Lord, and they insult me. And, above all else, *you will refer to me as Fra Giovanni*, is that understood?"

"Yes. I mean, Fra Giovanni."

The prior sneered. "I doubt it. Go find Fra Mariotto. The old man should have some menial task for you to do the rest of the day. Perhaps together you two might manage to make a single, passable monk."

Timo fled almost before Giovanni had finished speaking, and the prior's scowl followed him all the way to the kitchens. Then, it turned upon me.

"You." If anything, his glare darkened, though I could not imagine what I had done to anger him. "You're the girl who showed up smelling like someone's chamber pot." He pursed his lips as if to spit, though he did not. "A woman beneath the roof of holy men, now that *is* a joke. See already what you do?" He gestured at Fra Timo's receding form. "You corrupt. That is the purpose of your sex. A mistake born from the bone of Adam. Even here, you fill the weakest of our order with lust and foolish thoughts. Have you not done enough? If you had any respect, you would have left already."

I met his glare, but said nothing.

He sneered. "I will pray for you, girl."

"Save your breath," I told him. And, turning on my heel, I left.

I didn't know where I was headed. Too late I had realized that my room was in the opposite direction of where I'd set off, and I refused to turn back, so I wandered for a while through the arcades and chapels of the monastery, touring, yet again, the tired murals and reliefs that were by now all too familiar to me. Eventually my feet led me to the grand church room, where the angel had appeared. So many questions had been answered, but still, I had so many more.

Why would Oriel save me from the fire?

The sloppy sound of my boots as they slapped against the stonework. Red granite, smoothed by the endless footsteps of monks and laymen. Polished until the floor was a mirror.

What else must I do to find my vengeance?

The altar, regal in its seat before the empty choir. Almost a sarcophagus – styled and ornamented. Gold reliefs that tiled the walls of the unknown tomb.

Where is Mario il Topo?

The choir, like a forgotten room. After the imagined mosaic that had joined me with Oriel, the white vaulted ceiling seemed unfilled, like an untouched stretch of canvas within an otherwise finished painting. Like Matteo's painting. Untouched canvas, it seemed, burned alongside everything else. Whether in dust or ash, all ends. All ends.

How long is this path to Gilio?

Taken by some sudden urge, I began to sing. An old hymn. Older than me. Older than Gilio, or Matteo. The deep, delicate aria, caught up by the empty choir, shivered through the very beams of the cathedral. Voice overlaid the echoes of resonant voice, layering new colors – new sounds – in prismatic new ways. I was my own accompaniment. Tender inflections become harmonies, born all from one, undulate voice, rippling like breath upon wine. Harmony to chord. Chord to tonality. The timbre of life. Echoes like ghosts within a quiet sepulcher. As does a chorus, even the death of the song smoldered in slowly fading whispers.

My heavy breath felt too loud in the silence that followed.

"Bellissimo," Abbot Simone whispered. I had not heard him join me within the choir. "Che bellissimo. You did not tell us that you have the voice of an angel."

I studied the unfinished ceiling. "I do not know whose voice it is, but it is no angel's. Their chords are dry of purpose, or passion, or pain."

He was silent for many moments. Eventually, he spoke again. "And where is your pain, Amadora?"

I looked at him – held his old eyes in mine. "I have none."

"Is it from the child you bear?"

My arms went cold, and I hesitated too long to forge another lie. "How did you know?"

He smiled thinly, and laid a wrinkled hand across his stomach. "I saw. As now I see how the child brings you pain." There was no pity in his eyes, just empathy.

"You can't understand."

"I understand all too much of pain," he told me, and for the first time, I saw my own mirrored there in his eyes. "Life is pain. And loss. And guilt. Some learn this more quickly than others, but in the end, we all suffer."

"I was raped." I didn't know why I said that. Maybe he was the first I thought might understand. Maybe I wanted to shock him. Maybe I carried some sick pride in my pain.

He studied me under furrowed brow. "Yet you are alive." The abbot sighed. "Though I see you wish not to be. We all suffer, Amadora. It is how we overcome pain that describes who we truly are." He gestured around him. "When I first came here, I thought myself so pious, so righteous for choosing the path of God over the roads of man. Only now do I see it for what it truly was: the choice of a coward."

I didn't know what to say.

He laughed. "It is not what you expect to hear from the Father Abbot, is it – that he regrets his habit? Well, it is true enough, though I have never told my brothers. I've hidden from both my pain and the world behind the Lord for my entire life. I am a coward, and I weep to think the life I've missed within these walls. But I am old, and my choices have been made. All that's left to me now is the hope that, perhaps, I will be able to face my fears in the next life." His eyes flashed in the light. "But Amadora, you are tied to no such fate. Overcome your pain and find yourself again, or you will eventually come to share my regret."

I looked at the abbot, and it was as if I saw the man he truly was. *Is this what I will become?* A bare moment – a flicker of hesitation – stole through me, and for only a second, I yearned for the girl I once was.

Fire and anger boiled again to the surface. "I will not!" I cried out. "I welcome my path, Abbot. You waste your words on me."

His shoulders fell. Minutes passed, and he opened his mouth to speak no few times, though never did he utter a word. Finally, he turned for the door. "I cannot make you understand," he said. "But if you would hear an old man's plea: tell Timo what you have told me." His footsteps faded into the courtyard. "His response may surprise us both."

I am alone now, as I have always been alone.

I watched Signora Alba from across the ballroom.

I had been watching her all night – studying her mannerisms and memorizing her acquaintances. She did not seem like a woman in mourning. She was friendly with everyone, yet drifted between conversations so quickly that I doubted she had a true connection to any clique. I was beginning to suspect that, beneath her green dress, she was a chameleon.

The congregation and dissipation of dozens of meetings and a hundred conversations over the course of one night was an obligation of these parties, as I had quickly come to learn. It was like a dance – a social waltz of contracts and networks and schemes, all in the guise of merriment and festivity. I now understood that the entirety of Firenze was conducted at these galas. Women were married off, political offices were promised, trade deals were arranged – the lifeblood of the city pumped through the ornate pericardium of celebration. Everything and everyone had a purpose, a motive, a vascular function.

Except for Signora Alba.

She had no husband to represent, no goods to trade, no daughter to marry. She participated in no schemes and solicited no political promises. It was as if the purpose of her attending the festa was, in its entirety, *just to attend the festa.* It was nonsensical. So I watched her, increasingly sure that – as the only woman without enigma – hers must be the most immoderate. My heart sometimes raced at the thought, for immoderate secrets were what I most hoped to find. In the end, those would be what led me to Gilio.

Alba fluttered from place to place, a goldfinch, a chickadee. Occasionally, her migration would bring her close to where I sat with my harp, yet never did she say anything of any importance, just polite, hollow tropes of dialogue.

Lucrezia and Piero were in attendance, I knew. It was the first time they had heard me play in person, yet all I could think of was how I wished Lucrezia would confront the young dowager. She did not, and as long hours passed, I began to grind my teeth. By herself, Signora Alba revealed nothing. Less than nothing, but I was desperate to learn about her – to unravel that darker secret that would take me to Mario il Topo, and through him to Gilio. *She says nothing!* I cursed. *Mannaggia a lei!* The problem, I decided, was that there was no stimulus here to expose what I needed to know. She was too comfortable in the atmosphere of the party to let her mask slip.

A budding thought emerged within me, and I took to it with reckless impulse. Without taking my eyes from Signora Alba, I began to spin a web within the melody I was already playing. Small inflections; variations; deviations in theme. I picked apart the foundations of the piece until they very nearly crumbled, built new layers of arpeggio and harmony beneath it, then fixed a strand of resonance to each one. Soon the song was barely coherent, and my fingers were tied to the web that tentatively held it together. I waited, both the song and I balanced upon the edge of collapse. Shortly, the tone of the gala began to shift. I could see tensions rise – could hear it in the strained voices of those around me. Anxiety was bubbling, yet no one once paid me even a glance; it was as if I were invisible. Signora Alba, I was pleased to see, was not immune to the spell I wove. Once or twice I saw her smile begin to slip. Occasionally some stray word would catch her ear, and she would wince. *There she is. Finally, a woman with a secret.* The song wavered, teetering upon the edge of cacophony. I began to sweat, my fingers taut upon the fragile web I had woven. Someone dropped a cup of wine. The piercing clash of shattering glass drove a knife into the tonal discord of the festa. Dozens of people flinched. Alba nearly jumped out of her skin. The song wavered.

Then I pulled the whole thing down. It collapsed with devastating intensity, painfully inharmonious, revealing the assemblage of euphony and theme I had carefully hidden beneath layers of crumbling discord. It was a new song – a wonderful arrangement of passion and vice, of temptation and ecstasy that burst from the ruin of former disharmony like a rose growing through rock. It was a piece filled with all manner of affections, and I paid each its turn.

First: fear. It emanated from my harp in waves of silver and green, and I soon saw nobles begin to edge away from each other on the dance floor. Looks were cast, voices fell to a hushed whisper. Alba retreated into a corner, and seemed to recoil as one or two noblemen chanced to look her way, but otherwise her fear taught me nothing.

Frustrated, I moved on. Oh, how easily fear becomes anger – crashing notes and jarring resonances, deep purple and crimson hues. The effect was carnal. Voluminous voices were raised. A woman I knew to be the matron of the Pazzi family slapped her husband in full view of the gala. Yelling at the far end of the hall – about a twice-loved maiden, from what little I could hear – turned to fists in moments. As the duo of young noblemen took their brawl to the floor, a matched pair of far older men beside them fell to fighting as well. Even Lucrezia and Piero passed each other cross glances, yet through it all, Signora Alba taught me nothing.

I calmed the song. Anger melted away, and guilt was soon there to take its place. Deep yellow. The blue of a raw bruise. Slowly, the arguments and the fighting began to fade. Apologies were exchanged, and then exchanged again without a gaze once being met. A few people embraced. Lucrezia, it seemed, had finally heard my hand upon the strings; the look she gave me was sad, then curious. Her gaze followed my own, and soon she too was watching the widow as she wandered around the hall. But still, Alba taught me nothing.

Guilt festered and turned to sorrow. Deep, lasting sorrow. Grey. Grey. Grey and lifeless. Tears fell; remembrances were exchanged. Alba did not cry. She taught me nothing.

I wanted to scream. For a while, my song danced upon an endless bridge while I cursed and raved in the torrent of water beneath it. In my detention, a wayward soul found, by some means, reprise enough for a hesitant chuckle. *How could I forget?*

His laugher became the merriment of all as sorrow within my song was finally overcome. Joy is the blush of radiant cheeks and full lips. My fingers leapt from chord to chord and danced from string to string. Again, over long minutes, the ambient nature of the gala turned. Alba was again the chickadee. She taught me nothing, but I was not yet done.

Passion burns black as the night sky. Sultry as white silk. Bare as skin. Alba shivered. Flush crept along her pale chest and up her neck. I watched her steps quicken as she crossed the ballroom. Her fingers opened and closed again and again. All around her was a circus of whispered debaucheries and concealed vice. Wandering hands found supple homes. A playful giggle, then another, and Signora Alba's steps slowed to a stop. I watched.

Later, I reflected on how one look can reveal so much. A furtive glance when you believe no one else can see is no less telling than an absent word whispered when you believe no one else can hear. In both cases, it is not the glance or word that teaches so much, it is whom they are given to.

"Paula? Paula de' Ricci?" Lucrezia asked again. "Are you sure it was Paula de' Ricci?"

"A wide woman wearing a sickening yellow shawl and a great streak of mud upon the hem of her dress. I didn't know her name."

"That's Paula, there's no doubt." Lucrezia muttered. "Interesting, though I suppose it makes sense. Paula is the wife of Mario il Topo."

"The Rat?" I asked, suddenly excited. "Then there's no question anymore! Alba *is* having an affair with Mario. He must be alive!"

"Indeed." Lucrezia sunk into a thick, cushioned chair with a sigh. "I'll tell you, I have never been so exhausted after leaving a festa. I feel as though I've run across the entire city."

She was not the only one. As the party had drawn to a close, I had heard no few people say the same, though none seemed to know why. "What do we do now?" I asked. "I'm sure that Alba would lead us to Mario if we followed her. Have you talked to her? Maybe she will simply tell us where he is. If we could—"

Lucrezia held up a hand to forestall me. "I told you before, Amadora. I have other people to use for this. People better suited for it. You will stay away, do you understand?"

"No, I don't! Why haven't your people *already* found Mario then?"

Anger upon her face was a terrible thing. "Do not think to second guess me, Amadora. Whatever horrors you have lived, you are still a child in more ways than one, and if you cannot learn to trust me, then you will no longer be allowed to help me."

I seethed, but forced myself to play my part. "Fine," I said.

It seemed that was enough for her, for Lucrezia's steely glare began to dissolve. "Good. Then trust me in this: I *will* find Mario il Topo. Whatever it takes."

I was a fool, for in that moment, I truly believed that she could.

No words of man exist to explain the wickedness of fate – her tortured malice – and there is no hiding from her. She can find you in any cove or crevice, harbor or haven. She can find you in a bed, or a prison cell. She is persistent as the plague – and pernicious, as only she can be. A bloodhound. Fetor on the wind.

She found me in the market square, just when I'd begun to feel safe again.

After two months, I had fallen into a sort of routine around the monastery. Breakfast in the kitchen. A walk around the grounds. Some reading from the church's surprisingly ample library. Lunch; after which I tackled whatever chores Fra Mariotto had conjured up for me that day.

The chores, I was told, were a requirement of my extended stay – a way to 'give back,' as Abbot Simone said – but the longer I was there, the more I began to think the chores were, rather, a way for the abbot to belittle my tenancy before the judgement of the other monks. After all, Fra Gionvanni, made no secret of his *earnest* dislike of my presence. He seemed especially moved to brooch the topic whenever I was around, though he was far too clever to say anything within reach of the abbot's ear. Even the prior was not outside the abbot's rule, however much he liked to pretend otherwise. In fact, it seemed as though Abbot Simone and Prior Giovanni had recently become locked in an increasingly intense struggle for power. How I could be the cause of it, I had no clue, but many of the lay brothers now offered me far less welcoming prayers of well-being than they had when I first arrived. For that alone, I was glad for whatever inane conflict now split the monastery.

I wondered whether somehow it was my pregnancy that so divided them. There was no longer any hiding it; over the last few weeks it seemed as though my stomach had grown three-fold. I was a woman with child – a wayward glance revealed as much – yet I had been so far spared from the painful questions I had expected to accompany it. Even Timo, to my greatest surprise, had been silent on the issue. He hadn't asked any awkward questions or offered any clumsy remarks. In fact, it was as if he didn't recognize that I was pregnant at all. It only seemed as though he threw himself into the abbey's conflicts with increasing fervor.

I often saw him arguing with nameless monks on behalf of the Father Abbot, even though I never heard what they spoke about. Strangely, those grim, half-hidden conversations seemed to do something to him – to excavate the gravitas that Fra Giovanni so often reproved him for lacking. Watching from my seat against the well in the cloister, I marveled at how a stern countenance could make a man of a boy. Or was it more than that? He was taller than most of the other monks already, I realized. *How have I never noticed?* He looked so serious – so driven. For just a moment, Timo faded away, and in his place I saw a vision of the man, the monk, he could one day be.

He caught sight of me across the cloister, and the moment vanished. Quickly excusing himself from the brother with whom he had been talking, Timo hurried over to me with all the nervous exuberance of his boyhood reclaimed. Fortunately, he was caught just shy of his goal by the cheerful cellarer.

"Timo!" Mariotto called out, forgoing the brotherly honorific that defined their order. Yet again, I was reminded of how irregular the man was. "Just a moment, my lad." His jaunt had him breathing heavily – overlarge stomach stretching up and down with every breath. Finally, he said, "I need you to run to the market. I promised the abbot I'd make fungi di monte with that crate of mushrooms we received, but I've just found the last of our ginger ruined by mice." He growled heavily between breaths. "I've spent years asking for a good cat to keep around the pantry, but every time it's the same story about how monks are not to have pets. It's no pet; I've said so! I *need* a good mouser. We must be the only kitchen in the city not to have one."

"Can't you just make the mushrooms without ginger?" Timo offered.

Mariotto's frown deepened. "*Without ginger?*" he echoed. "Well then it wouldn't be fungi di monte, would it? No, it wouldn't be!" That seemed to settle the question in his mind. "I'll need you to bring me some from the market. That may be a bit hard as they've not quite come back into season yet, so you'll have to find some that's been preserved from last year's harvest." When Timo didn't immediately move, the cellarer huffed and gave him a small push. "Go on! Off with you, lad. Be back quick, or I'll carve *you* up for dinner instead." He turned to go, but paused after a few steps. "And see that you take Amadora with you!" he called out, gesturing at me. "She's got a good head on her shoulders. I won't have you getting there and forgetting the difference between ginger and garlic."

At once, Timo brightened up. As Mariotto disappeared, he turned to me – beaming –

any dissatisfaction with his chore shamelessly forgotten. "Well," he said, not even trying to hide his excitement. "I suppose we ought to get going, don't you think?"

My level glare followed him all the way to the market.

By now he was used to my odd, winding manner of finding a path through the streets of Firenze. He tried to help as best he could by walking in front of me, but still it took almost an hour to make our way to the Mercato Vecchio, all made worse by the fact that, because of the pregnancy, I stopped to rest every few streets.

Sideways glances shadowed us as we entered the piazza. *No, that's not quite right…* "Um…Timo," I said. "You can go on ahead if you want. I won't mind."

"We don't have to hurry," he replied happily. "Do you need to sit down?"

"No, it's not that."

"Oh. Then what?"

I hesitated. "It's just…people are staring…at—at you. They think you're the father. If you walk ahead, you won't look like you're with me. I don't mind waiting here for you to be done, really."

Timo stopped dead in his stride. He looked around, scanning, I could tell, for the truth of what I had said. I waited for his response – the unsettled embarrassment that was sure to come. He was only a boy, after all.

Then, he did something that surprised me more than I thought possible. He laughed.

Timo laughed long, and deeply. His pubertal voice cracked more than once, but he did not stop until his mirth had run its course.

"What was that?" I finally asked. His amusement was contagious.

"I don't know," he answered, still chuckling. "I guess it's just sort of…ridiculous? I mean, I'm not even allowed to…" he blushed. "Well, you know. But here they all are assuming I could father your babe. *Yours!*" He laughed again. "I'm flattered!"

"I thought you would be embarrassed," I said.

"Well, that's funny too!" he told me. "Come on, we had better get going. Good monks aren't supposed to laugh, so I had better at least get the garlic. That way I will have done *something* right today."

At that, I really did laugh, even though the sound of it sounded harsh and unnatural in my ears. "Ginger, Timo! We need ginger, not garlic!"

He stuck out his tongue at me, and together we dove into the market square.

As it turned out, ginger was not at all hard to find. There was a jar of it for sale at the first stand we approached, and the merchant seemed so glad to be rid of it that he practically gave it away for free.

"That was easy," Timo remarked as we walked away, the jar of ginger cradled in his arms. "Where should we go next?"

"Aren't we going back to the monastery?"

"Sure, *eventually*, but for now we should stay out and have a bit of fun." He smiled. "You are having fun, right?"

"I suppose a bit," I admitted. "It's been a while. I'd forgotten what it felt like."

"Feels a bit like being tickled, I think," he said. "And tastes like a good apple tart! Come on, let's go find one." Casting me a sly glance out of the corner of his eye, he added, "Just don't tell anyone when we get back. We aren't supposed to eat out of the monastery; fun in general is pretty strictly frowned upon." He mocked a serious face. "*Timo, you are an embarrassment to your habit. Stop laughing. Eat more vegetables.*" His impression of Fra Giovanni was eerily accurate, and it almost made me giggle. "I don't want to be like that! I want to be a good monk, I really do, but I just don't see how having fun should be bad. I think laughing can bring us all closer to God. After all, he must have some sense of humor. What else could explain why chickens walk like they do?" He launched into a fair imitation of a chicken gait. A few people jumped away as he pretended to peck at the ground.

"You sound like Fra Mariotto," I said, grinning at his antics.

"Is that so bad? I know what Fra Giovanni says about him, but the Father Abbot likes Mariotto. I mean, even though he doesn't always follow the rules, that doesn't mean he isn't a good monk. I just think that there's more to wearing a habit than all that."

"Plato suggested that the things we see in life are like shadows cast by the true forms of those things in the mind of God. If so, then I guess he was the first to laugh," I offered.

Timo smiled. "I like that. It sounds nice. I wish I could have learned about Plato, or to cook, or play the harp like you can. The monks taught me to read, but only ever from the gospels, or hymnals."

"Could your parents not read?" I asked.

"I don't know. I never knew them, not really. I only have a few memories from before they gave me to the church. I wouldn't even recognize them on the street." His voice had lost some of its vibrancy. I could tell that the topic was a tender one. "I love being a monk!" he suddenly exclaimed. "I don't mean to sound like I don't. I'm glad for what they did. I really am! It's just…" he trailed off.

"What?"

"It's just I wish that I could tell them that – you know, that I'm happy. I think that if I were them – if I had given my son away – I would wonder whether he hated me for it." He stood up as tall as he could. "But I don't! I love the church! I love being a monk! I want them to know how grateful I am for what they did."

"You can't send them a letter?"

He shook his head. "We don't keep records of the parents of our adopted brothers. If they had sent *me* a letter, then I might reply, but I've never received anything. Not even a word." Sadness returned to his voice. "We were poor; I know that's why they did it, but I always thought they loved me. I thought they would have written."

We walked in silence for a while. Timo had always just seemed so...simple. I could never have guessed that so much more lurked within him. He was in pain. We both were. Maybe the abbot was right. His words echoed like a whisper in my mind.

Tell him.

"I—I'm pregnant."

He raised an eyebrow, but he didn't say anything. That made it easier.

"I know it's obvious. I know you already know, but I never told you myself. It's...hard. To talk about, I mean." Suddenly defensive, I forced myself to meet his gaze. "It's not that I'm afraid. Don't you dare think that. I don't fear the birthing bed. I *hate* this...thing...inside me. I want it gone. It's not mine! It's—it's his." *Gilio.* I was breathing heavily. Slowly I steadied myself. "I—I didn't *want*...he...he took...he forced me to..." *Why is it so hard to say?* I had told the abbot without hesitation. I had told Lucrezia, and Antonia before her. But for some reason I didn't want to tell Timo.

"You don't have to say it." His hands were shaking, but still he managed to look in my eyes when he spoke. I was never more grateful to him than for that.

"I was an apprentice. Out west, in Montaione. I was an apprentice to the most wonderful artisan in all of Italia. The man…Gilio…he killed him. And he—he *took* me. And he tried to kill me too." A familiar smell broke through for a moment, and I began to follow it. "I've told others some of what happened, but…Timo, I've never told any of them all of it." I stopped for a moment. I wanted to see. I wanted to know what he would think. "Timo, I was *saved* from the fire that should have killed me. The workshop was like an inferno around me. I could…" I barely hesitated. "I felt my skin as it caught fire. I felt my hair as it burnt away."

Timo looked terrified, though I could see he was trying to hide it. "But then I woke up, in a bed, with no injuries except those I had before the fire." I put a hand to my distended stomach. "One, I still carry with me. But the others…they healed soon enough, though people knew enough to wonder how I had survived. Within a week they were all convinced I was some sort of witch – a *strega* – but that isn't true. It was an *angel*, Timo. I've seen him. He came to me in the church room of the monastery."

At that, Timo seemed to miss a whole step. He stumbled, and had to catch himself on a barrel of wine. "The inquisition showed up. A man in the town had called them. They said I was a witch. They said I killed Matteo. They told me how *I fucked the devil to carry his child*." Even the memory sent shivers of fury through my spine. That smell again. I turned left.

"I escaped, here, to find the man that did this to me. The inquisitor was right about one thing: he is the devil. And I'm going to kill him. I'm going to put a knife into him, and I'm going to watch him die." Timo watched me with wide eyes, but he said nothing. "Tell me I shouldn't'," I dared him. "Tell me it's wrong to want him dead, just like the angel did. He told me that if I killed Gilio, the baby would die. But I don't care. It's justice. And if it's revenge too, then all the better."

I had finally followed the smell to its source. Apple tarts. I took one. They were still warm. I paid the owner and handed the pastry to Timo. "You can't tell me I'm wrong." It wasn't a question.

He took the tart without looking at it. His mouth worked; I could tell he was searching for the right words – the right way to tell me I *was* wrong – but he said nothing. In the end, he filled it with tart, and for a while, we stood in silence.

"Can I have that one?" The voice of a young boy from somewhere around my ankles brought us both out of the spell my story had wrought.

"Not unless you can pay for it, you little urchin. Get out of here!" the man shouted, swatting at the lad, who could not have been older than six. He began to cry almost immediately.

"No, it's alright. Here you go." Timo seemed almost grateful for the distraction as he tossed a coin to the shopkeeper and squatted beside the boy with a kind smile. "Go on," he told him gently. "Pick out your favorite one."

The boy sniffled. Fighting back tears, he hesitantly pointed to a pastry near the top of the pile. Timo ruffled the boy's hair. "Good choice!" he told him, passing the treat to the lad, who held it as if it were made of gold. He looked first at Timo, then at me, then with no warning and less reason, leapt forward and wrapped his little arms around my midriff. I shifted awkwardly, unsure what I was supposed to do.

Timo laughed. "Look at that, I buy him a cake and he still likes you more! What's your name lad?"

The boy mumbled something into my inflated belly.

"We can't hear you," I told him, uncomfortable with his tiny arms resting upon my hips. I tried to pry him off, but somehow only ended up holding his hand.

He turned his head a little. "Francesco," he said.

"Ciao Francesco," Timo said, giving him a little wave. "Are you here alone?" It was clear from his clothes that he was no street urchin. He confirmed it with a quick shake of his head. "Are you here with your parents? Do you know where they are?" A nod told us what we needed to know. Timo smiled comfortingly. "Come on then, Francesco. Let's go find your family. I'm sure they're worried about you." He held out his palm. The boy hesitated for a moment, then – forcing the entire cake into his mouth – he reached out for it with his free hand, keeping the other firmly clenched around my own fingers. Soon, we were a family of three, wandering through the Mercato Vecchio with a jar of ginger.

"My name is Timo. And this is Amadora."

"Dora?" Francesco looked at me, then looked at my stomach. "Do you have a baby?"

"Uh…yes," I replied, unsure what to say. That must have been right, for the boy nodded happily and looked back at Timo.

"What's his name? Are you his daddy?"

My stomach twisted uncomfortably. Timo caught my eye for a moment, looking at once both pensive and concerned, then he turned back to the boy.

"His name is…" He hesitated, avoiding the look of alarm I shot him. "His name is Adamo. Because he has no father."

The entire world seemed to stop for a moment. *Adamo?* The buzz of the marketplace went quiet, and the ground beneath my feet seemed to fall away. I reeled. It was becoming too real. The child. What it meant. What I was headed toward. My legs shook. I could hear Timo saying something, but I couldn't understand it. I was being led toward the outskirts of the piazza. Next thing I knew, I was sitting on a bench. Francesco sat next to me, tightly holding my hand, and I could tell that Timo, looking worried as he knelt in front of me, wanted nothing more than to do the same.

"I'm fine," I said. "I'm fine." I squeezed Francesco's hand comfortingly. "Just dizzy."

I met Timo's gaze. He seemed desperately afraid of what he had done, and yet I could also see that he felt no shame.

"A name changes nothing," I told him. He just smiled, relieved, I think, that I was not too angry. He took a seat on the other side of Francesco.

"Do you come to the market often, Francesco?" Timo asked, prompting the conversation to move on.

"No, only sometimes," the lad replied. "Mamà doesn't like it."

She probably knows you might run off, I thought.

"But il mio papà said that we all had to come today, because he was meeting someone." Francesco smiled widely. He was still too short for his legs to reach the ground, so he swung them underneath the bench.

"Do you know where?"

The boy pointed to an alcove – built into the building above it and flanked by pillars —partially hidden on the corner of a street to our left. There were several people mulling around it, including a few guards.

"Is that them?" I asked Francesco.

He shrugged. "I think. Papà is inside."

"Well come on then, we had best get you back." Timo pushed himself to his feet, bringing Francesco with him as he did so. The boy stretched out, refusing to let go of my hand. "Will you be alright here?" Timo asked me. I nodded, but Francesco began to cry and clutch my hand even harder as soon as Timo tried to lead him away.

With a sigh, I stood. "How about I come with?" I told the lad. "Does that sound okay?" Sniffling, he nodded, and together we set off.

"I—I think I want to say something," Timo said after a moment. "Amadora…" he trailed off. For a while he was silent, and I began to wonder if he'd decided not to speak. But he found his voice just as we approached the meeting of Francesco's parents. "What if I—" A shrill cry cut through the air, and I never heard the rest of what he had meant to say.

"FRANCESCO!" Crying out, the boy's mother appeared out of nowhere. Running forward, she wrapped the lad up in her arms, adroitly ignoring how he squirmed and reached for me. "Where did you go, my beautiful little child?! You've had me so worried! I thought you might have been kidnapped! You know what I've told you about wandering on your own. Take a guard, always take a guard! That's what we pay them for! Don't you dare think about doing that to me again, you understand? Do you understand? Francesco! Tell me you understand!"

Whatever the boy mumbled, his mother seemed to take it as assent. Seemingly satisfied, she looked up, and for the first time she seemed to realize that Timo and I were standing there. "Did you find him? Oh, thank you for bringing him back to me! You must come see my husband, I'm sure he will want to thank you himself. Venite con me! Come!"

"Oh no, we don't…" Timo began to object, but the words were lost on the woman's ears. She was already gone, waving aside guardsmen so that we could follow into the alcove where her husband waited.

I caught Timo's eye and motioned that we could simply leave. He shook his head, and I had no choice but to follow as he forged ahead.

We entered the alcove.

The world narrowed into a thin sliver of sight, and my heart froze in my chest.

Francesco was the son of Gilio Salviati.

He stood there, like the phantasm of my blackest torments. He barely offered an unrecognitory glance before turning back to his conversation, but to me it was as if nothing else existed. Buzzing in my ears. And throbbing. I could hear the echoes of myself screaming in the most removed corners of my memory. Fire. Fire everywhere. I was breathing wrong. Time distended, my feet took a step towards him that lasted an age in my mind. My entire awareness moved as if trapped in mud.

"Amadora?" Timo's voice. Worried.

I am fine, I tried to tell him, but I couldn't move my head to look at him, couldn't move my mouth to speak the words. My feet took another step forward.

"Amadora…?" Another voice, echoing the first with the quiet tenor of imminent recognition. The voice was so familiar. It was poison in my veins but for that it did not kill me, instead, it brought me back to life.

My heart now thudded painfully within my chest. The world moved again, and for the first time I caught a glimpse of the man in a black cloak who had, until just moments before, been speaking with Gilio Salviati. Of course, it made sense, in some sick fashion. I was here by fate – sadistic in new form – and only he could deepen my tortures.

Fra Tomás, Father Inquisitor, hand of the church's justice. I looked into his eyes. And he looked into mine. Recognition broke upon him with sudden and violent purpose.

"ARREST HER!" he screamed, stretching his long, bent finger toward me. The shock of his sudden outburst sent a tremor of surprise through the assemblage. For a brief moment, all was silence as the Salviati guards hesitated.

Timo's hand was suddenly wrapped around my arm. "RUN!"

We did. My feet pounded against the flagstones. Timo clutched my forearm as he pulled ahead, urging me to move faster.

"Go get them you fools! For the Father Inquisitor!" I heard Gilio's voice, like a sickness, call out from behind us. In moments, we were shadowed by the sounds of his guards quick on our heels.

Gilio did not recognize me. I ran. I ran and I ran. Timo, yanking me this way and that, led us into the depths of the Mercato Vecchio. People shrieked and dove out of the way. A few, Timo pushed to the ground in our race to get away. My heart thrummed. They were right behind us. I could almost feel their feet on the ground behind mine. Ghost hands reached for my neck.

We burst around a corner. Timo threw me ahead of him as he dug his fingers into a mountainous stack of crated fruit and pulled it to the ground. From the corner of my eye, I saw the most immediate of our hunters trip and fall. Turning another corner, Timo pushed me behind an empty stall before diving in himself. Together, we crowded into the small space hidden below the vendor's booth. I was gasping loudly for air. Timo, his eyes wild, put a desperate hand over my mouth. Closing my eyes, I begged my breathing to stop.

Armored footsteps thudded past.

"Where are they?"

"Find them!"

"Close off the market! Don't let them out!"

The footsteps faded away.

I clutched Timo, touching him for probably the first time since we'd met. I could feel myself shaking – my bloated, pregnant body crying out in exhaustion.

"Take a few, deep breaths," Timo whispered to me, gently squeezing my hand. I held on tightly, wondering at how his touch did not upset me. "Be ready to run."

I was still breathing too heavily to speak, but he saw the question on my face.

"I'll lead them away. You get back to the Badia. Stay off the main streets." He sounded confident, but I could see the fear in his eyes. Timo was terrified.

He pulled his legs beneath him, but he did not run. Every few seconds he would twitch as if trying to jump out, and for a moment it seemed as though he had lost his nerve. He turned his head and looked at me. Hesitantly, he leaned forward, and he kissed my forehead.

Then, with a grunt, he leapt out onto the street and disappeared from view. I heard him yelling as he ran, and soon the voices of other men joined with him. In minutes, they had faded from hearing as Timo led the chase away from the monastery.

No time to think. I rose from behind the table. *Walk*, I told myself. One foot in front of the other, I slowly made my way past stall after stall, precariously balancing upon a knife's edge of composure as every second begged at me to run. *Blend in.* It was becoming more crowded. I tried to throw myself into the mulling masses. There were so many people – too many people. I gasped as the first man grazed a shoulder against mine. It seemed like every muscle in my body tightened at once, but I grimaced and pushed on. I sharply inhaled again as another man brushed against me. The next time, I let out a small squeal, then a cry of alarm. *There's too many people!* Men were everywhere, swarming around me like flies. *How much further? Please, let it be no further!* I bit my lip until it hurt, but still, panic wracked me. *Another few steps. Just another few steps.* I tried to dodge around a man who very nearly walked into me. My feet felt numb as they caught along the uneven cobblestone. The world tipped onto its side. I crashed against something heavy, but it was not the ground that I felt beneath me as I fell. My heart stopped.

"Ya' alright, lass?" said a deep voice beneath me.

It was too much. My chest heaved once. Twice. Three times. Then I screamed. Desperately, I lashed out, flailing in a frantic attempt to throw myself free.

"What the hell?!" The man I had fallen upon was clutching his brow – bleeding from where my nails had torn a thick gash almost to his eye.

The crowd was pulling back as I became more and more of a spectacle. I spun, looking for some sort of escape.

"What's going on there?" Soldiers. I didn't wait to see whose.

A gap in the throng emerged, and I dove through. I ran, ignoring my tired muscles and the cramps of my pregnant stomach and the bruises on my knees and the scrapes on my hands and the shouts of men behind me. I stayed off the main road, just like Timo had said. Alleyway after alleyway rushed by. Blood pumping, my vision blurred. I didn't tell my legs to stop, but in the end they did anyway. I collapsed upon the hard-packed dirt and stone. Gasping desperately for breath, I lay there for some time, certain that my pursuers would soon be upon me. They never came.

After a while, my eyesight returned and my breathing began to slow. Hesitantly, I pushed myself up enough to sit against the alley wall. My legs trembled and throbbed painfully. *I need to go*, I told myself, but my legs only shook more violently.

A muffled voice echoed down the empty alleyway from somewhere behind me. *No. Please, no. Oh god, they found me.* Dry, throaty sobs wrenched their way from my throat. *I need to go!* My fingers quivered as I urgently attempted to massage my legs back into life. I gasped at the pain as it shot up my midriff into my arms and chest. Tears poured down my face as I desperately kneaded my shaking thighs.

The voice was growing louder. No, were there two voices? A man and a woman. They were running, I could hear their boots slap against the ground.

I rubbed my legs harder. *It hurts!* Biting my tongue, I frantically began to recite the muscles of the leg to distract from the pain. *Lliopsoas. Pectineus. Adductor longus. Gracilis.*

"Castor, stop! Why are you doing this?!" The woman's voice.

Laughter. That was the man's voice. It was deep, and rough, and vicious.

The woman burst into view suddenly from a cross-street, lost her footing, and fell to the ground no more than a dozen strides from where I sat. I could see the crimson lines of blood where it ran down her leg. The wound looked…it looked like a bite from an enormous animal – a bear, I thought, or a wolf – but that didn't make any sense. The blood was fresh, and she was too far from the city gates to have come all that way injured. *Something is wrong,* a small voice within me whispered. *I need to go. I need to go!* I was frozen, trying to blend into the wall. *Please, do not look this way. Please.*

The man called Castor finally appeared, strolling into the alleyway as comfortably and calmly as if he were walking into a brothel. "Oh Dasy, look what's happened to your leg." His smile stretched from ear to ear. He licked his lips watching the blood pool around her knee. I could not see his eyes from where I sat, but the girl, Dasy, seemed to shrink beneath them. "You really should be more careful. After all, running away was your only gift. Who knows what might catch you now." The mockery in his every word made me shudder. It was like watching an animal play with its food. My fingers continued to knead my thigh. The pain seemed as though it was receding, but fear still froze me in place.

"Why are you doing this?" the woman asked again, her voice trembling in pain and fear. She seemed so small and frail, curled there upon the stonework. "We were friends. I thought we were friends." She seemed so confused – confused and sad.

"Friends?" Castor laughed. Sauntering a step forward, he kicked his boot deep into the woman's injured knee. She screamed, voice echoing among the empty backstreets of Firenze. "Look at us, Dasy!" he said. "Just use your eyes and look at what we are! I'm sick of it! I'm sick of pretending." He spat, then kicked her again.

Through her agony, she mumbled something that I couldn't hear. Whatever it was enraged the man. He growled like an animal. "Too many years." He took a step back, chuckling darkly as Dasy tried to push herself to her feet. She barely made it to her knees.

"This isn't you, Castor," she gasped. "Don't listen to him. He's making you do this."

"You still don't get it!" he yelled. "He *is* me! We're the same! I finally understand!" he licked his lips. "And we're finally going to kill you, Dasy. We're going to tear you apart."

Sorrow turned to anger, I could see it in the woman's eyes. She gritted her teeth. "You won't get the chance." For a moment, it seemed as if they had both turned to stone. A cloud passed before the sun, and a shadow fell over her face.

I blinked. *There is no cloud.* Her skin was darkening on its own. My breath caught in my chest. *What's happening?* Her eyes turned black. I could hear her hair break off and crumble away as the strange rot took over. Soon, her entire body was dark as the night sky. A loud crack rent the air, and deep fissures shot out across her cheeks and arms like jagged forks of lightning. Midnight skin crumbled away from the rifts like chalk dust.

My heart beat so loudly, I was afraid I would be heard. Fear seized me. The woman was dead. Horribly dead, but...how?

Scratching. It was so soft at first that I thought I was imagining it, but soon the sound had grown so loud it could not be ignored. It was coming from the body. From *inside* the body.

Castor laughed and took a step backward.

I would have screamed if I could. The woman's blackened chest began to shudder and bulge as the scratching grew louder. Suddenly, a piece of her – like a burnt log breaking apart in a fire – crumbled inward. The body was empty. Hollow. A charred husk. Another piece of the corpse broke off and fell into the darkness.

Then, the darkness moved.

And within the hollow corpse, a sick, yellow eye appeared.

I could not scream. I could not move. Every fiber in my body trembled from the terror that ran unchecked through my veins. *Run! RUN!* My legs lay useless beneath me. I could not even look away.

The beady eye flicked toward me, and I knew: it saw me.

In that exact moment – the moment when our eyes met – I felt a sickening jerk in my venter. A different monster, moving. A little, disgusting creature within me. Moving for the first time. Revulsion and despair filled my lungs like bile, and the spell upon me broke.

My heart beat so quickly it felt as if it were vibrating. Adrenaline coursed through me. I ran without a second though, legs desperately pumping. Everything was a daze of terror. I never looked back, but they did not follow.

Notes on Witchcraft

From a letter in the hand of Prior Johannes Nider:

> *"They could cause immense hailstorms and poison winds with lightning, cause sterility in humans and animals, injure their neighbors in body and property, drive horses mad when their wealthy riders mounted them, and travel through the air wherever they wished to go."*

The fallacious perception of demonic witchcraft is the product of common superstition, and superstition has plagued the social consciousness of the masses since we first evolved beyond the naked instincts of Adam and Eve. In that sense, witchcraft, by some style or another, has always existed as a system to explain that which we cannot yet explain. This alone – the need to ascribe meaning and purpose to the enigmatic – is conceptually harmless, benevolent even. Rather, it is the tendency of humanity to *fear* the unknown that leads to this, the greatest of casualties: the ascription and subsequent marginalization of social incriminates – those commonly called witches.

This was not always the case. The great Roman Empire of antiquity was a composite of new opinions, mythologies, and conceptions, and of these was the consideration that, rather than fear the unknown, mankind had the power, nay the mandate, to control that ineffable chaos which consumes the world. Witchcraft, still, was the system of explanation, but in a coordination that sought power over fear, witches were not perceived as the enigmatic harbingers of disorder and disaster. In that prevalent, contemporary schema which designed popular opinion, witches were a method by which to overpower the inherent tilt of nature toward entropy, and by this were shown a level of respect worthy of that social role.

A question of change is in order, for it is inarguable that the inclination of common thought toward the concept of witchcraft has shifted for the worse. Fear is now the currency of insecurity, and while others may postulate on the social indicators that mark this change, there is rarely an association so obviously stated as that of fear. Fear has impregnated modern culture; meanwhile, and by no coincidence, fear is the persuasion of the Holy Catholic Church.

Take this theory in conjunction with the recent restructuring of the Holy Inquisition under the pontificate of Pope John XXII to include sorcery and witchcraft in its mandate, and a strong argument can be made for some causal relationship between them. A public letter from the

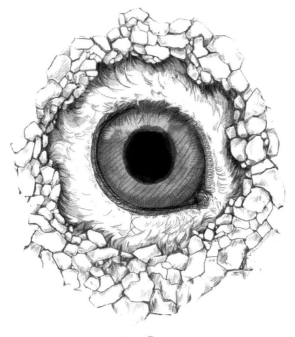

Benandanti

late Pope Eugenius IV reads exclusively on the public menace of witchcraft, naming it a perversion that stains the "simple-minded" proletariat of the Christian order, yet the entirety of his evidence in support for his remarks is the thrice-regurgitated backwash of hearsay.

Fear. Again I say, fear is the driving force that accepts such outlandish claims as these: that the work of demons is to mislead the pious, provoke storms and ill-weather, join carnally with men, or afflict with malady crops, cattle, and children. It is, at once, the more prudent and more frightening explanation that such effects as we see in death, disease, and disaster are more simply the work of an ever changing and unpredictable natural world, yet fear persists because the driving force of humanity demands an explanation of the inexplicable. We live with a need to satiate curiosity but have no predisposition to require truth as part of the fare.

Consider this with logic, would not the agents of the devil – demons, as we call them – be constrained by their own condition? Bereaved of any base requisite for existence, all animals seek restitution, and by what other style should we consider holiness for those creatures that were first made in the light of the Lord? Those fallen spirits were once radiant beings of divinity, created only for that one purpose, so it follows that they must behave with a driving need to return to that basal state of resplendence. In what manner does calling storms or impregnating women promote that ambition?

There is the greatest of theistic fallacies. These women so hunted by the Inquisition of Heretical Depravity are no more than social exiles ascribed the title of 'strega' by village idiots too emotionally impotent to exhibit empathy for the mentally disadvantaged or culturally disavowed. Those poor souls – misunderstood, persecuted, victimized, and tortured – are no more agents of demonic influence than the Pope himself. Scapegoats, sacrificial ransoms to a natural world that holds no grudges and accepts no gifts.

Even kings scarcely care for the afflictions of peasants. Consider then, how little such matters bear on the tortured expatriates of heaven itself. Fertility, livelihood, crops and cattle. Laugh, if you can, for the ambitions of the fallen suffer far greater stakes than those.

True demons will eat the world.

Who were they? What were they? I never questioned. I never cared.

By the next morning, Timo still had not returned.

I told no one. I couldn't. It was as if all that had happened was still happening over and over and over again in my mind, overwhelming all manner of rational thought. Even entering the monastery had felt like a dream; the wide wooden door swinging shut behind me was an eerily familiar feeling. It felt odd to walk after running for so long, as if I were moving too slowly as I crossed the atrium into the cloister.

Mariotto had been waiting. "Where's the boy with my ginger?" I remembered him asking. I must have responded, though I could not remember how. All I recalled was the cellarer storming off, muttering about what he would do to Timo if he did not show up in time for dinner.

He did not. And as I spent the night, awake, lying uncomfortably upon a comfortable bed, I wrestled with the notion that he would likely never return. What would that mean for me? *Ragazzo sciocco!*

I found no answers, but buried in my jumbled thoughts, neither did I find the dreams that had taken to haunting my sleep. No demons called to me. No angels counselled me. I was left with only my fears and my doubts, and somehow, that was worse.

When the light had finally broken through the gaps in my wooden shutters, they seemed to illuminate the only path forward that was left to me. I would quit the Badia – they were sure to expel me anyway – and I would go to Lucrezia for a new bed. Surely, she would know of a place where I might hide. *She needs me*, I managed to convince myself. *I play another gala just the week after next. She will have to take me in.*

My decision was made, yet still I lingered. My limbs felt heavy where they were wrapped in blankets, and exhaustion wore at me like an illness. There was little enough to pack, it was true. I could see my every belonging from where I lay. My harp; a small bundle of clothes: a few tunics, breeches, and the dress I wore when I performed; and a small purse of gold – the remnants of what Piero had paid for my story. *Enough to buy my way to Pisa.*

I sat straight up in the bed. "I am *not* going to Pisa," I said aloud, furious at the strange thought that seemed to have come from nowhere. "Maledizione!" Refueled by self-disgust, I quickly rose and began the task of rolling together my clothes. I would have to wear most of them in order to also carry my harp, but I thought I might be able to fit the dress inside the instrument's soundbox.

Suddenly, a knock at my door.

Merda! I looked around. What I was doing was obvious. I had taken too long, and someone had finally noticed Timo's disappearance; I was sure of it. *Now what?*

Another knock. "Amadora?" Mariotto's voice drifted through. I flinched as he opened the door.

His gaze seemed to take in the entirety of my room in one moment. There was no doubt he could see what I had been doing, for the look he then offered me was both sad and hurt.

"The Father Abbot wants to see you." He left quickly, and as he turned I could see the unoffered orange in his hand that had almost certainly been for me.

I looked back to my things. *Should I leave now?* I sighed. *Might as well go to the abbot.* There would be no sneaking away in any case, now that I had been found out. Something of Mariotto's look had gotten to me as well.

The abbot's study was no larger than the wide sleeping rooms that the monks shared, yet without the beds or chests, the room was left with plenty of space for a polished desk, a high-backed wooden chair, several shelves of books, and a small window overlooking the southern half of Firenze. I had only ventured into this room a few times over my stay at the Badia, and never with such a feeling of trepidation.

Abbot Simone sat behind his desk and seemed to study me with cautious eyes as I entered. Already with him were Prior Giovanni – his sneer, for once, one of worry rather than disgust – and…

"Timo!" I cried out, suddenly awash with relief. He was nearly unrecognizable without his habit, garbed as he was in the clothes of common folk.

He smiled but did not speak, and at once I knew something was very wrong.

"She is here," Giovanni said, cutting his words as short as he could. "Now I would finally like some answers."

"I as well, Fra Giovanni," Simone replied. To me he said, "It seems I must recant the words I gave to you when you first arrived. 'Your past does not matter here,' I believe I said. How I wish that were still true, but I have been convinced," his eyes flashed briefly to the prior, "that the safety of the abbey and its…mandate," he hesitated for a moment over the word, "must take priority."

I looked to Timo, but the boy seemed intent on his feet.

"Fra Timo arrived only a short while ago. You can imagine my surprise, as I had been given no news that he was even missing." At that, the abbot caught me with such a stern look of displeasure that I too began to study my boots. I didn't dare look at Timo again. "He has told me very little, I would assume out of respect for your privacy, and so I must ask you to fill in the gaps that he has left us – gaps that clearly go beyond even *my* understanding of your situation." At that, the abbot nodded surreptitiously to my swollen stomach, reminding me that he did indeed know of the child's aberrant conception.

"If you ask me, I say his silence is less showing of respect than desire. Clearly she has the boy wrapped around her finger," Giovanni said.

"Perhaps," the abbot admitted. "But it is not our place to judge a person's heart, only to guide their hands. Now Amadora, Timo has told us only that you were attacked in the market. I do believe he meant to use the word *inquisition* before he caught himself."

At that, Prior Giovanni sucked his teeth. "He *did* say it. *You*, girl, will tell us why inquisitors of heretical depravity are interested in you."

"I...don't know."

"She lies!" Giovanni cried out. "I told you, did I not? She has not even the barest of gratitude for our hospitality, nor does she have any respect for our order. This is a waste of time. She should have been put out months ago."

"Please, Amadora," the abbot entreated. "There is more at stake here than you realize. We *must* know if your presence endangers the Badia Fiorentina."

"I don't...they weren't looking for me. They just...*found* me."

"And now? Will they be searching for you now that they know you are in the city?"

"Yes. I mean, I think so."

"There!" Giovanni exclaimed. "Out of her own mouth! Simone, you must expel her. If the inquisition comes here; if they discover the—"

"Silence, Giovanni!" The abbot's forceful warning brought the prior short in whatever he had been about to say, yet one could not miss the anger still in his eyes. "I am still the abbot, whatever you may wish to the contrary, and you will refer to me as such."

"I don't understand," I said hesitantly.

"I apologize for that," Abbot Simone responded, though with a tone that made it clear he would not explain the matter to me further. "And also for this," he sighed heavily, "I'm afraid that I cannot allow you to continue your stay with us if it may pose a threat to the monastery, and as you still have not explained the nature of the inquisition's interest in you—"

"It doesn't!" Timo interrupted suddenly, speaking for the first time since I had arrived.

"Be quiet, boy!" Giovanni warned.

"No! I know what it is she won't tell you, and I'm saying *it doesn't concern us!* We're supposed to care for the sick and the homeless, not turn them away when it becomes inconvenient. She is our guest, and I swear, nothing that the inquisition wants from her could harm us."

"Is that so?" the prior made it clear what he thought of Timo's promises. "There is more than our reputation at stake, as you well know. Have you bothered to consider what would happen if they chance to look for her here? You were seen at the market too, boy. They might have followed you."

"They didn't," Timo said, his voice full and sure.

"And the girl?"

"They—they didn't!" Timo repeated, though less certain.

"Enough!" the abbot exclaimed. He sighed again. "Even if you were not followed, Fra Timo, they will have seen your habit. Eventually they will think to look for her in the city's monasteries, and without knowing what their response would be should they find her here…"

Timo opened his mouth to argue more, but the abbot forestalled him with a wave of his hand. "But yes, you also raise a valid objection: our order is sworn to care for the wayward. To cast that obligation aside should not be done lightly or without pressing need."

"Father Abbot—" the prior began, his voice harsh.

"I said enough, Fra Giovanni." Abbot Simone rubbed at his temples. "If Timo can swear to us that Amadora's presence is no threat, then I choose to believe him, regardless of whatever else I do not know."

Giovanni wore a mask of fury.

"Yet that means it will be upon *your* head, Fra Timo," the abbot continued forcefully. "You hold the safety of our entire order in your hands. See to it that Amadora is closely cared for. She will need to stay in her room whenever we receive guests or brothers from other abbeys. And *no more excursions.*" He said the last with tone that brooked no arguments. "If you are to stay here, Amadora, you are not to leave the monastery without my *express* permission. Is that understood?"

"What about my concerts?" I asked in return.

The abbot studied me over crossed fingers. "I will write to Lucrezia," he said. I blinked, surprised; I had no idea that the abbot knew I worked for the Medici. By the look on Timo's face, the name was a surprise to him as well. "But if you will agree to a few restrictions – measures of safety to keep you hidden as you leave and return – then I see no problem." He looked to the prior, whose brows were nearly quivering with rage. "Yes, I see you have much to say, Fra Giovanni, and I will hear it all." He made a motion to brush Timo and me toward the door. "You two can go."

The door closed silently behind us as we left, and though I desperately wanted to speak with him, we both walked in silence all the way to the Cloister of Oranges.

"I thought you had been caught," I finally said.

"It was close," he answered, tonally reserved yet clearly relieved that I'd broken the stay of speech. "I lost them near the Ospedale degli Innocenti."

"But you didn't come back here?"

"I thought they might still be looking for me. It just seemed safer to wait. One of my brothers in the Confraternity of Blacks spends his time at the Ospedale. He hid me for the night." His steps slowed to a stop. "You didn't tell them I was gone."

I flinched at the accusation in his voice. Suddenly, I couldn't stand for him to look at me. "I…" I didn't know what to say.

"You were scared," he said.

"Y—yes."

I heard his smile in his voice. "That's okay. I forgive you."

He continued on his trek across the cloister. His response confused me, but I followed after him all the same.

"The abbot was more upset than I expected," I offered, hesitantly watching to see if he had truly let the matter go. "Him and Giovanni both. Why are they so scared of the inquisition?"

Timo missed a step. "They—they aren't."

"Lying is a poor color for a monk."

He grimaced. "I'm not allowed to talk about it."

"Giovanni said there was something here."

He gave me a sharp look – as sharp as he could, anyway. "I said I'm not allowed to talk about it."

"Fine."

"It isn't just that I'm not allowed to say anything," he said after a minute. "If you're heard asking about it…well, I don't think the Father Abbot would let you stay if he knew, no matter what I told him."

"Is it that serious?"

He nodded.

Side by side, we leaned out over the courtyard below, enjoying the feeling of the sun on our necks. I shivered as a chill breeze ruffled my hair – a soft reminder that colder months were on their way. Already, the days had begun growing shorter, the nights trespassing sooner and sooner upon each evening. Winter was waiting its turn.

Life is little lived in little towns. Sheltered, secluded, unexposed to the grittier realities of the human experience – Montaione could never have prepared me for all I saw in Firenze. Simplicity is a lie. Life is complex, unkempt, and primal.

I now see how little I truly lived.

"Mario is dead."

"What—no. No that can't be true."

"He is dead, Amadora. Alba was a false lead. Leave her be. We will find some other path to Gilio."

She must have been mistaken. She must have been. Every whisper of my subconscious told me that Alba was going to lead me to Gilio. But she would not listen. All of my desperate refutations fell upon deaf ears.

In the end, I left for the gala frustrated. Lucrezia had been maddeningly close-mouthed on the matter, giving me little reason to believe Mario was as dead as she so enigmatically claimed. *She's given up,* I decided as I settled myself in for a long night of music. *She must think she would have found him by now if he was still alive.* But I knew better. Mario was crafty; I remembered as much from Montaione. He was still hiding, I knew, and the only way to find him was through Signora Alba.

My harp rested uncomfortably against my pregnancy, pushed away by the bulge of my stomach. My arms did not thank me for the extra reach. My fingers, as well, often missed their strings as the child moved – more and more often as each day passed – jostling both the harp and the music with his sickening acrobatics. I compensated, and in the end I doubted if even a few people caught the small tics in my performance.

Yet still the extra irritation was like a growing rash, and the uncomfortable need to act pressed upon me more and more as the night wore on. Alba swirled amongst the festa as she normally did. I never took my eyes from her. I *needed* to watch her; it was like a salve. I saw her secrets, the sly glances she stole and the too-even charade she performed. I itched to know more. I ached for the answers she held from me. She *would* lead me to Mario, and through him, to Gilio.

My music hiccupped as the child kicked again. *I'm running out of time.* It was true. Not for the child, though the day of his birth was stalking ever closer; he was just a reminder of what else waited for me in the city. The inquisition had my scent, and I could not hide from them in Firenze forever. Eventually, they would find me, and then my vengeance would never mature. *To hell with Lucrezia and her slow plots. She is wrong about Mario, and I'll prove it to her.*

My resolve sharpened to a point with sudden and spontaneous formation. With reflex bordering on impulse, I flew to my feet, the song I had played forgotten even in the throes of its climax. Patricians may have stared, but I never knew it. My gaze was locked upon Alba. Slowly, I packed away my harp. "Pregnancy sickness," I ambiguously explained to the nearest servant. Then, step by laborious step, I forced myself from the ballroom, out the palazzo, and onto the street outside.

The approaching onset of evening brought with it the relief of chilled air that one could feel even through the thick humidity that had appeared in Firenze several days past. From my perch upon the cobbled road, I could hear the gala as it continued unhindered by my absence. I knew it would likely continue on for many hours still, yet I waited patiently as night slowly wore on and dusk turned to darkness around me.

Eventually, the first patrons began to emigrate from the palazzo as the festa fell into its slow but inevitable denouement. I watched the egress without blinking, and was soon rewarded. Alba was never the first to abandon a festa, but would invariably excuse herself soon after the early exodus began. Tonight was no different, and it was with a flood of satisfaction that I saw her emerge from the wide gate of the palazzo.

Her olive gown danced around her legs as she set off. *Paula de' Ricci was not there*, I told myself as I followed Alba down street and alley. *Surely that means something.* I prayed I was right. If Mario's false widow was gone – on a trip, perhaps – then all expectations would be for Alba to seek out Mario in her absence. *That must be it.*

Sure enough, it seemed that Alba meant not to make her way home. Each turn took us further and further from her abitazione and into the eastern district of the city. My heart raced. Mario's home was somewhere nearby, I knew from my talks with Lucrezia. My skin felt almost like it was vibrating.

Then, suddenly, I turned a corner and she was gone. A sick weight settled in my stomach. *Where did she go?* I had only lost sight of her for a moment. My feet slapped loudly on the packed dirt as I ran forward, desperately peering down first one cross-street, then the next, until I was certain Signora Alba could not have gotten so far without me having seen her. Sucking in air, I spun around anxiously. *Where could she have gone?!*

A mellow sound burst through a nearby window. Laughter. I cocked my head. One of the voices sounded familiar. *Alba?* Hesitantly, I approached the shuttered casement.

Candlelight flickered through the slats in the window, but I could not make out more than vague shapes and dim outlines. My foot crunched upon a scattering of loose gravel as I tried to get a better perch by which to see, and I froze. Thankfully, it seemed that any ears within were deaf to my misstep.

There were voices, but so hushed that I couldn't make out whose or how many. *Was that Alba? Could she be with Mario?* I craned my neck, but could barely make out the impression of slow movement. *I need to see more.*

I could not hesitate. Reaching out, I lightly pressed my fingers against the window's closed shutters. Sweat had begun to bead upon my neck, but I managed to keep my breathing quiet as I slowly pushed against the painted wood.

The slatted panel shifted slightly. *It's not fastened.* I listened for a moment, but there was no pause in the hushed voices within. I pushed again, and the shutter slowly cracked open. My ears strained to hear any sign that I'd been seen as I continued to slowly – so slowly – force the window open a sliver at a time. It seemed like hours passed, though I knew it must have been far less. I almost forgot to breathe. Finally, when the gap had widened to the width of my hand, I stopped.

Creeping forward, I carefully stole a glance into the room within.

It *was* Alba. My breath caught in my throat, and my heart thudded against my chest. She was on her feet facing away from me, and though her long, coiled hair fell, untied, well past her shoulders, I could see the smooth, milky white skin of her back beneath it, trailing the entire way down to the exposed curves of her bottom. Beneath her lay the silky chartreuse folds of her recently discarded dress.

I was too excited to blush. *Mario must be here!* I could not see past Alba into the room, but I was certain of it. The rumors of her affair were proven true. I almost turned to leave, but something stopped me. *I should make sure. Once I've seen him, then I will go.*

Another voice appeared, muffled to my ears. I squinted, confused. That was not the voice of a man.

Alba stepped to the side, and for the first time I saw whom she was company to – her quiet lover in the secret places of the night. It was not Mario. I blanched, lost to the abrupt, alien mire that entrapped me. The puzzle of collected rumors that I had assembled shattered apart, and I desperately struggled to reassemble them in answer to my sudden, nascent disorientation. I was, all the while, barely aware – trapped in a daze of uncertainty and disorientation.

Paula de' Ricci stepped forward, and as I watched, playfully pushed Alba onto the fur-laden bed that shared the room. Standing over her, Paula slowly undressed herself, pulling one shoulder, then the other, away from the simple gown she had been wearing. She unlaced the bodice, and sliding it over the bud of her breasts, let it fall to the floor beside Alba's. Whispering something that I could not hear, the woman crawled atop her patient lover. Slowly, she began to caress the soft white skin of Alba's breasts, occasionally brushing her lips over the other woman's mouth and neck. A soft hand drifted down her stomach and into the dark fold of her legs.

Alba moaned deep in her throat. The sound of it was thick and trembling with carnal pleasure. It shocked me from my stupor, and for the first time I seemed to realize the scene before me. Bereaved of all restraint, I let out a squeaky gasp of shock.

Signora Alba's gaze flicked to me in the space of a moment. Her eyes met mine, and I watched as her expression became one of horror. My legs went cold. Paula spun around, and upon seeing my face in her window, cried out in alarm. I was frozen – turned, it felt, into a statue like as decorated the Medici garden. Seconds passed. Slowly,

Alba reached out an unsteady hand to me. It was somehow more alarming to see the tears in her eyes.

"Please…"she whispered.

I fled.

Would it be soft? I've never considered it before. There are always whispers, of course, and condemnations from the church. But I never paid them much mind. Now the imagery has taken root in my mind, and I cannot rid myself of the endless wondering. Would it be soft?

How would it feel, the touch of a woman?

Matteo had always been a trove of adages. 'More haste, less speed,' 'one butterfly does not a summer make,' 'many hands make light work.' His metaphors often grew tiresome, but I loved them nonetheless. As I raced back to the Badia that night – harp digging into my side with each step, heart pounding, feet aching, belly cramping – another of his proverbs found purchase in my mind. 'The last drop makes the pot overflow.'

The road I traveled had led me not to Gilio, but to a dead end. My revenge was thwarted. My life was threatened by the inquisition. The babe within me festered and grew more with each day. My home at the Badia was endangered. Fra Mariotto still would not speak to me. Timo hid something from me. And now I was confronted by the frighteningly alien idea that two women might lay with one another. My mind sought for some mental purchase, yet I had no framework by which to make sense of their relationship. How even could it be described? Lechery? Love? My pot was overflowing, and I no longer recognized the muddled path beneath my feet.

The gates of the Badia shut behind me. I raced through the monastery. I yearned for my room, for the solace of that private haven – a place to rest and think – yet in the Cloister of Oranges, in the midnight darkness, I hesitated. My tired feet slowed to a halt. The sweet scent of citrus filled my nose.

I found a seat against the well, tucking the thick folds of my dress beneath me as I sat. A soft breeze whispered along my forearms. My harp lay beside me. I closed my eyes, and slowly, I began to empty my mind of everything that so cluttered it. It was not quick, but as the darkness stretched on, the frantic fluttering of my thoughts finally quieted and faded away.

I took a deep breath of cool air. *One thing at a time.*

The next morning came and went while I lay sleeping in the warm embrace of my bed, and when I finally awoke, it was to the smell of food that waited upon the room's small desk. *I should visit Mariotto*, I thought as I hungrily devoured the meal, yet I did not move even after the last crumbs had long since disappeared from my plate. *One thing at a time*, I reminded myself. First, I needed to think.

But no sooner had the thought faded than there came a knocking at my door. I growled under my breath. "What is it, Timo?" I called out, already on my feet. "I can't—" My words were cut short as I opened the door not to find the boyish monk waiting for me without, but Lucrezia.

The Lady of Firenze stood, like a violent spirit, upon my stoop. Even from beneath her cloak, her fury was palpable. Everything from the stiffness of her shoulders to the fiery flash in her eyes told me that anger bubbled just under the surface. Not waiting for an invitation, she pushed herself into the room and quickly shut the door behind us.

"What did you do?" her words were low, but tense.

I didn't answer.

"What did you do?!" she repeated, stepping closer to me. "I know you disappeared from the gala last night, and one of my informants swears he saw you following Signora Alba as she left." She took a deep breath. "*Tell me you did not follow her home.*"

"I…"

The truth must have been evident on my face. With a fierce growl, Lucrezia turned to take a seat upon the nearest chair. Smoothing out her skirts, she seemed to think for a moment, then sighed. "What did you see?" The anger was mostly gone from her voice. If anything, trepidation now replaced it. I took the other seat, somewhat confused at her sudden turn of mood.

"I—I saw—" My cheeks bloomed crimson. "Her, and Paula."

"I see," Lucrezia said. "And you didn't think to come to me?" Her gaze was stern.

An abrupt realization struck me. I almost choked on my frustration "You already knew? Why didn't you tell me?!"

The glare she affected could have boiled water. "I am under no obligation to tell you *anything,* Amadora! If I thought to do what I could so that those two women might live out the rest of their days with some semblance of peace, that was my decision to make. They have both suffered quite enough, I think. They deserve what little happiness they can find." She reached forward and wrapped an iron hand around my arm. "You realize that if they were caught – if someone exposed them to the Ufficiali di Notte – they would be put to death?" She looked to me with heat in her eyes, and I saw what she was searching for.

"I won't say anything." Lucrezia's iron gaze studied me for a moment, then her grip loosened from my arm. Her shoulders relaxed, and she let out a quiet breath.

I could still see the fading marks of where her fingers had grasped me. I tried not to blush as a vision of Alba and Paula flashed within my mind. Slender fingers: gripping, wandering.

"Were you seen?" Lucrezia asked, interrupting my uncomfortable daydream.

"I…yes."

She cursed under her breath. "Did they recognize you?"

"I don't know."

She didn't reply.

"What does it matter? Like you said, they would be killed if they said anything."

"And you think they'll instead wait to see if you choose silence? The cornered cat has the sharpest claws, and I don't know what either of them might be capable of."

"So I hide here for a while longer," I said. "We didn't have any other leads anyway."

She nearly screamed in frustration. "You're like a child, and with all the patience of one! I had just begun to have you invited to galas sponsored by Gilio's supporters. This morning you even received an invitation to perform at the Palazzo Salviati itself!"

My breath caught.

"You see now, don't you? The last few months were only to get you to this point. If ever we were going to find the proof to bring Gilio before the Podestà, it would be at his own gala!"

"I—I can still perform!" I said. My words trembled.

"No."

It felt like I had been slapped. *This would have been my chance!*

"The gala is only three days from now. If you show your face there, who knows what Alba and Paula may do. No, I have already declined the invitation."

A shiver swept across my chest. My hands shook. "How—how dare you…"

"No, Amadora. How dare *you*? After everything I've done for you, you follow Alba when I expressly instructed you to *leave her alone.* Then you have the arrogance to act affronted when there are consequences?" She rose suddenly to her feet. "Leave town, Amadora."

"What?"

"Leave Firenze. You threw away your chance at vengeance. I cannot waste my time with you any longer, but neither can I ignore you. You know too much."

An uneasy feeling began taking root in my chest.

"I will instruct Abbot Simone that you are not to leave the monastery. Not for the winter. Come spring, I will send someone to escort you and the babe from the city. They will take you wherever you wish, whether it be Pisa or Portugal, and see you are properly settled." Her hand snapped forward like a snake, gripping my chin so that I could not look away. She fixed me with a cold stare that chilled me to my bones. "But believe me when I say this, Amadora. If you ever return to Firenze, it will not be Alba who presents you to the inquisition, it will be me."

She left without another word. As the door closed behind her, an intense rage took hold of me. A guttural scream tore at my throat. I reached for the nearest thing – my plate from breakfast – and hurled it at the door. It shattered, shards of porcelain blossoming into the air and tinkling across the floor.

I leaned against the desk, gasping for breath. After a few moments, I heard hasty footsteps outside, and my door was thrown open to reveal Timo. His panic seemed to fade as he saw me. Hesitantly, he took a step forward. "Amadora, are you—"

"LEAVE ME ALONE!" I threw something else, a cup I think. It broke upon the wall beside him, splashing him with wine and sharp fragments of debris. Overwhelmed, I collapsed to the ground. Curling up against the side of my desk, I began trying to control my ragged breathing.

I barely heard the sound of crunching porcelain, yet a half hour later when I again opened my eyes, I found Timo sitting on the ground to my right, leaning against my bed and looking out over the mess I'd made of the room. The wine had dried in his hair, painting dark crimson lines where it had dripped along the shaven sides of his head, looking eerily like blood.

He said nothing as I slowly moved to sit beside him.

"I'm sorry."

Timo glanced at me out of the corner of his eye. "The woman I passed outside, that was Lucrezia, wasn't it? Che cosa è accaduto?"

"She..." I hesitated. "She's sending me away from Firenze. After the baby is born."

Timo was silent for a moment. He didn't look at me when he spoke, "Maybe that's a good idea."

My heart sank. Confused and dismayed, I could not find the words to reply. More than anyone else, I had expected Timo at least would fight for me.

He studied his feet. "You probably haven't noticed, but things are getting worse and worse around here. Giovanni is becoming even more vicious in his crusade to evict you, and he has the support of most of the abbey now. It's only a matter of time until they all fall behind him. I'm worried for the Father Abbot. I think if it weren't for me, he would already have been forced to put you out."

"I—" I began, but Timo quickly interrupted me.

"Mi dispiace, Amadora, but maybe it's for the best." It looked for a moment as though he meant to put his hand on my arm, but thankfully he did not try. "Just…think about it, alright? All this – the drive, the anger – the man you're looking for has already taken so much from you. Even if you do manage to kill him, all that'll change is that he will be dead, and you will have given up everything else you might have had." Pause. "I just think that your life is worth more than his death."

He turned to look me in the eyes. "When we first met, you asked me why I fear the devil when it's God that hands out punishment. I think I have your answer." Timo took a deep breath. "I *don't* fear the devil. I pity him. I think he was just a sinner – the *first* sinner – and now he's stuck with that, fated to spend forever paying into an endless debt. I just…Amadora, I don't want that to happen to you. Think back to who you were before what happened. Maybe—maybe you finally have a chance to take something back from the bastard who did this to you. Maybe you could be that person again."

We sat in silence for a long while after that. The sound of my own breath, the creaking of the door, the distant noise of monks singing in the chapel; I was struck by how symphonic it all was – how appropriate.

Eventually, Timo rose and left, muttering something about finding a broom, but, forgetful as always, he did not return. He too, it seemed, was distracted by the echoes of our conversation.

Could I go back? Could I be that person again? The voice of my subconscious was abrupt, unanticipated, and surprised me so much that the muscles in my legs began to twitch.

"I can't," I said aloud.

You can try. You can live. The words came unbidden to my mind, yet though I did not want to admit it, I knew they were mine.

"Why?" I asked myself, anger piqued. "Why would I want to? I have nothing left."

You can find new places to call home, new people to love.

"He killed Matteo!"

You killed Matteo.

My stomach lurched. "No!" I yelled.

My voice reverberated against the empty walls of an empty room, and then died out to no response.

Notes on the Daughters of Iphis

I have found identity, as a concept, to be a mire of contradictions and inconsistencies. We are a people of many faces.

Consider the tale of Iphis, daughter of Crete, who, while disguised as a boy, found it in her nature to love another woman, the beautiful Ianthe. The mythology is clever to resolve this social conundrum of identity, for the goddess Isis is then invoked to transmute Iphis from woman to man. The issue is then, apparently, concluded within the bounds of natural law.

Can it not be said that this mythology, dictated by Ovid, was merely a construct of collective perception and dramatic inquest? If so – and I hardly entertain an argument to the contrary – then how must the tale be translated? Was the love between Iphis and Ianthe so damned as to warrant divine intervention, or was it rather conceived in a vacuum of explanatory prologue? That is to say, was perhaps the notion so new, so neoteric, that it could not function as an autonomous concept? If that were true, the expected outcome would be that as happened: force the condition into a preexisting definition – the natural coupling of man and woman.

Yet still it does not answer whether this was a failing of the individual or of the commonality. Is the love between two women naturally abhorrent, or does it only suffer from a lack of definition? Inarguably, it suffers from a lack of discourse. The absence of conversation in this regard is both troublesome and fascinating. Without a doubt, the lack of female voice in didactic literature is of primary consideration, but instinct insists that a deeper aversion to the matter haunts the missing void.

Perhaps that is too melodramatic. Certainly, there *is* an issue of definition, going back all the way to the Ancient Greeks, who in their pederasty, defined the members of an intimate relationship by action – penetration and reception. That definition is elastic in its use, and properly accounts for all relations of man with man and of man with woman. Here, of course, is where it fails: in the relationship of woman with woman, there are no concrete roles to assume; there is no one 'giver' or 'taker.' There is only a congregation of shared passion.

As a matter of identity, this lack of definition is particularly troubling. To be sure, the nature of an individual is ever-changing; it is an unavoidable process of life. Information, cultural stimuli, association with unfamiliar peoples: these are all catalysts for a shift in identity. Trauma, especially, can

Non dovrei essere innamorato dalla bellezza?

fracture and reform the individual perception of oneself. Such processes are natural, yet rely on predetermined schema to map and traverse. When there is no such schema present – when there is no definition by which to map that transition – how much harder must it be to know who you truly are?

In short, I wonder this: what do these women – these modern day daughters of Iphis – think of *themselves?*

I wonder at the nature of those voices so often heard within. They speak with the tenor and cadence of my own voice, yet I wonder…

Are they truly mine?

Demons and angels.

I felt them, more with each passing hour. I felt their pull, their desire. Perhaps it was my own desires that so divided me. Death and life. Vengeance and peace. Demons and angels. I could not be both. I could not have both.

It was the day of the Salviati gala. That night, some other musician would entertain the man that had destroyed my life. *What would I have done?* I wondered, then immediately rebuked the thought. *It doesn't matter. My choices never have.*

Indeed, the choice seemed to have been made for me: I was being forced from Firenze, forced to abandon my vengeance. Yet still…the decision yearned to be made as if Lucrezia's words had decided nothing at all – as if my own actions were all that could put me to either path. *Is my ego so stubborn that it cannot surrender control of even just one more choice?*

I plucked an orange from the nearest tree. The branch bent almost in two before relinquishing its fruit, then whipped back into place, bobbing momentarily before falling still in its prior seat, like nothing had happened. For a moment, I stood there, feeling as if understanding was almost within my reach – as if the pieces of my life almost described something. Then the moment was gone, and I was simply standing there, alone in the cloister, with an orange in the palm of my hand.

With a sigh, I wandered to the well. Finding a seat upon its sill, I curled my legs beneath my pregnant stomach and went to work peeling the stolen treat. Juice dripped onto my breeches and dribbled from my chin to my tunic. Lazily, I flicked the rind onto the grass.

Someone was watching me. From the corner of my gaze, I saw him – a figure in the shadow of the colonnade. *Giovanni?* As if he had been waiting for me to notice him, he suddenly stepped forward, approaching slowly from across the cloister. The rest of the abbey was still in the church; I could hear the morning lauds being recited even from here. *Why is Giovanni not with them?* An uncomfortable feeling found purchase in my chest.

He walked up to me, stopping almost within arm's reach. For a while, he stared at me – studying, it seemed like. Then, without a word, he turned and walked away.

That was...odd, I thought. Just as I was about to turn back to my treat, however, something caught my eye. A patch of white upon the ground: a bundle of parchment. Sliding off the well, I bent down to pick it up, having to brace my back against the weight of my stomach as I did so.

Did Giovanni drop this? I wondered, turning the small pile of papers over in my hands. They were all folded and tied together with a bit of string, but I could see writing inside. Careful not to bend anything, I slipped open the corner of the topmost piece of paper and read what I could.

My stomach fell.

I found Timo as he emerged from the church almost an hour later. The broad smile he always wore when seeing me slipped away when I subtly gestured for him to follow me into the empty Pandolfini chapel.

"Buongiorno," he said, though he made it sound like a question.

"I need to show you something," I replied, nervously toying with the packet of paper that I still clutched in my hands. "But…" My words died in the air. I didn't really know what else to say.

"What is it?"

I handed him the package.

He held it for a moment without moving, just staring at it, as if unsure whether he truly wanted to know its contents. Finally, he pulled apart the twine that bound it, carefully tying the string around his wrist to be reused when he was done. With deliberate lag, he peeled open the first page. His eyes moved across the sheet once, reading only the first line before he looked back to me.

"These are – are they all…?"

"Letters," I said with as much comfort as I could muster. "To you. From your parents." Something prompted me to add, "I haven't read them…only enough to know what they were."

He looked down at them again. "There are so many. Why would they suddenly send…?" He trailed off. "No, they wouldn't have. But then…"

"I'm sorry, Timo." He had worked it out more quickly than I'd expected. None of those letters had been sent recently. I had felt it; the parchment was too old – the bottom of the stack noticeably more aged than the top. The letters were years past delivery, but Timo had never received them. We both knew; there was only one person in the Badia who could make that decision. "I'm so sorry."

"How did you get them?"

I hesitated. "Timo…"

"Just tell me. Please."

"Giovanni left them for me to find. I think you know why."

I could see him thinking by the way his lips turned down. "He wants me to be angry…at the Father Abbot?" His eyes narrowed. "He wants to drive a wedge between us. If I confront him, the abbot will lose his trust in me, and then…"

"He'll send me away."

"You didn't have to give me these. You shouldn't have given them to me!" He thrust them back at me, hands trembling. "Please, take them! Please!"

"Timo—"

"Please!"

I did as he asked, thought hesitantly. "You can't ignore them, Timo. You can't un-ring a bell." I could almost hear Matteo's voice, giving me that same wisdom as he had hundreds of times before.

"Capisco. I know." He took a deep breath. "Will you take them back to the Father Abbot for me? Tell him what Giovanni did…but don't tell him that you gave them to me."

"You don't want them?"

"Of course I do!" His gaze flicked back to the letters for a moment before he could pull his eyes away. "But if the Father Abbot kept them from me… I'm sure he has his reasons. I trust him."

"Why?"

"Because he has always done his best to take care of me – of all of us."

"That doesn't mean he can't make mistakes."

Timo looked at me with sad eyes. "Everyone makes mistakes, Amadora. What matters, I think, is that you find someone to trust anyway."

"I trust you." The words were out of my mouth before I knew I had said them. *But it's true, isn't it?*

"You…do?" He looked astonished. And more than a little pleased.

"I think so."

"I trust you too," he said.

For some reason, that made me afraid. "Why would you say that?" I replied, panicked. "You can't. You can't say that."

"Why not? Amadora, I know what you've been through, but I think you're the last to realize that there is still something…" He blushed. "Well, something *beautiful* within you. You've just hidden it, I think, like a hermit crab falling back into his shell, but it's still there."

"You're wrong. I'm not that person."

"Maybe not right now, but I believe you can be again. I *trust* that you will be. That is the sort of trust I have in you."

"No! Stop saying that!"

"I won't! Amadora, I believe that—"

"TACI!" I screamed. "Sei stolto!" I was breathing too loudly, it seemed. "You're a fool, Timo! A simple-minded child who fell in love with the first woman who walked into the abbey! What, do you think I'm some deep mystery? You think I've hidden some wonderful part of myself away just so you can pick it free? Vaffanculo! Your infatuation doesn't make me special, Timo. It just makes you a fool."

In the silence that followed my tirade, I watched Timo's mouth open and close uselessly. His eyes darkened. Turning away, he tramped toward the chapel door. I watched, already imagining the way he would cry; he would come find me later, I knew, and beg my forgiveness like a child, desperately playing for whatever interest I might give him. It made me sick.

Yet, in opposition to all my expectations, he stopped abruptly before the gate. He seemed to waver for a moment, then spun back toward me.

"You know what I think, Amadora?" he yelled, his anger obviously surprising even himself. "I think you're scared that I might be right! I think you've wrapped yourself up in your game of revenge because you're scared to discover what you might be without it! You call me childish, but you've been running from your pain and your guilt like a little girl. You aren't the first person to ever suffer, Amadora, and now you're trying to push me away because I think you're worth giving a damn about. What, you believe that you don't deserve to be a good person? Che merda. You have the capacity inside you to do wonderful things!" Somehow, he made the compliment sound like a curse. "But that makes it all the more horrible that you keep throwing yourself at a path that wants to destroy you."

"I didn't choose this, Timo! This path was thrust upon me!"

"By whom? By Gilio? By God? You always have a choice." Suddenly, his eyes lit up. "And I can prove it! The angel, Oriel, you said he warned you against revenge, right?"

"Sì."

"Well there you have it," he said as if that was the end of the argument. "He wouldn't have warned you against a choice that you didn't have. That would be like…" his face scrunched up in thought. "Like betting on a lame horse. It wouldn't make sense!"

"That's a nice thought, but it doesn't change anything. I'm stuck here 'til after winter, then I'll be sent away. I have no more say in that than I have in anything else."

Timo was silent for a moment. "Maybe you're right, but you still get to decide how you deal with it. Instead of fighting, you can accept it."

"Accept it?"

"Take control, Amadora! Get out of the city! Take the baby and find a life for yourself!"

"Would—" My world shook. "Would you come with me?"

The conversation echoed in my mind for hours.

Even later, as I finally wandered up to the abbot's study, my mind was absently replaying the scene over and over into uselessness. I fidgeted with the bundle of letters in my hands.

"What do I do now?"

I hadn't meant to speak aloud, and the sound of my own voice surprised me from my dazed reverie.

"First, I suppose, you could knock." I nearly leapt from my boots as the voice of the Father Abbot appeared behind me. He must have come upon me as I stood outside his study door. Blushing, I stepped aside, only following him into the room after he had reached his desk. "What can I do for you, Amadora?" he asked, sinking into the wooden chair across from me with a heavy groan.

I hesitated. After a moment, I tossed the bundle of letters onto the desk. They landed with a satisfying slap of parchment.

The abbot's eyes glanced at the top page, then snapped back to me.

"Giovanni," I explained. My voice was unexpectedly curt.

"Did Timo...?" It was satisfying to see him so nervous.

307

I shook my head. The lying came easily.

With a sigh, the abbot turned his gaze back to the pile of letters. "Fra Giovanni is a good man, despite all that you've seen. He is so desperate to protect this abbey – desperate, but misguided." He looked back to me. "Thank you, for returning these. You could have done otherwise, but you made this choice. I am glad. It will save Timo much heartache."

My breath caught in my throat. It was as if a puzzle piece had clicked into place. The world fell away for a moment, and my mind raced with the genesis of this new realization. *'You could have done otherwise.'* The abbot had touched upon the issue without even knowing it. The same thing Timo had said – the same message: *'he wouldn't have warned you against a choice that you didn't have.'* Timo had been right. I *had* been given a choice. At that exact moment, as if to lend to my mental process, the babe kicked within me. *Of course!* The child was still alive, so somehow…somehow that choice was still left to be made. Somehow I still had the power to kill Gilio. Of course I did! Why would the angel have appeared otherwise? What use would his warning have been if the only future available saw me leave Firenze at the behest of Lucrezia Tornabuoni? Vaguely, I realized that my chest had begun to ache.

"Amadora?" The Father Abbot watched with questioning eyes.

As I rose from my trance, it was as if the world had somehow sharpened. Colors were brighter, lines crisper. The background chatter of my thoughts fell away, and each breath I took seemed somehow less strained than it had been before. I felt an overwhelming sense of calm as the pain in my chest blossomed suddenly into a comforting warmth.

"Why did you keep them?" I asked. It was the last question. I needed to know.

"The letters?" Abbot Simone brushed an absent hand across the pile of parchment. "They would only have brought him uncertainty. It's best that he keep his attention on his habit, and on the Lord."

"You are a damn fool."

Then I left without another word. I knew where I had to go – to whom I had to go: my only true friend in the monastery, in the end.

Somehow, I knew where he would be. A voice in my ear. Guiding. Whispering. Had it always been there, hidden beneath the clutter of hesitation and uncertainty? Well, the world was quiet now, and I had no reason to doubt it.

I found him, as I somehow knew I would, within the church. It was otherwise empty. His lonely voice sung into the chamber long after all the other monks had come and gone.

"Giovanni."

His song faltered. Hesitantly, and with obvious discomfort, he turned toward me. "What do you want? You are interrupting a holy man's communion with the Lord."

"I'm sure the Lord has better things to do than to talk to you." I took a step closer. "You want me gone."

Pause. "Yes."

"So do I."

His eyes sharpened, as if somehow my words were a trap.

"I'm done with this place. You want me gone, and I want to leave. Seems that there is a commonality between us after all." I waited a moment for him to catch up to what I was suggesting. "I need your help. The porter will not let me leave. The abbot has ordered him to keep the doors shut and locked."

Giovanni said nothing at first, yet eyed me with distrust. "Why would you leave now?"

"I have a gala to attend." The sun was falling further and further into the western sky. There wasn't much time. "Once I'm gone I won't return. I meant it when I said that I'm done with this place."

I could almost hear the gears and cogs of his mind grinding into each other.

One last push. "Just open the door, Giovanni. Just open the door – do that one, simple thing – and you'll be rid of me forever."

I had won. He squirmed for a moment, but in the end, I knew what his decision would be.

"One hour," he said, raising a knobby, wrinkled finger. "I will see to it that the porter is gone and the door is open." He growled in his throat. "If you dare try and trick me…"

"It wouldn't be worth my time. Just get the door open."

I knew where to go next. It was like an urge – an instinct – more than a voice. My room. As I entered, I noticed a tray of food upon the desk. An orange sat beside it. *Mariotto is ready to talk?* I ignored it. I no longer needed food. And I certainly didn't need the cellarer.

My gown was still folded in my chest. The urge *tugged* somehow at my consciousness, and I put it on. The long dress swirled about my legs. Another tug, and I looked to my harp. I could almost hear the words whispered in my ear. I obeyed without hesitation, packing the instrument into its rucksack and hoisting it upon my back.

My mind was clear – so clear – like I had finally woken from the fog of a long dream. For a long while, I stood there, alone in my room, savoring that clarity.

It's time.

My path was sure, and I walked with the confidence of one who had taken her road a thousand times before.

The murals of Saint Benedetto disappeared behind me. The Cloister of Oranges slid by without pause. The church room flickered into view for only a moment as my long strides took me past its open doors.

Giovanni was true to his word. I had known he would be. There, just ahead of me, the main entrance to the abbey stood open. Through it I could see the city street, the hustle of people, the turning light of the oncoming sunset. The sounds of Firenze – the background hum and thrush of her lifeblood – called to me.

"Amadora!"

I slowed to a stop. *This is it.* I had known it was coming – that he would be here.

"Where are you going?"

I turned toward Timo. Fate had shown me to him as I passed the church. He needed to be here.

"You can't leave! You can't! The Father Abbot won't let you return, and if you're seen…" his voice trailed off. "You don't care, do you? I can see it in your eyes, Amadora. Please, don't do this."

I didn't answer. I didn't need to. This was it, my choice. My hands began to shake. In the corners of my mind, I could hear his voice, answering me as it had that morning. *'I can't.'*

"You could have come with me," was all I said.

I turned, and took my first step toward the door. The second step was easier. The third, and there was no turning back.

"Killing him means nothing, Amadora."

No. Killing him means everything.

'I can't.'

Did it make it easier to blame Timo for what I did next? He made his choice, and I made mine. And while his explanation was lost upon me at the time, I remember it now as the first I had ever heard of the Gospel of Cain.

The strange confidence – almost like a voice of foresight – that had begun in the monastery grew stronger and more vibrant with each step I took. The warmth in my chest became fever, then fire, then burst up in a blaze of new energy that made me wonder how I did not glow with the incandescence of it. I was no longer Amadora; I was something new, something that could not be stopped. The crisp lines and bright colors of the world burned with fresh magnificence. I was drunk with the knowledge – knowledge as sure as any I had ever known – that I *could not be stopped.*

I am the shadow of death.

My harp was light upon my back. My dress wore upon my skin like air, flowing softly over the bulge of my stomach. The Palazzo Salviati was close. I could see its ostentatious spires even from the first. The marble statues that adorned its highest tier watched my short approach, seeming, each in turn, satisfied and saddened.

I could have closed my eyes and still I would have known what waited for me – every breath and fleck of dust, every word and movement – so strong was the spell upon me. The air around me hummed and sputtered as wave after wave of cold fire surged through my veins.

The gates are open.

I turned the final corner, and the face of the palazzo appeared before me. Its iron doors swung wide to accept the final few guests to the festa. The sun was setting, draping blood-red lace upon the marble plinths and columns.

Do not stop.

There were guards, one to each side of the palazzo ingress. They had not yet seen me. Still preoccupied with other guests. And within my dress, I did not stand out.

Look down.

A stone sat upon the cobble street – a piece of the palazzo fallen from above, it seemed. Bending over, I took hold of it. It fit perfectly within my palm. My skin felt like fire. Without looking, I tossed it to the side, where it clattered for a moment, then fell still.

Keep walking.

I approached the gates, still unseen. There was another company of guests behind me. I paid them no mind. Step. Step. The guards still had not seen me, though I was so close. Another few paces, and I would be firmly in their sight.

Do not stop.

The guard to the left suddenly cursed. He started back and began swatting at his shoulder, where a passing bird had left a streak of ordure. At the exact same moment, a small cry appeared behind me. The other guard rushed past to help the young noblewoman who had tripped upon the stone I'd tossed. Neither saw me as I glided, like a ghost, through the iron gates of the palazzo and into the maw of fate.

Ahead.

I entered the galleria. The long corridor stretched deep into the bowels of the building. It was flanked by stone men trapped upon stone pedestals, their hands, it seemed, reaching out as if to seize me as I passed. They knew – as I did – what was coming.

Left.

Through the courtyard. Up the wide, ornamented stairwell. Into the hall beyond. Stone columns and vaulted ceilings. A room of mirrors. There: Signora Alba and Paula de' Ricci. A candle flared, a curtain was caught by a stray breeze, a cry of alarm, and I passed unseen.

He waits within.

I floated into the ballroom. My feet barely touched the floor, and they did not hesitate. I knew he was here. In this room. In this very room. This would be the end. *Gilio Salviati.* I was a ghost – the ghost of vengeance. I laughed aloud.

Look.

To my left was a long bar.

The harp.

I placed the instrument atop, at the edge of the table. I knew it was right.

Onward. Do not stop.

Of course. The feeling of power grew even stronger. It was like being born again; for the first time, I was truly alive. The wind in my breath flashed like lightning.

There.

I looked at Gilio, where I already had known he would be. Beside him was the Father Inquisitor. I laughed again. I laughed and I laughed and I laughed without a single sound.

Step left.

My feet obeyed without question, taking me within inches of a passing nobleman. I held out my hand just as the goblet in his companion's fist splintered, drooling thick rivulets of wine across the marble stonework. I felt something brush my palm, closed my fist, and walked away as the knife pulled itself, unnoticed, from his belt sheath.

Soldiers are coming.

I turned again, and took another step to the side. I knew they were behind me: inquisition soldiers. If they saw my face, it would be over. Of course, I already knew they would not.

"Dora!" Francesco's voice. He could just barely see me from where he sat in the corner of the room. I watched his young face light up with joy. Jumping down from his bench, he tried to run to me, only to tangle himself in the legs of his nursemaid and bring them both crashing to the floor.

Now. Go.

The commotion had done it. I walked right past the inquisition soldiers without even prompting a glance.

Tomás and Gilio were waiting.

There.

Talking.

Unaware.

Do not stop. This is the end.

My feet fell soft upon the floor, yet I felt the vibration of every step like a shudder of pleasure through my frail frame. The child within me was kicking now – as if he knew his fate was being writ and was desperate to fight against it. The knife hummed in my hand.

Tomás looked up at me.

Do not stop.

An enormous crash echoed through the chamber, and the budding recognition that had not yet dawned upon the Father Inquisitor crumbled away as his gaze flickered toward the noise.

The noise of my harp, finally knocked from its perch upon that small table, shattering into a hundred pieces upon the polished stone floor.

Gilio.

Now there was only him.

A step closer. I could smell the fat of him.

A step closer. I could see the narrow slits of his eyes.

A step closer. I could hear the last breath he took.

A step closer, and he finally saw me.

Reaching up, I wrapped my fingers in his hair. He did not have time to react. I pulled his head down, bringing it close to mine, aware, for the first time, of the tears running freely down my cheeks.

I looked as deeply into his eyes as I could. Searching, there, for the light of his soul. I wanted to watch it burn.

I saw it. And I smiled.

You are mine, Amadora Trovatelli.

The knife slid quietly into the back of his neck, sheathing itself between the fourth and fifth cervical vertebrae. As he dropped to the floor – like a puppet with his strings shorn – the glaring fire within me, that had guided me, faded away, ecstasy turned to a burning pain in my chest, and I was left barren, looking down upon the warm, twitching corpse of my greatest accomplishment with the shuddering withdrawals of a cold and fervent joy.

Notes on the Orange Groves of Toscana

While the popularity of these sweet citric fruits has risen drastically in the past several decades, it should be noted that true oranges as we recognize them today did not reach Italia until the end of the 14th century, before when they had only been grown in the strange lands to the East, namely Malwa and the Empire of the Great Ming.

Yet while these treats are enjoyed by many, the medicinal uses of citrus are where their value truly lies. Scurvy, that common yet mortal ailment, was first acknowledged by Hippocrates of Kos nearly two millennia ago. In the many years since, the use of citrus in its prevention and cure has been repeatedly discovered, documented, and forgotten. Only recently have we truly began to appreciate the efficacy of the fruit in this regard, particularly in situations where proper diet is difficult, as in the case of a trading galley or desert caravan.

Surely this practical application of the Tuscan orange outweighs the already bright pleasure of its consumption. However, to make this argument is to separate the aforementioned facets of the fruit entirely from each other.

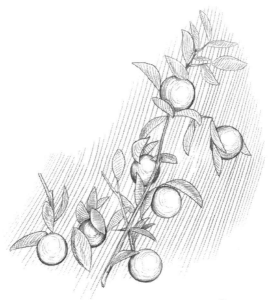

Chi si prende cura degli aranci?

Rather, I believe it is not beyond the grasp of reason to pursue the claim that both aspects – both the medicinal and the palatable – are branches stemming from a basal stalk.

Before moving further with the immediate theory, it first behooves both the botanist and the philosopher to take note of all benefits afforded by the orange tree and its produce. Perfumes and sweet aromatics can be manufactured from the oils of the orange peels, as well as the flowers that bloom within its foliage. The peel is also known to repel many insects and garden pests, can be used as kindling to start a fire or as a candle to light the home, and is a quick tool to remove grease and oil from a cooking pot. Even the wood of the tree is gifted, being strong and tightly grained lumber, as well as clean to burn, nonabrasive, and scented lightly with the sweetness of the fruit it grows.

It is a singularly invaluable crop, and the many farmers of Toscana have been quick to recognize and adopt it as the newest child of Italia. Today, it seems that orange trees are found in every corner of the contado, their sweet scent confounding even the most temperate dispositions.

WINTER

Causality is a strange beast – a leviathan who haunts the branching rivers of time. Who I am...does my definition not also encompass all the women I might have been?

Amadora. Not a musician. Not a painter. Not a wife.

A murderess.

I suppose these are aimless musings, for it is not the untried path that decides the destination. My death awaits, and the women I might have been: they can only watch as I slip into the abyss.

Lord. Please. I am so afraid.

I awoke to darkness and cold stone.

And laughter. My laughter. Piercing through the dead air around me. It seemed to echo overlong, reverberating amongst the stone walls of the room I found myself in. *My prison cell*, I supposed, not really caring. Still I was laughing. For many hours, it felt as though I might never stop.

But finally it did stop. Abruptly, and without cause, my mania softened. My arms tingled with the calming relief of a long-needed rest, and I slowly rolled over so that my back was flat to the hard floor.

I could see the room a little better from there. One heavy door stood to my left. There was no handle. To my right was a pile of moldy straw and a tarred wooden chamber pot. On the wall above was set a small window – barred and dark. *A cloudy night.* A small part of me knew it was not my first night in the cell, but I could not remember anything beyond that.

A sharp pain shot through my midriff as cramps wracked my venter. I began to laugh again.

I did not notice the darkness of the cell subtly recede to pale grey as the hours drew on, but I was aware of the soft rustle and quiet grinding of the latch being turned and my prison door creaking open.

Warm torchlight fell over me like a blanket where I lay upon the stone. I slowly turned my head to it and found myself meeting the eyes of a young man.

"Timo?" I asked. No, it was not Timo. He was gone, like so many others.

The guardsman recoiled as if my madness might pass to him like a contagion. I tried to stifle the boiling laughter within me, yet only managed in causing myself to gargle my mirth like a cough in my throat.

"What the hell are you waiting for?" Another husky voice hidden around the corner. "Grab the bitch and let's get moving. This cold is getting into my bones."

The first man spat once in my direction. Passing the torch behind him, he took a few hesitant steps forward. "Get up," he growled. When I did not move, he spat again. This time, I could feel his slaver slap against my neck. "I said get up." The toe-plate of his boot dug suddenly into my side, knocking the breath from my lungs. Bending over, he dragged me – gasping – to my feet. I hung limply from where his gauntleted fingers held my arm, sucking in air. "I ain't carrying you all the way. Get your feet moving if you know what's good for ya."

I didn't bother resisting. Why would I? As I let him push me from the cell, I finally got a look at the other guardsman, an older man with thin hair, and the thick iron shackles he held. Within moments, my wrists were locked before me between the narrow clamps. I could already feel the bruises start to well up where impatient hands had clawed them into place.

Stone corridors passed as I was herded forward, one guardsman in front, and one behind. Whenever my short legs would lag slow, a sharp blow to my ankles got me moving again.

I did not recognize where I was. Certainly it was not the Palazzo Salviati. I must have been moved.

Abruptly we were going down. Winding staircase after staircase until I was sure we had descended the height of a steeple, yet still I could see morning light as it shone through thin windows down adjacent hallways. *I was being kept in a tower?*

This was the Palazzo del Podestà then; it was almost certain. I was being held in the headquarters of the Podestà, one of the three foreign rectors that kept the law in Firenze. This must be what killing a nobleman got you.

Soon enough I found myself being ushered through a broad archway and into a wide chamber, noisy with the sound of turbulent debate, yet upon my arrival, all fell silent.

A lone, empty chair sat in the center of the floor, facing the far podium. Along the walls to my right and left, behind ornate wooden railings, were long benches crowded with dozens of men and women – nobility and wealthy merchants all, by the cut of their cloaks. Each looked to me with a different expression: fear, disgust, pity, anger. I paid them no more mind than a passing glance. Upon the walls above their heads, however, were hung fabulous paintings. One depicted the vast Florentine army – dozens of nameless soldiers dressed in armor and draped in the colors of their house – marching from Firenze's westernmost gate. On either side of that were two smaller paintings: to the left, that of a fierce battle – The Battle of Anghiari, I guessed at a look – and the victory of the Florentine army over Milan; to the right, a barren field of broken spears and armored corpses. I could see the small forms of carrion birds as they circled in the sky above.

Suddenly, blinding pain blossomed out from the back of my skull.

"I said *move*." The guardsman raised his hand as if to strike me again. I waited for the panic – for my phobia to take hold of me – but it never came. Just like it had not come when they'd pulled me from my cell, though I only now realized.

I almost laughed. Impulsively, I rammed my forehead into the man's nose, sending us both crashing to the floor. He struggled to throw me off as blood began to pool around his mouth. I thrashed around, but my manacled hands made it difficult to move. Suddenly, something was lifting me into the air. The other guardsman had me by the scruff of my dress. I stopped struggling, aware that angry voices now joined that of the bloodied man as he pushed himself to his feet. There was fury in his eyes. I met his gaze, and I smiled with all of my teeth. His hand leapt toward my throat.

"That is enough."

The voice rang clearly through the room, immobilizing the guardsman and quieting the discontent of those seated against the walls. I looked over my shoulder and, for the first time, saw the speaker, seated behind raised counter on the opposite end of the chamber. He wore a long velvet robe and cap of deep crimson. *The Podestà.*

He caught my eyes and held them for a long moment. Then, without looking away he gestured to the empty chair in the middle of the chamber before him. A deep sigh rumbled in his chest.

"Sit."

The hold upon my dress released, freeing me to approach the Podestà. I stood before him for a moment, then took the seat, instinctively smoothing my skirt as I did so.

"Grazie," he said, nodding to me. To the rest of the chamber, he continued, "We are here today to determine the truth of the crime committed by this woman here, whose name has been given by a witness as Amadora Trovatelli. She was arrested in flagranti for the murder of Gilio Salviati, well-known magnate of Firenze."

A dozen voices erupted loudly into the silence that followed. The Podestà waited patiently for a moment, then raised his hand. Silence fell again. I felt unexpectedly calm.

"There is no question of guilt. There were over thirty witnesses, and I have personally heard the tale from each of them. I do ask, however, in the interest of the assembly, that there be a public testimony." His gaze wandered the bench along the wall to my left. "Signora Salviati. If you would."

I recognized the woman that stood and stepped forward from my brief encounter with her in the Mercato Vecchio. She did not look at me, though I could still see the narrow slit of her eyes and the hard lines of her lips as they struggled to contain her vehemence.

However, from behind her hips peered another set of eyes that did not shy away. Francesco. Why was he there? I killed his father. If the angel spoke truly, that same act had doomed his brother yet unborn within me. He met my gaze, and for that moment, I understood him in a way I've never understood another. His pain, his anger, his grief: pale echoes of my own, but driven with new purpose. He had trusted me as only a child could. I looked into his eyes, and I saw the shattered pieces of what I had broken – the young and fragile faith that the world was fair and bright and good. Shattered pieces.

I looked away.

"…a Medici assassin I tell you! Who else would have done this! Who else?" Signora Salviati was speaking, I realized. I turned my attention to her, and never again looked back to the figure at her waist.

"Signora Salviati, I understand your frustration, but I called upon you for a testimony, not an accusation—" the Podestà said.

"SHE KILLED HIM. STABBED HIM THROUGH THE NECK LIKE AN ANIMAL, AND WATCHED HIM BLEED TO DEATH." She was screaming. Anger coursed through her words, and furious tears flashed down the sharp corners of her cheeks. She took a deep breath. "And you know what she did next? Do you?" She turned to the rest of the assembly, though noticeably avoided looking in my direction. "She *laughed*! She LAUGHED! And she didn't stop. No, even when my husband's soldiers took her. Even when they dragged her away. She was *still laughing*. I don't even think she knew where she was any more." Her voice turned and broke. "I can still hear it." She clutched Francesco closer to her. "We both can! And yet you ask me again to say what happened? Are all men so useless?! I want justice! I want her dead!" She was spitting with rage. "And I want the Medici *filth* who sent her hung! I want them all dead!"

The Podestà turned his gaze to me for a moment, sighed heavily, then looked out over the assembly. "Signora Salviati addresses what I believe to be the true reason for this trial. Motive. Yet we *must not*—" he let the force of his words linger for just a moment— "we *must not* allow passion to overcome reason. I will have the truth, nothing more." His thick voice boomed through the chamber.

Signora Salviati opened her mouth angrily, but was interrupted by the Podestà before she could speak. "You have said your piece, Signora, and you have made your accusation. If you have nothing else to add, sit. If you cannot do that, then you will leave."

The woman bristled, and for a moment I thought she might erupt. After a minute, she took her seat, but from then on she looked at the Podestà with resentment and new malice.

He sighed again. "Good. Is there anyone else here who wishes to share testimony?" Pause. "No? Not even you, Fra Tomás? You were so very...*vocal* when we spoke earlier."

The contentment I had enjoyed since first waking fled in an instant. A shiver rolled across my spine, and my stomach lurched. I grasped the arms of the chair to keep my hands from shaking as a soft rustle of fabric announced the rising of someone behind me along the wall to my right. I closed my eyes, trying to shut him out.

"You made yourself very clear as to what you thought of my mandate," Tomás said. His voice was horrible. It was dead. Emotionless. Everything I remembered. "The questioning and execution of this witch falls under the jurisdiction of the inquisition. This trial is meaningless. The Lord is her judge. As he shall judge you, signore."

The Podestà did not respond at first beyond a deep rumbling sigh. "I appreciate your concern, Fra Tomás." He did not bother to hide the sarcasm. "But I am only a man, and I require proof, which you could not give. If this girl is a strega, provide evidence to convince me of such. Otherwise, you have no more say in her fate than my wife's chambermaid."

His clear dismissal was met with a flurry of shocked whispers from the assembly.

"We will see," was all Fra Tomás said. I could hear him take his seat, yet it was several more seconds before I felt my breath return. Hesitantly, I opened my eyes. The Podestà looked down upon me. He seemed tired.

"This is a dirty thing. A dirty thing," he said softly. "So let us have the truth of it. Girl…Amadora, is that your name?"

I said nothing. Why would I?

The man sighed again. "Amadora, I am offering you an opportunity to explain yourself. You would be wise to take it, as I doubt you will have another. Now, tell us: are you an agent of the Medici, as Signora Salviati claims? Are you a strega, as Fra Tomás would have me believe?" Pause. "For what reason did you murder Gilio Salviati?"

I shrugged. "It doesn't matter."

"Perhaps," he replied. Sigh. "But then neither do you have any reason to keep the truth from me. I confess that when I look at you, I do not think I see a witch, nor an assassin."

At his words, Signora Salviati moved as if to speak, but with great effort, did not. I looked at her, and saw Lucrezia in my mind's eye. "No, I am neither of those things."

"Then why?"

"Vendetta. Equità." I shrugged again. "I am content knowing he rots in the deepest pits of hell."

Silence. "What was his sin?"

"The same as mine."

"Murder?"

I looked at the Podestà – met his eyes. He slowly nodded to my swollen stomach. "And the babe?"

"He'll burn for that too."

He brought his hands beneath his chin. The room was quiet as he studied me – his brow furrowed, his eyes tired, his lips downturned. It felt as though he was trying to look inside me.

Finally, he sighed. "I think I am beginning to understand."

The composure of the assembly was balanced upon the edge of a knife. A breath of wind felt as though it might knock the whole thing down. The Podestà seemed not to notice, or at least not to care.

"It seems that the character of Signor Salviati is being called into question." His words were stern, but tired. Signora Salviati's eyes seems as though they might bulge from her head entirely. I could see dark purple blotches appearing on her cheeks. "However," he added, "I will not conduct a case of public fame against the recently deceased. Not in this court. Suffice it to say, I have met Gilio Salviati on a number of occasions, and I cannot say with certainty that these accusations might not be founded in truth.

"As to the matter of witchcraft, I still see no proof. Her instrument was a knife, not some strange maleficium, and the death was natural enough." The Podestà looked momentarily to Fra Tomás as if expecting him to offer up some contention, but when it was obvious none was coming, he continued, "And in regards to the accusation of her association with the Medici…" he sighed. "Signora

Salviati, I realize this is difficult, but there is simply no proof. I have testimonies that indicate Amadora was employed by a noblewoman in Leon Bianco. In fact, there have been several reports from inside your household that *you yourself* invited her to perform at last night's gala. Simply put, there is no discernible link between her and the Medici.

"Yet this changes very little," he continued after a long moment. His tired gaze turned back to me. "Murder is a dark and terrible thing, and the law calls for the steepest of punishments."

At this, the precarious balance of the room seemed to slip. "The noose!" one person called out. "Send her to the rack!" another yelled.

Torture? Death? I found it difficult to focus on the concepts.

The Podestà raised his hand for silence. He looked around, and it seemed as though he was attempting to meet the eye of every person seated along the walls.

"The steepest of punishments," he repeated.

Mine was the last eye he met.

"Circumstances shape the crime. So too, it seems, can they shape the scope of its penalties." A deep, tolling sigh escaped his lips. "Amadora Trovatelli, you are hereby convicted of the murder of Gilio Salviati. I sentence you to *confinato a perpetuo carcere.*" An explosion of angry voices burst out almost at once. The Podestà did not look away. "You will spend the rest of your life behind the bars of a cell in Il Carcere delle Stinche." The buzz of enraged debate was nearly deafening. "Though perhaps one day you might earn the church's pardon. This is as much mercy as I can give."

What? It was hard to think through the fog upon my mind. I was confused. I didn't understand. *You're...letting me live?*

Suddenly, the tumult around me died. Tense silence took hold once again, yet it was not the Podestà who had called for it. I could hear the slow beat of a single set of footsteps behind me. My blood turned to ice as an emotionless voice appeared like a specter in the air above my shoulder. "I have a letter for you, signore. I think perhaps now you should read it." Slowly, Fra Tomás stepped forward. I was painstakingly aware of every movement as he reached forward and deposited a thick piece of folded parchment upon the raised desk. It was closed with a red seal.

Whatever insignia was stamped upon the seal wrote deep lines upon the Podestà's brow. Without a word, he broke the wax. His eyes drifted across the page once, snapped back to Fra Tomás, and then returned to the letter, more slowly this time. Finally, he set the parchment down.

"Why am I only receiving this now?" He did not hide his anger; his voice boomed with it.

Fra Tomás bowed his head. "My apologies. I simply did not wish to interrupt the..." he coughed into his hand, "proceedings. They were entertaining, after all."

The once tired eyes of the Podestà seemed filled with thunder. For a moment, I wondered whether he meant to strike Fra Tomás. Finally, his gaze fell. His shoulders seemed to slump, and he leaned back in his chair, defeated.

He turned to the assembly, "I have just received a bullectini." He sighed. "The Priors have decided that this case falls under the jurisdiction of the Holy Catholic Church. Amadora will be handed over to Fra Tomás and the Inquisition of Heretical Depravity for…" he glanced down at the letter, "for purgative torture. And subsequent execution." His eyes flicked to mine for only a moment, then looked away. "By fire."

L'isola delle Stinche. The prison. A place of pain and death. The last home I was ever given, and the one I by far most deserved.

There was but one light to be found in that miserable darkness, and I do not suppose I shall ever see her again.

"I deeply regret that we cannot begin the ardor of cleansing your soul quite yet, strega. It seems that the executor of the prison has not seen it necessary to outfit the proper instruments of torture. I suppose you do not mind waiting a few days for me to acquire that which you will need? No, I thought not. I can only say how deeply I regret the delay. Truly, I would begin our work within the hour if I could. There is much to be done. Your soul will require many weeks of attention to be truly cleansed. Many weeks. Alas, this is how the Lord has seen fit to use me, and a proper tool does not complain. This work we will do together…it is a thing of faith – a thing of *art* – and should be no more rushed than any other craftsman with his paintbrush, do you not agree?"

I could not shut out his words as I was led, still chained, down the single road that separated the Palazzo del Podestà with the city's prison. Fra Tomás walked beside me, seeming almost cheerful as he spoke with a guise of amicability.

"Regardless, it seems to me that art should only be produced as a service to the church, and through us, to the Lord. Any other form is apostasy. And then reasonably, would not my service also deserve the same appreciation? The strokes I employ are different than those of a painter and his brush, but often we produce the same crimson patterns. There is beauty there, I think. Yes, I do think so."

Cold seeped into my bones, but not from the chilled northern breeze of an early winter on its way. In my stomach I could feel the mire of inconsistencies – peace and horror seemed ill-suited bedmates yet were content to share in the turmoil of my state, at least for the moment.

"For now, it will be enough that you are neither fed nor watered. I have often seen that such a fast may soften even the most corrupt sinner and make him all the easier to remold into the Lord's image. That is what we are doing, you see. Your soul has been disfigured. Tampered with. Spoilt. Such is the cost of maleficium; only such a soul can commune with demons and their like. A pure soul is immune to such things. So, before you can receive judgment for your crimes against man," he made a motion with his hands meant to imitate the lighting of a fire, "you must be prepared to face the judgement of God. I will cleanse you. Remold you. Purge you. With my help, you may still be saved from the torments of hell. *That* is the work we do." He closed his eyes and took a long breath, savoring the air in his lungs. "It is a good thing we do together, Amadora. A good thing indeed. Even now, I can feel the gratitude of all the souls I've saved thus far. Hundreds of them. A good thing indeed."

We turned a shallow bend, and I suddenly found myself face to face with an enormous, monolithic stone structure. *L'isola delle Stinche.* It looked as though someone had built a small castle right into the heart of the city; large, uneven walls rose almost a dozen times my own height into the air, broken not by windows, but small, hand-sized openings that I imagined allowed some small flow of air to pass to the rooms within. High above, peeking out from above the high walls were three guard towers, though I could not see any shapes moving atop them.

The stillness was absolute, oppressive, and unsettling. *It's as if the stones themselves have died.*

Seated against the corner of the prison nearest us was a peculiar little kiosk, an aedicula, made all of marble, upon the front of which were a pair of small, closed panel doors. It was a street tabernacle – one of many in Firenze – a place for the layman to worship in the city, and a place for the condemned to repent as they were led to their execution. I knew that inside would be a painting of a saint, likely Saint Peter, so as to help guide the spirits of the devoted. As we passed it, Fra Tomás bowed his head and drew his fingers across his forehead and chest in the sign of the cross. I considered spitting on it.

We continued straight ahead, passing quickly into the shadow of the prison. A small door stood to our right, yet the top of the frame was no higher than my shoulder. Above it was a plaque inscribed with the Latin phrase, "*Oportet Misereri.*"

Mercy is necessary.

I had heard of this door and its reputation. Too small for any man or woman, made purposely so that prisoners felt the weight of the prison shutting out the world behind them. The people of Firenze had their own name for this door: Porta della Miseria.

The Gate of Misery.

I bent forward and stepped through, and that was the last I ever saw of the sun.

Cold. Dim. Rancid.

My eyes struggled to adjust as I was led deeper and deeper into the prison.

"I am pleased, at least, that you will not have means to corrupt the men of this place, sinners though they are. The executor has at least enough sense to keep his women imprisoned separately. A wise choice, though I believe he offers them too much comfort."

The air was heavy with the smell of rot and mildew. No breeze. No light. My feet slapped loudly upon the damp stonework. Everything I saw seemed to glimmer slightly with a sheen of moisture. No circulation.

Cold. Dim. Rancid.

Guards were posted occasionally at the doors we passed through. After a few minutes, we emerged into a small, shaded courtyard, filthy and layered with mud and sharp gravel. I could barely even see the sky above us. To the right, as I was led through it, I could see a stone lion beneath a mantle of mold. Next to him was inscribed, "*Videbunt Iusti Et Letabuntur.*" It was a quote from Psalms of David. *The just shall see, and rejoice,* it was supposed to read. However, the last word had been misspelled. Rather than *laetabuntur*, it was written *letabuntur*, which instead translated as:

The just shall see, and die.

I shivered as we passed through the other side of the courtyard and into the bowels of a prison that deemed death akin to joy.

"Here we are," Fra Tomás said after a moment. A heavy wooden door, with a small barred window, stood before us. Tomás' lifeless voice seemed muffled in the dead silence that lay upon Le Stinche like a curse. "You will be held here until we are ready to begin our work together. I ask that you exercise patience, if such a virtue is even still available to you. The wait will not be long."

One of the men with Tomás stepped forward to unlock the door, which screeched upon its hinges as it was pried open. Suddenly, there was a hand around my neck, and I was being lifted by my throat into the air. I gasped, struggling to breathe as the guardsman tightened his grip and full threw me through the opening. I hit the ground at a strange angle, and whatever air I had left was knocked from my lungs in an instant. As if through a fog, I heard the muted sounds of the door closing and the lock clicking back into place.

Tears of pain welled up, unbidden, as I desperately gasped for air. It was difficult to move, but after a moment I was able to pull myself up just enough to look around.

My cell was not what I expected. It was large – several times larger than the room within which the Palazzo del Podestà had held me. And it was not empty.

Another woman. Seated upon the cell's only cot with her legs crossed beneath her. She wore what once must have been a wonderful ormesino dress, though the grime of the prison was quickly reducing it to the state of a dish rag. The front lacing of her bodice was undone for comfort, and beneath she wore nothing but a thin white chemise. Her long golden hair was mostly tied up, but several stray locks had fallen around her ears to frame her soft green eyes, which studied me curiously. Vague familiarity itched at the back of my mind, as it seemed to do for her as well.

"Are you—" she begun to ask, before her eyes widened. "Wait, I *do* know you! The lost girl with the harp!"

At her words, a memory fell into place.

"The whore," I muttered in reply, remembering back to my first trip to the Mercato Vecchio and the courtesan who had shown me the way.

She frowned. Silence followed my remark, and I used it to study the rest of the room.

Stone walls. Stone ceiling. A small slit, no wider than a few fingers, made for the room's only window, yet through it I saw only the prison's outer wall.

Cold. Dim. Rancid.

"Are you hurt?"

My gaze wandered back to the woman, who was now eyeing my swollen stomach with an air of worry. I looked down to it as well. *He has not moved much today. Perhaps he grieves.*

There was a rustling of cloth and movement from the corner of my eye that made me look up. The whore had left the cot and now knelt beside me. She did not touch me, yet her eyes – those soft green eyes – brushed across my face and skin like satin.

"You'll be fine," she said after a moment. She offered her hand, and after I took it, pulled me to my feet. Without letting go, she led me toward the cot and pushed me to a seat. "Sit," she said as if I was not already. She watched me for a moment, to make sure I was following her direction, then backed away to find her own seat along the floor of the wall adjacent. She continued to study me; her curious green eyes seemed so bright, despite the mud streaked across her cheeks and in her hair.

"Isabella," she said, catching my gaze. "No more of this, *'the whore'* business. I didn't like how you said it. My name is Isabella."

I shrugged.

"Hmph." She blew a strand of hair away from her face. "I don't remember you being so *dull* when we met before. In fact, you were rather excited about something, as I recall." A sly smile played its way across her lips. "Would you like to see my tits again?"

My head whipped around, and a blush flooded my cheeks.

"Aha! You have some life in you after all!" She laughed. "So do you have a name as well, or should I call you by that wonderful hue you've just turned?"

"Wh—what?" I stammered.

"Your *name*, dolcezza! I want your name!"

"It's…Amadora," I finally managed to say.

"Amadora," she repeated. "That is a beautiful name. You should, I think, lead with that next time. It makes for a rather better introduction than asking me about my breasts."

"*I did not ask*—" I began to exclaim, but was interrupted by the sudden snort of laughter that exploded from Isabella. In that moment, every line of her face seemed to change. The corners of her eyes wrinkled, her nose scrunched up, her cheeks brightened. I watched dumbly as mirth overtook her. She was so out of place, so *ridiculous*. Incredulity. *Can't she see where we are?*

My chest heaved. My breath jumped in my nose. A strange sensation gurgled in my stomach.

And suddenly, I was laughing as well. My own voice seemed strange to my ears as it echoed and bubbled off the walls around me.

"There! Now that's much better! I was worried for a moment that I was to be stuck in here with someone boring." She muffled one last giggle. "But now I'm beginning to think that we might get along after all."

I didn't know what to say, so I stayed silent. But I could still feel the strangeness of a crooked grin as it pulled upon the muscles of my face.

"So tell me, *Amadora*. How long will you be visiting me here? I doubt I'll make my own freedom before you; I got hit with the double penalty of place, you see. Apparently the Onestà doesn't like us whores near the city's churches." She sighed. "It's just…they're so *wonderful*, don't you think? Santa Croce, Santa Maria del Fiore, Santa Maria Novella. They're so grand, and elegant – so beautiful. When the clouds pass by overhead, it almost looks as though they're dancing." She smirked. "Besides, I should think the Onestà would want us as close to the churches as possible, in case we catch some of that salvation they seem to have so much of."

"I…uh," I stammered, feeling unsure of myself. "I don't think I'll be here long. A few weeks, probably."

"They're letting you out that quickly? Beato te!"

I didn't bother to correct her. *Death will be its own freedom, I suppose.* But the thought of the inferno I was fated for set my stomach roiling.

Notes on Inquisitorial Torture

Pain is the truest harbinger of verisimilitude. Even I, after everything, admit to the efficacy of that dictum which is so central to the conduct of the Holy Inquisition. Pain will tell. It is an intricate tool that, like any pen, may transcribe both fiction and fact in its use.

The issue is then, of course, the fiction. When judicial torture is most commonly employed as a method of questioning, the interference of fiction corrupts the results gathered by its use. Most will do anything, *say anything,* to bring a stop to their pain, a clear and irreparable flaw to the institution, yet it is a flaw only worsened by each new development in the field. New tools – new tortures – new and heightened levels of pain are only met by the body's need to escape from them. In that way, each new device of torture is merely an additional motivation for untruth. Seemingly, this is a paradox of ideals: promoting fiction in the search for fact.

Unless, of course, truth is not its actual purpose. Do not forget the obvious cruelty and fundamental sadism of

Il dolore è nella mente

mankind. One only needs a description of the torturer's tools to understand his true function.

Throughout history, these tools have evolved, being more refined from one generation to the next. The earliest instance known is that of the Persians, who thought slaves less deserving of mercy than even the basest of animals. Those unfortunate enough to displease their masters were strung up between two poles, and the skin was slowly peeled from their bodies – piece by piece, beginning with the soles of their feet and moving upwards until even their eyelids were removed. Mercifully, the shock of this procedure was usually enough to cause death, but in the instances where oblivion was not so easily achieved – when the carver had been slow and meticulous in his work so that the victims did not bleed away – the men would continue to hang there, sometimes for days.

Imagine, if you can, the sensation of every nerve in your body being scorched at once, over and over again in every moment, every minute, every hour, for days that seem to have no end. The most meagre breath of wind feels like the cut of a new knife, the smallest drop of rain cracks against your exposed muscles and veins like the snap of a whip. You cannot blink, so your eyes slowly dry and shrivel and die. Every movement, every *moment* is a new and horrific agony. Until, eventually – mercifully – death finds you. Slow death.

That is the starting point – the foundation from which all tortures since have been improved upon.

The Romans, in particular, were powerful innovators of the craft. There are several accounts of the condemned being led to their place of torture only to find a donkey waiting for them. As they watched, the donkey was disemboweled – its stomach ripped open and the entrails removed. The beast would die in agony. Then the victim would be stripped naked and forced into the animal's belly, leaving only his head outside. As the corpse decomposed around him, he found himself eaten alive by maggots, vultures, and disease. Slow death.

Such animals were often used by the Romans as the tools of their inquest. The most horrific, perhaps, of their tortures was that enacted by rats. Captured. Starved. Then forced into a cauldron. Those condemned to this end were stripped, and the container of rats was affixed to their stomachs. The pattering of tiny claws against its brim. The feeling of unseen breath upon your belly. The iron was cold, for a while, where it met skin, yet it soon became warm, then hot, as the executioner held a torch to its end. The sensation of searing skin was soon forgotten as the rats within fled the fire by the only means available. Tearing, eating, digging. Blood seeping out from the seams between iron and skin. Something moving inside of you. Agony beyond words. Slow death.

Of course, these methodologies are outdated – barbaric by today's standards. Death is not a requisite of pain: we have come to understand. They exist freely, even independently from one another. The instruments in use today make use of that autonomy, incurring great pain without ending life. Whereas the tortures of the ancient world might construct an agony of days, the advances of the modern world can produce unyielding weeks of anguish, even months should it be required. Take away the victim's skin, and the medicines of doctors can keep her alive. Take an eye, or a nail, or a hand, and she shall live. Crush her bones, feed her poison, pierce her skin with needles and knives, cook her alive or leave her naked in the snow, and with the proper attention, she will live.

Yet what truly sets apart this modern age – what truly dictates the horrors afflicted upon the condemned – is a new invention of thought: pain is in the mind. Just as a man can forestall an aching back as he works the field yet curse and cringe as he attempts to sleep that night, so too may the pains of the torture chamber find themselves multiplied by circumstance. Anticipation. Sleep deprivation. Starvation. These are the new tools of the trade. And there is no slow death to escape a mental affliction.

But of course, even the most careful machinations of man cannot sway the ultimate laws of nature. Death may not be the cost of pain, but it shall never be free.

There is always a cost.

I quickly came to enjoy Isabella's company. She was bright, and clever, and she made me laugh more than once. It is strange that I should have found some semblance of joy again there, in the darkest of places.

No, that isn't quite right. Perhaps…perhaps joy is most easily found in such a place. Like a firefly on a moonless night, in misery joy shines brightest.

Tomás was true to his word; no food was delivered for me either that night or the next morning. It seemed that the other inmates of Le Stinche were served a meal twice a day, if they could afford it. Those who could not were allowed to beg for their food – through the proxy of a friar, of course – though often that earned them nothing. For me, even that miserable option was unavailable. My only course was to slowly starve, or so I thought.

"Do you not have anyone who can pay for you?" Isabella finally asked after, again, a meal was brought only for her. Concern was writ clearly upon her face. "Don't worry, I'll get word to Madelena la Donna. The brothel has plenty of soldi put aside for this sort of thing."

"I…can't."

She laughed. "You're worried about the debt? Don't be. Madelena won't force you into a bed, though I daresay you might benefit from the experience." She winked. "But there are plenty of other ways to repay the brothel." Her eyes suddenly lit up. "Perhaps you could teach us! You *can* play the harp, can't you? Oh, I would so love to learn!"

"It's not that."

"Then what? I know you must be hungry."

I bit my lip. I didn't want to say. I didn't want her to know what was waiting for me. "It's a—a part of my sentence." *Please don't ask any more.*

"Well that's outrageous; you're carrying a child. Here," she said, tossing half a loaf of bread in my direction.

"Really, I can't."

"Why, are you not hungry?"

"Yes, but…"

"Then eat!"

"If I'm seen—"

"Then you're seen eating. But honestly dolcezza, no one pays us any mind in here, and even if they were to look, none of the men care. Past keeping the doors locked, they can't be bothered with us." She smiled warmly. "Trust me."

From then on, Isabella insisted on sharing half of her food with me. I was afraid, for the first few meals, that Fra Tomás would appear any moment to wrack some new punishment upon me. He never did, but I knew too that I had not been forgotten. He would come to claim me soon.

Don't think about that. Don't. The torture. Oh god. What is he going to do to me?

The icy claws of inescapability were closing around me. At times, I felt as though I could barely breathe. Other times, it felt as though I was floating. The death of Gilio had lifted a weight from my back, but that weight had been my shield and without it…I was naked – left with nowhere to hide. Eventually, I began to wonder whether Fra Tomás had lied about needing time – whether the waiting was a torture of its own.

Torture. Don't think about that.

I tried to close my mind to it, but nonetheless my nights were endless, sleepless nightmares. In the quiet dark, my thoughts were quick to wander. I would imagine the pain – the *procedures* – he had in store. Would he beat me? *No.* Would he cut me? *Don't think about that.* Would he pull apart my bones? Would he burn me? Would he make me beg for death? *Stop! Please, no more!*

I could not quiet my thoughts, but at the very least they taught me something. *I will say whatever he wants. Whatever is necessary to make the pain stop.* I had nothing anymore to care about, after all. No one to protect. That was some small comfort. Perhaps it would be enough.

It won't be.

The days, like my nights, passed slowly, but not in silence. Isabella was an easy companion, quick of mind and soft of voice. She seemed content, as well, to allow me my reticence, though in time I always found my voice; she seemed to draw it out of me.

She talked of many things. Of Firenze. Of the brothel. Of dresses and women and culture. She seemed to somehow know whenever a topic hazarded too close to discomfort and would steer it a new direction as through she were captaining a ship, yet invariably her interests were drawn to music and art and all the ideals of my untold upbringing.

In such things, she was an utter novice, but her curiosity was bright and unquenchable. Though I spoke little, she held tightly to what I did offer as if it were worth more than gold. That look in her eyes – that honest desire...I began to develop a weakness for it.

I did my best to resist. Weakness. I needed...I didn't know what I needed. Not that. Not weakness. I needed to be strong for what loomed ahead like a sepulcher in the fog. My stomach lurched. *Don't think about that. Anything else. Think of anything else.*

"Chord. It's called a chord," I blurted out, interrupting Isabella's description of the voices she'd heard singing within Santa Croce.

"A...chord?" There it was: that earnest curiosity.

I nodded. "Two or more tones in harmony. A chord."

Excitement was clear in her voice. "How do you know what's in harmony or not?"

"You can hear it. A harmony sounds..." I paused to think, "...comfortable. Like two notes that belong together." *What am I doing?* "Here, sing something and I'll show you."

To my surprise, Isabella turned a light shade of pink. "S—sing? Now?"

I smiled. "It doesn't need to be anything extraordinary. Even just a simple sound will do."

The pink in her cheeks deepened, but she seemed determined all the same. "I—uh…okay. I'll try." Her brow furrowed. She bit her bottom lip for a moment. Then, hesitantly, she drew in a deep breath and let loose a timid note. It wobbled for a moment, unsure. She blushed even harder, but continued, clearly determined to make some sort of steady sound.

I watched her. I couldn't help it. The way her nose flared. The way her clenched fists still quivered. That light in her eyes.

After a moment, I joined my voice to hers. Swelling upward, I found the fifth – the happiest harmony – and held it.

The tremor was completely gone from Isabella's voice. Still singing, though seemingly unaware of it, her eyes sparkled with joy.

I rose to the sixth, creating a new chord – hopeful. Down to the fourth: calm, contemplative. Then I returned to the fifth before letting our little song die away into the echoing stonework.

Isabella panted for air as if she had just run a race, but there was no hiding the wide smile that stretched between her cheeks.

"That was fantastic!" she exclaimed, laughing between breaths. "È stato ottimo!"

"Harmony," I said, surprised to find that I was a bit short on breath myself.

"I see what you mean now, about it sounding comfortable. Were those chords then?"

I nodded. "Chords can be more than that too. More harmonies at once, like what you heard in the Santa Croce."

"Is it the same on the harp?"

"All music is made of the same parts. The only difference is in its expression. If your voice is the sigh of wind on a summer's day, then the voice of the harp would be like rainfall on still water."

"That's beautiful," Isabella said. Standing for a moment, she walked closer to take a seat next to me on the bed. Her hand gently brushed mine. "Where did you learn all that?"

"I…" Hesitation. Weakness. *What am I doing?*

"I was a workshop apprentice. My…father…was a master of many crafts." *Stop! This cannot last. You know what's coming for you.* "Music. Art. Literature. Natural Philosophy." *She will only make it harder to bear.*

"That sounds wonderful."

"It—it was."

"Tell me more? About music, I mean."

"What do you want to know?"

The smile she gave me was brighter than any I'd before seen. "Everything," she said.

I give up.

My voice – budding as it was in reply – caught suddenly in my throat. Sound. Noise from outside the cell. It was not time yet for another meal.

No…

My hands began to shake. My chest went cold. I could not breathe. Panic. Tears of horror suddenly staining my cheeks.

Please…

The door screeched open.

A figure stood in the darkness beyond.

"It is time to begin, strega."

I could not move, could not speak, even as the guardsman entered the cell to retrieve me, I could do nothing.

"What's happening?" Isabella asked from her seat beside me. She was worried. I clutched desperately at her hand, as if that could save me. I held to it like driftwood in a storm; even as the guards took me – even as they pulled me away – I held to her. "What's happening?!" she cried out, being dragged behind me. "Where are you taking her?! Amadora! What are they going to do?!" A heavy fist lashed out, and her hand suddenly disappeared from my own.

The door was closed.

It disappeared behind me.

I was being led away.

"Amadora!"

Her voice called out for me, frantically, one last time.

But I was already gone.

If I could cut away these memories, I would.
I wish death had found me first. But now it is too late.
Too late.

I was taken to a small room. Small door, small room.
The guardsmen did not enter. New men, instead.
New men, each with a black hood.

Inside the room. *Oh god.* Things.

A table with straps. A winch to pull. Spikes to peel my flesh as the joints in my arms and legs were torn apart.

I vomited onto the floor.

A fire in a low brazier. Implements of iron – knives, brands – already red hot in the coals.

Worktable. Upon it: pincer, serrated blade, knife with a point that jutted forward to pick and pry beneath my skin.

There. A clamp. Wooden clamp, but spikes inside. Close the clamp, close the spikes.

In the corner. Boxes. Closed, but I could smell something acrid within. *I don't want to know. Please.*

The child within my stomach moved suddenly, kicking and rolling and thrashing.

I vomited again.

"Ah, what is this?" Tomás. Behind me. Bending down, he smeared his finger through the recent contents of my stomach. I would have retched again but had nothing left to give up. "This was not an empty stomach, I think. Not a one of *fasting*, as I instructed." His narrow eyes did not leave my own as he stood up. Slowly, he reached forward and wiped his fingers clean upon the front of my dress, brushing the swell of my stomach. "We shall discover how."

"Come. Let us begin," he said, waving me forward. To the hooded men: "Prepare her."

I was stripped to my shift. The thin garment was barely opaque. I knew the dress was no armor against this room, but without it, the feeling of helplessness that already wracked my chest grew to a fever pitch. Exposed. I felt exposed. I folded my arms beneath my breasts in a feeble attempt to hide them from view. Dizzy. Disoriented.

The hooded men pushed me into a chair. I flinched back as they began to tie my wrists down with leather straps. Finally, the pressure in my chest was too much. Panic. Uncontrollable.

A shriek escaped me. All sense of control was gone. I thrashed, bucking my body back and forth. *ESCAPE.* Hooded men held me in place. I thrashed even more violently. My head cracked into the nearest. My vision blurred. Teeth. I tried to catch skin between my teeth. The last of the straps tightened over my wrists and ankles.

A pale laugh pulled apart my frenzy. "Ah, already the strega shows her true nature. But we have not even begun this work of art you and I shall create together."

My chair was turned to face the fire. I could feel its warmth lap teasingly against my cheeks.

"Perhaps I should explain. There are many devices before you, and I can only imagine you must be intrigued by their use? Yes, I think so." I could hear him move just behind me. I flinched as his cloak brushed against my neck. "You see, Amadora, we – that is, the inquisition – traditionally make use of three tortures. Those of air, of water, and of fire."

My skin was becoming hot from the heat of the brazier. I shifted as far away as I could.

"To be sure, each will have its turn with you, but in my travels, I have discovered many more things, more *procedures*, that I have found to be even more effective. It is exciting, is it not? No, do not ask me to say any more. The time will come for such things soon enough; there is no need to rush. We have many weeks together, Amadora. Many weeks."

Suddenly, there were hands at my throat, pulling back my head. Someone was moving in front of me. At the brazier. I could not see.

The scream that burst out from within me was sudden and piercing as blinding pain erupted from my right arm. My vision disappeared. Nothing but the pain existed. Searing, lacerating agony. My skin was being ripped away. I could feel it. Surely, it was being peeled back. Torn away. Ripped, shredded, burned. The pain – the screaming horrible blinding pain – was spreading, moving up my arm like the crawling of a white-hot spider. Screaming. Screaming without end.

I do not remember unconsciousness, but I awoke to the gasp of cold water splashing across my face. That gasp turned to a shriek as the pain in my right arm – like the quick memory of agony – returned in earnest.

The hands were gone from my neck. Shaking, barely able to hold my head aright, I struggled to look down at my arm.

Nearly a quarter of the skin on my forearm was bubbled and seared away. I could see, in places, the muscles and tendons that had been hidden beneath. Like peeling back the rind of a crimson fruit.

It felt as though I were looking at the charred remains through a long tunnel. As if a sick lens had fallen between myself and reality.

"No no, Amadora. You must not fall asleep. We have barely begun."

Where am I? What is this?

"Come. Again."

I was screaming even before the iron touched me.

Hours. Days. Perhaps only minutes. Consciousness and unconsciousness blurred together until the only reality left to me was pain. Endless and unyielding pain.

Through the haze that took me, I was vaguely aware that my arm had been completely peeled. Even the skin upon the back of my hand had been boiled away. A red and blackened mass. Agony through my stupor. My chest. I could not fully breathe.

Cold water across my face. The fog receded.

"You have done well, strega. Tomorrow, we shall work with your other arm."

"N—no…please…"

Tomás put a thin finger to my lips. "For now, we must protect you from infection. The rot is quick to follow such a procedure, and we must keep you in good health to do our work here."

I could barely see as Tomás bent over my arm. I weakly struggled to get away, but the straps held me in place. "Come now, there is no need for that." Tomás gingerly pushed my shoulder back against the chair as from his belt he drew a large flask. With one motion he popped the cork and upended it over the newly mangled flesh.

My throat burned as a new shriek tore out from my chest. The thick red-brown liquid sizzled and sputtered as it seeped into the tissue and muscle of my arm. The acrid smell stung my eyes as I writhed back and forth in my chair.

Time passed. Did the pain lessen, or was I simply becoming accustomed to it?

I was no longer in the chair. Moving stone. Doors and hallways and passing guards. And pain.

There was a tingling of familiarity as we came to the door of my cell. It opened. I was brought in. Set down. Collapsed onto the hard ground. Pain. The door closed behind me. Alone.

A scream. Suddenly, there were soft hands around my face.

"Amadora! Oh god, Amadora?! What have they done to you?"

Isabella cried out in horror as she finally saw the mangled skin of my arm, still dripping as it was with blood and brown mucus.

For a while, as I lay there unable to move or to see or to speak – floating lazily upon the narrow line between consciousness and unconsciousness – Isabella was quiet. Her hands were cool as they stroked my cheeks.

"Tell me again about harmonies. How do you make them into a chord?" Isabella's voice appeared from overhead.

What?

"Come now, I haven't forgotten. You said you would teach me, so teach me."

Even through the sea of pain I was drowning in, I could feel a sharp spark of incredulity.

"You promised!"

I did? "N—no...I..."

With extreme effort, I managed to open my eyes.

Isabella sat above me, cradling my head in her lap. Her cheeks had turned a pallid white, and tears were falling freely from her wide eyes. Desperation. She was trying to help, I finally realized – trying in the only way she could think. Anything to take my mind from the pain, to lessen it even just a little.

In that moment, I loved her with every ounce of myself – whatever little of that remained.

"Of...course," I whispered. It was hard to focus, hard to even think through the pain. My right arm felt as though it were still on fire. "I—I did promise...after all."

I spoke, I think, for hours. Quietly, maybe even too softly to hear, but Isabella never interrupted. She never asked questions, never needed anything. I don't even know what I spoke about – whether it had anything to do with music at all – but the act of moving, the struggle to do *something* helped. All the while, she stroked my face and pet my hair. Eventually, I recognized that the color had begun to return to her cheeks, though I knew she was avoiding the sight of my disfigured arm.

I was breathing heavily. That was the first thing I realized when I awoke. I didn't remember falling asleep, if you could call it sleep. I *did* remember the night. The pain. The cries of agony. The endless burning as my arm felt like it was being mutilated over and over and over again.

Consciousness was elusive, but I held to it as firmly as I dared. Isabella was still there, I could vaguely see, lying next to me. I bit my lip to stifle the shrieks of pain that still threatened to escape. She had fallen asleep as well, it seemed, and from the draw to her closed eyes, her dreams had been no kinder to her than mine.

Not dreams, nightmares. Incubi. Nightmares are things of fiction. Mine had become reality around me.

My stifled whimpers turned quickly to sobbing. I lay there, on the stone floor of a cell in L'isola delle Stinche, the husk of my arm cradled against a stomach swollen with the seed of murder and rape, and I wept.

Is it strange that I should still mourn my arms? 'They will never truly heal.' Ovviamente. Lo so. I am studied enough to recognize when skin has been damaged beyond its ability to reform.

It is strange. I lay here upon my frozen deathbed, and still I mourn that my arms would always have borne this disfigurement.

I am dying; no longer should it matter.

Strange.

"Today, Amadora, we will be working with something new."

I held both of my ruined arms beneath me like a charred babe.

The second arm had been worse than the first. Screaming. So much screaming. I had been caught in the throes of agony long after I was returned to my cell. Screaming long into the night – long after my voice had given way, I was still giving up noiseless shrieks of pain. For days, not even the gentlest words of Isabella were able to break the shell around my consciousness. I could not sleep. I dared not eat. Even the tiniest movement or breath of wind burned like white fire.

Yet I was again in the chamber. Nothing could stop that. Inevitable. Unbearable. I was shaking, desperately, as I watched Tomás peer at me from over his workbench.

"Please…" I whimpered, my tremors rising. If not for the hooded men with their hands beneath my shoulders, I would not have even been able to stand.

"Yes, I should think you would be excited! Molto bene!" He clapped his hands together and rose suddenly to his feet. His black robe swirled around him ominously. "I think, for now, that we shall leave the fire torment, as it is called. We may yet return to it, but I admit, I am impatient to move onto my own inventions." He said the word with the loving pride of a craftsman and his latest work. I began to weep.

"Yes! Sorrow! Regret! We are clearly on the right path toward cleansing your soul. Come, let us continue." His voice trembled with the cheap facsimile of excitement.

"No, no, no…" I shook my head as if in denial. Tears splattered onto my shift.

I was carried forward by the men who held me. I struggled weakly against them at first, yet as I saw where I was being borne, my fear quickly overcame my weakness. The table. Winches to turn, to pull me apart. I began to scream through my tears. Adrenaline coursed through me, but for all my thrashing, I could not escape. I shrieked as the barely-formed scabs upon my mangled arms were ripped painfully open. Blood began to seep out even before I hit the table.

"Today," Tomás continued without paying me any mind. "We shall learn something about you. You will share something with me – something you do not wish to share. Such secrets are a sin, of which I must purge you."

My shredded arms were pulled up above my head. The rough, splintery wood of the table scraped horribly into the exposed, bloody tissue, and I shrieked anew. I could not move. Trapped.

"Now now, Amadora, no need to look so frightened. It is a simple thing I ask for. A secret; that is all."

I cried out as I felt his hands touch my face. He was holding something. I struggled to see what it was. I could not focus. My vision was going white. Panic.

A small metal clamp. He fastened it to my nose, and immediately, I felt it become harder to breathe. The sobbing. The panic. I gasped in air.

"Let us begin."

Suddenly, there was water everywhere. I could taste the salt of it as it was poured into my mouth. I couldn't breathe. I thrashed around, desperate for air, yet heavy hands had appeared to hold my head in place. Drowning. I was drowning! My vision blurred. *No more!* My chest screamed for air. I tried frantically to fight down the instinct to breathe. Gulping down saltwater. Air. I need air. My head was pounding. I could barely see. Finally, I could control it no longer. Saltwater filled my lungs as my chest desperately tried to suck in breath. I heaved, gagging horribly into my own mouth, but the water did not stop pouring. Fog. I was losing consciousness. Blackness.

Then, coughing. Hideous agony as I bucked in place, half-vomiting half-coughing up an endless stream of saltwater. I gasped in air, but filling my lungs was a new torture. I choked as more and more liquid came sputtering up my throat.

"Now, a secret, or we begin again."

I gasped for air, struggling against the piercing pain in my chest. "I—I don't…know." My chest heaved. "Please…"

"Hold her down."

I shrieked as hands again pulled my head against the table. "NO! PLEASE! I'LL TELL YOU ANYTHING!"

Water. All that pain. I was drowning. I was dying. Saltwater flooding my lungs. Burning me from the inside out. I could not drink anymore, but still it poured down my throat. My stomach was distending, pushing now against the babe.

Air. Vomit. Spilling out the sides of my mouth. Could barely think.

"A secret, Amadora."

"I—I…" My head throbbed. Couldn't focus. Couldn't think. "Can-t…remember…"

"Ah, yes. Memory can be a fickle thing, is that not so? I am an understanding man. I am a *generous* man. So, what if I ask you a question – just one question – and if you answer me, you may return to your cell for the day? Will you do that?"

"Y—yes."

"Good. Then answer this: *who has been giving you food?*"

Isabella.

My jaw locked shut. I gasped for air through my teeth.

"How disappointing. Hold her down."

I can barely remember any longer. Has my mind rejected the memories?

Or are my experiences the first parts of me to die?

The sun is rising, but I cannot see it through the clouds.

"**W**hy are they doing this to you?!" Isabella sobbed as she held me. Her hands were gentle, yet desperate, where they wrapped around my chest. My shift was almost completely gone, ripped and bloody. Thick rivulets of blood still seeped out from the gorges torn from my back.

The lash had been sewn with shards of metal. It had not satisfied them to pull apart the skin of my back. They had taken my arms again as well, tearing new gulches into the raw, unhealed flesh.

I had screamed until my throat bled.

"Strega…they think…" It was hard to speak. "Sur— survived a fire…shouldn't have…wish I hadn't."

"You're no witch." Her fingers were in my hair now, caressing. "Even if you were, you wouldn't deserve this. No one does."

"Do—don't know how I lived…"

"Then maybe you are a witch." She smiled through the tears in her eyes. "My little witch. Come, use your magic to take us away from here."

I started to have dreams. Strange, half-conscious dreams haunting the nights I spent writhing in agony.

"Soon."

I heard the voice – as real as if it been spoken from a dark corner of the cell. The same word over and over and over again. Sometimes a whisper. Sometimes so loudly that I wondered how Isabella did not wake. Always the same thing.

"Soon."

I almost recognized the voice. Flashes of darkness. Of a fire without flame. A man that was not quite a man. *Moloch*. The name came to me. Or had it been spoken?

"Soon."

The lash was the torment of air, and was the last of my agonies mandated by the Holy Catholic Church. After, I was given completely into the hands of Tomás, to be used for whatever sick purposes he could imagine.

First, he robbed me of sleep. Four days tied to a wall in the torture chamber. Four days of hooded men with hooked knives. Cutting and slicing and carving my legs whenever my eyes began to droop. Tomás made me watch as they fed a dog with the pieces of me that were removed.

Next, they covered my head with a thick sack, stripped me of my clothes, and chained me to the courtyard stones overnight. Winter took me, and by morning, I could barely move. My fingers and toes had blistered thick and white in the cold, and my joints had locked up. Worse, though, were my arms and legs. The scabs had frozen, stretched, and burst as I was dragged back to my cell. Like a paintbrush smearing a crimson path.

"How dare they?!" Isabella had practically screamed. "You're carrying a child!"

"The child of the devil?" I could barely speak. "They don't care."

"Soon."

I lost track of myself. I barely even knew who I was.

Sometimes I would talk to the voice at night. Sometimes I would respond – ask him who he was, beg him to help – yet always he replied the same.

"Soon."

No more. Just let me die.

"Please, come in," Tomás said as I was carried into the room. My legs did not seem to work much anymore. Not like they were meant to.

I did not struggle as the men took me to the chair and lashed me in place. The width of leather strap over my wrists marked the only skin untouched upon my arms. Like pale white manacles.

"Look at me, Amadora." Tomás bent over my chair, his horrible eyes only inches from my own. Studying me. Devouring me. "Yes, you are nearly prepared to face the

Lord's judgement. This has been a long process. I know it has. Yours was a soul deeply rooted with demon's filth. We are so close now. So close. But I must have your secrets."

Not Isabella. I'll give you anything else.

"Let us begin."

Screaming. Endless screaming.

"BADIA FIORENTINA! I WAS THERE! WITH THE MONKS! THEY TOOK ME IN!"

Agony. Better to die.

"HIDING SOMETHING ELSE! THEY'RE HIDING A BOOK! STOP! NO MORE, PLEASE!"

Please let me die.

"A BOOK! A LIAR'S BOOK! I SWEAR! PLEASE STOP! I'LL TELL YOU ANYTHING!"

Please.

"HIDDEN! I DON'T KNOW! CAIN! HE SAID CAIN! THE GOSPEL OF CAIN!"

Timo? Was he there? No, it was just a memory. Another phantom to haunt my sleepless nights. That day, in the Pandolfini chapel. I had asked him to come with me – to flee the monastery, to run away and live a new life with me. And he had said no.

'I can't. I'm so sorry, Amadora. I just can't.'

You could have. Timo, why did you do this to me? You could have stopped all this. Why didn't you just come with me?

'I have to stay here. I have to. We…we aren't just an abbey. There's more that we do here. We…protect something.'

Protect what, a book? A dusty old tome meant more to you than I did.

'A gospel. A *hidden* gospel, Amadora. An account of the life of Christ that the church has been hunting for centuries. They want to destroy it, Amadora! Destroy the written words of the Lord!'

Why Timo? Why would anyone care? Why did you care?

'It's amazing, Amadora. The book – the gospel…I still don't understand it. But it's written by *Cain.* How can that even be possible? The son of Adam. The murderer. How could he have been alive to see Christ? He must have lived for thousands of years!'

You guarded a lie. What you said was impossible.

'The church says the same thing. They say it cannot be true, and that any such false scriptures must be abolished. But I know it's not a hoax, Amadora! I know it! So…I have to stay here. I have to protect it.'

Liar! You were a liar! You never cared about me! "Liar!" I cried out into the darkness.

"Soon," it replied.

Two days later, I was again taken from my cell.

"Please…," I whispered to Isabella as the door was pried open and the soldiers again came for me. "Let me die."

But she could do nothing as I was dragged away again to the room.

The room.

The room.

I knew I was near death. I could feel it all the time now. So close, like a companion hiding just there in my shadow. I had begun to hope that it might find me, that a slip of the knife – Tomás need only make the smallest of mistakes – might release me from that hateful room. But it never came. No matter how I tried to thrust myself into his machinations. No matter how I might goad him. His instruments never wavered. I could find no mercy.

But I was not taken to that room. Not today. No, today Tomás waited for me within the courtyard. It had snowed, though the heavy slush already was taking on a murky brown hue. There were the shapes of other men there as well. Prisoners, I assumed, as they were led along through the courtyard, beneath the stone lion and his misspoken words of justice and death, to the lower malevato, where they would live out whatever sentence awaited them. I paid them little mind.

"Buongiorno, Amadora." Tomás' voice no longer left me. It was with me every moment. In my nightmares; burned into the scarred husk of a body he had buried me in.

Only the guardsman's hand around my arm kept me from collapsing.

"I have decided that our time together must end. You are as ready, I believe, as you will ever be to face the judgement of our Lord."

I did not understand. Long seconds passed.

"Look at them, Amadora. You have finally revealed to me that secret that had been guarded most hideously by your heart. With this, you may finally find redemption." He set his hand gently upon my shoulder. His long, bony fingers brushed away the tears that were now falling from my cheeks. "I am proud of you, my child."

My chest was pounding, and a sick sensation filled me. I did not want to look, but I could not control my gaze as it was again drawn to the men shuffling through the courtyard.

I wanted to scream. I wanted to rage, or cry, or be sick as I finally understood. But I felt nothing. Emptiness.

Abbot Simone looked up as he was marched before me. His eyes: so full of sorrow and dread, and when they met mine, horrible accusation. Behind him, Prior Giovanni seemed to have given up all hope. His arms hung limply, his gaze seemed empty and useless, and his feet barely left the ground as one slowly shuffled its way before the other. I don't even think he knew I was there. One after another, the monks of the Badia Fiorentina, shackled and dressed in rags were marched before me.

Some, like the abbot, looked up at me with anger. Some spat, or cursed, or wept. A few others even seemed to pity me. I watched them all from a distance, hidden as I was in the furthest back corner of my mind.

Timo is not here. The realization came late, as the last of the monks disappeared into the dark maw of the prison. In fact, there were many still missing from the procession. A third, perhaps, were not with the rest. Timo. Even Fra Mariotto, the fat cellarer. *They escaped?*

Tomás came with as I was led back to my cell. "Most have already confessed to harboring that horrid apocrypha of which you told me. The fate of the unredeemable heathen awaits them, and any more whom I find had knowledge of this book." He sighed lightly as a false smile slipped across his teeth. "I shall bring them to Rome for trial, after your execution."

The door to my cell was opened. As my body was dropped to the floor within, even as Isabella rushed to my side, Tomás continued to talk, "I have already spoken to the Podestà. You are to be burned on the morn of this day next week. You have seven days. I suggest you spend them in prayer."

Burned. The door slammed shut.

There was still some breath of life within me – some porcelain piece of myself that had, beyond reason, survived the last weeks of agony, pain, and torture. It quivered, and shook, and finally as the key was turned in the lock, it broke.

I began to scream from my cold bed upon the stonework.

"YOU THINK YOU CAN KILL ME WITH FIRE? FIRE HAS NO POWER OVER ME. NON IL POTERE! I HAVE SURVIVED THE FLAMES, AND I WILL DO SO AGAIN. ME TU BRUCIA! BURN ME AND WATCH!"

I screamed until my voice gave way, and then I lay still. In silence. As if I were already dead.

The end is coming.
I can already feel the fire.

The babe no longer fought within me. It seemed that he had resigned himself as much as I to what awaited us.

I was content, in a way. Eager even, for the escape that death would bring. But the fire...I was so afraid of the flames. I did not want to die that way. *Qualcos'altro.*

Isabella was always with me. She stayed by my side day and night, doing her best to comfort me in whatever ways she could. We did not talk about what awaited. Instead, she seemed desperate to learn everything she could about my past. Montaione. Matteo. My tutelage and talents. My childhood hopes and fears. Many days passed before I finally understood: her questions, they were meant to save me – or at least save whatever parts of me she could. If at least she remembered who I was, I would not completely disappear.

It was utterly foolish; it was useless sentimentality, and yet...it comforted me.

So we spent our time within each other's voices. I emulated Isabella, asking my own questions of her past. I did not want to die alone. If a part of me could survive in her, then maybe…maybe I could have a part of her with me at the very end.

As if to further build the sensation of loss that loomed ever over me, I regained a little of my health with each day that passed. Even the pain in my arms began to slowly recede, and soon enough, I could stand – even walk – again on my own.

I wept at the cruelty of it, that such things as hope and well-being were given reign to so mercilessly mock me. They only made my coming death that much harder to bear. Let my legs be ruined. Let me die without hope. Let me beg for an end.

Instead, it was as if my body meant to somehow deny its impending riddance.

"Tell me more about Matteo," Isabella said as we shared our morning meal. With my health had come a deep, driving hunger. I refused to take more than half of Isabella's food, but such meagre portions left me entirely unsatisfied. Not for the first time, I found myself wishing for an orange from the gardens of the monastery.

Who tends the orange trees now that Timo's brothers are gone? Aloud, I asked, "Matteo? What else do you want to know?"

"I don't know," Isabella said with a nervous smile. "He just sounds so wonderful. Wise, and caring. I envy your upbringing."

I had shared much with Isabella, but I found I could only speak of my happier memories. She did not know of Matteo's death, nor did she know that Gilio had forced himself upon me. For these last few days of my life, I could almost pretend that none of it had happened – that Matteo and the workshop waited for me to return, as they always had.

"He snores," I replied. "And when the summer comes, his feet smell like bad asparagus."

Isabella chuckled softly. "Does he play the harp, like you?"

"That and so much more. The harp, the lyre, flute, portative. I believe he could make music from rocks and sticks if he set his mind to it."

"And he taught that all to you?"

"Only the harp. He meant to teach me more. I…would've liked to have learned." Pause. "I should have listened better. I should have been a better daughter. I—I miss him."

Isabella seemed not to know what to say, so for a moment we sat in silence.

"He loves you," she finally said. "Which is more than I can say of my…well, my mother. She never told me who my father was – probably some inflated merchant with a wife of his own and no interest in a bastard daughter."

"You never tried to find him?"

"Why would I?" she replied. "So he can take a dowry when he marries me off to some other man's poor bastard? Col cazzo!" She spat on the ground in an intensely uncharacteristic show of crudity. "I don't belong to anyone!"

Neither of us said anything for a few minutes.

"I think I understand," I said. "What you do – the...the..."

"Whoring," she offered.

"Yes. That." I took a moment to shift my weight, crying out as the scars of my arms stretched and moaned. I closed my eyes and waited for the pain to subside. Finally, I found the strength to continue, "It—it isn't like I thought it was. You aren't trapped, or cornered into it. You...*enjoy* who you are."

Isabella looked at me for a long while, then looked down. "It's not always like that. Some of the girls are like you say. They're ones that like to cry, you know, after they take a man. We try our best to help them – give them easy clients, teach them how to enjoy themselves – but usually...well, usually they can't handle it. They run away: to a convent, or another city, or wherever." She frowned. "I pretend otherwise, but truly, I've never understood that. It may not be the most respected profession, but what we do is honest. We're paid well; we only answer to ourselves; and if you do it right..." Isabella laughed. "Well, it *can* feel quite good. Most of the time anyway."

"I wouldn't know," was all I said. Thankfully, Isabella did not press for more. "You know, I used to tell myself that, one day, I would have my own workshop. I wanted it so badly." A sudden, angry laugh found purchase in my chest as I looked down over the mutilated remnants of my arms and legs. "Now I understand. It never would have been possible. I was a stupid, naïve girl, dreaming of freedom and love and other useless things. Matteo knew though. He knew how the world truly worked. Women are wives, or whores, or nuns. They cannot be musicians. They cannot be artists." I looked at Isabella. "I envy you."

"Maybe. I don't know. Maybe you could not have had the life you dreamt of – just like those girls could not have the lives they wanted – but that doesn't mean you give up. You find the next best thing, and you make the most of it."

"I don't really have that choice anymore."

Isabella looked down. "I'm sorry."

Silence followed, stretching on long into the evening. Even with my body recovering, sleep remained as elusive as it had always been within the cold prison cell. I spent the night harried by that same, horrible voice, speaking endlessly out from the darkness.

"Soon. Soon. Soon."

And as the dawn finally came, and the sunlight peeked hesitantly through the narrow window-slit in our cell, I realized that this was the sixth morning since the monks and the courtyard. A strange numbness seemed to come over me. The next sunrise would be my last.

I'm going to die tomorrow.

"What do you think it will feel like?" I didn't know if Isabella had woken, but my question hung in the air regardless. She did not immediately respond, and after a moment I gave her up for sleeping. I was surprised then, when several minutes later, her soft voice – trembling slightly – broke the stillness.

"I think dying must feel a bit like falling asleep. Like the entire world is a book, and you've reached the last page. As you close the cover, and you fall slowly into that long darkness, you know that your life helped shape the story, even if just a little."

"I…" My voice trailed off. *Whose story did I shape?* My mind flashed with images of those I'd hurt or betrayed. *Matteo. Antonia. Jacopo. Lucrezia. Abbot Simone. Francesco. Timo.* I had never been anything good to anyone. *I've even hurt Isabella, in the short time I've known her. She weeps to see me go.*

I closed my eyes to shut away the tears.

"I don't want to die."

It felt strange to spend my last day in silence, like I should have been doing something – singing, or dancing, or talking – anything to pull as much life from the day as possible, but it was as if an enormous weight held me down. Isabella could feel it as well, I knew. I counted the seconds, then the minutes, as the last of my hours fell away from me, wasted. I willed the sun to stop its path across the sky, but all too quickly it was falling – setting. My last sunset, and I couldn't even see it from my cell.

As the last auburn vestiges of sunlight faded beneath the snow-capped walls of the prison, as my last day became my last night, as the darkness began to encompass me and the damp stonework chilled my mangled skin and the frost of cold winter night set upon me, the rustling of footsteps echoed out beyond the cell door.

It's too early. No. Oh god, please no. I shut my eyes as tightly as I could. I grasped my knees tightly, pulling them to my chest, ignoring the pain as the movement stretched the scars upon them. Isabella was suddenly by my side as the footsteps grew louder. Her hands trembled as they lay upon me.

"It's going to be okay." I could hear her whispering. "It will be okay. It—it will be over quickly. Oh, my little Amadora. It's going to be okay. You'll be with Matteo again soon."

She knew.

The key turned in the lock.

My chest hurt. It burned. A sudden tightening in my venter made me shudder in pain.

"Soon." The voice was in my ear. *Moloch.* I felt the sick shivers of dread run down my spine.

The door opened.

The soft glow of a lantern illuminated the black-clad figure that waited without.

My breath caught.

"Timo?"

Notes on the Confraternity of the Blacks

The Compagnia di Santa Maria della Croce al Tempio, as the confraternity was originally known, can trace its origins back over two hundred years, and while the group's title has changed in that time, their original mission has remained more or less the same: to provide spiritual guidance and relief to those citizens of Firenze who most need it. In the early 14th century, this mandate narrowed somewhat, becoming especially focused on providing its services to those unfortunate souls who, by some sin or another, found themselves condemned to death; however, it was not until the confraternity of Santa Maria della Croce al Tempio divided itself in 1423 that the final arrangement of this mandate was achieved. The Confraternity of Blacks – so named for the black hood and gown worn by its members – was born, and their work was truly allowed to begin.

Now, to be clear, while the most recognizable of work undertaken by the Confraternity of Blacks is the comforting of the condemned, they in fact offer many charitable services. These are perhaps not as thrilling to watch or discuss as the accompaniment of a murderer or thief to his final stage within the Piazza della Forche, but what else they

La tua anima vivrà per sempre

offer should not be belittled by comparison. By means of land gifted to the group in 1361, their members take responsibility for burying the bodies of the deceased, mourning their memory, and comforting their families. And while the group may not directly involve itself in other philanthropic activities around the city, they are known to work closely with other confraternities in such endeavors, and so vicariously assist in a myriad of other altruisms. Yet while it is necessary that such pursuits are paid homage to, they do not define the group. To the people of Firenze, they are known as the comforters of the condemned.

And well they should be known, for they are arguably the most *visible* of confraternities within the city. No Florentine will miss an execution if they can help it, and so the walk of the comforter as he precedes the condemned – walking backwards so as to keep pious etchings raised and in total view of the condemned at all times – is easily recognizable.

Yet truly, what do these men do? So far we have spoken only of their public humanities, but have entirely neglected the full measure of their service. That is to say, the true worth of the Confraternity of Blacks was in the comfort they provide on the night *prior* to an execution. To remark only on the methods by which they accompany a man to the gallows is no different than assuming the entirety of a book by reading just the final page.

No, the night *prior* is where comfort is most needed. The condemned will not be able to sleep, so turbulent are his thoughts. Panic may set in, accompanied by desperate supplications for divine intervention. Never have those entreaties been answered. Never. And the silence that replies is deafening. Comforters fill that silence with prayers and hymns and gospel readings, deadening, in some small way, the plight of a man about to die.

Those of the confraternity come from many walks of life: farmers, craftsmen, bankers, nobles. Monks. Yet they are all taught that to rightly prepare the condemned for death, they must each take on the mantle of a merchant, for their work is in the procurement of merchandise for the halls of heaven. In the spirit of this role, many who take on their work share in a script by which they read upon entering the prison cell of the man about to die.

"This happens to you because it pleases the will of God our Lord. Not that God is happy about the violent death of anyone and especially not about the death of the soul, but he lets it happen and allows the punishment of the world to be given to the body so that the soul does not carry punishment and eternal suffering. And if the punishment of the body is not borne willingly, know for certain that it will not be worthy and God will not accept the soul to greater glory nor to the greater crown.

"I beg you to listen well to what I'm going to tell you

now. Man and woman are composed of two natures and two substances, that is, the body and the soul. Therefore, do not have your heart fixed upon your flesh and body at present, because it will soon return to the mud and filth from which it came. Now, lift your spirit, because your soul will live forever."

I'm sorry. Timo, I'm so sorry.
You never should have trusted me.

F ra Timo da Arezzo stepped into my prison cell.

It wasn't until the door closed behind him that I realized the black robes he wore.

"Amadora Trovatelli," he said, breaking the silence that had followed his arrival. "My name is Timo, and I have been selected by the Confraternity of the Blacks to comfort you in your last hours." His eyes were dark, and I could not make out his expression through the dim, flickering light that barely illuminated his pale cheeks.

Above me, Isabella had stiffened. Her hands moved almost instinctually to grasp my own.

Without waiting for a reply, Timo immediately began to recite some script about death being the will of God and the eternal persistence of my soul. It was eerily similar to the law of the abbey he had shared with me that first day in the Badia, yet I let him talk.

Why are you here, Timo?

He did not look at me. His voice was dry and passionless, and he spoke as if to the cell wall. "Therefore, do not have your heart fixed upon your flesh and body at—"

"Timo," I said his name softly.

His voice caught for a moment before he could continue. "—at present, because it will soon return to the mud and filth from which it came." He continued his recital – more loudly than before – and I could see him faintly shake his head as if to deny that I was truly there.

I squeezed Isabella's hand.

Timo continued in his work for hours, never once stopping or allowing me to speak. He prayed, and recited verses, and sang hymns all with the same, monotonous tenor.

I listened quietly, for the most part. Not to the words, but to his voice. I never thought I would hear it again, and much to my surprise, I was happy to be wrong. Isabella too, it seemed, was content to listen, though she never left my side or removed her hand from mine. I focused on controlling the pace of my breath and tried not to think of anything except Timo's voice, but every so often, a sharp twinge of pain would shoot through my stomach. The fire. *Don't think about it.* I desperately tried to take comfort from the dry thrum of his dictation.

Comforting. It *was* comforting, I supposed. Just his presence – as forced as it seemed to be – already had made the night easier to bear, even if just a little.

"Amadora…"

I had become so accustomed to Timo's monologue that several moments passed before I realized the silence of its absence. I glanced up, and was surprised to see a very different Timo than had entered the cell. Tears had appeared to trail their way down his pale cheeks. His fingers were white where they gripped the small book of scripture he carried, and it looked as though he was having trouble swallowing. He fell to his knees in front of me, and I could see his hands shake as his fingers hesitantly reached out toward the twisted remains of my arms.

"Wh—what have they done to—to you? Amadora…" Timo struggled to speak, and all trace of his previous apathy was gone.

"Timo?" Confusion.

"I—I had to wait for the guard. Had to be safe. Didn't want him to suspect." His voice was shaking.

Isabella reached forward. Her hand wrapped tightly around his wrist. "What are you saying?"

For the first time, Timo seemed to realize Isabella was there. He looked up at her nervously, his chin quivering slightly. "Who…? Can—can you help? Please…"

Isabella seemed to come alive. She was on her feet in a moment. "How?"

From beneath the loose folds of his robes, Timo brought out a small parcel of clothes – black – and identical to those he wore. "The guard…he does not stay all night. A new one takes his place. He will not know I came alone."

What? My mind was reeling, struggling to understand. Sudden hands pulled me to my feet. Isabella had wasted no time, and was urgently pulling the black robes around my head. I cried out as the coarse fabric scratched against my arms.

"What are you doing?" I didn't understand. It was like I could not focus. "Isabella, what—"

"Quiet, Amadora!" Isabella whispered under her breath. Letting the robes fall into place, she brought her hands up to cup my cheeks. Her eyes were wide, and shone brightly, and seemed to engulf my own. "Focus on me, Amadora. Focus! Listen to me. You are going to escape. You are going to live. Do you understand what I'm saying?"

It was as if the slowly moving pieces of my mind had finally come together. I looked down at myself, then up at Timo. *I...I'm going to live?*

"Why?" My question hung darkly in the air before us. "Timo. The monks. The Badia. You know what happened." His gaze fell. "I—it was me. So...why?"

A long moment passed. Finally, he looked up and met my gaze in a way he had never done before. His suddenly forceful eyes pierced my own. "I still trust you. I know the woman you can be." He looked for a moment to Isabella. "I think she does too."

Isabella's hand was in my own.

My stomach twisted violently, and my fingers instinctively tensed around Isabella's as I gasped from the pain.

Her eyes widened.

"What?" Timo asked.

"You need to go. Now." Isabella pulled the hood of the robe up around my head so that it hung low and shaded my face.

"Are you...?" I didn't know how to ask.

"I stay here." She smiled. "I'll be released soon, Amadora. Don't worry." She leaned forward, and kissed me. Her lips felt soft upon my own. "We will see each other again. But for now, you must go." Her hands fell away, and she turned to Timo. "Go!"

His eyes flickered between us, confused, then he nodded. Turning to the door, he began to knock loudly upon the wood.

"Ehi! You there!" he called out through the iron grate. I tried my best to fold my arms so that the sleeves of the robe hid the bulge of my stomach.

After a moment, a voice replied, "Che cosa vuoi, conforteria?"

"We're done," Timo responded. The strength that had so infused him only moments before seemed gone, and his voice quivered slightly. "She doesn't want any comfort, and I don't want to lose a night's sleep for nothing. My assistant and I would like to leave."

A face appeared on the far side of the grate, glowing softly in the light of Timo's lantern. "Your assistant?" His eyes turned to me. A tense moment passed. Finally, his gaze returned to Timo. "Alright, but are you really giving up, frate? The girl isn't like to do well alone the rest of the night. Don't you think she deserves a bit of the Lord's peace and all that? Been through hell, that one has."

"The Lord can't work with those who don't welcome him. We've tried our best, but she seems determined that we leave." Timo shrugged awkwardly. "If solitude brings her comfort, who are we to argue? Our work is a charity; I won't force it upon her."

The guard seemed to hesitate. As he opened his mouth to reply, though, Isabella suddenly screamed out, making both Timo and me jump in surprise. "GET OUT! I DON'T WANT EITHER OF YOU HERE! LEAVE ME ALONE!"

"Whoa! Va bene, va bene!" The key clicked in the lock and the door swung open. Timo nearly pushed me through before following himself. "I see what you mean! Well go on then, though I'm a bit sad to see the girl fight against you both. Surely she needs mercy more than most. Pity what all they've done to her. Got a daughter myself. Makes it hard to bear the screams sometimes."

I could feel my heart pounding in my chest. I struggled to keep my breath steady.

Timo's voice was significantly shaking when he responded. "Y—yes...that so—sounds horrible."

"You alright there, frate? Seems you've gone a bit pale."

"Fine...I'm fine. A bit tired, is all." He seemed to finally collect himself.

"Alright then. You two better get on."

"Grazie mille," Timo said with a grateful bow of his head. Then – motioning for me to follow – he began to lead a path away from my small prison cell.

I was nearly gasping for air by the time we turned our first corner and the guardsman disappeared from view. Leaning for a moment against the nearest wall, I struggled to subdue my panic and catch my breath. My lower back ached from standing for so long.

Timo's eyes nearly bulged from his head. "We need to keep going! Don't stop!" He sounded very near panic as well.

I took a deep breath, and pushed myself forward. Timo seemed desperate for me to move as quickly as possible, but my strength was already beginning to waver. Weeks of immobility had taken their toll on me.

Slowly – so slowly – we came to the dirty, snow-strewn courtyard. Every step seemed to take an age, and I could see panic grip Timo more and more with every passing moment. My legs shook. My back ached. My skin felt hot. Step forward. Another step. Another. I could see the dark sky above me; it was a clear night, and heaven's cold stars glistened brilliantly over Firenze.

"You leave so soon?"

The pallid voice seized me from behind like the ragged claw of some great beast. I froze in step. I could not move.

Shock made Timo turn too quickly, and he stumbled for a moment before catching himself. I could see his legs shaking. "I—we—we were not wanted…" Full panic had taken Timo. My chest began to ache as well as my back. "Didn't want comfort. She—the witch…didn't want…"

Timo, you fool! The lie was obvious! It was so obvious! *He knows! He must know!* My legs begged to run, but fear rooted me in place as Tomás stepped into the light of Timo's lantern.

"I…see." Tomás' voice was dangerous, like a viper's hiss. He looked at me, and my blood froze in my veins. Yet…from within the shadow of my hood, I could see no recognition in his eyes. After a moment, he looked back to Timo. "I see," he repeated. "You fear the witch."

What?

"W—we do," Timo stuttered out, recovering much more quickly than I. "Fear her, I mean."

"How disgraceful. You do the Lord's work. Are you so wretched that you believe this will not protect you? Disonorevole!" He looked again to me. "And you as well? You fear this…this *witch?*"

My stomach seemed to turn up into my throat. Several tense seconds passed. Finally, I managed a jerky nod.

"Shameful! Worthless! Faithless!" Tomás condemned, his gaze turning back to Timo. "Be gone with you then! The Lord shall judge your unfaith most harshly; I have every trust in that."

Then, beyond all hope, the Father Inquisitor turned and began to walk away.

One step away.

Two.

Three.

He did not seem to be slowing. His gait was drawing him further and further from us. I could feel Timo's hand as he pulled on my sleeve, desperate to get away.

Suddenly, a piercing, twisting pain in my abdomen. It wrenched at my venter, pulling and clenching and cramping. There was a slight sensation of bursting, and a gush of warm liquid spilled out between my legs.

I gasped, and from my mouth escaped a sharp and familiar cry of pain.

Tomás spun, his gaze alight with recognition and fury. "Strega!" he spat. Something sharp was in his hands.

Suddenly, Timo was running past me. I had a glimpse of his eyes – wide with terror and panic – as he threw himself at the Father Inquisitor. He gripped the lamp like a weapon. I heard a muffled scream. The lamp came down, shattering into jagged pieces of metal and drenching the courtyard in sudden darkness.

Silence.

"T—Timo…?" I whispered weakly.

A low, almost inaudible murmur replied from where I had last seen him in the darkness. I shuffled forward, heart pounding, legs dripping. *My waters broke,* I realized in some muted, dark corner of my mind. I pushed the thought aside.

My eyes slowly adjusted. Still forms seemed to appear out from the blackness, amorphous, then more distinct as my vision adapted further. Tomás lay unconscious, a dark trickle of blood falling from a wound on the side of his head. Beside him, I could finally make out Timo, hands clenched around his chest.

Around the hilt of a knife.

"Amadora…" he moaned, voice gurgling through the blood spilling out the sides of his mouth.

Everything seemed to slow, and my body felt as though it were caught in a thick pool of mud.

"Timo…" I muttered, suddenly dizzy. I couldn't focus. "I think I've gone into labor. I think I'm having the baby."

The starlight flickered in the tears that fell from his cheeks as his breath caught in his throat. His eyes were wide. He looked so scared. So scared. He heaved once, twice.

"Amadora…please…run."

And then his chest went still.

"Timo…?"

Silence.

"Timo…come on, Timo…please, we need to go…"

The world did not move, and for several seconds, I was trapped in the darkness.

I heard the vague sounds of shouting in the distance. Guards. We had been heard.

Then, I turned, and I ran.

I ran until my strength gave out, and now I am dying where I fell.

I did as you asked, Timo.

But I don't think it was enough.

Forgive me.

The night sheltered me like a dark cloak as I fled the abandoned alleyways and familiar streets of Firenze. I was gripped with some strange strength. Was it fear? Sorrow? Anger?

Relief?

The sounds of the prison and her guards slowly faded behind me.

New snow had begun to fall, and I could feel it crunch underfoot with every step.

I needed to get out of the city. The blood thrummed and rushed through my veins as I loped past house and home on the road towards the eastern gate.

Below the strada, to my right, I could hear the steady sounds of the Arno – that immortal river that runs through Firenze. It flowed west, as always. I could almost feel the push of it against me as I forged my way onward.

I clenched my teeth to stifle another cry of pain as my womb pinched and contracted. *Too soon*, I remember telling myself. *It's not time. Months too soon.*

My cheeks were cold, I realized, from the tears that had somehow found their way upon them. The salt droplets froze, cracked, and fell away like hail, sparkling dangerously in the starlight.

Finally. Above me loomed the dark outline of the Torre della Zecca, the final turret of the city wall and the tower that stood guard over the open gate – the Porta della Guistizia.

Suddenly, in the distance behind me, erupted the deep brassy toll of bells – the alarm bells of the Palazzo della Podestà, echoing through the silent city, sending a signal to the fourteen gates and their guardsmen. 'Close the doors. Let no one through.'

They were too late. I was through the portal and out of the city before even the first toll had faded away. I heard the shouts from the tower behind me, fighting to be heard above the bells, but it would be hours before they discovered where I had gone.

I fled along the road that paralleled the Arno. Through the Piazza delle Forche and out into the gaping darkness of a Tuscan winter night.

I do not know how much time passed.

My arms froze, and burst, and bled, leaving a splattered trail of red snow behind me as I walked. My feet swelled and went numb. The contractions that wracked my body grew more and more frequent as the hours passed. Soon, they were upon me almost as often as not. I vomited several times, but my feet never stopped moving.

The Arno disappeared. I could barely hear it anymore, somewhere to the south. I forged onward. The snow was falling ever harder. The ground beneath me sloped up and up and up, and I realized – somewhat belatedly through the fog in my mind – that the white skies had begun to lighten.

As I continued higher and higher into the cold, white, desolate hills that stretch far outside the city of Firenze, the sun finally crested the horizon, yet I could not see it. Hidden – both its light and warmth – hidden behind the thick, grey clouds that lay now across the sky, weeping snow. Weeping. The world was weeping.

Trees. I had not noticed them appear, but now there was an entire forest crowded around me. Were my feet still moving? Yes. One after another. After another. Boots pushing snow aside. My hands were red. Blood? And white skin.

I screamed suddenly into the crisp air. The contraction that enveloped me was worse than any before. It felt like my hips were being pulled apart. The ground rushed up to meet me as my legs finally gave way. I panted desperately, crying out again and again as my insides were twisted and pulled and squeezed.

My muscles relaxed, and the pain subsided as the contraction passed. But I found I could not get up. My legs did not obey. They wobbled, and slowly shifted, but I could not put them beneath me. I could not get up.

I crawled backward into a snowbank underneath the stark eaves of a white oak tree. I wrapped the black robe around myself as tightly as I could, but it could not shut out the cold.

Again. The pain. Deep pulling and thrashing as another contraction took me. I gritted my teeth, but could not stop the sob that wrenched its way out my throat.

Breathe.

Another contraction again so soon.

Breathe.

Again.

Like waves upon a stony shore. Crest and subside. The incoming tide, lapping closer and closer and closer.

Push. The thought broke upon me through it all. I pushed. I pushed, and the agony climaxed, and I screamed, and still I pushed.

A minute to breathe as the wave fell away. Then it was back.

Push! I screamed again and again into the dead forest. My back felt as though it was about to break. Searing pressure.

Breathe.

The pressure was getting lower. Moving downward.

Again. *Push!* My voice crying out between the trees and snowy knolls. I could feel the stretching and tearing as the baby pushed his way through me.

Burning. Burning as his head crested between my legs. My hands could feel his scalp. His thin hair. I screamed again. *Push!*

My heart stopped as my baby fell into my hands.

My baby.

The world seemed to shift as I brought him up to my chest. My chest ached, and my skin shivered. Everything else – the pain, the blood, the cold – all fell away until there was only him. *Adamo.*

Overwhelming. I looked at him, at the shape of his mouth, the soft curve of his ears, the gentle pads of his small fingers, the way his nose curved like mine.

And I fell in love.

How could I have ever done anything else but love him? My Adamo. My sweet baby. I finally understood; he was all that had ever mattered. He was the most important thing in the world. My masterpiece. I began to weep, tears choking the breath from my lungs as they rolled down my cheeks and fell into the snow, a halo of glistening diamonds. Crying, sobbing, I became a slave to the passion that flooded me. The love. But even more than that, the crushing, inescapable grief.

For my baby did not move.

He did not cry out, or shiver, or grasp at my hands. He could not see me, could not feel me. He was still, and quiet, and dead.

I barely recognized my own voice as I held him to my chest and began to wail. I howled with a new sort of pain. A deeper pain. My chest swelled and shook like it meant to burst. I rocked my baby side to side in arms that could no longer feel the cold.

"I did this," I moaned softly. "Adamo. I did this. I'm so sorry. I should have listened." The energy of the birth was beginning to leave me. My head felt heavy, and fell back into the snow. "Oriel. I should have listened. I'm sorry."

From the corner of my vision, I could see the deep crimson patch that was growing wider and wider in the snow between my legs. The umbilical cord still trailed inside of me. I knew it needed to come out, but there were no more contractions. *Something is wrong.* I felt heavy. Drowsy. My head swam.

Oriel.

"Oriel?" I struggled, but could not move. "Oriel?!" Desperation found purchase in my voice, driving it to jagged heights. "Why Oriel?! You could have stopped me! You could have saved him! Why?!"

"I tried."

I had heard that voice before. That bottomless, wondrous voice that could never belong to either man or woman. Straining, I managed to turn my head just enough. Beside me, standing in the shade of the white oak, stood the angel from the church room – the one who had appeared to me on the summer hill beneath a different tree. His wings were whiter than the snow around him, and the bottommost feathers lay soft upon the fresh powder.

"Oriel? Why?"

"I tried, Amadora. I warned you of this path. I tried to save your son."

"You…tried?" Momentary heat welled up within me. "Y—you never tried! YOU NEVER TRIED!" I gasped for air. Looking down, I pulled Adamo closer, nestling him in the crook of my neck. "Words. That was all you could offer?

407

I know you could have done more! You could have! You pulled me from the fire! Why then? For what?" I glared up at him, filled with rage and grief. "Is this what you saved me for? Is it? Bastardo! The fire was a kinder fate than this!"

I was shocked to see the tears in his eyes. He did not speak for a moment. "'Twas not I, nor any agent of the Lord, who delivered you from the fire."

Silence.

A cold, awful weight settled within me.

I closed my eyes, desperately willing for any other answer. But I knew, immediately. I had always known.

When I opened my eyes, the angel was gone. The only things that remained of him were the shallow grooves where his wings had brushed the snow, and soon even those disappeared beneath the falling white flakes that were beginning to bury me as well.

I brushed the ice from my son's cheeks. *My beautiful son.* My heart trembled. I would do anything. I would *give* anything to save him. *Including this.*

"Moloch?"

Silence. Not even a gust of wind.

"Moloch!" I said again, crying out with my tired voice.

"No need to shout."

I jerked around. The voice had come from behind me. I struggled to turn – to see – as out from the corners of my vision walked the devil of my nightmares. Stretched. Pale. With skin that pulled too tightly across his face and neck. Ash-gray hair fell halfway down his back. He wore no clothes, and yet was no man. A crudely hewn replica.

He circled around me, quietly smiling with a mouth that seemed to cut his face in two. Finally, he stepped closer. Squatting down, he settled himself on his thin, spindly calves and rested his arms easily across his knees. I tried to shy away, but it was hard to move. I couldn't feel my arms.

"Hello, Amadora." He spoke in a raspy whisper. "I told you didn't I? *Soon*. Over and over, I said it, and yet it feels as though I've waited an eternity to meet you. How wonderful that our time has finally come. If I may say so, you look delicious this morning. Simply delicious."

"M—Moloch…?" My voice quivered.

"Had we not already established that? Really, I was under the impression you were one of the more *intelligent* ones. It seems dying has made you quite stupid." He laughed mockingly. Then, looking down at me as I lay in the snow, he absently licked his lips. "Yes, I am Moloch. Moloch, *the sceptered king*. I was called that once, and I quite like it."

"Why…everything…" I struggled to form coherent thought. "What do you want with me?"

He laughed again. "What do *I* want? That seems rather personal, I think. What's more important here is what *you* want." His eyes drifted to the still form of Adamo in my arms. "Of course, I think we both know what that is, don't we?"

"Can you save him?" My voice shook. My throat was cold.

"Save him? I have no idea. I doubt it. But I *can* make him live. Isn't that what you want?"

409

My thoughts were slow. I couldn't focus. "Yes. Please, give him life."

"What, for free?" His thin voice cracked and sputtered as he laughed wildly.

"What do you want? My life instead? Take it."

"Your life? Your life is over. Useless. Expired. Truly, I'm insulted by the offer."

"Then what?"

His too-large eyes sparkled like polished obsidian. "Your innocence."

Confusion.

"You know, Amadora, you aren't quite so wicked as you pretend to be. I mean *sure* you've killed a few people. You betrayed a whole monastery too; that one was my favorite." He chuckled quietly. "But somehow, you've still got a touch of innocence left in you. Makes it difficult – so difficult – to claim your soul."

My soul?

His fingers leapt out. With otherworldly speed, they grasped my chin. He leaned forward until his eyes were only inches from mine. I could smell him – like rotting flesh.

"Give it to me," he growled with sudden, terrifying malice. "Give it to me, and that putrid *corpse* of a boy in your arms will live. Give it to me!"

I held even tighter to my baby.

"Y—you swear he will live?"

"Yes! Fine! He'll live and dance and *fuck* for all I care! *Now give it to me!*"

It was hard to think. Even harder to see. The corners of my vision were blurring – distorting.

The world was heavy.

My innocence.

My soul.

Adamo.

Slowly I lifted my son from my chest. *It's enough.* With trembling arms, I reached out toward Moloch.

"Yes. Please, do it."

He laughed then. Shrieking with joy, he reached forward and plucked Adamo from my hands. In an instant, the baby burst into angry black flames. The fire itself seemed to writhe and squeal as it consumed him. For a moment, I thought I could hear the cry of a babe from within the inferno. I screamed, but before I could do any more, Adamo was gone. Vanished.

"He lives!" Moloch spat, interrupting my cries of alarm. Standing, he bent his hands backward and stretched his arms behind his back, groaning softly with relief. "Ah, that's better. Much better. Now, I really must be going. Ciao, Amadora. By the look of it, I will be seeing you soon." He gestured cheerfully to the blood still spreading beneath me.

"I thought...you wanted...?"

"Your soul? There wasn't much to take, really." He raised his fingers, and for the first time, I saw that there was something in them: a butterfly. Small, almost colorless, it writhed weakly between his thumb and first finger.

A wave of weakness crashed over me. I gasped for air, struggling to breathe, and by the time the world swam back into view, Moloch was gone.

Adamo was gone.

I was alone.

So I closed my eyes and prepared to die.

I am cold.

"Forgive me," I whispered.

There was no pain. No, the cold had taken the pain.

Darkness fell upon me, obscuring everything in thick mist.

In that moment, I could see the face of everyone I had once known.

Matteo. I wept even as my consciousness began to fade away. *Matteo, I did this. I did this. I'm sorry. Please, I don't want to die.*

I could almost see the hellfire. It was crawling closer, like some hungry beast. It was so close.

Antonia. Jacopo. No, please don't. Don't laugh at me. I'm so scared.

I could feel it lick at my feet. The fire without flame.

Timo! I wanted to go with you! Don't leave! Help me! Please!

I began to scream wordlessly in the fading chambers of my mind.

"Wait a moment, Amadora. Let's not be hasty."

A sudden gasp tore its way from my chest. Light flooded back into me. My eyes flickered open.

Alit upon my nose: the butterfly. Its wings had been torn, and it flapped them uselessly.

Behind it, standing over me, was Moloch. Back. And with something in his stare.

"I'm feeling a bit strange. I think…I think I've had a change of heart. I think I *do* want your life."

I still could not move. The darkness was not far off. It had only been pushed back somehow.

Wh—what?

"Your life. You offered it earlier, and I think I want it after all." He laughed. "I really couldn't have expected this! Amadora, you are a woman of many surprises. Let's make a new deal. A *better* deal."

My consciousness wavered, and my eyes closed once more.

Suddenly, his voice was in my ear. I could see him through the darkness, as if he had stolen onto the canvas of my mind. "Your death will lead to fire. Dark fire. *Eternal* fire. I have been there. I have burned in that fire since the world began."

I know.

"You don't. You don't know. You cannot imagine." He seemed to lose control of himself. His face contorted, and in that moment I saw fear in his eyes. "There is no escape from it, Amadora. Never. You and I shall burn together for all of time."

I was barely aware of myself.

"But…I can offer something else. The next best thing."

The next best thing?

"Time," he said. "I can offer more time."

How?

"Let me in. Let me share in that wonderful body. I will keep you young, and strong. You will not burn if you cannot die."

Why? Why would you do that?

The fear in his gaze sparked once more. "As long as you live, I too, elude the fire. I am…making a wager, shall we say. On you. There's something about you." His eyes burned. "I *like* what I see in you."

The fire was back. Coming closer.

I could feel it burning.

"Decide now."

Yes.

A long, pale finger reached forward and touched me upon the chest.

Blinding white light.

Then nothing.

Notes on Winter's Child

The winter solstice has always been of notable cultural significance. This is unsurprising, as the ebb and flow of the seasons has dictated the prospects of humanity since the first days of Eden. Like a cheironomer leading a liturgical chant, the cold months of winter conduct vivid movements of action, respite, and above all else, transformation. Rain becomes snow. Day is swallowed by night. Trees change their function, beasts change their color, and even people change. People change.

Take, for example, the story of Persephone in Greek tradition. Claimed by Hades as his wife, carried across the Acheron, against her will she was made queen of the underworld. Demeter, her divine mother, wept and cursed the ground, causing the plants to wither and die and the land to become desolate. This was the first winter, and as Persephone must return to the underworld every year to fulfil her deific obligation, winter returns – mournful anew.

Yet the most overlooked aspect of this tale is also its most significant. Hades – the loneliest and least loved of gods – found chance to find a wife. The god of death fell in love.

Farfallina mia

Even within the context of the Greek pantheon, this is far without the expectation of his character, much less of his symbolic theme. It bespeaks something basal about not only the lord of the underworld as he exists in the Homeric Hymns, but also the common tradition that his mythology represents. For what are the old gods if not demonstrations of social thought? In this, it suggests a wonderful common agreement, something unspoken even by the modern masters of art and literature: no one is exempt to change – even death might fall in love.

And so we return to that which is seemingly most assured: change. Transformation. This is Winter's true Child, and it reveals something within us all.

Written in the hand of Isabella d'Esposito.

End of book one.

Historical Notes

Here, I have attempted some partial record of the research that was compiled into *Winter's Child* in the hope that no few of you may find this watershed period of history as fascinating as I did.

All locations and major historical figures in *Winter's Child* were accurate to as high a degree as I was capable of producing, but, of course, historiography can hardly offer a complete picture of every instance. For many things, I was forced to extrapolate – to fill in those gaps of knowledge with educated estimations of reality. That is the curse of historical-fiction.

If you have any questions about specific resource material, or anything else, contact me and I'll do my best to answer.

Montaione

In the summer of 2013, I, with my parents and younger sister, traveled to Italy on what was both a vacation and research trip. At the time, I was well into the first draft of *Winter's Child* but was quickly becoming aware that my narrative suffered from my lack of experience with the setting. Pictures do not quite capture the immensity of a location, and history books do not make memories. It was my hope that even a few weeks in Tuscany might be enough to inform my draft and bring some level of realism to the setting.

Of course, to me, it was no less crucial that I bring Montaione to life than it was Florence. The small town sets the stage for Amadora's journey, but even more than that, village life – especially in this region, *especially* in this time period – is fairly underrepresented in contemporary literature. There is a certain magic to an old town like that. It has this element of mystery, of long lost history, that just doesn't exist in newer countries like the United States. That first night in Italy, I slept in a building that had been standing since before the first pilgrims landed on the shores of America. I've never felt so small, or been so inspired.

Yet, the problem with representing the history of a small country town like Montaione is what also builds that air of mystery and excitement, that is, there is very little history to represent. For small towns, historical documents are sparse, often unshielded, less sought after, and certainly less analyzed than they are in a cultural giant like Florence. There is no quick Google search to find the Podestà who held office in 1449. There is no published map to see where the old town walls used to sit, or where their roads once lay. In fact, I was nearly forced to give up any claim to historical accuracy with Montaione at all.

I should say here that you need not worry. In the end, I was able to find the information I needed. Montaione hosts one, *very* small museum, and though the exhibits are entirely geared toward artifacts of Roman antiquity, the museum's front desk had for sale a couplet of books on local history.[1,2] These two texts have singlehandedly informed the account of Montaione you'll find in *Winter's Child*, and while I will never meet their author, I would like to take a moment to thank Rino Salvestrini for the incredible work he did at putting these histories together. I hope that my translation did the books justice.

Art

There is, frankly, little to say here except that the art of 15th century Florence is both captivating and discerning. The transition from the iconography of medieval art to the realism of Renaissance art marked the early rise of Renaissance Humanist philosophy and all the social revolution that followed. Lest you miss any chance to experience the artworks I've cited in *Winter's Child* for yourself, here is a quick guide.

Page 10: there is a reference to a fresco on the wall of the Brancacci Chapel in Firenze. The fresco mentioned is "The Expulsion from the Garden of Eden", painted in the church

[1] Salvestrini, Rino. *Montaione e la sua storia*. Vol. 1. 2 vols. Poggibonsi, SI: Arti Grafiche Nencini, 1997.

[2] Salvestrini, Rino. *Montaione e la sua storia*. Vol. 2. 2 vols. Poggibonsi, SI: Arti Grafiche Nencini, 1999.

of Santa Maria del Carmine by the artist Masaccio around 1425. [3] For reference, the painting was completed about four years before Amadora was born.

Page 92: the towering golden doors of the Baptistery of San Giovanni are one of the central artistic foci of Florence, even today. The eastern doors (now set on the north side of the baptistery) were created by Lorenzo Ghiberti over the course of 21 years, consisted of 28 panels depicting the life of Christ, and were not completed until 1424 (five years before Amadora was born). Later, Ghiberti was commissioned for a second set of doors for the baptistery, a total of ten panels which took him an additional 27 years to complete. These were not quite finished by the time Amadora visited the baptistery.

Page 103: I describe a mural circling the second story walkway of the Badia Fiorentina. The fresco cycle was painted between the years of 1435 and 1439, which would have put its completion only ten years before Amadora was welcomed into the abbey. The attribution of these murals is somewhat debated, but while some claim they were the work of Portuguese painter Giovanni di Consalvo, most agree that they were likely done by Zanobi di Benedetto Strozzi. [4]

Page 106: here is a somewhat roundabout reference to a mural not yet painted in Amadora's time. The strange things

---

[3] Masaccio. *Cacciati dei progenitori dall'Eden*. 1425. Santa Maria del Carmine.

[4] Di Benedetto Strozzi, Zanobi. *The Life of St. Benedict*. 1439. La Badia Fiorentina.

she sees above the choir in the Badia Fiorentina hearken to an actual set of frescoes painted by Gian Domenico Ferretti and Pietro Anderlini sometime around 1734, nearly 300 years after Amadora's vision of them.

Witchcraft

Witchcraft! If I'm being honest, the history of witchcraft – its perception and ecclesiastical inquest – hold the highest tier of fascination in my mind. How fear, superstition, and ignorance were catalyzed by the growing influence of the Catholic Church to create an environment in which inconformity might lead to accusation, inquest, and execution – it is nothing if not interesting, morbidly so. In contemporary texts, such as *The Malleus Maleficarum* by Heinrich Kramer (a 15th century German witch hunter),[5] the darkest imaginations of the public become perceived fact – fornication with the devil, the black Sabbath, infanticide. These fireside whispers were the horror films of the Renaissance age, but without any suspension of disbelief, or indeed any disbelief at all.

Much of my research into pre-modern witchcraft was facilitated by a college course I was lucky enough to attend at the University of Washington, but I will do my best to outline the most influential texts I referenced while writing *Winter's Child*. First, *Witchcraft in Europe: 400-1700: A*

---

[5] Kramer, Heinrich, and James Sprenger. *The Malleus Maleficarum.* Translated by Montague Summers. New York, NY: Dover Publications, Inc., 1971.

Documentary History, edited by Alan Charles Kors and Edward Peters.[6] This book might be the most complete compilation of historical texts on witchcraft in the world, and the commentary that Kors and Peters provide for each document do wonders to contextualize its significance in relation to the movement as a whole.

Next, and perhaps the last of the most applicable resources to witchcraft in Amadora's story, is a book by Carlo Ginzburg, *The Night Battles: Witchcraft & Agrarian Cults in the Sixteenth & Seventeenth Centuries*, which discusses the most unique instance of documented witch-trials in history – the only time when a coordinated group of people actually claimed to harness power similar to witchcraft.[7] Within, Ginzburg explores trial documentation on a group that referred to themselves as the Benandanti. They were, by his estimation, a type of agrarian cult, and they believed that, at certain points of the year, they would rise from their bodies in the dead of night and fight evil spirits to ensure the fertility of the next season's harvest. It is a fascinating account by any standard.

The Badia Fiorentina

---

[6] Kors, Alan Charles, and Edward Peters, eds. *Witchcraft in Europe: 400-1700: A Documentary History*. 2nd ed. Philadelphia, PA: University of Pennsylvania Press, 2001.

[7] Ginzburg, Carlo. *The Night Battles: Witchcraft & Agrarian Cults in the Sixteenth & Seventeenth Centuries*. Translated by John Tedeschi and Anne Tedeschi. New York, NY: Penguin Books, 1985.

I had the intense fortune of foresight to visit the Badia during my 2013 research vacation to Italy. It is truly marvelous, and it easily surpasses my best attempts to describe it within the story. It has been around since well before the 11th century, and was a chief site of importance in medieval Florence.

In 1307, the belfry of the church was demolished in order to, apparently, punish the monks within for not paying their proper taxes. This was followed, in 1330, with the construction of a new campanile above the abbey. Very little has changed in the Badia Fiorentina since then, aside from a suppression of the monastery in 1810. That is, except for one key transformation.

Here, unfortunately, is where a bit of historical inaccuracy comes into effect. The church of the abbey – the room in which Amadora first meets the angel, Oriel – was remodeled in the Baroque fashion between the years 1627 and 1631. To my chagrin, I was unable to find any information regarding how the church appeared before that transformation, and so the setting described in the pages of *Winter's Child* is somewhat different than the church of that time would have looked. Instead of pointlessly guessing at a pre-Baroque design, I merely described the church as it existed after the remodel. You may disagree with the decision, but it seemed better to retain some semblance of accuracy, even if its effective date was off by nearly 200 years.

Of all the locations in *Winter's Child*, the Badia is the least sure of its accuracy overall. Between the suppression and the remodel, it is difficult to discern what the old abbey must have been like, though I hope I was close.

In regards to the Benedictine monks that occupied the Badia in *Winter's Chila*, I can only hope I did the order justice. All information on their methodologies and strictures were taken directly from the monastic code outlined in *The Rule of Saint Benedict in English*.[8]

People

I suppose I get to brag, just a little here, about some of the more subtle Easter eggs I left hidden in *Winter's Chila*. Most, I assume, would only be found by (and indeed, relevant to) those with a fairly extreme bent toward Renaissance history, but I enjoyed the opportunity to plant them nonetheless.

Andrea del Verrochio. You met him, briefly, in the workshop of goldsmith Niccolo Torrini. While Niccolo may have been a character of fiction, Andrea himself did exist, and was about 14 years old at the time of Amadora's arrival to Florence. He is thought to have been apprenticed to a goldsmith in his youth, and, upon becoming a master himself, apprenticed none other than Leonardo da Vinci in his own workshop. You might remember that Andrea said he would not want to paint anymore if he could not be the best? Well, he did just that. Giorgio Vasari, in his *The Lives*

---

[8] Fry, Timothy, O.S.B., ed. *The Rule of St. Benedict in English.* Collegeville, MN: The Liturgical Press, 1982.

of the Artists, wrote that upon seeing the work of a young Leonardo da Vinci and recognizing its superiority to his own, Andrea set down his brush and never painted again.[9] More information on Andrea can be found in the aforementioned text, which was published in the mid-16th century.

Francesco Salviati is another character with real historical significance outside of *Winter's Child*. Indeed, I attempted to tie the fictitious events of the story into the factual actions of Francesco later in life. On April 26th, in 1478, nearly thirty years after Amadora's murder of Gilio Salviati, Francesco was executed – hung from the wall of the Bargello (also called the Palazzo del Podestà) after he and a group of cohorts attempted to assassinate Lorenzo and Giuliano de' Medici (sons of Piero and Lucrezia) and displace the Medici family as the rulers of Florence. The plot is now known as the Pazzi Conspiracy, and has found a small place in popular culture, being reenacted through paintings, operas and plays (such as Vittorio Alferi's *La congiura de Pazzi* in the late 18th century)[10], and has even been experienced as a playable event in the *Assassin's Creed* gaming franchise.

Criminal Law

---

[9] Vasari, Giorgio, Julia Conaway Bondanella, and Peter Bondanella. *The Lives of the Artists: A new translation.* New York, NY: Oxford University Press, 1991.

[10] Alfieri, Vittorio, Pietro Bettelini, and Carlo Dionisotti. *Tragedie.* Pisa: Presso Niccolò Capurro, 1826.

Of all the historical facets of *Winter's Child*, those regarding criminal law and how it operated in 15th century Florence were the most time consuming to research because they were, by their very nature, the most complicated. I won't try to summarize what I found here, other than to say that there were three foreign rectors (judges) – the Podestà, the Captain of the People, and the Executor of the Ordinances of Justice – that presided over mostly separate aspects Florentine law, though parts of their duties were also diffused amongst other groups and councils, such as the Priors, the Gonfalonieri, the Otto di Guardia, the Onestà, and more.

For more information, I suggest you look at the sources I found so invaluable in the course of my own research. *The Criminal Law System of Medieval and Renaissance Florence*, by Laura Ikins Stern, was *by far* the most informative and digestible text on these topics, though I'll admit it took me far too long to discover its existence.[11] Stern's text focuses heavily on the jurisdictions of Florence's courts, and discusses key points at which the legal system shifted in new directions.

Crime, Society, and the Law in Renaissance Italy, by Trevor Dean and K.J.P. Lowe addresses some of the same topics as Stern's text, but less thoroughly.[12] Instead, the

---

[11] Stern, Laura Ikins. *The Criminal Law System of Medieval and Renaissance Florence*. Baltimore, MD: Johns Hopkins University Press, 1994.

[12] Dean, Trevor, and K.J.P. Lowe. *Crime, Society, and the Law in Renaissance Italy*. New York, NY: Cambridge University Press, 1994.

chapters within offer a much wider breadth of information, ranging from legal systems in other Italian city-states, to common punitive outcomes, to discussions of the crimes themselves.

To further explore concepts of corporal punishment, specifically the death penalty and judicial torture, I turned to three academic articles by Marvin E. Wolfgang. The first, "Crime and Punishment in Renaissance Florence", dealt in part with the concept of punitive imprisonment, but also covered some applications of judicial torture.[13] The second, "Socio-Economic Factors Related to Crime and Punishment in Renaissance Florence", offered details about the death penalty, torture, and the legal bias toward women in court.[14] The last, "Political Crimes and Punishments in Renaissance Florence", covered multiple arenas of criminal law, but the explorations of torture, location, and precedent were what most obviously made their way into *Winter's Child*.[15]

L'isola delle Stinche

---

[13] Wolfgang, Marvin E. "Crime and Punishment in Renaissance Florence." *Journal of Criminal Law and Criminology* 81, no. 3 (1990): 567-84.

[14] Wolfgang, Marvin E. "Socio-Economic Factors Related to Crime and Punishment in Renaissance Florence." *Journal of Criminal Law and Criminology* 47, no. 3 (1956): 311-30.

[15] Wolfgang, Marvin E. "Political Crimes and Punishments in Renaissance Florence." *Journal of Criminal Law, Criminology, and Police Science* 44, no. 5 (February 1954): 555-81.

The prison house of Florence in *Winter's Chila*, the Carcere della Stinche, no longer exists. It was demolished in 1833, and upon the land was built the Verdi Theatre that still stands in the Santa Croce district today.

This created, for me, a frustration similar to what I experienced with the Badia Fiorentina; there is very little to suggest what the old prison looked like. We have, from my understanding, a floorplan of the building itself, though it lacks any sense of description and fails to explain any floors above ground level. So, while useful, it cannot describe the prison interior to the degree necessary for me to faithfully reproduce it in *Winter's Child*.

This is where a wonderful text, *Criminal Justice and Crime in Late Renaissance Florence: 1537-1609*, by John K. Brackett became invaluable.[16] His exploration of the prison interior was incredibly thorough, using secondary documentation to suggest a detailed explanation of the extant floorplan and highlight key features of the building. It is from his book that the Stinche in *Winter's Child* gained life.

To fill in the remaining gaps, I turned to an article by Guy Geltner, "Isola non isolate. Le Stinche in the Middle Ages."[17] His essay describes the sociological impact of the

---

[16] Brackett, John K. *Criminal Justice and Crime in Late Renaissance Florence: 1537-1609*. Cambridge: University, 1992.

[17] Geltner, Guy. "Isola non isolata. Le Stinche in the Middle Ages." *Annali di Storia di Firenze*3:7-28. doi:10.13128/Annali_Stor_Firen-9847.

prison, as well as listing the prison staff and offering tables of applicable statistics.

The Confraternity of the Blacks

The Confraternity of the Blacks – also known as the Company of Blacks, or more simply just "the comforters" – was a quasi-religious organization in Florence that operated independently of the legal system to provide comfort and last rites to criminals sentenced to death. The group was not a niche movement, and played host to numerous members of historical significance, not the least of which was Lorenzo de' Medici, the Magnificent (son of Piero and Lucrezia). While his use of the confraternity to boost his own political significance did not occur for nearly 30 years after the fictitious events of *Winter's Child*, his involvement illustrates the importance of the group to the city of Florence, and helps explain how similar organizations found cultural purchase elsewhere in Italy at the time (specifically the Company of Death in Bologna).

Their practices and procedures are explored in a critical text by Nicholas Terpstra, *The Art of Executing Well: Rituals of Execution in Renaissance Italy*.[18] In addition to boasting a full translation of the four books that, compiled, made up the Comforter's Manual, the text offers contemporary

---

[18] Terpstra, Nicholas. *The Art of Executing Well: Rituals of Execution in Renaissance Italy.* Kirksville, MO: Truman State University Press, 2008.

accounts of these comforters in action, and contextualizes these events with well-structured analyses.

Misc. Resources

There is an abundance of reference material that, rather than showing its immediate usefulness in *Winter's Child*, helped weave the tapestry of world that sits behind the narrative. If nothing else, these resources influenced the tone and direction of the story, but more than that, I found them interesting. Intensely interesting.

First is the account of Sister Benedetta Carlini – a 17th century nun at a convent in Pescia – who was the subject of ecclesiastical inquest when she was discovered to be having sex with another woman of the nunnery. There is a wonderful book by Professor Judith C. Brown that explores the records of what happened, as well as offering insightful commentary about the historical and social ramifications of the trials. [19]

Looking back, I never expected that trends of fashion, clothing especially, would prove such a frustrating challenge to research. There are documents, paintings, and other accounts of the Renaissance world that offer hints of what people wore, but many such articles fail to account for regional differences in style. Venetian robes were far different than those of Florence, after all. In the end, I

---

[19] Brown, Judith C. *Immodest Acts: The Life of a Lesbian Nun in Renaissance Italy.* New York: Oxford University Press, 1986.

discovered a pleasant compilation of knowledge in a new translation of Cesare Vecellio's *Habiti Antichi et Moderni* – an illustrated compendium of style written in 1590.[20] The drawings alone were worth the read.

Another interesting book, if you've the time, is George Elliot's *Romola*.[21] George Elliot, whose true name was Mary Anne Evans, is widely considered a master of the Victorian era novel and is mostly known for *Middlemarch*, though she herself once said that she considered *Romola* to be her finest creation. The story itself is set in late 15th century Florence – not long from the events of *Winter's Child*. It is a breathtaking look into the time period, and should you find yourself wanting more of Renaissance Florence, *Romola* ought to be your next look.

---

[20] Vecellio, Cesare, Margaret F. Rosenthal, and Ann Rosalind. Jones. *The Clothing of the Renaissance world: Europe, Asia, Africa, the Americas: Cesare Vecellio's Habiti Antichi et Moderni*. London: Thames & Hudson, 2008.

[21] Elliot, George. *Romola*. New York, NY: Oxford University Press, 1994.

Made in the USA
Middletown, DE
12 August 2019